Rachel Billington has published fifteen novels, including *A Woman's Age*, *Loving Attitudes*, *Theo and Matilda* and *Bodily Harm*. She has been President of PEN, and is co-editor of *Inside Time*, the national newspaper for prisoners.

By Rachel Billington

All Things Nice
The Big Dipper
Lilacs out of the Deadland
Cock Robin
Beautiful
A Painter Devil
A Woman's Age
The Garish Day
Occasion of Sin
Loving Attitudes
Theo and Matilda
Bodily Harm
Magic and Fate
Tiger Sky
A Woman's Life

NON-FICTION
The Family Year
The Great Umbilical: Mother, Daughter, Mother

FOR CHILDREN
Rosanna and the Wizard-Robot
Star-Time
The First Christmas
The First Easter
The First Miracle
The Life of Jesus
The Life of Saint Francis
Far Out!

A Woman's Life

Rachel Billington

ORION

An Orion paperback

First published in Great Britain in 2002
by Orion
This paperback edition published in 2003
by Orion Books Ltd,
Orion House, 5 Upper St Martin's Lane,
London WC2H 9EA

A CIP catalogue record for this book
is available from the British Library.

Printed and bound in Great Britain by
Clays Ltd, St Ives plc

To Kevin

The Waking

I wake to sleep, and take my waking slow.
I feel my fate in what I cannot fear.
I learn by going where I have to go.

We think by feeling. What is there to know?
I hear my being dance from ear to ear.
I wake to sleep, and take my waking slow.

Of those so close beside me, which are you?
God bless the ground! I shall walk softly there,
And learn by going where I have to go.

Light takes the Tree; but who can tell us how?
The lowly worm climbs up a winding stair;
I wake to sleep, and take my waking slow.

Great Nature has another thing to do
To you and me; so take the lovely air,
And, lovely, learn by going where to go.

This shaking keeps me steady. I should know.
What falls away is always. And is near.
I wake to sleep, and take my waking slow.
I learn by going where I have to go.

THEODORE ROETHKE 1908–63

Constance O'Malley
b. County Mayo, Ireland, 1940

Fay Blass
b. Chicago, United States of America, 1940

Nina Purcell
b. Sussex, England, 1940

1965

The urn, crumbling at the base, was planted with sweet-peas. Without supporting canes, they trailed wistfully down the sides. How inappropriate, thought Fay, for a mental hospital. So unstructured, so childishly pretty when surely we aim to teach our patients to walk tall, to brace themselves for the world, to find courage and strength. But, then, the whole hospital was peculiar, even by English standards, she assumed, although as a newly arrived American, she could not be certain. Twenty or more wards, long, brick, two-storey buildings, had been grafted together around the remains of a grand house. A hundred years ago it would have stood outside London but now the city, residential streets and tall apartment buildings, had grown to enclose it. Nevertheless the grounds, with stately oaks and Wellingtonias, still discernible walks and stone parapets, had survived. Hence the crumbling urn. But who had planted the sweet-peas? Gardeners did little more than mow. Perhaps it had been a patient.

Fay looked down at the large folder she carried, filled with patients' notes, sad stories she had found herself reluctant to read. That was what she had been doing in the garden, sitting on a parapet in the not very warm sun. Walking with more resolution, she crossed a courtyard and entered a small black door opening almost directly on to a functional flight of stairs, which she climbed at a run, arriving at a long corridor. To her left was the group-therapy room where she was due later. To her right at the end of the corridor, bathed in the sage green of its walls, a queue had formed in front of the kiosk from which pills were dispensed. Despite the occasional date with group therapy, Fay had already noted that pills were the principal treatment in the hospital and that most of the inmates wore the habitual droop of the heavily drugged. Or, in her view, over-drugged. But how could she know, a mere doctor in training, what stories of horror and anguish were made, by the use of chemicals, dully acceptable?

'I beg your pardon!' She had apologised automatically as one of the pill-takers, a young woman, as if to contradict her thoughts, broke away from the herd, dashed down the corridor and knocked her against

1

the wall. Fay, irritated, decided to block her way, 'Please don't bother with an apology.'

The girl shook her head, loosing a mass of red-black hair. 'I'm sick. I don't have to dispense apologies. I'm way past apologies. Apologies are over, out.'

'Who said?' They stared at each other. Fay noted that she was very beautiful, Irish colouring to match her Irish accent: thick dark hair, white skin, vivid blue eyes and a perfect oval face that made her seem like a child, appealing.

'I don't even bother to apologise to my maker any more.'

'What maker is that?'

'I'm not joking, you know.'

Fay tried to remember any notes on a hyper-manic Irish woman before deciding the repartee had gone on long enough. She held out her hand, announcing formally, 'I'm Dr Fay Blass. I don't think we've met.'

'You refer to one of those unmerciful group sessions, I may assume.' The tone was petulant but she put out her hand politely. 'My name's Connie O'Malley.'

'Please to meet you, Connie.'

'It's my pleasure too, Dr Fay.' Again she was mocking.

Fay said nothing. She represented authority here: there was no need to say anything. She wondered, however, whether this was the sweet-pea-planting patient.

Fay watched as Connie signed the Name of the Father across her breast and walked away without saying goodbye.

Fay next saw her later that day. Group therapy was held at three o'clock in the afternoon. Fay hadn't yet worked out how compulsory it was for the patients but there was always a large group sitting in a circle, heads down, hands limp on knees or one hand grasping a cigarette with weary vigilance. Everything was dangerous to these people on the edge. Words were infrequent, occasional explosions blasting apart the dust trapped in the shafts of early-afternoon sunshine.

Fay was only an observer, noting the slack atmosphere, noting Connie sitting by the door – propped open for those with a claustrophobic fear of no escape. She was obviously paying no attention to the group but staring dreamily towards the corridor outside.

Suddenly she rose to her feet so violently that her chair fell over, shrieked, 'Hubert! You disgusting man!' and dashed out.

Subdued panic followed. The smokers stubbed out their cigarettes as if in agitated preparation for their own departure. Those who were temporarily without one in hand lit up at once and puffed passionately. Calm was gradually restored and, in the course of this, a woman was uncovered to Fay's view whom she hadn't previously noticed, which was odd because she was large, tall and solid. Perhaps it was because she had been sitting back silently but now leant forward, even half rose as if she planned to follow Connie. Fay, attention drawn, thought she looked too much a regular person to be one of the patients. Perhaps she, like herself, was an observer.

'I know that girl,' this woman said out loud.

'Excuse me?' enquired the facilitator, in a kindly voice. But the woman said nothing more and hunched further back into her chair as if that made her invisible.

Connie reached her room with a big bearded man hard on her heels. Flinging herself on her bed, she buried her head in her arms. Humiliation and rage churned about her brain, slowing now and again for simple misery with images of Rick: Rick at the seaside, Rick in her bed, Rick in Paris. Her heart and stomach became squeezed with pain. Rick wouldn't come to see her. Rick had abandoned her. Instead she had this huge person, this gargoyle, this Hubert, his father. Now anger beat out all other emotions.

Crouching tigerishly, she yelled, 'I don't know why they let you in! This is a closed ward! I am a closed person!'

'I'm sorry. I know my way around these places, I'm sorry to say.'

'Sorry and sorrow and sorry again. I'm sorrowfully sorry to see you here. Visits by invitation only. My own family debarred.' Connie sat on her bed, back defiantly against the wall.

Hubert, apparently downcast, certainly old, perhaps penitent, sat on a chair. 'I've brought you some bananas.'

'Bananas. Ugh.' She pushed away the brown paper bag. She thought, Of all things, bananas! It should be laughable. 'Ugh,' she repeated.

'Bananas were rarely to be had in my youth.' He was trying to smile reassuringly but it came out as a leer.

'Your beard needs trimming, cutting, shaving right off. You're disgusting!' But it was she who was disgusting. That beard brushing over her naked skin. He hadn't raped her. Oh, God, if only he had raped her!

'I'm glad you've lost none of your fire,' he said sadly. There was a pause while she tried to hold on to her fierceness, staring above his head, waiting for him to go.

'I'm sure Rick would come from Paris if he knew.'

That was IT. Leaning over to where the bananas had spilled on the floor, Connie grabbed and split the bunch, peeled each in turn as Hubert sat amazed, then threw them at his face. One found its target. Hubert looked as if he was going to cry but, backing away from the onslaught towards the door, began to recover.

'I have been working on a sonnet,' he cried, 'with all the principal words in brackets. It was to begin with your name in double brackets, a tribute, but now I shall substitute Rick's mother, my lady wife, who, I may say, has been very gracious to me lately. And let me add,' he ducked further out of the door, 'that you're a great fuck and that your religion expressly forbids any self-harm.' Happily for Connie, his foot then caught one of the banana skins, with which she had followed the bananas, and he slid out of her view, crashing resoundingly on the well-polished corridor floor.

The moment he was gone, Connie fell forward flat on the bed, head dangling to the floor. She thought she might vomit, which would have been a relief, but she didn't. Instead she shut her eyes. Maybe life upside down would be better.

A few minutes later there was a tap on the open door.

'May I?'

Connie opened one eye and looked through her hair at the dark legs of what, even without raising her gaze further, she could identify as a priest.

'Welcome, Father O'Donald.' She could see at once he was used to hospital, even mental hospitals. It was the way he took off his coat and hat and laid them neatly one on top of the other on the window-sill of her little room, the way he did not bring his chair too close to the bed where she spent so much of her day.

'I only just received your message,' he said.

He knows I am a murderer, she thought, and he thinks if he had got my message earlier he might have stopped me. She imagined the conversation, about the sanctity of life. 'What God has given, let no man take away.' Except that it was Hubert who had given it to her. Or Rick. No. Rick had been in Paris. She would never cry in front of a priest. She thought of the orphanage she'd visited with her sister, Eileen, a grey granite building on the outskirts of Dublin, where rows of babies, born out of wedlock, were tended by their mothers before being shipped out for adoption. She had thought it a terrible scene but Eileen had been impressed, wondering cheerfully whether a couple of her children wouldn't be better off there.

'Turn your mind to it, Father. Spending nine months producing a

4

baby and then giving it away.'

'I beg your pardon?' said Father O'Donald. He looked so unknowing that Connie realised all of a sudden that he didn't know of her terrible sin and was merely visiting a poor Catholic girl who'd taken an overdose. Well, why should he be let off the hook? She stood in front of him, hands on hips, bare feet planted defiantly.

'I was going to have a baby when we met on that boat to France – twice we met, wasn't that odd? Going and coming back – but now it's gone. The baby, I mean. I killed it. Well, I paid thirty pieces of silver. Anyway, it's all over now.'

The priest looked serious.

'This isn't a confession,' continued Connie. 'I haven't repented. I'd do the same again. And if I don't repent, you can't forgive me.'

'That's true enough.' The priest sighed. 'Although that's going by the book.'

'The Holy Book,' confirmed Connie.

'I didn't know. If you'd told me on the boat . . .'

'No, you couldn't. I told you already. You would never have persuaded me.'

'It wouldn't be me.'

'What do you mean?'

'I would have listened. And then I would have asked you to listen. But it's too late now.'

Connie began to cry. 'There you are. I knew you'd make me cry. But it doesn't make any difference. I still think it was the right thing to do. I could never have given away my baby. Never!'

He sighed again. 'No. I see that. You were so unhappy before and now you seem even more unhappy.'

Connie stopped crying. 'That's just for now. I keep hearing my aunt, that's all. Sister Mary Oliver. She was a nun. She took me to Knock on my twelfth birthday and we recited the rosary by the gable wall where the Virgin appeared in the rain, although there wasn't even a puddle where she stood in her blue cloak. We filled our jam jars with holy water. My aunt was very, very holy. She died, you know, soon after, and I expect she's shaking her finger at me from God's right hand.' She flashed a defiant look at the priest. 'But I'll soon get over her. And then I'll be better. And I won't have a baby no one wants. I'm going out of here quite soon, for sure. There's nothing wrong with me. I meant to kill it, sure enough, but I didn't really mean to kill myself. It was just showing off, to God I wouldn't be surprised, in a low moment. I don't know why they brought me to this sad place. I'm not mad or anything.'

5

'Just unhappy,' said the priest gently.

'Much less unhappy than if I were still pregnant.' They looked at each other. 'You see what I mean? A baby is real. It's about feeding and dirty nappies and sleepless nights. I've seen that. My big sister had five under eight last time I saw her.'

'I'm sorry.' The priest stood. He glanced at his watch. 'Perhaps we could say a prayer.' He looked a little more hopeful.

Magnanimous in her victory, Connie said she would really like to say a prayer but she was still surprised when he dropped forward on to his knees. She felt obliged to join him, conscious of her bare knees on the lino floor.

'Make us, O Lord, understand the purpose that we are sent her for, and give us the joy that comes out of true understanding. Amen.'

'Amen,' echoed Connie.

'Not very elegant, I'm afraid,' Father O'Donald got to his feet in a tired, lop-sided way.

Connie saw him down the corridor and stood to watch his black hat and overcoat disappear. He was all right, except that he reminded her of her weekend in Paris. Of those roofs. Of that sex. Of Rick who had given her a letter to read on the boat. 'Dear Connie, you are so special but . . .'

Nina turned the taps so that they ran quietly. She was in a sterile cream-painted hospital lavatory, which was reassuring. It also had a basin. She was trying to keep her breathing regular, not to panic, not to scream. Just wash quietly and leave the room after a few seconds like any normal person. But she knew she needed longer than that. There was general washing first, up to her elbow, thorough, thoroughly thorough. Next were droplets, clean droplets splashed at her neck and face, flicked at her legs. She was panting. She must control her panting. Thank God there was no mirror to reflect the flush of panic on her face. Now for the serious part, each finger washed ten times under running water, and three ten times again and, just in case she had miscounted and to be quite certain everything really was absolutely all right, even those uncertain and unknowable things that were beyond her powers of prediction, three times more. No towel, of course, with the horrors of filth that it might be harbouring. Breathe evenly, she told herself again and, at last, ritual completed, was free to do so. Slowly and carefully, she unbolted the door and sidled out.

Gaining courage, she made her way down the corridor towards the kitchen and only recoiled a little when she saw the American doctor holding the coffee jar. There was something calming about her slim quietness, the dark hair pulled back tidily, red lips, glasses, clipboard held protectively under her arm.

'May I?' Carefully Fay tipped a spoon of coffee into two cups and waited for this large anxious-looking woman – the same who had cried out in the group therapy – to pour in the hot water.

'You're a doctor, aren't you?' she asked, kettle in hand. The hand shook a little, Fay noticed, then wondered about her drug dose.

'I guess. Fay Blass. I'm over here on a residency as a post grad. Over from New York, that is.'

The woman poured some hot water on to the coffee powder. Her manner was tentative and suspicious, as if she trusted neither herself nor the hot water. She did not pick up on New York nor did she supply her own name. Even her voice was doubtful. 'I come in three afternoons a week. Under Dr Halpern. It's a break from my children.'

'Children? More than one, then?'

'Two. Two babies, born in Malaya.' She paused, as if picturing her children or Malaya, while Fay waited patiently. Eventually she started again in a rush. 'My husband's in the army. I mean, that's not the reason I have two children. Anyway, we're in Germany now.' Her face became bright with colour and embarrassment. 'Actually, I'm here to try to break the cycle of my obsessional washing. Dr Halpern believes in behavioural therapy. But I expect you know all about me.'

Fay took a calm professional breath. So that was the problem. 'Not really. Ritual purification isn't my field.'

The woman took a step backwards. 'Oh, I don't think it's got much to do with purification.' She sounded shocked.

'I'm sorry.' Fay frowned. She felt much more out of sync with England and the English than she had ever expected. There was a lack of openness, she thought, that bordered on the devious, and she replayed to herself the map of central London with all its crazy crescents and mews and gardens. 'I'm over here for two rotations of six weeks,' she explained. 'I'm on a bit of a learning curve here,' she added, in order to be non-threatening.

The woman asked, with sudden intensity, 'What do you make of the girl who left our group? I know I've seen her before.'

'You mean Connie. The Irish girl. She had a guest. Unwelcome, it seemed. What's your name, if you don't mind me asking?'

'Mrs Purcell.' She rethought. 'Nina.' She held out her hand. 'Americans are more informal, aren't they?'

'If you'll let us be.'

Companionable now, they left the kitchen. 'When I was asked how I wanted to spend the afternoons,' said Nina, 'I answered, "Paint." Heaven knows why.'

'That sounds great,' encouraged Fay. 'I'd love to see your pictures some time.'

'Oh, no, they're not pictures.' Nina, returned to nervous mode, backed away. 'Just daubs. Colours. You know. A child would do better.'

'Not me,' persisted Fay, holding out her hand palm upwards like a wild-animal tamer. 'I've no sense of colour. In fact, I suspect I'm colour blind. Except then I'd almost certainly be a man.' Suddenly Fay smiled. 'My mother, on the other hand, has a thing about fuchsia.' And when, except in England, did she ever think about her mother, let alone bring her up in conversation? The fuchsia climax had been in Orbachs after a solid afternoon's shopping – the only reason she came to New York from Chicago as far as Fay could see. She'd gone on and on about how she was one of the lucky few who was enhanced by a vibrant colour like fuchsia. In the end Fay'd given in and got the wretched garment knowing she'd never wear it. And then her mother had begun boasting about her daughter, the doctor.

'Fuchsia would mean a flower not a colour to my mother.' Nina stared over Fay's shoulders. 'She has a big garden with big flower-beds. When I try to talk to her, she throws withy-winde and ground-elder and nettles at me. We're very close.' She began to walk way but quite slowly, talking over her shoulder. 'In fact, I'm living there now.' Fay watched her go, disappointed.

'Did you plant some sweet-peas in an urn?' she asked, hoping to recall her but Nina didn't hear or didn't answer.

Nina sat by a window in the painting room, watching the clouds go by. 'You've got the whole afternoon,' Dr Halpern had said when she first arrived, and she had vaguely remembered that time had once been a source of pleasure. 'The whole afternoon.' Clearly, he expected her to respond in some way, with thanks, suggestions or even merely comments. He had been sweating rather heavily, his skin red and freckled, his shirt collar rising above a pull-down tie. He was a fitting part of the ugly world she had created for herself. Even his white coat had a button hanging down, like an eyeball gouged from its proper position. Actually, there had always been too much time in her life.

Nina returned to the clouds. It was a cool, late-autumn day but the sky was blue with a tumultuous selection of grey and white moving slowly across it. Unfortunately, from Nina's viewpoint, across the hospital garden to the world outside, the clouds had to pass behind a tall apartment block. Twenty-nine floors, she'd counted. At first she found this jutting intrusion frustrating each time it interrupted the flow of her observation. Moreover, she noticed that a cloud entering the space barred to her eye in one shape emerged on the other side subtly altered. Because the sun was fairly low and behind the clouds, she could see their outline sharply etched, frilled like a shell, often black-edged with a thin, shimmering halo. Sometimes, when a cloud was big enough, it showed on either side of the block. What horrors were created by man, thought Nina, and, holding up her finger, was delighted to see that as swiftly as that, with one finger raised, she could obliterate the whole concrete hideousness. And then, as she watched, concentrating hard, one finger in front of her nose, she saw a cloud with billowing perimeters like a ballet dancer's skirts enter the space behind her finger. But how would it emerge? Smiling to herself, she tried to imagine, waited patiently to see if she might be right.

'Could I be disturbing you in the ancient ritual of raising the left forefinger?'

Nina turned quickly. She wanted to talk to this beautiful Irish girl, who was shifting about, pushing back her thicket of hair. 'I've seen you before.'

'Is this a way of avoiding my question? Anyway, you've seen me all over the place, throwing my weight around—'

'No, really,' Nina interrupted, frowning. 'I did see you once. In a hotel in Hastings. But we haven't met.' She, who was usually so private, was tempted to tell this stranger more, tell her that she had been on her honeymoon, lunch each day in the formal restaurant, William so handsome, both of them so formal, despite the nights in that big white bed.

But Connie, grimacing and looking as if she might burst into tears, had dashed over to the table and plunged the biggest brush into a pot of red poster paint. 'Blood!' she exclaimed, scrawling and dipping over a sheet of paper.

Nina watched the ugly redness spread from the paper to the table and wondered if she wanted to talk to such a crude self-dramatist. It

9

was all so obvious. Abortion. Suicide equals blood. She went over to the table. 'I did see you, about four years ago. You came in with a man, both of you looking so wild and happy. William, that's my husband, and I watched you. You joined an elderly couple who were half-way through their lunch and we knew it was your friend's birthday because the man, who was huge with a beard, shouted it out to him. He was your friend's father, I think. Oh, you looked so happy,' repeated Nina, sadly. 'I've always remembered.'

Connie daubed even more angrily for a few seconds and then laid down the brush, her expression changing. 'Oh, we were happy! We'd been to the sea so Rick could wear his birthday suit, he said. So I wore mine too. How we made love among the dunes – with the sand in every cranny of us but we didn't mind. It didn't feel wrong either, not like hell and damnation, more like Adam and Eve before creation.' She paused. 'Or was it after? Anyway, you know what I mean. Rick buried the condom, you know, with a little ceremony for the precious seed. Oh, God. Oh, God.' She began to cry, tears dripping freely. 'The sun glittered on the sea and I never found my knickers at all.'

'I'm so sorry to have upset you so much,' began Nina, horrified at Connie's anguish, although she seemed determined to continue speaking through her sobs.

'That was my first meeting with the disgusting Hubert, you see. He who came visiting me a few days back. At least I caught him with the bananas. You were in that summer Sunday dining room so you saw he licked the salt off my arms. But you couldn't see that he had his fingers running up my legs. Between my legs. Still wet from sex with his son. I should have known then. Like father like son, whatever that foolish phrase may mean. They were both my ruination one way and another.'

'Oh dear,' began Nina again, but saw, to her surprise, that Connie had stopped crying and even produced a bewitching smile.

'They're in the past, that's what I say to myself. Now, you tell me what you were doing in that gloomy dining place spying on a poor Irish girl.'

'I . . . I . . .' Nina realised how unused she was to confidences. What should she tell her? About the wedding night when she, a virgin, had been whiter than the white sheets and William had told her it would be better next time. No, that would be disloyal. 'I was on my honeymoon,' she said briefly, adding, to avoid further questions, 'You know you asked me why I had my finger raised. Shall I tell you now? I mean, it is quite interesting.'

'Do that. It might take my mind away from the weakness of the flesh.'

'I was looking at the clouds,' explained Nina, in a clipped voice, 'and I held up my finger to obliterate out that depressing apartment block.'

Connie picked up the brush again, still dripping blood, and held it towards the window. 'That's outlandish!' she cried. 'The brush is greater than a million tons of concrete!'

So they sat side by side, monitoring the progress of clouds behind finger and brush and, after an hour, the sun had delighted them by moving through yellow to orange to mauve. Time was very slow in the hospital, particularly in the afternoons.

Rubbing their eyes, which were squint sore, they moved over to the table where paper and paints were still scattered around.

'I saw you with a priest.' Nina took up the brush.

Connie stared, began as if to mock and then began again: 'A friend. All the Irish have pet priests. He's mine, although I only met him once before. On board ship. But, in case you should ask me, I won't tell you about that trip because we've had enough tears for one afternoon.'

'I'm sorry,' said Nina.

'Father O'Donald was sorry too.' Connie sat down and put her feet up on the table. 'I told him enough to shock him, poor man. Although I didn't tell him about the crème de menthe I vomited over the Algerian boy with long eyelashes and a stiff you-know-what. I didn't want to absolutely revolt him. It was bad enough revolting myself.'

Nina, head bent over a painting, found nothing to say.

'Have you been long in the married state?'

'Five years. We've been abroad most of that time. My husband's in the army.' Was this the most defining truth about her? It seemed so. She tried to think of any other personal information but instead remembered watching William's stalwart legs when she had been ten and eating cucumber sandwiches under the shade of a table. He had been playing tennis on their grass court with her father and his father and someone else. At fifteen, he had seemed very grown-up. His legs had been pink with exertion and covered with blond hair. His feet, in particular, had seemed enormous and she kind of thought he had been wearing sandals. Or maybe she was remembering his toes from later assocation.

'The British army.' Connie dropped her voice to a whisper before resuming at her usual high pitch. 'If I told my da I was associating with the wife of a British army officer – he is an officer, I assume – he'd cast me off without a penny, although as he hasn't got a penny and I've already cast myself off, it would not count as relevant. I had an uncle, joined the British army during the Emergency and his name was never spoken in our house, although he was Da's best beloved younger brother. I never even knew he existed till he was dead, killed by a German bullet, a traitor to his own country as even his own father admitted, though his mother had more sense, I was given to understand by my sister. We women tend to be more balanced. Are you inclined to nationalism yourself?'

'Why do you call the war the Emergency?'

'It was your war, not ours. I was only a little girl. It meant nothing to me, whatever it was called.'

Nina looked up from her painting and spoke slowly. 'I think the war, war in general, has been the most important thing in my life.' This was better. This was saying something true and new about herself. Should she add, 'You see, my father was held in a prisoner-of-war camp from the time I was born till after my fifth birthday?'

But she could see Connie was not listening. She crowded over Nina's shoulder to look at the painting. 'Heavens above! You've drawn God's finger wagging at creation.'

Nina looked. 'I didn't mean to. I was just trying to put down what I saw.'

'Let me tell you, what you saw was the great policeman in the sky. I would say Gardai but I've always pictured him British.'

Nina washed her brush deliberately in a pot of water. 'You're going out soon, aren't you?' She was surprised to feel a sense of desolation.

'Everyone knows everyone else's business here.'

'Sorry. I just wondered.' She looked down shyly. Why shouldn't she do something for herself? Something out of character. 'Perhaps you'd like to visit me in the country.'

Connie walked restlessly round the table. She held Nina's picture, which she flapped as if to cool herself. 'That's very kind. Most kind. But I'm not too drawn to the country. I was brought up there. My formative years in rain and cow shit.'

'It's not very like that in Sussex,' said Nina earnestly. 'At least, I suppose it does rain and there are cows. I just thought you being out of your own country ... It's my mother's home, really, although my husband bought it from her. It's called Lymhurst.' She hesitated. 'My father's dead, you see.'

Connie stared at her. 'Well, I'm sorry.' She turned away and looked relieved when Fay, white coat plus clipboard under the arm as usual, entered the room. 'I was going to clear up.' Fay stared at the red paint

12

splattered over the table. 'That was me expressing myself!' Connie cried. 'Now don't go disapproving, Dr Fay. Just address your eyes this way.' She hung Nina's painting from her arm like a flag. 'Give your honest opinion. Do we have a Picasso in our midst?'

'Oh, Connie.' Nina took back the painting protestingly.

'I don't pretend to be an expert on painting.' Fay began to screw tops on to the paints. 'Please call me Fay.'

Nina began to help her as Connie watched them both consideringly. 'Picasso has invited me to stay with her in the country, at a house called Lymhurst,' she announced, addressing Fay. 'She has taken pity on me as an expatriate. It seems to me you might qualify on the same grounds.'

Nina looked at Fay. 'That would be awfully nice. It's rather a big house.' Her heart beat fast. She never invited anyone to Lymhurst.

'I'm not sure—' began Fay.

'Apply for permission,' cried Connie. 'We are the only women of the world in this home for lost souls. We must stick together.'

'What happened to all your *old* friends?' Veronica grumbled. She and Nina were digging over the flower-beds, laying them to rest for the winter. Her voice, although not bad-tempered, carried forcefully over piles of ragged flax, Michaelmas daisies, far-flung roses, some still flowering.

'It seems a pity to cut them all down.' Nina snipped a white bud and put it behind her ear. Her mother knew perfectly well that she had no old friends. Ex-friends, perhaps, blotted out by William. Childhood friends, perhaps. What were their names? Juliet, Angela, Phoebe, roped in by Major Launceston-Smith to help celebrate the Queen's coronation in their paddock. And William lecturing her about his national service in an 'officer potential platoon', until he had suddenly grabbed her arm and told her his parents were divorcing. 'My mother's bolted,' he had said, in imploring tones. As if she, a twelve-year-old girl, could help him with that one. Divorce happened in the films, as far as she was concerned.

'Why are you smiling? Her mother straightened her back for a moment.

Had she really smiled? 'My new friends are not staying,' she said, sticking her spade in the soil. 'They're just coming for lunch. Nor are they mad, Mummy, in case you wondered. One is an American doctor and the other Irish. I think she tried to commit suicide. She's quite a drama queen.'

'I never think autumn's a very good time for visitors. You can't sit out but it's not cold enough to enjoy toasting fires.'

'I like autumn.' Nina stood straight and looked around. 'It's such a relief from all that green.'

'You've always been very colour sensitive,' agreed her mother amicably. 'I remember those summers after the war when I filled the beds with colour and you sat there matching up the colours with your paintbox. But green always wins. So many lawns.' She stopped working, too, and surveyed the offending grass, long and spongy due to inattention and late growth. 'And then there's the field and trees.' She bent sideways and expertly wrenched out an anonymous tendril. 'I think I'll take the children into town when your friends come. Then you'll have more time to talk. Less of a strain.'

Vaguely resentful of her mother's attitude, Nina reminded herself that Veronica, the fairly new widow, had a right to a strong and supportive daughter, not an anxious obsessive. 'I am almost entirely well,' she said, in cheering tones.

'That's good news.' It had begun to get colder, dank odours rising out of the newly turned earth, a misty cloud compressing the air.

'Poor William,' said Nina suddenly. 'All alone in rotten Germany.'

Veronica looked up but said nothing.

'A house with a driveway!' Connie exclaimed.

Fay, sitting beside her in the back of the taxi, reckoned this was only a preliminary. 'Go on, share it.'

'There have been two driveways in my life. One, in Mayo, good, leading to the convent where on special holy days the nuns gave us cream teas. One, in Hampshire, bad, part of recent disagreeableness, although it seemed fun at the time. I became disgracefully drunk there and drowned a poor innocent Mini. I'll tell you about it one day. It casts a shocking light on the British class system. I should have known better. Hubert warned me. Horrible Hubert with the beard spoke truthfully for once. He said, "There are two sorts of people, the insiders and the outsiders, and one sort has a fence around them and the other is free as air."' She had become abnormally pale.

'I'm sorry.' Fay took her hand, reminding herself that Connie had

14

only been out of hospital a few days. But Connie shook her off. 'That drive was as long as the road to heaven. But it went badly from the beginning. Rick was ashamed of me, you see, so I took to the champagne.'

They stopped in front of a slate-roofed house, much disguised by creepers. Fay found her purse and struggled to work out pounds, shillings and pence – like the class system, another black mark to torturous English minds. Ignoring her problem, Connie got out of the car and stood staring at the house. 'We do have buildings of this pattern in Ireland,' she announced, 'but they belong to that mongrel breed, the Anglo-Irish.'

'Welcome! Oh, I say. Welcome!' Nina burst out of the house. She was wearing a baggy sweater and a skirt of some tweedy material, and she appeared to Fay enormous and assured. Yet she seemed uncertain whether to kiss her visitors or shake their hands. Instead she did neither and continued with hearty salutations until the taxi driver, at last paid, made a slow turn and disappeared down the drive.

'What a beautiful house,' said Fay.

Nina stopped on the threshold. 'Do you really think so? I'm so glad. I absolutely love it. But then I can't really be objective.'

Fay was surprised at this level of emotion but since she really did like the house, she enlarged. 'It's exactly how I imagined an English country house should be. Carrying great age gracefully. Just look at that engraving on the down pipe.'

'Oh, the guttering. It tends to leak, I'm afraid.' She paused. 'Actually it spews out tears every time it rains. But William's mended most of the others. He bought the house from my mother, you see.'

They went inside and Fay found herself in a dim hall with dark wooden flooring, low windows and one table lamp. There was a comfortable-looking sofa, a chair, a brass bucket filled with cricket bats, walking-sticks and tennis racquets. One or two were square-shaped and looked very old. A large bowl of purplish daisies and a flower shaped like a red lantern stood on a round table, alongside magazines, newspapers and a few books. Four doors led off the hall. The one immediately to the left was wide open and Fay looked into a small marble-floored room with a tiny round window filled with topaz-coloured glass. Coats and mackintoshes hung in rows, below hats and above boots, all bathed in a topaz glow. Two guns were ranged in a rack and prints of men in uniform hung on either side of a splendid wash-basin. An open door led to a lavatory, which Fay could see was majestically wood-framed.

'I think of it as a gentleman's lavatory,' said Nina, appearing at the door with Connie, 'not that my father ever used those guns. He was a teacher after the war, when I knew him.'

'A gentleman's lavatory,' repeated Fay, in a satisfied voice. Although temperamentally in favour of the present over the past, she found herself seduced by this modest and tranquil corner of history.

'I know it sounds silly,' continued Nina, 'but I always think William, that's my husband, likes this room best in the house.'

'Men like peeing. Next best thing to sex.' Connie placed one of the hats, a brown felt Homburg, over her brilliant hair.

'Oh, William prides himself on his self-control,' said Nina. Then, hearing her words, she blushed, and loosed a mild giggle.

'It has to be a man's place,' said Fay. 'There's no glass above the basin.'

'Perhaps you'd like to see the rest of the house?' Nina led the way to a wide, L-shaped room furnished with soft sofas and a grand piano.

'Do you play?' Fay asked her.

'My mother did. But she gave up, except for teaching purposes. Would you like a glass of sherry? We'll go to the dining room.' Fay opted for water but saw Connie watching enthusiastically as Nina poured a small amount of amber liquid from a chunky cut-glass decanter into a thistle-shaped glass.

They followed Nina up scuffed, uncarpeted stairs with a balustrade made shiny by sliding hands. Fay admired the landing ceiling, which was decorated with plasterwork, roses and crowns. 'All that remains of a much older house,' Nina told her. They peered into large rooms with small windows and low window-sills, into square rooms, tall and light. They entered a children's room with a frieze of goblins parading near the ceiling. 'Helen and Jamie sleep here,' said Nina, looking as if her children were still a surprise. 'They like creatures with pointed ears because they've lived abroad so much.' Fay thought this a possibly revealing *non sequitur* and decided to pursue it later.

They resumed the lower landing, where Fay asked about old portraits and discovered Nina knew little. 'My father inherited the house from an aunt,' she explained. 'I suppose I'm not very curious about information. You must be starving. I've got a cottage pie in the oven.' She took them back to the dining room.

'Did you have a nanny?' asked Connie suspiciously, but Nina's face wore the deaf look of someone preparing to extract a hot and heavy dish from the Aga. Crossing herself with an ironic expression, Connie took her place opposite Fay at the wide mahogany table. She fixed her with what Fay was beginning to think of as her confiding face, 'Oh, 'tis sad to think on the Irishman's fate, who must seek fulfilment far from home. Of my five brothers four have fled across the seas. Only Michael who's cut of my father's cloth has stayed to grow old there and become silent and arthritic like my da in an evil-smelling, sodden hovel that even the rats disdain. Yet it's sad, too, to be without a home altogether, to remember the sweetness of peat fires . . .'

'How long have you been in England?' asked Fay, wishing to interrupt this mournful saga.

But Connie was vague. 'Years and years. I never take much account of time. Ah, Nina has come back to us.'

Indeed Nina had now re-entered bearing a stained brown pie dish from which she began to serve. 'So the house has been in the family for centuries?' enquired Fay. Her tone was purposefully reverential but she was thinking that the room was one of the coldest she'd ever inhabited. Nor did she much like the look of the cottage pie though. She sighed and hardly heard any of Nina's tentative historical references until they ended abruptly with a question. 'However did you become a doctor? You must be dreadfully clever.'

The correct answer would have been, 'Yes.' Then she could have expanded with, 'I'm not only clever but also hard-working and ambitious.' She faced Nina's open, admiring gaze with a little despair. How could she explain? 'I was born and raised in Chicago,' she said, and bravely placed a small piece of potato in her mouth. Would that tell them anything? Connie's attention, she noticed, was riveted to the sideboard where a bottle of red wine stood open. She could have told them she was the daughter of Jewish immigrants, but something about the room made her feel the word 'Jewish' was not appropriate.

'Do you cut up dead bodies?' asked Connie, interest still centred on the bottle. 'I worked in a medical hall in Dublin and the students liked to make us shudder with their grisly tales.'

'Oh, do you?' repeated Nina, eyes wide.

'Certainly do. In New York I'd get up at dawn, pick up a jelly donut on the corner of First Avenue and Sixty-ninth Street and head for the labs. They were open from five a.m. It was only a couple of blocks to walk but it got my circulation going. That and the sugar from the donut set me up for playing about with a naked corpse.' She paused.

'Please go on,' encouraged Nina, as if Fay were telling a children's story.

Fay pushed away a bit of gristle. A corpse was never a pretty sight and got worse as the semester proceeded, five students using it to practise their knowledge, cutting and peering, snipping and stitching. 'To be truthful,' she said, 'I always enjoyed my time in that lab, on my own, book in one hand, checking up on veins and arteries, gut and sinew.' She had never found the dead flesh revolting except for her first two or three sessions. The smell had been bad, of course, but that wasn't the corpe's fault. 'I used to want to be a surgeon and now I'm beginning to think about it again.'

Smiling to herself, Fay remembered licking the red jam from the donut off her fingers, and feeling more at home in that cool, silver-lit basement room with the chopped and churned-up corpse than she had parading fuchsia garments for her mother.

'I'm just so jealous.' Connie waved her hand round the room, ending with fingers pointed at the bottle of wine. 'Do you mind if I release this poor wee bottle from limbo?' She rose and snatched the bottle.

'I'm a terrible host.' Nina offered her glass to be filled while Fay put her hand over hers.

Fortified by the wine, Connie became expansive once more. 'I'm fed up with working as an idiot barmaid,' she said. 'I'm not going back to it. I'm looking to be a political columnist. Politics is the only subject worth the newsprint.'

Fay was impressed. 'There's so many newspapers here. In New York you only have to bother with the *Times*. Much simpler.'

'William has a cousin who's a journalist,' Nina got up to clear the plates. 'Merlin de Witt. He works on an evening paper. For the gossip column.'

'Political gossip?' Connie frowned, while reaching forward to pour herself another glass of wine.

'Back home we rate our political journalists higher than we do our politicians,' Fay remarked, overlooking the fact that she found the English newspapers disconcertingly lightweight. For example, the coverage of the Vietnam war. Nor, now she came to consider it, had the subject been mentioned in any conversation since her arrival.

'Would it matter you being Irish?' enquired Nina, returning from the kitchen with a glass bowl filled with pale green goo. 'It's gooseberry fool,' she added. 'We had such a glut of gooseberries this summer that Mummy and I bottled them so I'm trying to use them before they rot.'

'Another new experience!' Fay picked up her spoon.

'You certainly don't have a sweet tooth.' Connie pulled a face.

'I've forgotten the sugar again!' Nina dashed from the room.

Gooseberry fool certainly vanquished politics, thought Fay later, after intense discussion about the level of sweetness necessary had been followed by coffee (tasteless), chocolates (good) and the suggestion that they should go for a walk. Fay noted that Nina went upstairs to wash and returned with hands held damply from her sides. Ritual incomplete, she estimated.

Nina began leading Fay briskly out of the front door, then hesitated and turned back. 'When I told the doctor in Germany I thought I was going mad because of all this washing – he was British, of course – he asked whether my children were still in nappies and whether I had a washing-machine. Then he suggested I came home. So here I am. It is better.'

Flattered by this confidence from one who was so obviously private, Fay took her arm, swathed thickly in a tweed coat. 'Doesn't your husband mind?'

'Oh, Williams's older than me. He's fearfully busy. Important. Very handsome, too.' Nina blushed. 'Our first years were in Malaya and he was often away for a month or two in the jungle. I've known him since I was ten, you see.'

It had begun to drizzle lightly when they came out of the house. Connie, who was already outside, held up her hands in welcome both to them and to the rain. It's in my blood, she thought, holding her face up too.

'Let's go,' Nina pushed Connie forward, 'before it really pelts.'

They both turned to see Fay carefully extracting a plastic envelope from her handbag. The next moment she was entirely encased in transparent plastic.

They were amicable. They walked down the drive, a little way on the road, along which few cars passed, and then turned up a track that led across fields, up a hill towards a wood on the top.

They stood together on the edge of the wood, a mixture of oak, ash and tall, dark pines, which gave them some shelter. Below them they saw the way they'd come and the road with its sprinkling of red-brick houses and, set back, Nina's house, considerably larger than the others, encircled by its lawns and gardens, half obscured by trees.

'It's a very ancient wood.' Nina turned to stare into the dimness behind. 'I was too frightened to come up here as a child. In midsummer, the heavy weight of the leaves cut out most of the light. It is supposed to be an ancient burial ground and somewhere in the middle there's the stump of a yew tree under which sacrificial practices were observed. Or so the tradition goes. I always preferred the Downs, so open, with so much sky.'

'That's just so interesting,' said Fay, glancing down at her soaking shoes.

'Do you mean you've never found this sacred yew?' asked Connie, already in among the trunks. The other two followed, hesitantly. Even though so many of the leaves lay on the ground softened with the rain, the wood was still a dire and murky place. Nina looked up for the sky and found that what light there was ran down the tree trunks. Connie, having elected herself as leader, hair frizzed up in witch-like rebellion, plunged on, ignoring dead sticks, nettles gone to seed, brambles with withered berries, saplings bare of leaves, standing whippily upright.

Nina, began to search carefully, removing long tendrils of ivy when it sat, wig-like, on an interesting shape. Fay began a city girl's imitation, peering eagerly from under her plastic brim.

But time passed and no age-old stump was discovered. 'I'm beginning to lose my faith in the story,' said Nina. 'It should have to be an enormous trunk if it's hundreds of years old.'

'There's plenty of trunks,' pointed out Fay, trying to be fair.

Connie stared crossly around as a bird made a loud squawk above their heads. She picked up a bit of dead branch, and squinted upwards. 'Just watch me knock if off its perch,' she began, then stopped. 'You know what's bloody well above our heads,' she said. 'A yew tree.'

They all began to scrabble, bare hands dirtied and scratched as they revealed the grey-black wrinkles of the massive trunk. Its spread seemed too great for a single tree and yet the bark, although sometimes taking an inward curve, did not separate.

'It's one vast tree!' Fay stood back, awed.

'If it's over a thousand years old,' said Nina, who was so hot she'd thrown off her coat and sweater, 'it would have to be vast.'

'Come on, you two!' called Connie, who was still frenziedly tearing and clearing. She, too, had thrown off her jacket and wore only a tight black sweater over her short skirt.

'The reason we couldn't see it,' said Nina, staring upwards, 'is because it's still growing. We were looking for a stump.'

'I'd love to find out just how old it is.' Fay was sweating under her plastic mac. She took it off with a brave air.

'We could cut down the tree and count the rings,' suggested Connie.

'We could measure the trunk,' Nina laid a proprietorial hand on a cleared portion, 'but I don't expect it's a hundred per cent accurate and I'm sure we haven't got a tape measure.'

'I like to be prepared.' Fay delved into her handbag and produced a very small tape measure, hardly more than a yard long, but nobody was in the mood to give in. 'We just take it hand over hand,' instructed Fay.

Connie laughed because she felt pleased to be under the spell of this magic yew tree with these two weird people. These women. Women had never engaged her much.

It was not at all easy to measure the tree. Essentially, it lacked a waist. Fay and Nina became even more determined, very hot and rather scratched. Half-way round, they paused for a moment. Nina licked her reddest wounds and Fay put her hand to her head. A few minutes earlier she had removed her glasses, which had become misted over when they weren't hooked on predatory creepers.

'I'll tell you what,' called Connie, from a little mossy pad she'd cleared of twigs, 'when you've finished the statistics, I'll teach you how to do an Irish jig, the two of you. There's not an American who hasn't got Irish blood in his veins and Nina has the upright build and the light foot.'

'Dancing? We're dancing now.' Fay looked shocked as she tried to follow Connie's instructions. But Connie was stern. 'Fay, you may have many letters after your name but you have a shocking tendency to spread your knees. "Knees together at all times," as the dear nuns used to say – would that it had been to more effect. Knees together, Fay, it's the lower leg that moves. And absolutely *no* hip work. Hips are out! Forbidden! Besides there is no room for hips on the wood door we're dancing on.' She paused for a touch of education on how Irish dancing took its straight-laced form, not just because of the dear nuns but because a hard flat surface in the miry bogs of the west was hard to find and a door off its hinges, laid at a crossroads, made an acceptable surface, except that there was not much foot room. 'Remember that, Fay, small as you are, with your skinny hips and pointed elbows, keep them to yourself if you're to stay in line on the door!'

Nina, despite her size, picked up the steps cleanly and lightly, until Connie's wrath descended. 'Is that an Irish jig you're doing, Nina? I do not think so. You are doing a Scottish jig, which is not at all the same thing!' Once more her voice rose and Nina admitted meekly that she had been thrown back to her dancing-school days with Miss del Monte who wore pleated black sleeves like a raven's wing. 'But I dare to hope there's universality in the Celtic—'

'Celtic!' screeched Connie, and they all began to screech and laugh and dance (even Fay, particularly Fay), and soon they were steaming and hot and out of their minds.

'I can't keep it up,' pleaded Nina. 'I'm too fat!'

'Coward. Back, kick, feet together. Forward, bend and step together,' commanded Connie.

'I wonder if the ancient rites were anything like this,' panted Nina, since she no longer needed to count, 'or were they more threatening?'

'Nothing could be more threatening than Irish dances!' exclaimed Connie. 'The skirl of the pipes, the kilts knife-edged, the black curls flying...' She began to sing:

> 'In Mountjoy one Monday morning
> High upon the gallows tree
> Kevin Barry gave his young life
> For the cause of liberty...'

Fay, smiling, partially blind without her glasses, danced: 'One, two, three, forward kick, back kick, bend, cross over. One, two, three.' And then began to sing herself:

> 'Give me your tired, your poor,
> Your huddled masses yearning to breathe free,
> The wretched refuse of your teeming shore...'

'Whatever's that from?' Connie asked jealously.

'The Statue of Liberty,' replied Fay. 'Do you want more?'

Nina sank down, smiling. And looked at her watch. 'Oh dear. Oh dear. Oh dear.'

The other two stopped dancing to stare. Had Nina lost her nerve, Connie wondered, a crisis of confidence or, alternatively, could it be the need to find a washbasin? They panted in a dishevelled fashion and could not estimate the seriousness of Nina's panic.

'I'm awfully sorry, I'll have to rush. My mother will have brought the children back for tea.'

That was all. Children. Motherhood. Domestic responsibilities. Connie moved away a step or two.

But Fay was immediately sympathetic. 'We'll hurry too. After all, I guess we should be thinking of what train to catch.'

'Thanks be to you, O brave and everlasting tree,' intoned Connie, bowing to the yew so that her wild hair tipped right over her head. 'Thank you for receiving us your humble servants and extending to us the beneficence of your pagan wisdom – which may also have a Christian element, depending on your age and the company you've mixed with...'

'Forward,' insisted Fay, taking her arm.

'I planned to apologise for the lack of sacrificial victim,' grumbled Connie.

'There is a victim.' Fay pointed to the sloughed-off plastic mackintosh and only allowed Connie a guffaw and a backward glance as they followed Nina, already crashing her way through the undergrowth. They caught her up at the edge of the wood. She was standing, apparently no longer in a hurry, staring at the sky whose previous unexceptional grey had changed to a subtle inky wash.

'I am watching the moon arising.' Nina turned to them. 'I much prefer it to the sun. I'm so sorry for behaving in such a hysterical way. Really, there's no hurry.'

'Understood.' Fay stood closer to her.

'I can never remember if the moon's real,' said Connie, 'or a shadow of the sun. It certainly doesn't look real.' They all considered the moon, which did indeed look as transparent as white gauze.

And just as Fay started to give accurate information on the moon, Nina shouted, 'Let's run!' and set off at a madly dangerous pace down the steep hill. They were idiotic, running, whooping and shouting as if they were children. 'I'm going to fall over, I'm going to fall over . . . I've fallen over.' Nina, hampered by her tweed skirt and ungainly stride, hit a tuft of grass and tipped, breathless, into the ground where she sat, smiling, and watched the other two race past her.

Connie zigzagged, arms outstretched, shrieking, 'Oh, Mother of Mercy, look at me, I'm flying. I'm flying.' And certainly she was the first down to the bottom.

Fay steered a straight course and wore on her face a mix of wonder and bewilderment. 'Why are we doing this?' she panted. 'There must be easier ways to break a leg.' But then she, too, was at the bottom and watching when Nina rose and picked her way slowly through cow-pats and nettles.

When they drew together, it was still light enough to see each other's exhilarated faces. Linking arms, they set off down the road.

The house was silent. Nina, lying in bed, realised this with surprise. It was usually noisy, wind rattling the creepers against windows, blowing at the chimney tops, a gutter banging or pipes sighing and clattering, mice scuttling under the floorboards, starlings whistling in the roof, the noise of two children from what always seemed like dawn. She stretched her legs and, rather guiltily, wondered whether William was awake in their bed in Germany.

Whenever she was away from him he reverted, in her imagination, to the age he had been in the early fifties. When she had fallen in love with him, she supposed. In the silence, she listened to his deep eighteen-year-old's voice. 'I'm in a potential officer platoon, you see, but that doesn't mean I can always avoid a wigging from the regimental sergeant major. He has to keep us in line. The only thing I'm not mad keen on is blancoing webbing and buffing buckles. But you can't choose in the army, that's for jolly well sure.' That had been on Coronation Day, the same day he had looked so strong and handsome and told her about his parents' divorce with a discernible tear in his eye.

Nina sat up in bed and looked out of the window. She had not drawn the curtains so she knew from the darkness that the moon had made its exit. Perhaps that meant it was nearer morning than she thought. Or maybe it was cloudy. As she looked out, the darkness became patterned with lighter tones of black. From outside she felt a breath of wind.

There were six people in the house. Fay and Connie were sleeping in unused rooms where dead butterflies lay on the window-ledges and cobwebs were decorated with flies. They had stayed over to continue the search for the book about trees. According to Nina's mother, it would reliably inform them of the age of a tree whose circumference they had measured unreliably as forty feet. 'A monster!' she had proclaimed. It was a dark blue book, she had said, without a dust cover, with gold lettering on the spine. She had last seen it on the dining-room table, about ten years ago.

They had not found it. Instead Connie and Fay had come to watch Nina as, lap spread wide, she received the bathed and milky sweetness of her naked children. By then it was too late to catch the last train back to London.

Fay, too, was open-eyed in the darkness. She had been woken by unnatural creakings, and stayed awake to examine the startling discovery that she did not intend to pursue her career as a psychiatric doctor. Her decision to join the profession, she now realised, had been based on the false premise that her detached nature was perfectly fitted to psychiatry. But recently she had come to understand two things: first that her nature was not as detached as she liked to believe and, second, that in exploring the labyrinth of the tortured mind, she was pandering to her own ghosts. She would move into surgery, learn about sharp knives and clean cuts.

Fay turned over again to sleep but a familiar scene entered her consciousness. She was nine or ten, apparently captive in the dark corner of a kitchen. On the other side of the room, her grandmother stood at a table under a window in a brilliant triangle of light as if she were on a stage. Fay had been sent by her mother with a message. She had been interrupted as she lay on her bed reading Oliver Twist, her short-sighted eyes close to the print. Her mother hated this absorption in a world over which she had no control and often disturbed her in this way. Now, in a small act of rebellion, Fay had forgotten what the message was and stood, in darkness, watching her grandmother, although her thoughts were still with the oily riverbed where Dickens had been leading her. Her grandmother was merely a picture, wispy white hair, pudgy face and knobbly fingers.

'I have a message,' began Fay, but too softly to break through her grandmother's concentration. Deafness was another reproach. Her lack of English worst of all. She was making bread, kneading the dough on the marble slab, grasping in her fist flour from the tin on her right and throwing it at the lump. White specks were caught by the sunlight and hovered in its beams. Impatiently, and forgetting she could not remember the message anyway, Fay raised her voice. 'I have a message from Mother ...'

The old woman turned sharply. As she did so, she put up her hand to brush the hair from her face. 'The trouble is,' continued Fay, taking a step forward, 'I can't remember—' She stopped abruptly, the image in front of her so distinct in its stage-lit intensity that she felt herself become the audience. Where her grandmother's arm was raised the sleeve had fallen back, revealing a row of small blue numbers. The arm dropped, the sleeve fell. Fay's grandmother blinked enquiringly, her left hand still resting lightly on the dough.

Fay wanted to flee but instead she froze. The whole scene froze, the sleeve for ever fallen back, the numbers revealed. She knew she could escape if her mother called, 'Where are you, Fay? Did you ask

Grandma?' But she never did. The scene remained until she managed to wake, gasping with dread. Then she was able to remind herself that her mother had called and she had escaped.

Fay woke up fully and reached desperately for her glasses.

Connie had eventually prised a bottle of wine from the sideboard cupboard and drunk most of it herself. Before she had fallen asleep, she had pictured herself as the man in a household of women. She could see that from the outside that might seem absurd – she was so obviously carved in the shape of Eve – but nevertheless her reaction to the little children, the mother, grandmother and widow had been, she felt certain, like a visiting man. She wanted to admire, command and go her own way. She wished to carry trays, not lay them, to open bottles of wine and drink them, to lead conversations instead of following them. She tried to imagine Nina's husband, who seemed to be a shadowy figure in the family's life, and decided that shadowiness, too, would suit her. She would like to own a wife at home while she paraded in the field.

Tonight she would have only happy dreams. She was sixteen, living with her sister Eileen in Dublin, filled with confidence, going out on the town in Eileen's swirly pleated skirt because she was fat and pregnant and borrowing her highest stilettos too. Soon she was interrupted by her little nephews, red-cheeked, hair standing up in peaks, socks round their ankles. 'Auntie Connie!' They looked in awe at their smiling film-star auntie. Above her skirt she wore a pearl-buttoned blouse and pale blue cardigan sent by well-wishers in America.

'Oh, boys, boys!' She had hugged them both and was off, teetering a bit on her unaccustomed heels. They had a special purpose because tonight Diarmuid Ferguson was bringing along his Yankee cousin.

It was summer, even along the bricked-up walls of the river Liffey. Flies danced above the dark waters, eddying the air so that the buildings behind, the heavy power of the Guinness distillery, wavered too. Five of them jostled each other along, voluble about the merits of Presley in *Love Me Tender*.

They were showing off and knew it. In their midst, a head taller, twice as broad, the cause of all the jostling, strode Billy Ferguson. While the other males had slicked-back hair over pale, mostly pimply faces, greyish shirt over dingy flannels and dusty black brogues (proudly bought with their first earnings), he sported a crew-cut over a sunburnt face, a white T-shirt under a tartan shirt, canvas sneakers and, best of all, only previously seen in the films at the Palace, blue jeans.

And it was not just his clothes and healthy golden body that enthralled them. He also brought visions of a world where 'Dad's car' could be taken out for a run, where gum was for chewing rather than gluing paper, where there were fifty flavours of ice-cream, where chocolate came out of machines, where hot dogs were sold on street corners, where children slept not just one to a bed but one to a room, where the sun shone every day through the summer and in the winter the snow was pure white and never turned to slush. Tall Billy and slouching Diarmuid were so unlike it was impossible to believe they were cousins, although true enough.

It was no wonder that boys and girls alike took Billy round the sights of Dublin as if he were a film star. It was no wonder that the girls set their hearts on capturing his. During the first hour in Billy's company, Connie used up witticisms that should have lasted her weeks. 'Do you know the story about the two tailors? One said he was so keen on the job that he could fit a man with a suit if he only saw him going round the corner. "That's nothing," said the other tailor, "I can fit a man with a suit if I only see the corner he went round."'

But Billy, it seemed, was not choosing in a hurry. He talked to them all equally, admired the bullet holes in the main post office without taking the gum from his mouth, sidestepped a priest politely enough but made no move to cross himself as they passed St Patrick's Cathedral.

Finola fell back to join Connie. 'How long is he staying, then?'

'Until he goes to college. Eight weeks, minus the week for crossing the ocean.' Connie had invited Finola along because it was she who'd got her the classy job in the medical hall, she had plenty of money, which might come in useful, and she was exceptionally plain. The night they'd had the longest mouth-to-mouth kissing competition, Finola had not found any boy willing to accommodate her. Connie had won with a count of a thousand, although she'd never spoken afterwards to her partner who kept trying to break the rules by parting his lips. I'd part my lips for Billy, thought Connie, as she bent to place her licked finger over a rising blister on her heel.

Ahead, the boys had stopped, turned round laughing, not at them, probably, but it was enough of a challenge to have the shoes off Connie's feet and her running along the warm pavement. If it was a tomboy he wanted, then she could be that too. And she'd got him. Hard kisses in dark streets. Bodies pressed urgently together. Yearning, ignorant lust. Nothing more but it was enough.

Turning in her bed, Connie admired the sweet simplicity of her past.

Waking further, she stroked sympathetically her rounded breasts and narrow waist. It wasn't their fault things had turned out badly. Tears dried slowly on her cheeks.

Stealthy as a burglar, Nina felt her way out of the bathroom and down the staircase. She was fleeing, she supposed, touching the old panelling with extra-sensitive fingers. She glided through the kitchen where she found a torch on the dresser. But after she had unlocked the back door, she found the torch was not necessary. A smooth grey light, which felt as if it had no connection with the sunrise, made it easy to find her way to the little potting shed by the overgrown vegetable garden.

She wondered what visual memory had led her to its dark, thick-smelling interior. She listed the smells to herself: earth, rotting onions, tarred strings, sacking, fertiliser, chemical sprays, mice, rusting iron, birds' droppings, and wet vegetation pushing in through a hole in the window.

Nina pointed her torch towards a wooden workbench. *There* was the blue book, now mottled a greenish-brown with the damp, cover curling at the corners. Brushing off mouse droppings and a ragged corner of cobwebs, Nina took it outside towards the lightening sky and, opening it randomly, prepared to read as she wandered back to the house.

'So you found it, then.' Her mother stood at the door to the kitchen, wrapped in a heavy plaid dressing-gown.

'You're early.' Nina frowned. She had been happy alone.

'Your father wanted breakfast at six. During his last year, when he slept badly, at five. I think he remembered starving in the camp. Come in. I'll make us a cup of tea.'

Nina followed her obediently but she was surprised by the confiding expression on Veronica's face, by this recollection of her father's past. Her mother had always been secretive and encouraged secrecy in her. She sat at the wooden table and opened the book. The clock on the wall struck six.

Veronica brought a pot of tea, cups and saucers, and Nina was about to remark how many of the book's pages were stuck together, when her mother spoke in a hushed, emotional voice: 'Roger couldn't help himself. Men are like that. I was just surprised he would do it. I suppose I thought he was too old, too settled. It didn't seem in character. But I should have guessed when he started reading poetry. He used to read it aloud when we were first married. I learnt some Wordsworth to please him:

> "It is a beauteous evening, calm and free,
> The holy time is quiet as a Nun
> Breathless with adoration; the broad sun
> Is sinking down in its tranquillity..."'

She spoke the lines in a sing-song old-fashioned way tinged with a kind of ruefulness. 'Once learnt, never forgotten. But I didn't know he had a book of his poetry in the camp. I only found out when she told me. She knew all sorts of things about him I never found out. That's what hurt most. I never knew why she wanted him. Not that she really wanted him. Not to marry, so he told me. She wasn't trying to take him from me. But she did, of course, although we never spent one night apart until he died.'

Nina wanted to protest. Why was she hearing this now? Her father had died two years ago. Was it because she had brought new friends to the house?

'He told me ten years ago. That book you've got there lay on the dining-room table. Seeing it just now brought it all back. I was amazed. He was such a controlled man. But later I began to understand. There were things he couldn't bring himself to tell me, when he first came back, about what went on over there. Do you remember – what were you? Five or six – he was so fat when we had expected a starving skeleton? Now you're plumper you sometimes remind me of him as he was then. It soon dropped away again. It had taken months for him to get back and he'd eaten all the way. He would only talk about that, the being-hungry part. He said it was reason for staying alive, being hungry, and once you lost that obsession you died. But he never talked about the brutal things. I was young, and I supposed, I still suppose, he didn't want to spoil our happiness with horrors. And then, when he did want to talk, it must have seemed easier to start afresh with someone new. Someone who hadn't known him before the war. I don't know. He might even have believed he was being kind to me.'

She stopped here and Nina felt she was open to questioning. What question? Facts? The woman's name, perhaps? But she didn't want to ask questions, she didn't want to hear this at all. The dust and mould she had picked up in the shed without any worry began suddenly to irritate her hands. Longingly, she looked at the taps above the old basin. But she could see her mother hadn't finished. She was looking at her directly, almost challengingly.

'She was – is – a fellow teacher, of English. But her name is not important. Perhaps in time I'll even be grateful to her for teaching me things about Roger that I would never have known otherwise. We did meet once. She was at the funeral, although you wouldn't have known. One of the things I learnt from her was that, despite everything, starvation, illness, the deaths and suffering around him, he found a kind of happiness in the camp. He felt his strength and was proud of it. That was what he couldn't bring himself to tell me and he told his mistress. His friend, shall I say? Mistress is too strong. He was an old man and never very well. They beat him often, she told me, more often than most, and each time it made him stronger.'

She's telling me my father was a hero, thought Nina, and shuddered a little. It's not enough that he was a survivor, he has to be a hero and now he has a mistress too. 'I can hear the children,' she said, with relief.

'Yes, you go to them.' Veronica put out her hand to Nina. 'I didn't mean to upset you. It was just seeing the book. I suppose it was a self-indulgence. We won't speak about it again. Forgive me.'

'No, please,' cried Nina, heading fast for the door and then, with a sudden change of direction, for the garden.

Connie heard Fay leaving, Veronica driving her on the way to do some shopping. Fay had been determined to leave early. Connie could hear their voices on the driveway beneath. She liked the way they didn't fetch her, as if she were quite independent and could choose to lie in bed all day if she liked. She was just thinking this, naked and warm, when the door opened slowly and a small round-faced child, about five years old she guessed, holding the hand of an even smaller child, appeared. They stood there staring silently.

Connie laughed. She could see they thought her beautiful, her black shiny hair streaming over her white shoulders.

'You are right,' she pronounced solemnly. 'I am the Princess Gloriana come from the Emerald Isle to bring magic into your mama's life. You may kiss my hand.'

Detaching herself from her brother's hand, Helen came over and carefully placed her lips against Connie's outstretched fingers. 'Can you really do magic?' she whispered yearningly.

'Helen! Jamie!' called Nina from below, and the children began to go, although Connie could see in Helen's eyes that she waited for an answer. She put her fingers on her lips; it was a secret between them. Noisily, the two children scrambled down the stairs.

1966

Fay typed a letter to Nina. She was sitting in her railroad apartment. This was four small rooms, one leading into the next. The room, where she worked, had no windows and would have been very dark, had she not imported a spotlight.

March, 1966. NY, NY

Dearest Nina,

I think of you often, picturing your house and garden, your children and your dear mother. I can't really picture William, of course, since I've never met him, but I did spot his photograph on the piano. It had to be him, a very upright sort of man in his uniform, fair and handsome. *Very* English. Although as I write this, I realise it just might have been your father. Do the generations of military men look different? Perhaps I could tell with an American. I don't think I told you – in the end we talked so little – I have a younger brother, Daniel, born in the year World War II finished. He is in college now so exempt from military service. I try not to imagine what will happen if the war in Vietnam drags on.

I am much more settled now I've decided to work towards becoming a surgeon. I've never minded working hard – although sometimes I look at my poor skinny body and wonder just how it can carry on up to sixteen hours a day and so much of it bent over a book. And then there's the challenge of being a woman in a man's world. Our lives are so very different, yours and mine, which is perhaps why I treasure our fledgling friendship. Next time you write, try to make it a little more legible and informative. For example, are you finding time to paint? And, if this is not too upsetting a question, how are your ablutions? I'm addressing this to you in Sussex, assuming your mother will forward it to Germany.

Very best wishes from your American doctor friend, Fay.

PS Do you have a new address for Connie? Why do I worry about her? Is it because she's so beautiful?

'You come from a farm in Mayo.' Merlin de Witt confirmed Connie's information. 'Your family are manual labourers.' His small dark eyes gleamed admiringly. 'You're working in a pub yet you're a friend of my cousin William's wife.'

'A very old friend.' Connie crossed her legs under the table. 'Although I cannot disguise from you that we have nothing whatsoever in common.' At least that was true.

Connie got the job. She joined ten other extroverts on the *Evening Standard* diary page. They sat at a large table surrounded by wastepaper baskets the size of dustbins. By eleven o'clock in the morning these were already overflowing with white paper like froth on badly pulled beer, as Connie, the ex-barmaid imagined.

'Who wants Mary Quant's fashion show?' asked Merlin, waving the invitation like a huckster at a fairground.

'Me!' yelled Connie, grabbing it before her rivals.

'And I'm going with you!' exclaimed Zodiac, the only chic woman in the room, Connie thought. She lived in a houseboat on some forgotten inlet near Tower Bridge where her mother created feather and sequin appliqué work for an East End shop.

Soon everyone knew that Connie's mastery of words was reserved for the air. Someone had to write up her exploits from her illegible notes or her descriptions. Yet her reports on sinking barges, two-headed cows, copulating guardsmen, angry boxers, would-be moon walkers and suicidal models were so vivid that as long as someone else pinned them to paper, she was considered an indispensable part of 'the team'.

'We're a team, of course,' Merlin addressed Connie and Zodiac, with his unconvincing vowels. They looked at him tolerantly. It wasn't easy pretending to be one of the fashionable working classes when every word proclaimed you Eton and Oxford. 'But if you buzz off together, who's doing the Chelsea flowers, the Lord's cricket and Twiggy on a tandem bike?'

'Oh, we'll do them too.' Connie tapped him sweetly on the cheek. She knew that familiarity had been noted by Merlin as a sure sign of the lower classes so he encouraged his staff in such demonstrations.

Connie had discovered the expense account. After a month of lifting a finger for a taxi she could no longer conceive of wasting time at a bus stop or making her way to a smelly old tube station.

Mary Quant's show was a disappointment. 'Her clothes are like school uniform,' Connie objected, as a flat-chested model, pale as paper, hair black as ink, paraded a tunic with inverted pleats below a white band.

'But it's so beautifully made,' drooled Zodiac. Connie left her to it and went to the flower show. It had begun to rain heavily, a summer rain that made her think of sodden Irish leaves, of the field she had to cross to bring home water from the well. She spread herself out to dry in the taxi's warm, padded interior. At least, she thought guiltily, her parents' home was on the mains now, a ceremony – according to her sister – that had drawn as near fanatical a celebration as the day the Holy Virgin clinked her rosary at Bernadette. I must write home, Connie told herself. Then, to divert herself from the knowledge that she would not, she started a conversation with her driver about President Kennedy. 'In a country of the young, he had been the youngest ever president . . .'

Connie looked about her and saw that in London there were no rules, neither of dress nor of much else. It seemed she could be exactly what she wanted to be.

Fay went home to Chicago for Seder, determined to have a good talk with Daniel. Her uncle Larry was there and he reminded her of how his military cap had given her lice at the end of the war. Then there was his wife Vera and their son, David, and various other cousins. They were all squeezed into the same small, over-furnished room in which she had grown up. She felt particularly irritated by the dim wattage of the light-bulbs that made relatives, hardly able to see each other, communicate at louder volume than normal. Eventually, after the ceremonial meal had been eaten, the guests had left and her mother had gone to bed, she managed to get Daniel to herself.

'I dreamed about you,' she told him.

'A dream or a nightmare?' He lounged on the only comfortable chair. He was a spoilt mother's boy, Fay thought, who was about to graduate from the University of Chicago. And then what? That was the worry. That was why she had to talk to him.

'You were drafted,' said Fay simply. It was frightening that, as in her dream, he had grown his hair long; despite his jaunty manner, it gave him a sacrificial Christ-like appearance. His eyes were too big and dark, she thought, for the sixties. She found her heart thudding in a way it never did during the toughest operation. 'It was a stupid dream.' She calmed herself and managed a smile. 'You're savvy enough to figure out it's graduate school next.'

'You're assuming I want to dodge my patriotic duty?' He wore sneakers, pale trousers, a shirt and tie in honour of the occasion, the last chosen and knotted by their mother. Probably it had belonged to their father, and been packed away for the son. There was nothing wrong in that, Fay told herself, except that her mother had despised her husband when alive – why should she want a dead man's noose round the neck of her son? Daniel, she observed, had a strong neck and broad shoulders.

'Do you play games?' she asked, surprised at the question and that she didn't know the answer.

'Sure. Softball. But swimming's my thing. I'm no slouch, Fay. Your little brother's been growing up while you've been doing all that studying out East.' His mocking, yet tender voice, as if he were the elder, made her assess him all over again and for a moment she saw a strong young man, no easy battle fodder.

'I may not get to see you often but I worry about you like a sister.'

'I kind of intuited that when you settled down at my feet.' It was true: she was crouching at his knees in an attitude of feminine supplication.

'I guess you have a bit of experience in that line.' She smiled and nodded in the direction of their mother's bedroom.

'We get on OK. She knows my boundaries.'

With her mother's bedroom so close, Fay was worrying that they should not be having this conversation but Daniel remained easy. 'I am going to graduate school.' He paused. 'But, if you want to know, I don't feel too special about it. Politics don't interest me much but draft-dodging doesn't feel like a good way to kick off things.'

Fay, concern rising all over again, noted nevertheless that he still seemed relaxed. She decided to risk going a little way down the line. 'Uncle Larry fought.'

'Different time, different place. All the same, I don't go along with this demonstrating. It's not showing respect for those who fight.'

'I should think they have to face worse things than lack of respect.' She looked down and saw her hands were shaking. Where had this fear been lurking?

Fay's mother had made up a bed for her on the uncomfortable sofa. The room was very warm and still smelt of food, coffee, cigarettes, bodies. Fay, lying awake, thought about germs. She calculated the number that each member of the family had brought in with them.

To say the least, she was bedded down in a hostile area. She'd be wise to prescribe herself a preventive dose of antibiotic. Still unable to sleep, she switched on the light and reached for her book but was diverted by the beam from the light, which showed a multitude of nearly invisible specks – of dust, skin, hair, food particles and something else: the memory that was always there. Her history.

Fay lay down again and realised that what had been odd about the conversation between herself and Daniel was his calm, her intensity. How well had he known their grandmother? He was born in 1945, she had come to America in 1948 and died in 1956. Was it possible he had lived in the same small apartment as her without having seen those blue-grey numbers? Certainly he would never have learnt about her in conversation because nobody ever talked about her past. Or the past at all. Daniel would have been too young to remember her arrival. He would have taken her presence for granted, her premature old age – she was still in her fifties when she died – her ill-health, her lack of English. It seemed likely that he had never lived with fear and guilt as Fay had. Fay pictured his open, frank face. Surely that should make him safe, at least from her kind of demons.

Back in her apartment Fay rose early to study. Dust from her medical books rose up to her spotlight. She pushed them away and turned to her typewriter.

April 1966, NY

Dear Nina, I went home recently and saw my brother. It struck me just how unlike we are. He's just so relaxed. I wonder why our generation seems beset by such demons. Can it be because we were born during a world-wide war? Perhaps that's one of the reasons I feel I can talk to you, despite that huge Atlantic between us. Your father was a prisoner-of-war, I know, although that's about all I know. You once said in the hospital that war had been very important in your life – or something like that. Tell me, some day, how long he was away, how it affected you, just being with your mother, the two of you so close, not knowing when or whether he'd come back. Oh, we're an odd generation. And now it's war that's on my mind again. I guess over your side of the Atlantic you hardly think of Vietnam. Daniel's OK because he's going to graduate school but how long will it all last?

Fay put down the pen and found, as always after writing to Nina, that she felt curiously soothed, as if posting letters half-way across the world put things in better perspective. The truth was, she worked too hard. Which you certainly couldn't say about Nina.

Nina picked up a squashed wax crayon that was lying on the kitchen floor. She like the idea of writing to Fay with purple-crayon inefficiency. 'Why are you smiling?' William stood at the door. He had been

35

having a bath and now he came into the room with a towel round his waist.

Nina looked at the crayon in her hand. She had already forgotten why she'd been smiling. 'It's Jamie's.' She went over to William and put her arms round his naked chest. His flesh was warm, pink and hard. His arms came round her. They were still damp and smelt faintly of soap and even more faintly of William's own body, a smell she had known since she was a child. 'I had a letter from Fay.'

'Your American.'

'She's not mine.' Nina removed her arms and stood a little back to see William's expression, although she knew what it would be.

'Well, she's certainly not mine.' He was frowning.

'If she comes over again, you could meet her.'

'Make her mine, you mean.'

'Oh, no.' Nina laughed. 'I don't think there's any chance of that. I wouldn't say she's your type at all. Far too independent.'

At this William lost interest, as she had known he would, and started to approach the table in a way that meant he was wondering why she hadn't started making supper.

'Grilled chops,' said Nina. 'They'll be done by the time you've dressed.'

William didn't comment on this obvious untruth. As a soldier, he dressed with a speed and efficiency that, in the morning, left her filled with lassitude. 'Go and see if the children are asleep,' she suggested.

'OK.' He liked kissing them when they were asleep. He liked kissing her when she was asleep and she liked it, too, because it transported her beyond the reach of rational thought. What would she write to Fay? She began to plan a letter in her head: 'Dear Fay, It is spring now but in this ugly little German town, you would hardly know it. Helen and I both miss the English countryside so much that we paint strange green water-colours. Hers are better than mine because they are freer ...' Would this constitute the sort of news Fay asked for? She doubted it. 'Dear Fay, William has been promoted to Major. He leaves every morning at eight o'clock and returns at seven ...' This was news but not hers. 'Dear Fay, Helen is begging to go to boarding-school in England. I tell her she is hardly more than a baby. She has a very strong will ...' This was not her news either. Slowly Nina walked to the sink and turned on the taps. 'Now I shall turn them off without washing any part of my body,' she told herself. This she did, carefully studying the drips that lingered temptingly after the main flow had stopped.

At the door William made throat-clearing noises. There was an element of reproach that he could not yet smell sizzling lamb but only as an undercurrent because he wanted to believe in her as a successful wife and mother.

Dear Fay, I am so lucky to have such a wonderful husband and children and mother. Families are just the most important thing in the world. Someday I'd love to meet yours. Are you close to Daniel? Years ago I used to think of William as my older brother but when he became my husband, I had to drop that idea! The first time we met he was learning to drive and shunted me up and down our driveway in his father's car about a dozen times. I was so impressed. It was a beautiful sunny afternoon and my father had organised a tennis tournament on our lawn. I'd had to mow it over and over again. The mowing always put me off tennis. But, then, I was never any good at sporting activities. Not competitive enough. I fear I really disappointed my father. You asked about that wartime period when my mother and I were together. The truth is I only remember happy country days. It was when my father came back that things were less fun. But he thought William was wonderful. Another soldier in the family. That sent my stock up no end. Yes, I really would like to meet Daniel.

Connie stood with a notepad outside the heavy doors of Biba in Kensington Church Street. Not that they appeared heavy the way teeny girls swung in and out of them.

'Excuse me. I'm doing an article for the *Evening Standard*.' The girl she had addressed, perhaps seventeen years old in a pink mini-skirt swirled with lime green and purple, stopped for a second, then shook off Connie's hand and dashed into the shop. After this had happened twice more, Connie realised her mistake. She was standing in the way of shopping addicts and their fix. She must grab them coming out, buzzing with exhilaration, pupils dilated with the thrill of a satisfying buy.

'Excuse me. I'm doing an article for the *Standard*. I wonder if you would show me your purchase.'

And how they did! Jersey knit dresses, the size of jerseys, feather boas dyed shocking pink and violet, hats the same night-club colours, jackets so tight at the waist and high on the shoulders that it was a wonder they'd do up, tights in every colour, and gloves made of tigerskin or mauve lurex.

'And how much did you spend?' asked Connie.

'Altogether, you mean?' The girl, draped in gold vinyl, considered. 'Do you mind my asking what you earn?'

'I'm a secretary. Twelve pounds ten a week and I spend six or seven pounds on clothes, usually here. I mean, this is the cheapest and the most with it. I come in from Chingford.'

'So you spend half your wages on clothes?'

'I know. My mum says I should be saving for my bottom drawer but she lived in a different age. I'm earning good money so I can choose how to spend it. Nothing wrong with that.'

'No,' agreed Connie. 'I'm with you there. Nothing wrong in the world.' She saw in the glinting lights that revolved outwards from the store's spotlights and the low sun over the street that she had a good story here, a story about youth and freedom, sex and money and a new kind of power.

The light caught in Connie's eyes. A young man was approaching her, with dark hair flopping across his forehead, horn-rimmed glasses and a small-knot tie. Rick was thrusting his way through the crowded pavement like a pre-programmed missile. She felt pierced already, heart thudding, knees wobbling, and tried to summon up her newly acquired journalistic skills to defend herself. But the images his presence conjured up were too powerful.

Evenings in the pub had been hard work, certainly, but before midnight she had cleared up and was off, new friends around her, white lips, blackened eyes, tight black skirt, hair backcombed and sprayed, and heels as high as she could stand in on the underground escalator without falling.

Then it was dancing, sweating out the dregs of glasses swigged during the evening, not caring who squeezed her flesh, slipped their fingers under her straps. That was how she had met Rick, who took her back to his bed-sit in Kilburn and kept her up till three showing her his books of paintings. And almost without drawing breath, he had a condom out of a packet and his cock out of his trousers, and her on the bed half undressed and too sleepy to really partake but dazzled by something about his pale round face and his glasses and the way he talked so interestingly about his books, and then the sudden thrilling switch when he turned to concentrating on her body. She fell in love, she supposed.

'I don't want to see you standing there in front of me! Sure, I do not! Take yourself out of my sight!' she screamed, had become an Irish milkmaid, quivering in front of the young master.

'Connie!' He was still not close. He shouted through heads that hardly bothered to turn.

'Don't! Don't dare to come near me!' She pushed past his pale, tight, cruel face into Biba, although she hardly knew she had moved. Her hands waved and shook as she tried to hide among the racks of feather boas. Dangling purple and pink fronds blurred her sight. She was underwater, drowning in bright weeds.

'Connie! Please, Connie! Connie, come out.' Thank God she could hardly hear his lying voice. He had taken her to dinner with his friends once. In the city because he worked there now and wore a suit. She had spent a week's wages on a pair of earrings that looked like liquorice allsorts.

All his friends were men, pale indoor faces, smooth white hands on the starched white tablecloth, all wearing the same expression – not quite leering, not quite lecherous. Connie had gathered that Rick was showing her off for the wrong reasons. Absentmindedly she snapped off her new earrings and laid them like an offering on the nearest table.

'I gather you work in a public house,' one of the friends, the tallest and most languid, had commented.

'I understand your family have a few acres in Ireland,' said a second after a suitable interval. Perhaps this was a kind overture, an invitation to expand, in the Irish way, on peat water so clear that the little folk could admire their pointed ears and on air so fresh that one gulp would last you all day . . . 'I will arise and go now, and go to Innisfree . . .' But Connie had thought of the rain and the mud, her father's solitary gloom and her mother's brave smiles.

'Do these belong to madam?' An elderly waiter bowed to Rick over a silver platter on which lay the liquorice-allsorts earrings.

It was after this evening that Rick had begun to accuse her of smelling of drink and cigarettes. She had told him she was a bar-girl and that drink and ciggies was what bar-girls smelt of. And then he had gone to Paris.

'Bloody hell, Rick!' Now she would crisp him with her wrath. 'Can't you tell when a girl's working?' What was he doing seeking her out as if it were a normal thing to do? 'You bastard, Rick!' She enjoyed pronouncing the word, although its weight seemed to have silenced her. What did she want to scream? *Look what you made me do. So. So, I hurled a bunch of bananas at your father but that would be too good for you. Besides, I'm stronger than that now.* Stronger? Hiding among the water weed. She watched as the lurid feather-boa fronds parted slowly, revealing his once beloved face. But there was no love in it. Never had been, if truth be told. His father Hubert, the rat, had more love in his corrupt, degraded soul.

'Connie. We don't have to part like this—'

'Yes. Yes. Yes. We do.' She fled back on to the streets, past open-mouthed gargoyle stares. In her haste she had not realised she was hooked to a row of boas, which fluttered dramatically behind her like ragged pennants. Some way behind raced a bevy of mini-clad shop assistants.

Soon Kensington Gardens appeared on her left. She dashed through an opening and flung herself on to the grass. Pink and purple feathers continued to eddy round her for some time.

Connie's article, about young buying power, written up entirely by herself with ferocious wit and energy, caused a minor sensation. A startled readership wrote in to the *Evening Standard* expressing their shock and outrage:

'Selfish, silly and frivolous. Are these the children for whom we won the war?'

'My daughter had all the high ideal of motherhood before she went to London and now she's only interested in the length of her skirt . . .'

'They talk about psychedelic colours and then they say clothes have nothing to do with a drug culture . . .'

'When I visited a changing room with my daughter it was not only communal, which was bad enough, but a man was in there!'

Ecstatic at this tribute to her skills, Connie sent copies to everyone she could think of, including Nina and Fay. When the outrage wore thin, a line of heavyweight defenders appeared:

'If being frivolous is not getting involved in things like Vietnam then I'm all for it,' wrote Mary Quant.

'In London now a girl can walk down the Kings Road dressed in anything, even in two banana skins, but they must be well designed banana skins,' commented Ossie Clarke sagely.

Finally the Chancellor of the Exchequer joined in: 'The new fashion industry for the young has resulted in a very promising export trade . . .'

The editor-in-chief of the *Evening Standard* summoned Connie to his office. Only partially disguising his surprise at her outfit – tight high-heeled white boots below lurex tights and a dress trimmed with fake leopardskin fur – he congratulated her on a piece that was utterly of the moment.

'That is the essence of journalism,' he advised her sententiously, while Connie tried to look abashed with a modest smile. He sat forward in his chair. 'So, what would you like to take on next?'

In order to gain time, for she had no ideas for another article 'of the moment', Connie crossed her legs and noticed that her knees, previously plumpish and dimpled, were now tapered to an elegant point. It was fame, she supposed, that gave her no time to eat.

'The models are very thin.' She batted her false eyelashes. 'Just look at that Twiggy. Almost skeletal. And, of course, the young girls want to look exactly like them. It can't be healthy, can it?'

In less than a year, Connie had become a leading feature writer. She sat in the diary room still, but only because she enjoyed it. She was presumed to be in touch with the kind of people that the editor and Merlin could only guess at. One evening Merlin took her to supper at the new Italian restaurant in Soho. Mario and Franco's was notable for the lack of Chianti bottles, fishermen's nets and pictures of Sorrento. Connie thought it also lacking in atmosphere.

'This is where all the film and advertising people come,' said Merlin longingly.

'I don't know why you want to be something you're not,' responded Connie, swigging her Verdicchio as if it were water. 'Why not use your proper name, Merlin Regis de Witt?'

'Sssh.' Merlin looked round anxiously.

'Trying to pretend you're Merlin Derwitt just shows a lack of confidence. Take a leaf out of Justin de Villeneuve's book.'

'The de Witts are mentioned in the Domesday Book. With a family history like that how can I pretend to be in touch with modern life?'

'You take too much note of our editor. Come to that, I can't imagine why you want to be a journalist at all with the knowledge you have in you.'

Merlin looked hunted. 'Now, Connie . . .'

'You should be a professor. Why shouldn't you be a professor?'

'My father was a professor.'

'Oh, well, then. But at least you could be a serious writer. You could write more about politics.'

'My uncle is a junior minister.'

'Oh, well. That is bad luck. Why don't you write about antiques?'

Despite Merlin's gloom at his establishment background, by the end of the evening he had revealed quite a different person from the old fusspot, would-be swinger, that Connie had identified him as in the office. Mysteriously, it turned out that he knew a great deal about

41

antiques, and when he asked her, 'Would you like to see my etchings?' it was no joke.

Nina was overawed by Connie's meteoric rise to a narrow but high-profile fame. She wanted to talk to her about William but guessed she would never have the nerve. In the end she made it impossible by coming to see her in London with both children. They were meeting in Merlin's flat.

'They've been to the dentist, I'm afraid,' apologised Nina, 'so they're not very jolly.'

'Can't they put in a word for themselves?'

Nina thought it was not only her children who found it difficult to speak out, she could hardly put in a word for herself. 'Normally they would eat.'

'Oh, Mummy, we can still *eat*!'

'There's my girl,' said Connie.

They repaired to the kitchen, where the atmosphere improved and Nina became curious. 'So are you living with Cousin Merlin?'

'We're certainly not lovers, if that's what you mean.'

Casting a glance at her children, who were munching their way through a plum cake found at the back of the cupboard, Nina tried to decide if she were prudish or Connie vulgar. Because she disliked criticising others and was accustomed to criticising herself, she decided on the former. 'I once met Merlin's mother, before she died.'

'It would have to be before she died, wouldn't it now!'

'Louisa Regis de Witt was a formidable woman.' Nina tried to hold her ground. 'An American heiress. The Regis came from her. She fell in love with this rather ordinary Englishman and never recovered when he was killed in the war. Lived here alone in this flat and died about five years ago. Her heart had broken and never mended, so the family say.'

'Surely little Merlin made her feel less alone?'

'She didn't rate him highly, I'm afraid. But of course he's ended up awfully rich. She collected antiques and apparently had a frightfully good eye for them, quite apart from all the money she had before.'

'Merlin told me his father was a professor and his uncle a politician.'

'Absolutely right. The sort of dim professor who wears a fob watch.' Nina took a large cherry from the cake. 'He was known as Witless de Witt. That was why it was odd Louisa so adored him. William thinks that, being American, she couldn't tell one sort of Englishman from another.'

'How odd. I'm Irish and I can tell with perfect ease what sort of Englishman I'm faced with.'

'Can you?' Nina failed to disguise her doubts. Connie's own description of her love life with the notorious Hubert and Rick showed outstanding talent for misjudgement.

'Well, I can if they tell the truth about themselves.'

Nina sighed. 'If they know it. Why don't you bring Merlin to stay at Lymhurst? I don't go back to Germany until the weekend.'

'Merlin and I don't travel together.'

'Come yourself, then.'

'I just might take you up on that kind offer. Now, children, before you finish that cake, I've just remembered that it was presented to your host by his mother on her deathbed with the instructions that he should use it for his wedding cake and think of her. I thought he was making a joke at the time but now I'm inclined to think he was telling the truth. Here, we'll put it back in the box and he'll be none the wiser.'

'He will on his wedding day,' observed Nina, smiling.

'Not at all. His bride will put it down to ants or earwigs or mice—'

'Or snakes,' suggested Jamie, perking up.

'There's a bright boy. Or rattlesnakes or cake-loving cleaning ladies . . .'

'Or tooth fairies.' Helen entered the game.

'In other words,' continued Connie, 'the bride will have many explanations at her fingertips without blaming two poor hungry children, just back from the dentist and starving because their mother had not thought to provide for them.'

'You invited us to tea!' protested Nina.

'And, above all, the bride will be delighted that she doesn't have to be lumbered with some dead mother's maudlin fantasy. In all honesty, we have done Merlin a favour. Children, do you think we should finish it?'

'No. No. They'll be sick.'

'Sorry, kids. Regretfully, we must close the tin.'

1967

Nina watched washing-up liquid bubble off her pink rubber gloves. 'William, do you think the Americans are right to be fighting in Vietnam?'

He was already dressed in full uniform. She was late, washing up Jamie's supper with a deliberation that had drawn William's stare. 'Why don't you go and change,' he said, 'while I think of an answer? I'm only a soldier, you know, not a politician.'

Surprised that he had not answered 'yes' to her question without needing to think, Nina went upstairs obediently. While she brushed her hair, which was now long enough to twist into a little knot in her head, she reread Fay's letter:

Vietnam dominates everything. Family and friends are torn apart. They've always wanted to be one hundred per cent American and now that seems to mean sending their beautiful boys off to a war that they can make no sense of. Parents are sick with it all and feeling guilty about half-made plans to get their sons up to Canada. And then the pros and the cons argue with each other. It's a bad time. And the worst thing for me is that I don't know what I think, which is not my usual style. I envy you over there. But I guess I should be asking for your advice. Or William's. You see, I'm beginning to think I don't understand war at all, the purpose of any war. So maybe you should ask William. Or your mother. Or you. I suppose from the moment you could think there's been some war in your life. I know World War II had some pretty strong justification but all the same, with all those soldiers fighting for freedom round the world, it didn't save the lives of six million Jews, did it, happening behind their backs, under their noses? Perhaps there was some other way of stopping that. Something that didn't include sending ignorant young boys to be killed and to kill. Or to be maimed. My mother wrote me last week that my cousin Josh lost an arm and an eye ... He's the same Josh whose maternal grandparents died in concentration camps. I know there isn't any link but it feels like there is.

'Nina! What are you doing?' William shouted – with justifiable anger, she thought. She slashed a bit of lipstick across her mouth and hurried down. She could see it wouldn't be quite the moment to question the nature of war. After all, here they were living in Germany, the country that had caused so much suffering to both her family and Fay's. But that was over twenty years ago now, she told herself reprovingly, and she should hold individuals responsible, not a whole country.

'Has the baby-sitter arrived?' she called and war disappeared with anxiety about Jamie's single-child status since Helen had gone to boarding-school in England.

Their bed had grown smaller, Nina decided, and then recollected that she had grown bigger and that William, previously broad-framed but not fleshy, had too. When Jamie joined them for a cuddle on Sunday morning, it was more of a crush than a pleasure. At night, the two of them were thrown together in involuntary intimacy.

'Do you think we might get twin beds?' She spoke above Jamie's head, placing her palm on his fair hair.

William lowered his paper carefully. 'My parents bought twin beds the year that they divorced.'

Fay lay on the floor of her apartment doing sit ups. Thirty of them and then ten press-ups. It was Saturday evening, the sort of time other women had dates.

With pleasure, she felt her heartrate rise. A surgeon has to be as strong, calm and fit as a top athlete. When had she decided she wouldn't have dates? Let's put it graciously. A long time ago now. 1960.

He had been called Christopher, a ridiculous WASP name. Alone it would have been enough to shock Fay's mother. But that wasn't the worst of it. The best of it was pretty good: he was serious, hard-working, also aiming for medical school, nice-looking without being handsome, dark, crimped hair, well-spaced eyes, delicate fingers. It was the fingers Fay had fallen in love with, surgeon's fingers, she teased him, and perhaps his shoulders, their square simplicity. They went swimming together and, even when she was mostly naked, he still talked to her as if she were a human being.

In the spring of 1960, he asked her to be his partner at a dance. It was a great date, all her friends told her, the big one when men threw everything overboard. Fay knew that they meant marriage proposals, because that was what they wanted. With at least five more years of study ahead of her, she wanted no proposal except a place at Columbia.

But since no one was likely to believe her, she kept quiet and admitted she did want this date.

If they had known the worst of it, they would have guessed just how much. 'I am not a natural liar.' Fay had stared at her pale face in the mirror, into her own dark eyes, and they stared back, defensive, defiant, ashamed, exhilarated. She had just telephoned her mother in Chicago and told her she would not be spending Seder with the family because she had promised to spend it with her grandmother in Brooklyn.

'I felt sorry for her,' she had explained to her mother, 'spending Seder with poor deaf Grandfather, sad Uncle Morris and that weird cousin Elsie to keep her company.' Then she had rung her grandmother, her father's mother, whom she had got to know over her last three years on the east coast and, sounding sorrowful, complained, 'My mother insists I spend Seder with her and the whole family. A dreadful nuisance to do that journey when I could be with you.'

The beauty of this deception was that her mother and her grandmother had never liked each other and now seldom spoke. So both, however cross, were most unlikely to compare notes. Besides, the telephone was only for emergencies.

'You look great. Just great.' Compliments from Christopher were rare but Fay, the realist, knew he was right. She was wearing a pale blue dress, cut tightly to her small waist, and she had folded her hair into a chignon so it was like a shiny dark cap. She felt *soignée*, as near beautiful as she could be. She put her arm through Christopher's and smiled with Grace Kelly charm.

Fay had a glorious night and did not regret her lies. She kissed Christopher with the promise of more as they parted – five in the morning, a slick sunrise filled with song-thrushes and the revving of returning revellers' cars. But, inwardly, she knew it was over. The price had been too high. She would tell him she wasn't like other girls, that she had no room for anything but her ambition to be a doctor. Goodbye, Grace Kelly.

So. That was enough of Memory Lane. Fay lay back and stretched her arms over her head. I need sex, she found herself thinking. Sex is healthy. It's just the dating part I don't want. No Nina with her husband and children, no Connie in an emotional mess. Clean, ordered, healthy, man sex, that was what she was after.

Connie had formed the habit of visiting Father O'Donald every couple of weeks. He had been transferred to a Soho parish where he had inaugurated a shelter for heroin addicts and alcoholics and any other 'dregs', as Connie cheerily referred to them.

'How are your dregs this afternoon?' she called out now, as she descended to the neon-lit basement room.

'You don't treat me like a priest,' grumbled Father O'Donald.

'That's because you don't treat me like a sinner.'

'If it's a theological discussion you want I'm not your man, but it's true I harbour a soft spot for you. Not for your sins, you understand.'

The priest was buttering bread for Christmas-party sandwiches and immediately gave Connie the task of blowing up balloons. 'Couldn't we change jobs?' she objected. 'Surely spreading butter on bread is woman's work.'

'And you so full of hot air.'

'So, who will you be entertaining?'

'A fair amount of our countrymen, I expect. Christmas draws them to the priest and if there's a bit of warmth and food thrown in, they'll just settle in for the night.'

'One of them could be my own brother. Two of them came to England in the war when I was just a wee baby. But I heard about it, all right. My da never forgave them and my mam never forgave him. At least, that's how I figure it now. Kevin went to America, Finbar and Joe to England and Michael stayed at home. That's the history of the men in our family.'

'So where's the one in England you do know about?'

'Joe?' Connie made a face, then smeared her mouth with butter as if it were lipstick. 'He's up in the benighted north of this great country, and I'll thank you not to remind me of that drunken oaf who thought to use me as a skivvy in his best friend's house.'

Connie wasn't going to bother telling the story of her first impression of England, although she could remember it well enough. They had seemed very big the night she arrived at Warrington station, three of them, a welcoming party, and Connie couldn't tell which was her brother. Then the train had moved, the light changed, and she saw that the biggest of them had the reddish black hair and the blue eyes of Michael and herself, their nose too, straight out of the forehead, and the wide bony shoulders of her father. The other two were smaller men, who'd slicked back their hair and rubbed up their jacket for this occasion, meeting an unknown sister from back home. Between them they held a large piece of brown paper on which was written in white chalk, CONSTANCE O'MALLEY.

She'd put down her case. Then, looking around, she took in the coils from steaming chimneys that tore into the dark sky, the raging noise of machines, the sulphurous smell even in the cold night air. It seemed the station was surrounded by factories.

'You're an O'Malley, that's certain.'

'I was thinking the same about you.'

The two friends had stood back respectfully while the brother and sister shook hands. They were too shy to kiss on this first ever meeting. Well, the first that she could remember, at any rate. Nevertheless, Connie had noticed that there was the smell of alcohol about him.

'This is Timmy and this forward fellow's Pat. It's in Pat's house you'll be lodging.'

Connie had looked at Pat's pale thin face, the scarf choking his neck, the hands, too big, hanging out of his jacket. She could see him any day of the week in Dublin so what was her big brother, who'd escaped to England, doing to put her with a no-hoper like him?

'My wife's on nights,' said Pat, 'but she worries should the baby wake. It's a big enough room for two.'

Nights with a squalling baby. Connie had spotted it at once and thought, Isn't that what I've saved all these years to escape? The end was there at the beginning.

No, she would not share these gloomy memories with the priest who was having trouble putting air inside a long green balloon.

'You're supposed to be blowing up the balloons, not your cheeks,' commented Connie, watching his face swell alarmingly. 'Here, I'll stick it with a knife so you don't have to admit defeat.'

'The O'Donalds,' said the priest, laying down the balloon, 'are a close-knit family.'

'The O'Malleys are romantics,' responded Connie solemnly. 'To take a current example, I am planning to go to America and search for my long-lost brother Kevin. God willing, he'll be smarter than the man up north and I'll never return to this meagre land.'

Father O'Donald made an odd movement, as if flinching. But there was nothing, Connie thought, for him to flinch from. Curious, she leant forward just as he raised his eyes to hers. That strange plum-brown of the red-haired, they fixed on her with intolerable pain and emotion.

'No!' she exclaimed involuntarily, and looked away at once. If she had ever thought he liked her in that way, she'd never admitted it.

'No,' he repeated soberly. 'Certainly not.' The pause was brief enough but the 'not' rang heavily through it. 'I shall think of you often on your quest.' He had recovered his self-possession and could play the part of the kindly priest again.

'Oh, Father.' Now she could not even hold out a hand to him.

'I'll offer you up.' He smiled ironically. 'Tell me, when are you off?'

'This week, next week,' said Connie airily.

But when she got home a letter from Nina made her change her plans.

'William is away.' Nina showed Connie into her neat army house. She hugged her as if to soften the blow of arrival, of alien organisation, of a foreign country, of a friend perhaps not what she expected. She had not meant to sound pathetic in her letter but she did need someone to talk to.

'I hope I've not driven him off.'

'He's away often, I'm afraid.' She paused, suffering from honesty, but if you could not be honest with a friend what hope was there? 'I'm not altogether afraid.'

But Connie hadn't heard and continued into the house where she found Jamie lying on the floor studying the underside of a miniature jeep.

'Hi,' said Connie, 'you look comfortable.'

He did not deign to answer.

'I brought a bottle.' Connie reached into her bag – large and embroidered with bells. 'Actually, I brought two. It's so extraordinary having money. I send some to my mother, you know. Oh, what a lamentation!'

'Food,' said Nina to Jamie, who rose automatically from the floor.

'I might as well open the bottle now,' suggested Connie, failing to remember what she had in common with this worthy wife and mother. She had been summoned, that was it. She must recall that behaving well was not always its own reward. They were friends, once holed up in the same loony bin. They had danced by the sacred yew. 'Do you keep the bottle-opener concealed for tactical reasons? Perhaps Jamie has shown a tendency to dipsomania?'

While Nina put Jamie to bed, Connie sat alone drinking in the living room. She was surprised to see how ugly it was, the furniture a strange burnished orange colour that effortlessly dominated a vase of flowers and one or two prints on the walls.

At last Nina came down. She looked exhausted, ugly, dark circles under her eyes. She was dressed in a shapeless smock over baggy trousers.

'Are you pregnant again?' asked Connie.

'Of course not. I suppose there're no fat women where you work. And you're so skinny yourself.'

'Slender.'

'Anyway, you look jolly elegant and pretty.'

There was a pause while Connie searched for anything nice she could say about Nina's looks and decided it was best to change the subject. 'Any luck with the painting?'

'No. Jolly kind of you to ask. I don't know where the time goes. I do read. I'm reading Dante at the moment. "El Paradiso".'

'Heavens. I thought you were an atheist.'

Nina gasped, put her hands in front of her face, then resolutely removed them. 'The truth is I'm most awfully depressed. The washing's not too bad but I just can't see any reason to do anything. William can't understand. How I seem to have no time for anything. With Helen away, there's only Jamie.'

'Where's Helen?' asked Connie, who hadn't noticed her absence.

'At school in England.'

'But she's a baby!'

'She insisted on being taken out of the boarding-school she started at. There was a rookery nearby that made scary cawing after dark so she's being a day girl near Lymhurst and my mother's looking after her. They get on very well. She's learning to play the piano.'

Connie took another drink and settled herself down to listen. She saw that this was why Nina had invited her. She wondered when she would get round to William.

But her problems were more general, it seemed. First, there was being so much alone with only a three-year-old boy as companion – 'It's not at all like Malaya where we all knew each other and forged a real community!' This was delivered so earnestly that Connie felt the need to nod in agreement, although 'a community' conjured up prison images.

Then there was her inability to pick up her paintbrushes, which she had bought at great expense in London. 'At least they're useful for getting down the cobwebs.'

'What cobwebs?' Connie wouldn't imagine anything as friendly as a cobweb in this nasty little house.

'I don't know.' Nina looked round vaguely.

There was the problem of the house in England. William had bought it from her mother but was unwilling to pay for its upkeep. 'He says the money is for the children, which sort of stumps me because I would have thought the house is for the children.'

Connie's spirits began to sink under the predictability of this narrative and she decided to test the full-frontal approach. 'How are you getting on with William?'

'Oh, William's very well.' Nina gave an infuriatingly general smile, as if she had answered a question put to her by a stranger at a cocktail party. 'His new job is very demanding.' She paused. 'There was something . . .'

'Ah,' encouraged Connie.

'Do you ever think about war?'

'What? Why war?'

'You see, it's rather in my mind at the moment. Partly because Fay writes to me about Vietnam. She sort of assumes it must be the most important thing in my life, what with my father in the camp and his health never really recovering so he died youngish and then me being married to a soldier. Well, here I am in a country that wanted to take over England. I try to talk about it to William but he doesn't seem very interested. But there's something more confusing. You see, I'm beginning to think I married William because I thought he understood, and now I'm beginning to think he doesn't. Or perhaps there's nothing to understand. War exists. The stronger tries to bully the weaker so we all need armies. I suppose I hero-worshipped William, particularly when he wore his uniform at breakfast. I thought he was strong and manly, a moral force for the good, a soldier in every way. I'm still trying to keep that feeling alive but it seems to be necessary, if I'm to manage it, to stay on the side of war. If that's the right way to look at it, which it probably isn't.'

'Phew, said Connie.

'When I was about sixteen, I saw William in a newsreel. I'd gone with some schoolfriends to the local cinema. He was with a whole lot of other soldiers mounting the gangplank of a ship. They were on their way to Egypt. You know, the Suez canal thing. I'd never have recognised him, except he was suddenly in close-up. And just at that moment, when I was thinking, Gosh, that's William, doesn't he look handsome?, some youths at the back of the cinema started shouting – booing, actually. Anyway, a fight broke out between some officer class sitting near us and these youths at the back, shouting, "Murderers!" and that sort of thing.'

'I don't quite understand,' said Connie, as Nina paused again.

'I've just been thinking that maybe they were right and soldiers are murderers.'

Connie took a really large gulp of her wine. 'No wonder you're depressed. It strikes me you think far too much.'

'I hate thinking!' Nina cried vehemently.

'What do you like doing?' Connie commended herself for her patience.

Nina sat in her chair, hands on spread knees, eyes straight ahead. 'I like looking. Perceiving. I like losing myself in what I'm looking at.'

'Looking? Looking at anything?' Connie peered to see what was presently transfixing Nina. It seemed to be a bare patch of wall with a faint shadow of a faded potted plant. 'A kind of meditation, you mean?'

'Oh, no! Take no notice of me.' Nina stood up abruptly, as if she had knocked herself out of her trance. 'I'll get our supper.'

In the night, a loud noise entered Connie's dream and she knew there was a man in the house. She came downstairs for breakfast with trepidation. The smell of kippers filled the kitchen. William's broad back, at least she assumed it to be William's, bent over the stove.

'Good morning. You must be Connie.'

Connie was surprised. It was all very well to write off someone's husband in the abstract but when presented with a large, attractive, confident male person, the situation seemed to shift. Nina had never mentioned quite how fair, how fit, how sexy he was. She drew the sash of her mauve silk kimono tighter at the waist.

'Yes. I'm Connie. Do you really like kippers?'

'I love kippers.' He was very serious. 'But I only have them in Nina's absence. She has taken Jamie to school. I don't expect I can tempt you to one?'

'I wouldn't consider it. Your personal treat? It would be criminal.'

'I don't love them that much.'

'Stewed tea is my delight from this nice fat pot.'

'I'd forgotten,' said William, 'that you were Irish.'

Nina found them on either side of the table, companionable.

Connie knew that William was prolonging his departure, relishing this sparkling friend of his wife's on whom he hoped he was making a good impression.

'I shall have to go.' He was regretful, shook Connie's hand then kissed her cheek. He had the flattering air of a man who longed to exchange a dozen pressing engagements and the command of hundreds for another cup of tea poured by the white hand of this Irish beauty.

'You can see,' said Nina, clattering plates together, 'why I love him.'

'I'd better dress,' said Connie diplomatically. They had planned to go for a walk, despite Nina's dire prediction that there was nothing worth seeing in this part of Germany. But rain began to fall and soon turned to sleet, so they sat down once more in the living room and resumed their conversation of the night before.

'You think it's all my fault,' began Nina aggressively, 'now that you have seen him. And you're right. He is what he is and always has been, and probably always will be. There's nothing wrong with him.'

'I must admit that before I saw the golden hunk of him I would have advised you to take off for Sussex. But now I'm not so certain.'

'You mean because he'll take a lover. Oh, he doesn't need me away to do that.'

'Oh, no, surely—'

'The worst of it is that I don't care. Not really, truly, agonisingly. I certainly don't blame him with me looking like an old bag and half off my head too. I'm still washing, of course. Don't believe me if I tell you I'm not. But if he has taken a lover, it hasn't lessened his need for me.'

Connie began to feel depressed. She saw that there was a tangle here beyond the nimblest of fingers to unravel. Listening, she recalled to herself, was her original brief. And she made a note that marriage was only to be entered into under circumstances of extraordinary, and probably unattainable, certainty.

After Connie's departure Nina cleared up. She swept about her room, smelling of scents and creams. She crept into Jamie's room, and admired his sweet sleeping body before tucking him comfortably into his bed. She cooked the supper and left it to keep warm in the oven, then went to the dining room, which they hardly ever used, and laid newspaper over the mahogany table. She flicked through her sketch book, pleased to see studies of a candlestick, a window, a tree outside it. She took her canvas and paints from behind the dresser and began to squeeze out two or three colours. A limited palette, she told herself, admiring the cobalt blue curl like a shell. Cobalt blue, yellow ochre, Vandyke brown, raw sienna . . .

At ten, William came home and Nina, pale and worn, kissed him kindly. He went up to Jamie first and then they ate supper together quietly.

'Why ever did that friend of yours come here? We don't seem her style.'

Nina saw that William's admiration of Connie was to be disguised as criticism. 'She's going to America soon and she wanted to ask me about Fay. I reminded her that Fay was serious, hard-working, had no interest in men and no sense of humour.'

William laughed. 'That was a little mean. Not like you at all.'

It wasn't. Nina looked at him with the same kindness that was to do with three hours of painting. 'I'd rather be me than either of them,' she said.

'I should hope so too,' smiled William, with boyish affection, blue eyes wide.

Seeing this, Nina smiled too, but her heart, bolder than usual, gave a lurch of recognition. This was how William looked after making love, his relaxed, conquering-hero look, as she described it to herself. And yet he had not bothered to make an excuse for being late home and she had been too uncaring to ask for one.

Fay had borrowed a car to meet Connie at the airport. It made her feel old, as if Connie were her daughter. She sat in the bar, drinking black coffee and looking at her watch now and again. She knew how long it took for foreign nationals to pass through Customs, and she did not plan to stand waiting for every plane load. Her working day had started at six with her habitual jog and she had been on duty at the hospital at seven thirty. It was tiring being in demand. Why had she said she'd put up this wild Irish girl, whom she'd only known for a couple of weeks under circumstances too strange to make a real friendship? Oh, God, that crazy episode with the tree. How could she have forgotten that? Now, if it had been Nina, that would have made more sense. Nina and she corresponded regularly. In fact, she had a half-read letter in her purse now. Fay found it, with its German postmark:

I've just reread your letter and feel filled with admiration for your energy and organisation. You're the only woman I know who has a proper career or even the ambition to have one. That seems odd even to me, and to an American it must seem positively outlandish, as if we were Maori women or had our babies strapped on our backs, a pot bubbling on the fire and our men out sticking unwary beasts! It's even odder since I only have one child at home and the other in England being looked after by her grandmother. What I'm saying, I suppose, is that it must seem to you as if we're living in the Dark Ages not the late sixties when women like you are taking on a man's world. Perhaps I am the last of the generation who'll be quite so spineless . . .

In complete agreement with Nina's view of herself, Fay glanced at her watch again and thought that at least Connie seemed to have developed a career.

Connie charmed her way into the shortest line through Customs and was into the airport in a flash. She was not put out when there was no sign of Fay but went immediately to the bookstall where she spent every dollar she had on the *New York Times*, the *Washington Post*, the *Daily News*, *Time* magazine, *Newsweek* and then, with a mounting sense of excitement, *New York* magazine and the *Village Voice*. Clasping this challenging bonanza of American newsprint, she staggered joyfully to the nearest bar. Centuries of inherited Irish experience told her that anyone worth meeting would, sooner or later, be found in a bar. She ordered a highball and overcame her disappointment when, instead of being shaken to within an inch of its life by a man's thick arm, it was poured ready-made from a bottle.

Connie recognised Fay and leapt to her feet, waving her arms. 'Fay! Fay!' This caused the newspapers to cascade from the bar top.

'Welcome to the land of opportunity,' said Fay drily, as Connie stood looking, somewhat bemused, at the chaos about her.

Together they knelt to collect the papers. Another occupant of the bar joined them, a large man with wide hips crawling, catching, folding. Connie stood up, clapped her hands, laughed. At last the final pages had been compressed into her shoulder-bag and it was, of course, drinks all round.

'Trigear,' said the large man. He volunteered that he was heading for Mexico or, as he put it, 'thereabouts', which made Fay suspect he was up to no good. He had the bulging greyness of a man loaded with secrets, and when he drank he looked around as if to check out who was watching him. He wanted to know why Connie had such an abundance of newsprint. She began to explain. 'I'm a journalist,' she started clearly enough, but as she continued, her Irish accent with its long soft intonation becoming more and more pronounced, Fay felt certain that Trigear didn't understand a word she was saying, although his attention never flagged and he stared at her as if an exotic bird had appeared in their midst. 'And as an Irish woman, I'm accustomed to being a stranger in a strange land. My own voice speaks of the dark and dangerous riches of a people not only caught in the web of their own imaginings but also at the mercy of another race intent on enslaving the glittering life and brilliant dreams that showed up their own dull paucity. They were relegated to pig-sties, like the prodigal son, except that they were not guilty, the riches they had known were thrown into the mire, their princes became paupers, their women drabs, their only poetry in prayer until that, too, became part of the infinite repression. But the voice survives. My voice. Voices in these newspapers. The voice in words. More words!' In demonstration of her point, Connie grabbed a corner of the newspaper and, evidently fearing she was about to shake it open again, Trigear crouched forward on his stool, but Connie smiled. 'I shall desist.' She was obviously pleased with her performance and was about to accept another drink when she saw Fay looking unhappily at her watch.

'You're a perfect angel, Fay.' Connie took her arm affectionately.

They both watched as the big man took the hint and, crying, 'I'll be back, you little beaut!' bounded from the bar. Connie smiled as she noticed him tug the label off her case.

Fay drove them into town. She said, 'I would not have recognised you, so thin and chic.'

'And you just the same,' Connie replied contentedly. She was staring at the American night, the roads so expansive she could hardly see the countryside beyond and then, poorly lit by street lights, European-sized streets and houses, although the slatted wood was unfamiliar. 'How long have we to go, Fay?'

'We'll be at the Triborough bridge in a few minutes, so look out for the skyscrapers. You won't have seen anything like them.' Fay seemed softened at the prospect of showing off Manhattan marvels.

Apart from its strange consecutive layout, Fay's apartment was exactly as Connie would have pictured it: small, neat, decorated in shades of green and grey. There was a sofa-bed already pulled open. She had never seen such a thing before and marvelled at its comfort and efficiency. Fay showed her how the mechanism worked and advised her, in a slightly threatening way, how to shut it up in the morning.

'I'm entranced!' cried Connie. 'And you say it's called a Castro Convertible. How bizarre. I thought America was at war with Castro.'

'I'll leave your political education for the morning.' Fay excused herself for the bathroom and prepared for bed.

Connie found a notebook and began to scribble ecstatically about the American genius in breaking down the distinction between day- and night-life. On her pillow was a map of Manhattan but she barely glanced at it before sliding it to the floor, only rethinking when Fay reappeared with pale, creamed lips and an efficient smile: 'Did you see the maps I left you?'

'I most certainly did.' Connie scrabbled under her bed, rose with map triumphant. 'I'm putting it under my pillow, see, and in the morning, every street will be running alongside the arteries of my brain.'

Inwardly Fay grimaced at this whimsy. 'Sounds like you'll have an energetic night.' She went into her bedroom and closed the door.

Left alone, Connie felt far too revved up to sleep and let herself out into the warm night.

Nina was staring through the kitchen window. She had to remind herself that this was Sussex in May. Five minutes ago, the lawn had been green, varied by brightish patches of moss, the flat greyer leaves of plaintains, the bobbing white heads of daisies and the occasional tow-headed dandelion. It was the same lawn that she had looked on with baby-blurred vision, taken her first steps on, turned cartwheels on, entertained William to a glass of wine on . . . But Nina did not want her thoughts to take her too far from the scene in front of her, so she stopped there and took a step nearer the window-pane.

The lawn that had been green for as long as she could remember was now unnaturally white. For heaven's sake, it's nearly summer, thought Nina, and just look at the lawn. She said it aloud to her mother: 'Just look at the lawn!' But her mother's head remained bent.

'It's white,' said Nina quite loudly, since clearly it didn't matter if she spoke or not and she needed to be definite about this phenomenon. The green lawn had become white in a matter of minutes. First the sky had turned black, unnoticed as she and her mother ate their omelettes. Next, crystals the size of jagged ping-pong balls, had been ejected from the skies as if a giant hand had pulled back a spring. Millions of these irregular missiles had targeted the lawn, reached it, like an invading army, bounced once or twice then settled blanking out the green.

Nina stared at it, amazed, disquieted, exhilarated.

'Look, Mummy, the lawn is white!' Turning swiftly, Nina passed her mother and stepped through the door to the garden. The path, crunching under her feet, led her to the lawn. The sky had already

57

cleared above it, although blue-black clouds lay all around. The sun, revealed again, shone directly on to the crystalline surface. Soon, Nina could see, it would pick up rainbow colours, individual diamonds, reflecting on each facet the sky, the flowers, the world around. And after that, warmth would turn them into glistening pools through which the grass would pierce and then the lawn would be green again.

Nina stared at the white mirage and willed herself to recapture that startled moment of first sight. It had told her something important that she had been aware of without it quite reaching her consciousness. Now, with the cold air fresh on her face and hands, it seemed it was gone.

Nina glanced at her watch. It was Helen's half-term. If she were to clear up the kitchen and not be late picking up the children from the next village she must hurry. But as she went through the necessary actions of the day, she retained a rectangular image of glaring whiteness, a screen that had suddenly gone blank, a painted canvas going into reverse and wiping out the picture.

Late that night, when she lay awake, thinking as so often about William, she found that in the course of the day she had arrived at a new estimate of his character. William was selfish. He lived his life for his own purposes. He loved her only so far as she appeared within his range of needs. Outside the magic circle of himself, she did not exist. From the beginning, he had demanded her complete indentification with him without even knowing he was asking it, and she, being trained in that mould, had been more than eager to give it to him.

But if a green lawn could turn white in May, anything was possible. She wouldn't go back to him at the end of the week. She would ask for a separation and live at Lymhurst with her children and her mother. She thought lovingly of the countryside enfolding her in its exhilarating embrace. Even in this moment of truth she didn't dare put her painting into the equation.

Nina had known the fields around her house ever since she could remember. Now that she was walking every day, she began to be more adventurous, striking beyond the woods she knew to pastures that were sometimes hardly larger than her paddock and seldom more than three or four acres. There was no ploughed land here.

At a leisurely pace, she crossed the largest field into a wood at the bottom. A group of young bullocks, red, black, and spotted black and white, grazed in the middle and she skirted them warily. The sun had come out but it did not reach the edge of the field where she skulked along trying not to draw attention to herself as drops of water fell from the overhanging beech and lime.

With relief, she climbed the barbed-wire fencing into the wood and immediately found herself bathed in patterns of pale green where the sinuous trunks of young trees and the fallen trunks of old made right angles with each other. She wished she had brought her sketch-book. Spirits rising, she promised herself to return. The trees did not have the darker depths of the wood where the sacred yew stood. She could see bright fields on either side, a choice of destinations. Jumping the sludgy stream, its bank slippery with yellow clay, and avoiding the clumps of soon-to-flower bluebells, she walked quietly, enjoying the mindlessness and gentle light. She half expected to see a deer or two but there was nothing.

Moving out of the other side of the wood, bending through more wire, she entered a small field. She passed through an opening in the far corner and found herself in another, slightly larger than the first and grazed by a flock of sheep with long Roman noses. Choosing the nearer path of two, she found herself in a third field, again like the others but sloping unevenly downwards to a muddy patch of water, guarded by briars. At first glance she saw no way out until, beside the trunk of a young oak, she spotted a path trampled by animals. She felt how strange it was to be walking from one enclosed space to another, as if she were exploring secret rooms in a house. The sun was covered now by a smooth ceiling of low clouds and the bright saplings in the woods around formed the most elegant of wallpapers.

The next field was much bigger than its predecessors and sloped upwards to a mound, so smooth and regular as to appear man-made. It had been appropriated as a playground by rabbits of all sizes and shapes, which ran and jumped on its glossy surface. Well, she would join them.

As she approached the rabbits dispersed at top speed. She spread her jacket on the damp grass and sat down. Despite being on a higher point than previously, she was still enclosed by the woody walls and she realised, by the hard throb of her heart, that she was frightened at her disorientation, as if she had entered a maze and had no option but to walk continuously forward into an ever deeper sense of isolation and unreality.

Trying to change her mood, she reminded herself that she was less than an hour distant from fields she had known since childhood, that there every dip and tree was known to her – but it changed nothing. She had never felt so alone. She was forced to confront the knowledge that it was not this unknown landscape that frightened her but her separation from William. She had chosen aloneness, which seemed now no different from loneliness and, probably, she would remain this way for the rest of her life.

Connie, who as the seventh child of a seventh child had a witch's intuition on the rare occasions when she thought of someone besides herself, wrote to Nina on a yellow pad with a red pen.

> The Big Apple, July 1967
> Dearest Nina, this is my latest US published article. Treasure it and posterity may thank you. Fay says it stinks but she works too hard. Moreover, she's kicked me out. You'd never guess it, but she has quite an active sex life – for medical reasons, you understand. The men are very clean and bring their own toothpaste. My article, as you can see, is an interview with Gloria Steinem. Heard of her? You will. Beautiful, bossy, glasses, a kind of female Clark Kent, who thinks she can be Superwoman without a man in tow. (Although, of course, she has many men queuing for the honour.) Not my style. We're from different planets. Which made interviewing her kind of interesting. Now I'm leaving Fay in peace, how about you taking my place?

Rightly, she had not thought it necessary to sign her name.

Informed of this invitation, Fay felt curious to see Nina after so long. In fact, curious to see the three of them in one place. She sent a telegram:

CONNIE IS BIZARRE BUT PLEASE COME STOP FAY STOP

Nina was used to arriving in strange countries but neither Malaya nor Germany had made her feel so peculiarly English as the Customs hall at New York airport. She had half expected Connie or Fay to meet her but they had not. She fought for a yellow taxi and, on a blue and yellow afternoon, made her own way to Manhattan and an address Connie had given her.

The wide expressways, the spacious cars that gleamed tinnily impressed her with their differences even before she entered the city. They crossed a bridge called Williamsburg. Giving up her attempt to recall American history – Gettysburg? Williamsburg? – she looked out and saw, through the struts and frets of a long bridge, the serrated skyline of Manhattan, the dazzle of spires, square-topped mostly but some surprising with a bulbous dome or a needle point, and that one, she thought, was the Empire State Building. In that moment of visual excitement she lost all doubts about her visit. 'I shall jettison my scruples,' she said out loud, and found she was crouched forward on the edge of her seat, like a jockey urging his horse at a big jump.

Over the bridge, and they were down among the roots of the skyscrapers, taking their place with all the other traffic, grubbing noisily through streets unpenetrated by sun. 'Washington Square?' she enquired nervously, but the driver only twitched his shoulders.

The handcart was moving precariously, pushed by a group of young people, sex indeterminate, who seemed more interested in an animated discussion than moving forward. Swaying above them was a crude wooden-slatted box, like a giant rabbit hutch or orange crate. It was trailed by an everlengthening parade of cars hooting aggressively before they managed to overtake. It was Nina's taxi's turn. As she swivelled round to stare, she recognised one of the ineffectual pushers as Connie. 'Stop!' she cried excitedly.

At first her driver ignored her and then, at a second command, stopped so abruptly that she fell off the seat. Meanwhile, the handcart trundled towards them.

'Connie!' shouted Nina, forcing open the door.

'Fifteen dollars,' demanded the driver, uncoiling from the car with surprising energy and hauling Nina's case from the boot. She had not meant this but felt unable to communicate.

'Nina. My sweet darling.' Connie approached casually. 'What timing! You can open your New York experience inside our cage. Do you see?' She gestured proudly. 'It's built especially for tonight's event.' Bewildered, Nina stared at the wooden construction, which was the size of a small room.

'Forward, folks, please,' encouraged a young man, as he threw her case onto the cart. 'We'll give this a ride too.'

Nina stood inside the box with fifty other people, men, women, children, old, young, a baby and a dog. It had been set up inside a dark gallery adjoining a large church and they had all been led inside and the planks nailed back around them. They were prisoners. Outside, those who couldn't squeeze in stayed as spectators, sitting cheerfully on fold-up chairs. Two spotlights had just been illuminated and above their heads a tape began to play in a wheedling voice: 'Tea for two and two for tea, Me for you and you for me.'

Nina's neighbour offered her a cigarette. 'D'you know what's going on?'

'I thought you might.' Nina was regretting her bulk, which made her presence in this confined space so obvious. Her neighbour, a man of about her age with a dreamy pale face and a long scarf knotted at his throat, was probably half her size.

'It's the war, I guess,' he said. 'Caged in. I was curious. Came off the sidewalk.'

'It's about Vietnam,' Nina told him. 'At least, this event is one of a series on the theme of destruction.' She remembered Connie's explanation before she had disappeared, and sighed.

'Perhaps we're supposed to break out?'

'That idea appeals.' A wiry older woman, smoking a sweet-scented cigarette, banged her fist against a plank that shuddered but did not budge. The noise level increased inside the cage, people knocked against each other, banged their prison walls, shouted, the baby cried, the dog barked and the tape, becoming louder, imitated a train entering a tunnel.

'It's a very New York experience.' Nina's neighbour sounded doubtful.

'Don't you come from here?'

'No one comes from New York.' The wiry lady had slipped her fingers between the planks and pulled determinedly at a nail.

'I want to go into publishing,' continued the neighbour, 'but the only thing published in Chicago is *Playboy*.'

'I come from England.'

The woman cast them both scornful looks. 'You know, there's quite a gap up near the top. A child could get out that way.'

Nina peered upwards, trying to avoid being blinded by the spotlights. She thought of Helen, her supple, determined body. 'I have a daughter . . .' she began tentatively.

No one was listening. A hot argument had started about the morality of using innocent passers-by for an artistic experiment, a form, perhaps, of torture.

'My lunch hour is up!' cried one girl.

'If it's anger they're after!' cried another. But others began to laugh, except the baby and the dog, who howled in unison.

Nina thought of her own secret paintings, quiet and yearning, with panic. How could they exist in a brash world like this? It was at this point she spotted Fay, standing with awesome calm outside the cage.

'Fay! I'm right here.' But the hubbub drowned her voice. It was good-natured now and the tape sang in a boy's piping voice, 'Oh, say, can you see, by dawn's early light, America the brave, home of the free,' followed by the sound of slamming doors, gunfire, flushed toilets, running water and, suddenly, the live sound of cheering. Nina looked up and saw the wiry lady emerging like a snake from a top corner of the cage. As she jumped down, more figures insinuated themselves out of it, leaking from all sides, children first, adults after. Nina saw her neighbour go, one arm, torso, one leg, the other arm, the other leg. Before she could see if this miracle would work for her own larger proportions, Connie reappeared with her handcart colleagues and they gimleted open a doorway. The experiment, event, political protest, artistic happening, was over. Everybody seemed pleased with themselves.

Fay, Nina and Connie, a handcart pusher called Serge and Connie's beefy friend, Trigear, went to have a Chinese meal. Connie looked over her spare ribs with ravenous, joyous eyes. 'It's the new religion!' she rejoiced, between bites. 'The religion of protest.'

'This was a protest of unbelief,' objected Serge. 'You can't fling in religion as and when you please.'

Fay, about to defend Connie, thought better of it. Connie needed to break her habit of dragging religion into everything.

'Did you think it was a success?' asked Nina.

But the word 'success' satisfied Serge as little as 'religion'. 'It happened,' he announced, then relented. 'It happened differently from our expectations. There was no violence. No breaking out. No breaking.'

'So what did it mean?' persisted Nina, adding placatingly, 'I thought it very exciting.'

'It could mean art triumphed over violence,' suggested Fay, smiling. 'Nobody wanted to destroy such a lovely wooden box.'

'Cage,' amended Connie.

'It could mean the man off the sidewalk is wilier than the artist,' contributed Trigear, lighting a cheroot.

'I guess you're keen on meaning?' enquired Serge, estimating Nina with a sorrowful tenderness.

'I guess I am.' Nina, Fay thought, looked depressed and tired. This sort of argument could go on all night. In a few minutes she would take pity and find them both a taxi. She glanced disapprovingly at Connie, who was leaning closer to Trigear, despite the swirling cheroot smoke.

Serge sighed. 'Tell me now, the meaning of sending out brave boys to kill other brave boys. To kill and be killed. Or to be maimed. Or driven out of their minds. Tell me the meaning of Vietnam.'

Trigear folded his powerful arms and, barely repressing a little smile, leant back in his chair. His eyes half closed. Connie laid her hand on his bare arm.

'Balls,' pronounced Trigear.

'Time for bed, Nina.'

Fay had moved into a new apartment on the Upper West Side. As they bumped up Sixth Avenue, she pointed out buildings to Nina who seemed too exhausted to care.

Fay was disappointed at this lack of response. Trained to carry on however tired or discomposed, she could not understand why Nina should present such a vacuous front. Was it merely Englishness?

They arrived outside the apartment building, dated 1910 and ornamented with huge chunks of carved stone.

'Oh dear,' Nina looked round helplessly. 'I'm afraid I've left my case in that cage.'

'Box.'

'Well, I certainly left it there.' Suddenly she became animated. 'I hated everything in it anyway!'

Inside the apartment Nina sat down to ring home while Fay made tea. Fay could hear her murmured answers to what must have been childish questions: 'The Empire State's too high to see the top ... I'm afraid I didn't notice what plane I was on ...' Listening to this proof of Nina's motherhood, she found herself both impressed and put off.

'How is Lymhurst?' she asked, pronouncing the name with a kind of reverence. After all, it was the house that had first bound them together.

'Great. My mother and I are planting a herb garden.' Nina, gulping her tea thirstily, began to talk, but not about Lymhurst. 'Perhaps I was born out of step. In London the streets are filled with spindly girls in mini-skirts and here in New York I find people far younger than me, like that man tonight, Serge, engaged on a serious artistic endeavour, a serious struggle. In other words, they have a sense of their own importance. I don't mean they're immodest, merely that ...'

Fay watched Nina, her pearly English skin crinkled now with difficult questions, her generous shoulders hunched. She imagined how she

64

might have been in another age. Large, sensitive, obedient, loving, perhaps even beautiful, her *décolletage* low enough to show off her white bosom, a powdered wig to frame the regular oval of her face with its neat, unremarkable features. 'You don't have the problem of Vietnam your side of the Atlantic,' she said. 'Excuse me for stating the obvious. You don't have the draft. You can talk about dominoes as if it really were a childish game. You had a straightforward war that unified the country, did not drag it . . .' Fay paused. Now, she thought, they would have to talk about the breakdown of Nina's marriage. About William. Surely she had come to New York for just such intimate discussions. Nina stood up and went over to place herself beside the small uncurtained kitchen window. Discussion postponed as too painful, Fay presumed. She had forgotten how difficult the English found it to share.

The window framed a view of the building across the street. She turned to Fay. 'Is it a hospital? They look like dummies.'

'It's the last port of call for our city's senior citizens.' Fay tried to understand Nina's mood. 'I guess you're feeling contemplative?'

'Oh, really!' Nina seemed shocked, as if this were an insult. She swung away from the window. 'I was fascinated by the cage experiment. I tremendously admire Serge for what he's doing – they're all doing. It's group art, Connie informed me. And if it comes to that, I suppose I'm pretty jealous of Connie being right in the thick of things, although I found her boyfriend somewhat alarming.'

'You should be terrified. He stole Connie's baggage label at the airport the night she arrived. She elaborated on the wordy nature of the Irish. For some reason this had him hooked. Mostly, he's away cooking up wars in some unfortunate country and then Connie gets involved with quite reasonable sorts of men, rat-faced magazine editors, illiterate Wall Street bankers, all married of course.'

'Doesn't she ever go for nice men?'

Fay laughed. 'Ask her. She says she feels safe with Trigear because he's big and strong but I guess she's turned on by danger. At least he's not a drug dealer – not as far as I know anyway.'

Connie looked at Trigear. He made it clear that he liked sitting with the three women. He spread his well-muscled thighs, and his tree-trunk neck grew longer and stronger. He looked like a Samoan chief with three wives. Connie was as proud of him as he was of himself. She felt she could rest in the palm of his hand and be secure for ever.

'Trig's just back from . . . where is it, my heart's ease?'

They sat in Connie's apartment, one large room in a converted warehouse in the East Village. The autumnal weather had suddenly reverted to a steady eighty degrees Fahrenheit with brilliant summer sunshine. The room had no air-conditioning and the unplastered brick walls and glass windows intensified the heat. Nina, dressed in the wool skirt and sweater she had arrived in because her case had not reappeared, had turned bright pink. Trigear seemed unconcerned by the sweat that rolled from him, producing dark, maplike blotches across his shirt. Connie, lolling beside him, looked equally hot and unconcerned.

'I guess he just can't share with us the latitude and longitude of his last assignment.' Trigear remained silent. 'So how did you pass the daily hours?' Connie turned her attention to Nina. She wanted her to show off a little, be clever and English and make Trigear understand that she, Connie, wasn't any old tart. On the other hand, perhaps she was.

'Can't we open a window?' murmured Nina, 'I only have these silly clothes.'

'I fear not. Not for a century, I'd say.'

Connie watched as Trigear got to his feet. Dignified and slow, Samoan chief, he made his way to the window where he removed something small and hard from his inside pocket with which he tapped the window before returning it unseen. The glass shivered, splintered, fell outwards and crashed on to the sidewalk below.

'Oh, my God!' Nina ran to the window.

'She's quite right.' Fay joined her. 'Someone might have been killed.' Trigear smiled.

'Of course he looked first,' said Connie. 'This is just the sort of thing at which Trig is expert. Expert,' she repeated. 'No one has been killed or even injured. Thank you, dear heart.'

'You're welcome.' Trigear bowed. 'Who says I fix us a drink?'

Connie looked at her man, standing there so courteous and caring, and felt she was melting too. Fay might lecture her about morality, or rather Trig's lack of it – according to Fay, he was involved in destabilising the whole of Central America but what would a doctor know about a thing like that? 'There's a six-pack in the fridge.'

They all opened cans, except Fay who found herself a glass of water. Nina, who hadn't realised women drank beer, found she liked the taste of this light American stuff, and Connie added a drop or two of something stronger to hers. Trigear piled up three cans at his elbow.

'Nina did all the right things,' said Fay. 'She went to the Met and the

Museum of Modern Art where she saw the Jackson Pollocks. Did you like the Pollocks?'

Nina's face returned to its pink colour. 'Not really,' she muttered. 'All that desperate masculine energy. I did see some other paintings . . .' Her voice tailed away so only Fay heard the word 'Rothko'.

'Nina's always terribly secret about her likes and dislikes,' sighed Connie. 'So, did you have a thrilling time, my darling?' They would go soon, she thought, and then there would be just Trig and her. She glanced at the pile of cushions in the corner, which was her bed although Trig preferred the floor. 'You know what you're up to with a solid wood floor', that's what he said. 'Get more of a purchase.' Connie smiled at the thought.

'I had a super time!' enthused Nina.

'And what about your day?' Connie, as if she were an old-fashioned hostess, turned to Fay. They could describe their days and then go, she thought, for how could friendship compete with sex?

Fay smiled. 'You don't want to hear about my day. Let's just say I did no lasting harm and, in one or two places, might have done good.'

'Done good. Wow!' Connie forgot Trig for a moment. 'I wrote up the show, you know, but dear Max seemed decidedly unkeen to publish.'

'Are you writing a lot?' asked Nina.

'Sure. That's what pays my bills. For *Time* when they dig me, or the city mag, the *Village Voice*, and I just turned in a piece on transvestites for the *East Village Other*, although their idea of a fair wage is a joke. That's what I'm doing here, Nina, darling. I'm a journalist, the candy-coloured flavour of the moment. Dancing in all kinds of circles. Doing good when I can. Listen, this gem of the Emerald Isle is not going down without making waves.'

Nina turned to Fay, who nodded. 'Connie's all the rage. The beautiful wacky Irish girl. They all want her writing for them.'

'And you've only been here six months!'

Nina was invited by Fay to the hospital. 'So you can picture me when you're sitting in your garden back home,' she said. She showed her everything as if she were a witness or an inspector. When they reached the operating theatre, Nina felt too exhausted to continue so Fay looked at her watch and gave her five minutes in the canteen.

'How can you take the responsibility?' Nina tried to sound admiring rather than despairing. It was not Fay's fault that this evidence of her extraordinary success made Nina feel such a failure. She had wanted to talk to Fay about William but their separation would seem so negative unless she could explain who she was going to become in place of the good wife. Yet she hardly knew herself – that was not quite true: the paintings she had admired the day before were by Mark Rothko, huge colourful abstracts that had made her head sing. Standing gazing at them, she had known that her future lay with painting in some form or another. But she was far too lacking in confidence to mention that to Fay.

'I'm afraid I'll have to leave you.' Fay stood. 'I'll see you later. Have a good day.'

Nina, going slowly out into the bright, noisy street, wondered what would make it a good day for her. She should search for her case, she supposed; Connie had suggested asking Serge to help her and given her the name of a gallery where he worked. For some reason her spirits rose.

Serge was at the Judson Gallery, hanging paintings of sky, clouds, smooth, blue, white and grey. She instantly forgot the ostensible purpose of her visit.

'Fay told me you have some kids?' Serge came down off the wall. He wore baggy shorts and a string vest. Nina had never seen anyone, adult or child, dressed like this in a city. A fleeting image of William appeared, as if in competition with him, in ceremonial uniform.

'I do, Helen and Jamie.'

'That's just so great.'

Nina turned away under his admiration. It had just happened, she wanted to say, but did not wish to appear rude. Moreover, she felt in more than her usual muddle when confronted by Serge. Where was he to be appropriately docketed? Man? Boy? Clever? Uneducated? Middle class? And then there was the matter of sex and war.

'Hey, do you want a coffee?'

Serge and Nina strolled through Washington Square, where huddles of chess players were interspersed with groups of men intent on something else.

'Drug dealers, pimps, their prey,' Serge informed her nonchalantly. The autumn sun had turned into a dusky evening and under the plumed plane trees with their splotched trunks, the shadows were deeply purple. Nina was glad to have an escort, even if he was a pacifist. She wanted to ask him what he would do if she were attacked, her bag raided. Would he defend her with raised fists? Or was that a ridiculously naïve idea?

They walked some distance. Nina thought how odd they must look –

she in her English country wool, he in his shorts. He led her down steep steps into a small basement room where three or four tables were set up.

'Hi, Nora.' Serge greeted a young woman of some dark-skinned race Nina couldn't identify. 'Do you want to eat, Nina? Nora's a superb cook.'

They sat at a table and Serge ordered beans and pulses, squash, pumpkin, beets, kale and all kinds of vegetables that Nina had previously thought of only as decoration. 'I guess you're used to the famous English meat and two veg.,' he commented.

Nina realised he was a quiet person. His ideology had made him seem loquacious on the night of the cage demonstration but now that they sat together in the dank little room he seemed in no hurry to start a conversation. 'I wonder if you'd mind me asking . . .' she began.

'Please. Go ahead.'

'. . . how you avoided the draft?'

'With difficulty.' He smiled. 'But not as much as some because I was brought up a Quaker. When my papers came I applied to be registered as a conscientious objector. You could say I'm lucky.'

'You mean, not having to flee the country?'

'Or marry or carry on studying till you're bored out of your skull, hoping the war will end before your deferment does.'

'Is that what your friends do?'

'Yup. There's a whole lot of ways to avoid doing your patriotic duty but it makes it easier if you don't believe in the war in the first place.'

'Or in any other war?' Nina felt anxious at questions she wanted to raise: he was, after all, her host and even now a steaming mound of food was arriving.

'Correct. I'm a pacifist.' He began to eat, surprisingly greedy in his slim pallor. She found she was not hungry but tried, out of politeness, to match his helping.

'You know my husband was, I mean is – that is, he was my husband but still is a soldier.' Confused, she abandoned her food, pushed away the plate. She felt daring beyond her limits and ridiculous for feeling it.

'Lots of the best guys are soldiers.'

'He's in the regular army. A professional soldier.'

'Grounds for divorce?'

'No! No.' But maybe, she thought, a bit yes.

They were out on the streets again, Nina unsure whether she could or would explain. How could she begin? 'My mother's life was ruined by the war'? But that seemed too vast and pretentious a way to describe a comfortable country existence.

To celebrate her fourth birthday her mother had made a kite out of pink parachute silk, usually used for her underclothes. They had bicycled to the Downs – Nina on a seat at the back – and loosed the kite into a turbulent sky. 'Listen carefully,' her mother had whispered confidentially, 'and you might hear the sounds of guns from across the Channel. Last night our army set sail to end the war and one day soon your daddy will come striding back.' On the way home, the turbulent sky had poured rain on them. How they had shuddered and laughed!

'This is Eighth Street.' Serge took her arm. His fingers were cool and gentle. 'You should look at it since you're a tourist. Best movie house in town, best theatre, best cafés, most action . . .' He had turned into a tour guide. Obediently, Nina looked into the muddled darkness of people.

'I've got to get something to cover my legs,' said Serge eventually. Nina was embarrassed to have kept him.

'Oh, I'm so sorry.'

'They're not your legs to be sorry for.' Nina stopped herself apologising again. 'I live here.' They were back at Washington Square. 'Want to come in?'

It was a student room, or so Nina, who had never been a student, imagined – small, unclean, cluttered with books and paper, an unmade bed the only discernible furniture. It smelt quite strongly of man. They sat on the bed and Nina realised that he assumed they would make love. At once he laid his hand, slim and pale, on her tweed-covered thigh. It seemed extraordinary that he should desire her. Curiosity overcoming embarrassment, Nina looked into his face. His grey eyes smiled in a serious way but she saw none of the hot lust, the male-beast urgency that William displayed on such occasions. Reassured, she smiled back.

'Let's take off our clothes.' He had started as he spoke and Nina was flustered into following suit. Just an American experience, she thought, to quieten her fears.

'You're beautiful. You've the finest skin.' He touched her shoulders, her neck, her breasts. 'Untie your hair.'

She took out the pins, let the softness hang about her nakedness, let this stranger fluff it about his hands, let him slide behind her and kiss the beads of her spine, tickling butterfly kisses. His light hands made her beautiful, her curving belly, her wide thighs, her smooth woman's plains.

70

'Touch me,' he said.

It was warm in the little room, dim streaks of light coming from outside, the noises of the city – cars, police sirens – receding as the two white bodies wound together, stroked, caressed, admired, examined, whispered, loved and finally closed together.

Red, yellow, blue-green, blurred edges, floating horizons against a floating background. Colour suspended in space, colour against space. Suspended shimmering. Translucent black. Into space.

'I love ... Rothko,' murmured Nina.

Unhearing, Serge lapped around her. 'You are lovely. Beautiful. Thank you.' Silence. 'Time is very slow tonight,' he murmured.

The sounds of the city slid back into the room. Nina realised they had used no contraceptives. 'Do you have a bathroom?' Her voice told her she was happy.

'Down the hall.' She ran along a dark corridor. She washed slowly. She waited to see if her voices would whisper into her ear and command her to wash again or again and again. But they did not. She felt absurdly lighthearted. Serge sat sideways on the bed when she returned, his smooth boy's face solemn. 'Aren't you on the pill?'

Nina blushed at her childishness and listened as he lectured her. Indulgently, she thought it could have been about Vietnam, about truth, about ... 'I am listening,' she cried, catching his expression, 'but, to be honest, I'm terribly hungry.'

They went out again. The night was occupied with people and cool. Nina, pleased at last with her one hundred per cent pure wool clothing, hugged Serge's thin body. She was grateful to him. He found them another strange little café. This time a man with white hair fanned over his shoulders served them dark-coloured rice and corn.

'Please will you tell me more about being called up – drafted.'

'I was in the country. With country boys in a bus. Big nice boys with heavy red hands and sunburnt friendly faces. We were taken to this hall, lined up, stripped. Their sunburn marks were the division between light and shade. I was light all over.'

'But why take that trouble with you when you were already accepted as a conscientious objector? They knew you weren't going to fight.'

He shrugged. 'The system. Punishment? They had us bend over. Medical examination. "Haemorrhoids! Roydes has haemorrhoids! Roydes has haemorrhoids! Roydes has haemorrhoids!" They called it along the line. That was bad. But not so bad as shoving a stick of gelignite in a man's mouth. Or ass.' He leant forward. 'You said your husband's a soldier?'

71

She leant back. Did he want her to disown William? But she couldn't do that.

'William fought in Malaya. We lived there together for two years. The country's no different from Vietnam, jungles and things. But we did it differently.' She heard her voice take on a proud British sound and wondered if it was how she really felt. She remembered a young soldier she had seen in hospital there. Her stomach was domed with Helen, due to be born in few weeks. He had a dome over his leg where it had been blown away by a mine. 'Are you in my husband's company?' she'd asked, in a severe little voice to hold back her tears.

'Just finished his jungle training, too.' The doctor had been jocular, but the boy – he was hardly yet a man – remained silent.

The doctor had left her with him and eventually he had spoken to her, telling her about his fear of snakes, his eyes filled with tears. 'Keep your head down, we were told on the training, but how could I when I had to keep an eye out for the snakes? We'd just got across a river. It got lighter and we were warned. This is a nasty bit, plenty of mines. But I thought there were sure to be plenty of snakes too. And there one was. Well, it wasn't. Just another creeper. But I looked up, and that's how it happened. Gave away our position too. Messed up the whole plan. What a racket!' He had stopped abruptly and closed his eyes.

Nina had been about to speak when he opened them again. 'I don't know what my mum's going to say, and my dad. He'll blame me for sure. And what'll I tell my mates? They're not going to want a cripple down at the local. Pity I wasn't finished off, that's what I think.' It had been a speech about the reality of fighting and then she had been proud of the boy.

Nina looked at Serge. She was still proud. 'We fought on the ground. We got to know the people we were fighting for. We had to fight a second battle to win their hearts and minds. That was the order.'

'Hearts and minds?' His face was calm again. 'Well, as a slogan I guess it's better that "Search and destroy". So why aren't you married any more?'

'It was killing me.'

After they had finished eating, they went back to Serge's flat and made love again. This time he slid on a condom, which Nina found peculiarly exciting. When he entered her she cried out.

At dawn, drifting through the noises of a strange city, she remembered her wedding night in that hotel in Brighton.

William had taken off his clothes beside the bed, as if there was no time to be wasted. In unsoldierly fashion, he dropped each item on the floor.

'I'm singing!' Nina had cried, hearing her voice rise like a seagull. It had seemed easiest to take off her clothes as she came towards him, the momentum helping her out of a static scene of conventional bliss. She was not blissful. But she had a chance of being ecstatic. She reached William's arms with her underclothes intact. The room was dimly, coolly lit, but she had time to notice the darkness around his cock, as if his blond head belonged to someone else. His hands, as if he had done it before (and she had been glad of that), unhooked her bra efficiently and pulled off her pants.

He held her breasts. She was so pale. Nina felt her whiteness as a barrier, wished she was the gold of Tahitian maidens. White was cold. But he had snatched at her body, stroking, kneading, pulling her on to the bed. 'Before I get too carried away, I want to say I love you.'

Nina had a manic urge to laugh. Instead she found herself responding passionately, 'I love you! I love you!'

They had moved to the bed. What next?

'Oh, darling, darling Nina!'

Nina had looked at the knotted curtains, a prisoner's knotted sheets, a princess shimmying down her plaited tresses. 'Touch me,' she murmured.

But William was otherwise engaged, living up to the images of strength and power, love and gentleness. It was all very complicated. 'I want you so much,' he breathed into her hair.

'Oh, yes.'

'Can I . . . ?' He did. Nina felt her legs open accommodatingly. It was a good thing to do, she thought, to open her softness to his hard probe.

'Does it hurt?' He was tender, loving.

'No,' she lied. But only a little. She was happy.

'My darling. My darling Nina. Oh, my God! Please. Oh. Darling.'

Words, Nina remembered thinking. What can I say? I must enclose him, love him, hold him. Darling William with his red-brick skin. The shuddering strength of him. The needing and giving, the joining. 'I love you, William.' The room seemed to become black and silent.

Gradually, lightness seeped in from the edges. Nina had opened her eyes. She looked at William who seemed to be asleep. She put her hand on him.

'It will be better next time,' he had said, without opening his eyes. Nina had felt a little affronted at that. How should she respond? Surely

73

not 'Good.' That would hardly be polite. Better to stroke him, say nothing, let her eyes drift towards the windows. Wait for dawn.

Serge got up quietly, sliding gently into the day. Nina watched him and felt reassured. When he came back from the bathroom, she took his hand. He bent over her, pulled back the bedclothes, ran his hand over the length of her body. Nina realised she wanted him again and felt a little ashamed of herself. But he bent closer, took her nipple in his mouth and put his hand between her legs. She was still wet there.

'I have to go to work,' he said. But he didn't go immediately.

'Can we make love every day of the week I'm here?' whispered Nina. How had those words come so naturally?

'Of course.' He was smiling at her.

1968

The voice was completely unfamiliar but indisputably English. Connie, asleep in her tumbled bedclothes, did not even bother to open her eyes. Why ever had she lifted the receiver off the hook? But then the bell had been right in her ear and, through her dreams, she had dimly suspected, hoped, despite her present circumstances, it might be Trig 'Who is it I'm speaking to?'

'Merlin Derwitt,' stuttered the voice, sounding hurt.

Even now, Connie hardly felt like reacting. Merlin, although recognised, was from another world in England, and here he was a freak. She grimaced, coming more awake with her rise of emotions. 'Darling, lunch perhaps. Are you here long?'

'I'm not there yet. I'm coming in the New Year.'

'Is that so?' That was ages away. 'Lunch then. Call me when you arrive, darling Merlin Regis de Witt. The Blessed Virgin smiles on friendship.'

Lester Loughran removed his face from Connie's pubic hair and growled, 'What's all this Catholic stuff? You haven't been to church since you were a child and yet you behave as if it's the number-one item on your agenda.'

'How do you figure that out?' Connie was only mildly interested in the answer. Lester hardly knew her after all. She was only with him in Trig's absence.

'Don't you know you drag morality into every last moment? Each fuck is scented with incense.'

'I brought that back from India,' Connie lied, not caring to give him the credit for speaking figuratively. 'Do I talk about God?' she asked, a little more energetically.

'God, Jesus, Mary, in every gesture.'

Connie gave Lester a closer look. In her experience, men were not usually keen to talk about religion, unless you counted priests and, since leaving London, she had had no replacement for Father O'Donald of O'Donaldstown. Sadly, he was too busy to write and she too lazy. Lester was a pick-up. She had seen him arrive at a party and been turned on by his broken nose and camel-haired coat. She had worn the coat back to his apartment and they had made love on its cream satin lining. He must be at least forty, she guessed, although somehow his prematurely grey, crew-cut hair made him look younger. He worked in Wall Street. A rich banker. The truth, now she took the trouble to think about him for a few seconds, was as clear as a mountain stream: he was an Irish American.

Connie rolled on to her stomach, conscious, because she had been told it often, that the curve of her back was one of the prettiest parts of her body. 'I suppose your family is Irish Catholic,' she said.

'Correct.'

She noticed now that he seemed less keen to continue the conversation. 'I have a brother who might almost be you. You'd have to alter your name to Kevin, however. It might be that I came to America just to seek him out but I got sidetracked.' Lester was silent. He stroked her bottom, as she knew he would sooner or later. 'I never knew him at all. He was the eldest. Left after a storming row, I'll be bound, because my da never raised his name in our home. How old are you, Lester, if I may be so bold as to enquire?'

He was still silent but his stroking continued appreciatively, suggesting to Connie that he had not been offended by her question, although why she was giving him so much consideration, he a married man going with a girl nearly half his age, she couldn't tell.

'I guess I might be acquainted with your brother,' Lester drawled. Inconsequentially Connie noticed that he had a lovely voice and thought that a lovely voice often went with lovely hands. 'Kevin O'Malley. He lives in Washington. Businessman?'

'I don't believe you!' She rolled away. She'd given up thinking of her brother months and months ago.

'No? That's too bad.' He sat on the edge of the bed, his big shoulders hunched. She could see he was as discomforted as she was. No longer a random Irish girl. Now a girl with a family. Or at least a brother.

'Is he married? He can't be married or he'd have been in touch with Ma.' She heard her voice, whining, miserable. She wished they were still talking about Catholicism. She wished they were still making love. Or whatever it was they did.

'Yup.'

'May I ask what you mean by "yup"?' It was a relief to feel angry. Maybe she could blame him for this whole scenario.

'He is married. His wife's called Shirley. I could put you two together. He looks very like you. Your hair, eyes. Striking.' Lester had begun to dress, his lovely hands whisking on shirt and trousers, doing up buttons with a twist of two long fingers, flicking his tie into a superior knot, flying into his jacket, socks and shoes, which were very shiny.

Greedily following this dextrous male performance, Connie hoped she was falling in love. Falling and drowning. But surely it was Trig who held her captive? Could she drown in love for two men at the same time and both of them so unsuitable? Concentrating on Lester's face, still flushed from their previous occupation, lips full so she wanted to kiss them again, she managed not to recall Rick and his father.

'I'll call you with that address. You should meet with your brother.'

He, an adulterer, advising her about family duties. For once Connie held her tongue, which was the right thing to do if she were in love, and even more so if she wanted this brother in her life. 'Let's hope he's better than my other brother, the one I found under the factory chimneys, drinking himself into oblivion.'

Lester seemed startled but Connie knew that that was to her advantage and smiled sweetly. Another fact about Lester was that he was an important backer for the weekly that published most of her articles. Perhaps she could love him for gain.

Fay couldn't believe the presumption of it. Connie had arrived at the hospital and demanded to see her. But she had come as soon as she had a moment, thinking that people always did what Connie asked.

'Trig has never been away so long before.' Connie, dissembling because Trig was not the reason for her visit, rolled her eyes pathetically.

'You know my views on Trigear. He's a killer. Literally.'

'Well, maybe he's been killed now. I only mentioned him in passing.' She paused as Fay looked at her watch. 'Just because you have the ability to save lives, you despise those who have the ability to rub people off the face of this earth. The world must have a balance, you know. Give and take. The hunter and the hunted.'

Fay refused to be amused. 'May I presume you've given up on Judson and pacifism?'

'That was last year wasn't it?' Connie swung her legs like a child on a stool. 'Nina took over Serge. What a surprise that was! One-night stand from our country girl and a serial follow-up. Besides, you must have realised I'm not a serious person.'

'I'm sorry, Connie, I've got to split. Unless there was something special.'

'But there is. Extra special. Would you come to Washington with me? You must have a day off every few months. Tell me yes. Tell me you will come and be my friend for I go to meet my long-lost brother, the famous Kevin O'Malley. An American, I am given to understand, yet issued from County Mayo, from the loins of my own poor deserted ma and da . . .'

'Connie, you're full of surprises. Whatever put you on to him after all this time? Of course I'll come. I'm flattered, intrigued. But don't be upset if I run off now. I need to draw off the blood of a child.'

'Witch!' called Connie, as Fay retreated briskly. 'Saw-bones!'

Fay, negotiating corridors (how many hours a week did she spend negotiating corridors?), thought how odd it was that her job, her whole life indeed, had become a joke between them. She had become a paediatric surgeon. It was a rarefied world inhabited, apart from herself, entirely by men who had the guts, stamina and precision to cut into small bodies and tender skins. It was a *summa cum laude* club to which she had gained the right of entry. But Connie professed herself disgusted by such elective professional detachment and used mocking abuse to make her point. Fay had begun to wonder seriously how they could remain on good terms. Yet here she was summoned to this family reunion, given the role of closest friend.

Fay sat under her spotlight in her railroad apartment – she could well afford something better if only she had the time to choose – typed a letter to Nina. The words buzzed off her fingers like theorems:

Can you believe, he thought I would marry him and settle down and have kids? He likes my mind, he said, but he likes my butt better. You see what we learn in medical school. I only have to peruse my alumni magazine to see which side of the fence I'm putting my butt.

Bright girls reporting their news, except it's all about following their
husbands! I guess I never told you about Babs, my roommate in
college. You know why we were put together? Because we were both
Jews. We were about as unlike as

Fay paused. She thought, As you are to me, but since that contradicted
the point she was making, she wrote instead

Nixon is to Ho Chi Minh. The only thing I learnt from Babs was
how to smooth my hair on huge rollers and how to approach dates
with the young blazers at Amherst with the suitable inviting-yet-cool
smile. Not useful for the future as it turned out.

Fay paused again as she remembered those dates. Would Nina, in her
Englishness get the point?

The boys were called Ken and Gordon, which in itself was a surprise.
Ken, who belonged to Babs, was rugged and blond and played football
so he always had a bandage on some injured part of his body. He had a
very short nose, which made Babs sigh with love: 'Just think what
beautiful children we'd have with the neatest noses.'

'Hi! Hi, Ken!' Babs liked to stand on the tips of her toes waving at the
approaching car. She waved too. Gordon was a nice rich boy who
planned to follow his father into the real-estate business.

Within the car, cream-leather-lined, chrome-plated, open-topped,
fin-tailed, Ken, in the driver's seat, spotted the girls and biffed Gordon
on the shoulder. Fay had watched keenly.

'Here we go, picking up our two sporty Jewesses.' Ken had said the
words with just too much exultation so that Fay had caught them –
with no sense of surprise and, perhaps oddly, no rancour. That was the
way it was. She wouldn't be around in their world for longer than
necessary.

Fay laid her hands on the keys of the typewriter but not to convey
this little story to Nina.

Babs married her college sweetheart [she continued] and now I read
about her husband, Ken, who's in the oil business and has just been
relocated to Tulsa which makes a big upheaval for the children . . .

Fay began to tap with more vehemence.

The man who raised this marriage business is nothing like at my level

78

as a surgeon. He probably just wants me off the scene. I can't tell you
the lack of camaraderie in a hospital. We're all jockeying for the
major ops, as if we were ad agencies trying to catch the big accounts.
Anyway, I won't get into that. Just don't believe saving lives gives you
a higher view on life ... particularly if you're a woman. The main
point is I've never planned to marry and just at the moment the idea
of putting another human being into this world gives me the shakes.
I'm so fearful for brother Daniel that I've more or less banished him
from my life. Do you know what happens to a bone when it gets
whacked by a bullet? Well, if you don't I guess I'll show a bit of
mercy and leave it that way ...

Again, Fay stopped, figuring Nina didn't need to know all this. A new
thought struck her:

Hey, how ever did I get to inherit Connie? She's asked me to escort
her to visit her long lost brother in Washington. What a journey that
will be!

Nina had taken Fay's letter to her studio. This was an innovation built
from the stable where her pony had lived. There were cobbles
underfoot, two high-up windows, through which she could see only a
branch or two, and two large new windows in the roof, through which
she could see the sky in all its temperaments. The children were
banned. Her mother was banned. Sometimes she did not paint at all
but sat unoccupied in an old armchair, pink and bulging, she'd brought
in from the house.

She sat in this chair while reading Fay's letter, which was longer than
usual and struck her as filled with energy. There was a postscript: 'Have
you taken advice yet and signed up for art school?' Nina could not
remember receiving this advice. Was such a thing possible?

After a while she began to feel cold and went back to the kitchen
where her mother was preparing to go to bed.

'You don't seem very sorry for William,' Veronica said suddenly.
'What will he do for Christmas?'

Nina looked up, astonished at her mother's making such a
statement, and rather late in the day. It was already the end of
November. Nor could she tell if there was a question mark at the end of
the statement, or a hint of one. Veronica was holding her tapestry and a
glass of water. What had prompted her to speak? Was it a compulsion
grown since Nina's return from America? Had she noticed a hardening

she disliked? Was it a moral lead? Or had William been in touch? And, anyway, was it true? Did Nina feel little pity for William, reserving it all for herself?

'I'm thinking of the children, of course. They will soon know how you feel.'

'I am never unkind about William.' It was shameful, she supposed, that she had not realised it would be the children who concerned her mother.

'They will see his point of view as well as yours.'

'I know. Of course I know that!' She felt her cheeks burn. Did she hate William, after all, for taking away so many years?

'It was not as if anyone forced you to marry him,' said Veronica, as if reading her daughter's thoughts. 'Nor is he such a bad man. In fact, I don't believe he's a bad man at all.'

'No! No!' But I *was* forced, thought Nina, hardly understanding what she meant by that, except that that was how it felt. And he *is* a bad, destructive man, at least for me.

'Well, I'm going to bed.' Veronica turned her cheek for a kiss, which Nina gave. 'Goodnight, my dear.'

It was impossible to sleep after such an attack. Nina crept back downstairs to the hall where the only telephone stood. She rang asked the operator for Connie's number, thinking as she did so that she would never believe in technology that could cross oceans. She was surprised when there was no answer. She asked for Fay's number. It was, she reckoned only six in the evening on East 78th Street. But there was no answer there either.

'Hello, Fay. It's Nina. Nothing to say in particular. I hope all's well with you.'

Feeling guilty at the expense of such a pointless message, Nina returned to her bed. The room had become brighter, a full moon risen strong enough to pierce the curtains where the lining had become thin or even tattered. Nina tried to think the silvery beams beneficent and soothing but instead she felt the old anxiety, the suffocating tension that had led to her obsessions. Determined to break the spell and feeling the pangs of night-time hunger, she slipped out of bed and once more went downstairs.

The light was glaring in the larder: it illuminated shelves filled with home-made jams and chutneys, bottled plums and damsons, the jars all neatly labelled. It was her mother's place and somewhere, she knew, there was a tin of biscuits, kept hidden from the children.

She saw it too late – too late, that is, to pretend she hadn't seen it. It stared up at her, its shiny round eyes still appealing for help even after death. She trusted, at least, that the mouse was dead. Blood of a brilliance she had never seen stained the trap, the smooth grey-brown fur, trembled on one of the whiskers. The cheese was untouched, a little crumbled bait.

Nina stared, head burning, feet icy, body trembling. She saw the glassy tearfulness of the mouse's eyes turn into a man's. She saw William lying there bleeding.

'Oh. Oh. Oh.' Now she fled, back to the sitting room where the embers of the fire still gave a faint warmth. Why would the pathos of a trapped fieldmouse make her pity William? It was ludicrous, unwanted, illogical. But it had happened. For the first time, she cried for William. But not for a moment did she regret leaving him.

1969

'He just could be a paid-up monster.' Connie settled herself in the seat opposite Fay. They were taking the train to Washington because Connie said it would give her more time to prepare herself. Looking at her now, Fay thought she would need every moment. 'I've got a commission to do three thousand words. They'll run it on St Patrick's Day.'

'Does he know?'

'My long-lost brother? Certainly not. He might not like it.'

'Cashing in on your relationship?'

'That sort of ugly scheming thing.'

'So what's my role?'

'Now you're angry.'

'Call it bewildered. I intuited you wanted me along because you were nervous and here you are treating it all as theatre.'

'Theatre can't do without an audience, Fay, my darling dear.'

Fay stared out of the window for a few calming seconds while she tried not to think about the meetings cancelled for this trip, put off, month after month, by Connie. Connie was sitting cross-legged, tight crimson boots discarded and her face showing the signs of makeup imaginatively applied many hours earlier and never freshened. 'Where were you last night?'

Instead of answering, Connie produced a grubby cigarette and lit it.

'You can't smoke that here!'

'It helps when I'm tired. Sorry.' Taking one more deep drag, she stubbed it into the palm of her hand.

Fay leant forward, horrified, and saw that Connie held a coin in her palm. For some reason this little bit of trickery – perhaps because it was prepared and executed with such deftness – exhausted Fay's patience. She stood, swaying with the movement of the train. 'I'm carrying on to Washington,' she announced, 'but not with you. I want to see the Air and Space Museum but I want to see it on my own. Goodbye.'

She had gone several paces before the sobbing penetrated her anger. Resignedly she returned. 'Where were you last night?' she repeated.

'It was a magical evening,' snuffled Connie, thin shoulder-blades heaving under Fay's comforting hand. 'I just didn't get much sleep.'

'What are you chewing?'

'That illegal substance you were complaining about, Doctor. Getting rid of the evidence. It tastes pretty good and anyway I was starving.'

'Oh, Connie.' Fay gave up and began to laugh.

Connie looked up at her from under her eyelashes, dripping equal parts of tears and mascara. 'You wouldn't believe me if I told you. There was this pale rabbity person who pronounced one word, "Wow". It issued from his rabbity little mouth at long intervals, conveying not the smallest sense of enthusiasm. It was, you might have it, a word without expression. It was a Word of Art!'

'Whoever was the rabbit?'

'Andy Warhol!' Connie was triumphant, but this was only her curtain-raiser. 'Besides him there was this singer. His voice was the kind that would empty any bar in the Emerald Isle. His face too, broad as the shield of St Patrick, ugly black glasses, ugly black beard to make up for the hair he had mislaid on top. He sang for six hours without stopping.'

'And what was his name?' asked Fay patiently, knowing the answer, although not necessarily prepared to believe it.

'Oh, you'd have liked him. Sure you would have joined in our final chorus of "Prajna Paramita Sutra" before we headed downtown for a night of loving meditation.'

'Allen Ginsberg,'

'Right on.' Connie looked exhausted, ashen, but rather happy and relaxed as if the memories of the night were altogether beneficial – as if she might sleep for the rest of what should be a traumatic journey. Her eyes even closed briefly.

But now Fay had become irritably involved. 'He's only a Jewish boy from New Jersey. Just like I'm a Jewish girl from Chicago. I hate this guru thing. It's Fascist stuff. Babyish too. Hero worship is ridiculous. What's he doing about righting the world? What's he ever done, except have a good time, write a few poems and spin off to India when he feels a bit jaded? He's a poseur and a charlatan. And don't tell me that handing out drugs to anyone who wants them is going to change the world for anything but the worse. He should try visiting Bellevue after midnight. So should you, Connie.'

There was a pause. Then Connie cleared her face of surprise and said, 'Wow!'

Fay was not amused. 'Be serious, for once. Pay me the compliment.'

But Fay knew that it was impossible for Connie to change her character for a discussion.

'Ginsberg's on your side. He hates fans. He hides under chairs. If anyone tried to Heil Hitler him he'd slug the laurel wreath back on the bush it came from. He likes people, Fay, that's all. He's big-hearted. He doesn't like killers. He doesn't like the regular rich. He likes helping people. He likes loving people.'

'Thanks,' said Fay bitterly. She felt cold, but she wasn't sure whether to blame the temperature of the train or not being in tune with Connie or her own life.

'Your brother's done well for himself.' Fay stood staring upwards at a large, elegant corner house, with cream shutters and a cream magnolia tree.

'Fay, I'm scared. I'm scared witless, shitless.'

'You're never scared . . .' began Fay, before turning to Connie and seeing her chattering teeth and ashen face. 'Look, he's your flesh and blood.'

'You don't know. Oh, the wrath of God!'

'He's not God. He's Kevin O'Malley. He's got a wife called Shirley. Has he got kids? You didn't inform me on that one. In fact, you informed me on zero minus one. He's probably got a boy and a girl, Kevin Junior and Mary Jay. They're in there now, all expectant to meet unknown sister, auntie . . .'

'You don't know. OK. Ring the bell.' Connie grabbed hold of Fay, who marched her to the door, which was gleaming with new paint so that Connie could actually see reflected her terrified face. Fay could not be expected to understand her feelings. Kevin was as near as she would get to her father, that was it.

A black maid in white and black uniform opened the door. Connie

83

was leaning so heavily on Fay that Fay was afraid she had fainted. 'We have an appointment with Mr and Mrs O'Malley.'

'Please follow me.' The maid smiled warmly and Fay felt Connie straighten, become vital again.

'Oh, thank you,' Connie said to the maid, and to Fay, 'Such a gracious home.'

The room into which they were shown was decorated in yellow and cream and overlooked the street. Fay thought it had the formal air of a reception room rather than a family home.

'I've got a piece in this.' Connie picked up a magazine from the orderly ranks laid out on a low central table. 'About Leary. Freaky, sneaky Leary. Turn on, tune in, drop your drawers.' She was crouched over, enjoying her turn of phrase, when a woman quietly entered the room. She stood at the doorway, hand to her mouth, staring at Connie, who had not heard her and continued to read aloud admiringly. Fay was surprised by her age: this woman was well into her forties, fair-haired, blue-eyed, expensively dressed.

'You must be Connie,' she said at last. 'I'm so very happy to meet you. I feel dreadfully selfish dragging you all the way here but Kevin's so taken up with work that he hardly ever leaves – unless it's on a plane to some production crisis point.' She looked at a small gold wristwatch. 'He's promised to be back by midday, anytime now.'

Connie leapt towards her. Fay noted how immediately she warmed to this woman, grasping her hand lovingly. 'I'm so happy to be here too.' She laughed. 'Happy. Terrified.'

'Yes.' As introductions were made, the maid returned with drinks and sandwiches. Fay saw Connie's eyes flick over the jug and glasses. No alcohol. She took the drink.

'You're extraordinarily like him. It's weird. I'm sorry. I don't mean to be rude.' The woman seemed confused and, waving away the sandwiches, knocked her hand against a potted plant, which rocked precariously. 'We did try to make contact. When we married. Kevin wrote. At my suggestion. That was a very long time ago, just after the war. He'd been here already over ten years with no contact. I don't quite know why. Perhaps it was the war – he fought, you know. But men are strange that way. Cutting things out of their lives. So, when we married in 'forty-nine, I made him write.'

'Oh,' said Connie. 'I was nine.' Fay could see she was conjuring up an image of herself as a little girl. What had she been like? she wondered. Wild, definitely wild.

'Yes. You were just nine. Kevin wrote all about our marriage. I helped him. About himself and me. I thought his parents would want to know. But that was the trouble. I wasn't Catholic, you see. That's it. A mixed marriage, really. They wouldn't have anything to do with us. That was the bad start of it. When Kevin comes, he'll tell you the other side. You haven't heard of the GI Bill of Rights, I expect? It guaranteed education, you see. Even when I met him he was out ahead of the others. He'll come soon, I promise you . . .'

Fay saw Kevin's car first, big and black with smoked windows. The man was big too, having a word with his driver before entering the house in a rush.

'So, you've arrived. You've been made welcome. Shirley has made you welcome.' He stared as he talked, focusing on Connie, who was as pale as the couch she sat on and wouldn't meet his eyes.

'We must celebrate with a little champagne.'

'Now I recognise you as my brother.' At the mention of alcohol, Connie went towards him. But as they were about to embrace, a cat, previously unseen, striped golden with green eyes, wrapped itself around Connie's legs and flung her forward. Kevin caught her, arms outstretched. It was love at first sight, as Fay commented afterwards.

Connie, whom Fay had never heard speak of her life as a child, except in flamboyant asides of a disparaging nature, began to describe fields, lanes and buildings in delicate and apparently affectionate detail, as though the sight of her brother had caused a longing to share memories of a place she had determined to forget.

'Are you telling me the old house still has a fuchsia in flower just about the whole year through? But electric light now? When did that come?'

'Just as far as the village. We were still on kerosene when I left. Smelly stuff, though the peat in the fires helped. I'm telling you we lived as if the twentieth century hadn't begun.'

As they talked, they drank, Connie so small, her brother much larger, but both showing an identical tip of the wrist. Fay, watching silently, the designated audience, noted that neither asked the other the reason for their leaving home so thoroughly, as if the answer was understood between them. When they had covered every acre of ground around the house, picked over the village school and the church, laughed at the three bars that served not many more adult men, Kevin, examining the empty champagne bottle with surprise, became more reflective. 'One day I would like to take Shirley back.'

Shirley, Fay noticed, looked staggered at this ambition, which suggested it was an entirely new idea, but she did not intervene. The maid brought more champagne and sandwiches.

'Did Shirley tell you she converted? Five years into our marriage. She's very religious now. Chairman of the Sorority of Mary.'

Fay looked at Connie but her face still wore the blush of new love. Depressed at her own realism, Fay thought that if Connie could love Trigear, then she would have no trouble loving a brother who upheld the religion that, most often, Connie blamed for all the troubles in the world, or, at the very least, her own troubles. 'That sounds impressive,' said Fay. 'Do you get to wear a nice-coloured sash?'

Shirley turned to her. 'I was Episcopalian, of course, so I didn't have too far to go.'

This was, Fay guessed, a reference to her Jewishness. She had no objection to the assumption and for a second wondered whether to throw in her own lack of faith before deciding no one present would be the least bit interested. Besides, Connie, now sitting on the sofa holding Kevin's hand, had turned her starry eyes to Shirley. 'So why shouldn't you go to Ma and Pa now? You could bear the olive branch, a peace-maker, a new face to the ancient kingdom. They would surely love you.'

Before answering Shirley looked at Kevin. 'Yes. Perhaps. I don't know.'

Kevin put Connie's hand in her lap and stood up. 'I'll tell you the truth. Shall I tell them the whole story, Shirley? It's Shirley's story more than mine.' Shirley seemed to nod or blink or purse her lips. He was clearly going to tell the story to this new-found sister so it hardly mattered. 'Here goes with the brief version. After we'd been married a few years, we found we weren't to be blessed with children. About then Shirley made me very happy by becoming Catholic. I can't deny I'd done well. Started with an automobile business in Virginia. Soon had more than one and moved into property—' He broke off and tried to look modest. 'But you don't want to hear about business. More luck than judgement in the end, plus a good decision to base in Washington. Politicians ensure stability, I knew that. So we weren't short of money and we decided to adopt. We got this idea that we wanted to give a chance to a child from a poor home in Ireland. A home like mine, you might say. The place was filled with babies. It seemed just the answer. And then I had this other idea . . .' He paused, dramatically. Connie leant forward with a hero-worshipping fervour. 'You tell her,' Kevin turned to Shirley. His voice dropped. 'It was a fucking stupid idea.'

'You see, he wanted to adopt you,' explained Shirley simply. 'Your father never forgave him for asking. From that moment to this there's been no contact of any sort.'

'Da shouldn't have bothered,' said Connie, blinking back tears. 'He lost me anyway.' By now they were all blinking.

Fay visited the Air and Space Museum on her own. She came back on the train by herself. She felt that Shirley and she could be friends. 'You'll come to Manhattan very soon, please. I can give you a tour of the hospital.'

'I'd like that opportunity,' replied Shirley seriously. 'We have quite a line on hospital funding.'

Connie, of course, stayed on.

As Nina left the post office the woman caught her arm. The sudden physical contact was a shock. No one touched her now, except the children and her mother. But the woman's fingers held her tightly: she could feel their warmth through her sweater.

'You're Nina Purcell, aren't you?'

She began to deny it, resentful at the intrusion and at that old name. She would not return to maidenhood, whatever the distance between William and herself. In fact, her visit to the post office was in order to post a letter discussing this very point. She had written, 'I'm not trying to deny or wipe out our marriage. How could I with Helen and Jamie belonging to both of us? But I can't continue in it. If you think this is because I'm "sick in my mind", as you said, then maybe you are right. I've no reason to offer ...' The lines were still running through her head when the hand had clamped on to her arm.

'I'm sorry. I gave you a shock. I just wanted to talk to you for a moment.'

Now Nina looked and saw a middle-aged woman with strong features, fair, greying hair and direct blue eyes. She wore a thick sweater, hand-knitted in a complicated pattern. She did not look the Ancient Mariner type. 'We can go to the Three Wishes.'

The woman didn't introduce herself until they sat at a table with tea and scones.

'I'm Lisa Beckett. Your father was in love with me.' She stopped abruptly. Her face had become very pink and there were tears in her eyes.

Nina stared. The sun was shining through the leaded window-panes, cruelly picking out every wrinkle on the woman's face, highlighting the fine blonde hairs quivering on her chin and above her lips. 'What do you want?' she asked.

'Just to talk for a moment or two. Talk about your father, I mean. I'm sorry.'

'So am I.' Nina clamped her lips shut, then opened them to take a large bite of scone.

The woman shielded her face with her hand. Eventually, she whispered, 'I miss him so much. He was the only man I ever loved.'

'Did he love you?' Nina, judge and jury, took another bite of her scone. What was love, after all? One man's meat, another's poison. She could not feel her father had had enough love in him for two women, and he had certainly loved her mother.

The woman stood, becoming dignified instead of abject. 'I'm afraid it's all too painful. I had hoped . . .' The sentence remained unfinished. Stumbling slightly against the table, she moved towards the door. A bell tinkled as she left and her bowed figure hurried across the window.

Nina drank her cup of tea and then a second one. She thought of Serge and how, although he had made her feel so happy, she had never confused it with love. Nor had she any particular wish to see him again, although she had loved the sex. She thought of her father less gently, the way he had squeezed the life out of her mother and herself in the name, she supposed, of love.

Nina walked back past the post office and, once again, her arm was taken. 'I'm sorry I fled so rudely. I didn't even pay my share of the bill.'

'I'm afraid I was rude too. Perhaps we can walk and talk. It's such a lovely day. You're a teacher, aren't you? I suppose that's how you met my father?'

They headed towards a small park where an iron bandstand, painted a lurid turquoise, rose out of variegated laurel leaves. 'I hero-worshipped him, at first because of what he had survived during the war and then because of what he taught me.'

'I did know of your existence. My mother told me.'

'After his death, I expect.'

'Why do you say that?'

Lisa looked surprised. 'She didn't want anyone to know about me, least of all, you.'

'Perhaps she didn't think it so important.'

It appeared that Lisa did not feel the need to defend herself from this accusation. They were walking side by side, quite fast, and now Lisa pushed open the gate into the park. Nina asked, 'He talked to you about his time in the camp?'

'Yes. He thought about it all the time, of course. The not talking had become a nightmare. It was what made him so complicated, so unhappy.'

'I didn't know he was so unhappy. He didn't seem unhappy to me.' She knew she sounded resentful.

'Shall we sit down?' Lisa indicated a bench and they sat side by side. Nina watched a young mother drag apart a boy and a girl who were squabbling over a snail. The boy wanted to stamp on it and the girl wanted to give it into her mother's safe-keeping. On the whole, the mother seemed to favour her son's point of view. Eventually she picked up the snail and threw it as far as possible into the depths of a holly bush. Both children began crying. But in another moment the boy had run off to the bandstand where his crowing voice filled the little park, 'I'm the king of the castle!'

'There were two sides to your father,' Lisa moved closer to Nina, 'or I should say three. But the two are most important. You see, but for his experiences in the war, he would have been someone quite different. Even, perhaps, a soldier.' Nina looked quickly at Lisa but she seemed unaware of having said anything especially significant. 'He grew up in that confident generation when men were quite unafraid, quite certain of their place, well, I'm not afraid to say it, their superiority. He entered the war like that. Handsome, clever—'

'Happily married,' interrupted Nina.

'That too,' agreed Lisa sadly. 'And soon he had a baby. In fact, he had everything on a plate.'

'Go on,' encouraged Nina, putting out a hand. Something had changed again. How weird it all was.

'I think what happened was this. In the camp, one side of him, the one that already predominated, the tough survivor, grew even stronger. He wasn't a popular figure. He was often cruel to people weaker than him. He despised anyone who gave in and didn't hide his contempt for them. But there was another he was thoroughly ashamed of and tried to keep secret – from everyone.' She stopped and Nina saw the tears had returned. 'Sometimes, he told me, at night, he couldn't stop weeping. In other circumstances, he would have been diagnosed as having a nervous breakdown. It was most uncontrollable when the malaria was bad, although he used to pretend it was sweat rolling down his cheeks, not tears. It was during one of these bad periods that he took a book of poetry from a man who'd died. It became the most important thing in his life, so he told me. He could even forget the humiliations of starving. He could put himself into a kind of trance where food had no place. Or, rather, its place was taken by poetry. Beauty. Harmony. Rhythm . . .'

'But why couldn't he tell my mother that? She was a musician. A professional once. Her life was all about that, even if she only taught children.'

'I know. I suppose their marriage had started off in one way and couldn't change.'

'He'd been away for five years. Surely they could have begun again differently?' He did read her Wordsworth. I suppose the book was Wordsworth's poems?'

Lisa shrugged. 'The story isn't finished. He came to me in the summer of 1955. So I had him, part of him, for eight years. We read poetry together, we made love.'

'And this story?'

'Yes. Yes.' She looked down and away, as if suddenly reluctant. 'Have you read about what went on in the camps?'

'I saw the film. The one with Alec Guinness playing the brave officer.'

'The brave officer. Yes. There were those. I told you about the book of poetry. That was what caused the trouble. One of the Japanese officers noticed how attached Roger was to it. He made him read bits from it, took him to his hut, gave him cigarettes. He knew a little English. He wanted to learn more.' She paused.

Nina frowned. 'Do you mean he was fraternising with the enemy?' The words sounded stiff and unconvincing, taken from an earlier age.

'Nothing so simple.' Lisa even smiled a little. 'It was understood that you couldn't say no to a Japanese officer whether you liked it or not. The main bartering card played by the Japanese was the sick. They couldn't understand why the English cared about them so much. Eventually this officer was posted to another camp but he wanted the book so much that he tried to barter better treatment for the sick. But your father wouldn't give him the book.'

'Why didn't he just take it?'

'Your father buried it when he was out in the jungle working on the railway line. The officer took his revenge not on your father but on the sick. For a year no one in the camp spoke to Roger.'

Nina stood up and stretched out her legs, stiffened and aching with the tension. She felt there was nothing to be said. If she had loved her father more, she supposed she might have been sadder. 'So he was punished too.'

'His own shame was his worst punishment. He could never forget it. He no longer believed in himself. But I gave him back something. By loving him as I did, by making him talk about it, I helped him.'

'You mean I should be glad that you were his mistress.' Nina did not sit down again.

'I told you. There were two sides. I expect he loved your mother in another way.' She looked down at her hands. 'You look very alike, as I expect you know. But I won't bother you again. It's just . . . I loved him so much. When he came to me, he could have been anything, done anything, and it wouldn't have affected my love for him.'

Now Nina felt like crying. Not for Lisa but for herself because she had never felt this kind of love and suspected she never would. And then she thought that now her father was no longer a hero, just another survivor.

Nina opened the letter from Connie with the hope that the dramas of Connie's life might shift the perspectives of her own.

I'm writing this in luxury!

wrote Connie, on notepaper headed 'Georgetown' and with a hovering magnolia.

You know how little I care about such things. But it has been thrust upon me. I have found my eldest brother, Kevin. He's on the way to making a fortune. Not crooked, as you'll be thinking. He's big and gorgeous with the authentic O'Malley blue eyes. This is, you might say, the announcement of the birth of a new brother (and an opportunity to use this slick paper and sit at a cute desk). I am staying here for a little while for a getting-to-know-each-other session. He has a sweet darling wife called Shirley who has tube problems and can't produce little Kevins. When I was a child, they had this passionate longing to adopt me so it is too romantic that I have found them now. Please rejoice and drink a stiff sherry with your mother to the present joy of your friend, Connie. PS God moves in mysterious ways. Shirley is an altar girl, actually something grander you wouldn't understand, at the local Catholic church.

The telephone rang at midnight. Both Nina and Veronica stumbled out of bed and groped their way to the hallway where Nina's hand reached the receiver first. It could only be an emergency.

'Who? Sorry.'

'It's Merlin. William's cousin Merlin. In New York. I can't find Connie O'Malley.'

Veronica stumbled up the stairs again, while Nina, at last grasping the situation, went to find Connie's letter. She had always suspected William's cousin was foolish enough to be in love with Connie.

Fay's telephone rang at midnight. She reached for her glasses and the light switch. It must be an emergency. But she wasn't on call.

'Thank God, Fay, you're there.'

'It's the middle of the night, Connie!'

'Is it? We've just got back from dinner. *Such* grandeur. All hawks, I'm afraid. Do you think politics is a matter of conscience?'

'I'm sleeping, Connie. I have a call in for six.'

'Sorry. Sorry. You're so directed.'

'I don't want to cut you off . . .'

'OK. It's Merlin. You remember? Nina's cousin, Merlin de Witless. He calls here all the time. The maid won't shield me another day. He says he only came to the States to see me. I don't dislike him. It's just an inconvenient moment. I tell him he's spoiling a lovely friendship. Will you look after him?'

It seemed easiest to agree. 'OK. Give him my number.'

Merlin could not be stopped from coming to Washington.

'Show him the cherry blossom!' Fay had advised with spinsterish asperity.

Merlin and Connie met at the Jefferson Memorial. The weather was cool but spring-like. Connie could see that Merlin was deeply affected by the sight of her. Although she didn't take it seriously – there was no sense in him loving a girl like her – she was moved and flattered. To calm himself, he read the inscription on the monument: ' "I have sworn upon the altar of God eternal hostility against every form of tyranny over the mind of man." '

Connie kissed his flushed cheek. 'If only that sort of thing weren't so complicated. Kevin's making a fortune out of the war.' She sighed, with a touch of theatrical mournfulness.

'If only everything wasn't so complicated.' Merlin gulped and took her hand.

They began to walk, following the edge of the Potomac, where the pink froth of the cherry trees spread above their heads like upside down ballet dancers, as Connie suggested, pleased with the image. They stopped to watch the reflection in the wide pool of water between the Jefferson Memorial and Lincoln's even grander one. Connie shivered in the breeze, before the marble whiteness of the monuments against the blue sky. Merlin took off his coat and put it round her.

'I'm sure you were never in love with me in London. I'd say hardly at all in love. It was just hanging about in New York gave you strange ideas.'

'Who said I was in love with you?' Merlin had remembered who he was, his success as a journalist, his flat in Albany, his spectacular collection of eighteenth-century prints soon to be added to by judicious buying, his interesting circle of friends. 'I am in love with Japanese cherry blossom, with a new world of galleries and museums.'

'Oh, is that it?'

They began to walk again and Connie noticed that Merlin was tall and slim and his coat was made of fine wool. His English accent made her feel homesick – for what it was hard to say.

'Where are you staying?' He was in an expensive hotel. 'You could give me tea there?'

Looking unnerved, Merlin prodded his finger at the guidebook. 'You can walk to all the principal sites in Washington.'

Connie laughed. 'That doesn't mean you're obliged to. I'm serious. I want to come back with you.'

Merlin's room was large and ornate, impressing Connie, who only briefly considered her aim in inviting herself into Merlin's bed. It would make his journey worthwhile.

Merlin watched her undressing with concentration but made no attempt to remove his own clothes. It took her only seconds to reveal her nakedness. Connie was pleased by his look of awe and posed a little, pushing out her hips and cupping her breasts in her hands. But then, as he put out his hand to her, she felt a sudden sense of wrong-doing. 'But, Merlin, we're friends!'

'Yes. I know.'

The awe had gone and she could see that he was striving to express complicated feelings. This made her feel very unsexy and, taking up her skirt as a covering, she sat on the bed away from him. 'We don't need to make love. We get on perfectly well without it.'

'I've been thinking of you all day, all night. For days.'

'That's jet-lag, Merlin.'

'Don't make fun of me. I love you!' How could she resist that and the tearful eagerness with which he pounced on her and whisked off his clothes.

What is fucking? thought Connie. Answer: fucking. He knew how to do it at least and she had always been fond of him, if only to use him as the butt of her jokes. She remembered the wedding cake eaten by Nina's children.

'You haven't got married yet?' she asked.

'No. No.' She could tell he thought they were making love. When they had finished, he told her how he dreamed of marrying her, of bringing her into Albany, of exploding the constrictions placed on his life by his mother. He would stop trying to be a journalist and become an art connoisseur, doing a bit of dealing on the side. Connie would be his iconoclast. His most precious art object in his new life.

Fay had yet another midnight call. 'Fay, you've got to come to my succour. You bear a heavy burden yourself, sure you do.'

Fay thought that whenever Connie reverted to Irishisms, storm-clouds followed.

'It's Merlin. He's asked me to marry him. He thinks he's utterly in love.'

'Surely you said no?'

'How could I be so cruel?'

'What do you *mean*, Connie?'

'We'd just made love. His eyes were like stars. He was in heaven – if it exists. I said I'd have lunch with him in New York on Tuesday so that he could leave happy. He's booked a poolside table at the Four Seasons, but of course I'm not going.'

'You want me to go? You want me to go and tell this man I've never met that you were just playing around? And that your true love is, at this moment, divided equally between a hired assassin and a married man . . .' Fay felt so filled with anger that she could hardly hear her own words. Faltering, she gave Connie her chance. Nothing. 'Fuck you, you fucking asshole.' She put the phone down.

Connie, sitting at her typewriter for she was late delivering a piece on women warriors, swore some more, then typed out a row of expletives. What did Fay, with her cold sex for health reasons, know about emotions? Determined not to feel badly about Merlin, she typed, 'I WAS ABUSED' several times, although she knew perfectly well that the best she could do in the line of abuse was Hubert. She had not thought about Rick's father for at least two years and didn't plan to ever again. 'I

AM NOT THINKING ABOUT HUBERT IN PARTICULAR I AM NOT THINKING
ABOUT THAT DRUNKEN NIGHT WE FIRST HAD SEX NOTE NO MENTION OF
LOVE I WAS A CHILD PLEASE GOD REMEMBER.'

It was Hubert caressing her. She had known that, although the drink
made it less obvious. He was an older man, his hands moving over her
skin with a savouring slowness. When she put out a hand to touch him,
he took it and put it back to her side. His breathing was heavy but
controlled, and after his hands and then his lips smoothed across her,
she felt the scratchiness of his beard.

She had tried, just for a moment, to face the wrong she was doing,
but it was far too late for any last-ditch strength of character. The
decision had been taken that night when he came to the pub, drunk.
She had been drunk too. Perhaps it had been taken before that, weeks
ago when Rick had suddenly announced, in public, not warning her
beforehand, that he was going to Paris. 'I am being transferred to Paris,'
were his words, cold, anonymous words, she decided. A week later he
had gone. He must have known for ages. Anger had squeezed out
sadness, squashed it into a tiny corner, until she was on top form.

The night after Rick's departure, in the pub, his father had confirmed
this: 'You're in fine fettle, my girl. Oh, my God, I feel the spirit of poesy
waving her magic wand.' There and then he had composed a poem,
writing the first line carefully on the inside of his arm when she had
declined the honour.

> The Fine Fettle Girl
> Is shaped like a skittle
> (Though you can't knock her down)
> Is bright like a kettle
> (And whistles like one too)
> She pestles my mortar
> She pounds my aorta
> That fine fettle girl.
> That fettle fine girl
> That skittle, kettle, pestle, fine fettle girl
> (Who whistles me to her).

Naturally, she had objected, pointed out that any drunk in Mayo could
do better, had even quoted a line or two of childhood remembrances to
prove her point. She had ridiculed his sense of rhyme, rhythm, his
repetition, totally unsuccessful, in her view, of the whistle theme.

He had ignored the criticism and enjoyed the attention. 'You do not understand the importance of the bracket,' he had stated solemnly. 'I do not hold that against you. It would be straining the realms of the unlikely too far that an illiterate poppet from the distant bogs of Ireland could appreciate the merit, the distinction, the gorgeous subtlety – if used in the right hands – of the bracket. A bracket in one magnificent, yet delicate sweep both denies and impresses the importance of the words within its embrace. Brackets are the unsung heroes of grammar, patronised, spat upon, seldom allowed to enter the golden realms, the rarefied heights of poetry, yet representing a meritocracy that cuts through the moribund hierarchy of the English language—'

As he took a quick breath, Connie interrupted, 'Go see the Book of Kells, and call me illiterate then!' It did not matter that she had not seen the Book of Kells, she thought excitedly, because it was in her bloodstream, it was her inheritance.

'Well!' Hubert had exclaimed. 'I may have to write a new poem called "Hiding Your Light Under a Bushel". Bustle, hustle, works well.'

So they batted the words backwards and forwards because it was Connie's evening off and she had time to sit with the customers. Athough by closing time they were surrounded by the wilder elements, something irreversible had been struck between them so that there they were, a fortnight later, in Hubert's mucky flat, in bed together. Or, to be more exact, he knelt on the floor.

'God!' raged Hubert, struggling with a condom. 'The man who invented these things deserves no quarter.'

'Perhaps it was a woman,' Connie had suggested, giggling weakly from his love-making. She was putty, jelly, cotton-wool, liquid amber, pale flame . . . How had he done such a thing to her when all her love was reserved for . . . But then he was clambering up to her, his engorged sex magnificent and apparently fully arrayed. What could she have done with such grandiose conquering?

And now she had Merlin de Witt to deal with. Nothing very grandiose about his conquering. Connie picked up the telephone and dialled Fay's number again.

Fay hurried to the Four Seasons. She had dressed carefully, the ghost of her mother hovering anxiously, although from what Connie had said Merlin de Witt would not be difficult to impress. I am one of the few women surgeons in Manhattan – she allowed herself a moment of inward congratulation.

'Mr de Witt's table,' she told the *maître d'*, arriving late after her bleeper had caught her just as she was leaving the hospital.

'Mr Derwitt has already arrived.'

Fay looked at the width of window with its geometric view of mid-town Manhattan as she followed a waiter across the restaurant, hoping in that way to avoid a sighting of Merlin de Witt's face. She was like the soldier or policeman, she thought, who comes to bring news of a death.

'Madam.' The waiter bowed. He stood at a table occupied by a handsome and prosperous-looking Englishman. Very English in a pale, dandyish suit and with long but smoothly brushed hair.

'There's some mistake . . .'

'Connie sent me.' Fay sat down quickly so that the waiter should remove himself. She saw that the moment Merlin had taken in her alternative presence, his face had assumed a mask of politeness. Thank God for the English stiff upper lip.

'I suppose she got held up in Washington. Perhaps you'd like a drink. Perhaps you'd like champagne?'

Fay saw that it stood ready in a bucket. She let him pour her a glass, although she would not drink it. 'I understand you have to leave tomorrow.'

'Yes. Early tomorrow.' A crease of pain wriggled out of the mask before it was swiftly contained. 'You're a doctor. A surgeon. Tell me why. I would be very interested to know why. How you came to climb such a pinnacle.'

There was a need for conversation but Fay would never have told him so much about herself if she hadn't believed he was truly interested. 'It began,' she said, 'with my childhood.' And who had cared to dwell upon her childhood before? 'You may have guessed I am Jewish.'

'Oh, well,' began Merlin, in the English way of looking for the road of least offence. Or perhaps he was thinking of Connie.

'There're a great many Jews in Chicago. My mother came over from Poland as a teenager in the early thirties, leaving behind her mother, father, most of the rest of the family, a younger brother and sister, aunts and uncles. She married just before the war. I was born in 1940, my brother in 1945.' She stopped. The story, told like this, seemed almost a cliché, if the definition of a cliché was something expected, without surprise. She saw that Merlin had put aside his champagne, in deference to tragedy. Yet she liked him enough to go on.

'Yes. They all disappeared. That is, were wiped out. At least, not quite all. In 1950 my grandmother emerged. She had survived. I can imagine what she survived but I don't know exactly because it was never and is never talked of. She lived with us. I can't explain what it was like. She died anyway when I was fifteen. She had always seemed old to me but quite recently I worked out that she was probably well under sixty. I never knew her exact age.' She stopped again, thinking how old she herself was now and yet how these details of her growing were still, apart from becoming a doctor, the most important facts in her life. She remembered suddenly how she had refused to mourn at her grandmother's funeral. Sad, but a fact. Just like her death. Of course, that was not how it had been received in the family. It was as if the whole Jewish story had come alive with her dying. Simple words, 'Oh, what she has seen!' opened wide the years of the Holocaust, of the tortured deaths of millions, of ovens, shower rooms, starvation, of lampshades, mothers separated from babies, of cruelty, humiliation, nakedness, revulsion, shaved heads, girls who became old before they could become women. Disgusting, shameful, unbearable happenings that she was determined to keep out of her life.

She had gone up to her bedroom and, sitting on her bed, opened her mathematics revision book. She was surprised but not alarmed at the pleasure it gave her. With every equation her own equanimity was restored.

When she had eventually returned downstairs, she wished she could slide in through the door, over the window-sill, undetected, just a cold draught, invisible, cloaked in the hieroglyphics of her maths papers. But she knew that was impossible. She was a major player in her grandmother's death, the eldest grandchild, clever, sharp, modern, part of the great United States of America. She was not a boy, it was true, but that could not be held against her. That she had a *shiksa* expression about her sometimes was not so good, but that was the price you paid . . . Stopping these voices before they drove her back upstairs, because she was angry and because perhaps, just maybe, she had loved her grandmother, Fay turned the handle of the door. 'Dear Fay,' her mother had said, with a proud smile, 'we were just talking about your high ambitions.'

'You must be very clever,' ventured Merlin, as the silence lengthened. 'Is your brother the same?'

Ignoring the question – this was her story, not Daniel's – she fixed Merlin with an intense stare. 'If you mean clever because I had none of the obvious advantages, that is true. I was clever enough to win scholarships. But I had one very strong incentive, the urge to escape.' She paused and looked beyond Merlin, saw that the table and diners shimmered with sunbeams. 'And perhaps to atone.' She launched the words on to the ripples of light.

'To atone,' repeated Merlin, who had picked up the menu. She felt it was less in self-defence than to protect her.

'I had survived,' she said simply, and found that, mercifully, she had been given the ability to smile.

Connie telephoned Fay at a respectable hour. 'Has he gone?'

'I presume you are referring to Merlin?'

'Sure I'm referring to Merlin. Did you have a miserable lunch? The trouble with Merlin is he's a character waiting for a plot. Did he manage to keep his stiff upper lip in place? At least, stiffer than something else I could mention . . .'

It was then that Fay put the phone down and did not pick it up again when Connie rang back, neither the first time nor the second.

Instead, she went out of her apartment – it was a warm sunny evening – and visited a large supermarket where she spent a long time staring at the display of vegetables and fruit. The brilliant colours of the red, yellow and green peppers, the purple aubergines, crimson apples, pale melon and orange pomegranates made her think of Nina. Her letters were filled with intense references to colour, most of which Fay skipped over. She would write to Nina as soon as she got home.

My dear Nina, I am sorry that this will be a dismal letter. But I thought you should hear it from me. I have had as much as I mean to take of Connie. To be precise, our friendship is over. I have lost all respect for her. No need to burden you with all the circumstances. Her treatment of your cousin Merlin is part of it. I suspect we were always far too different to get along for long. I regret our yew tree bonding. If that's what it was . . .

Nina wrote back quickly to Fay. It was half term and she had been listening to Helen's exhortations to buy her a pony. New York seemed very far away.

'Dear Fay, Oh dear. I am so sorry. Of course Merlin is William's cousin, not mine . . .'

Then Nina wrote to Connie. 'Dearest foolish Connie, What have you done to upset Fay so much . . . ?'

She hardly expected an answer. Connie liked to quote Dr Johnson. 'No man but a blockhead ever wrote, except for money.'

Connie swivelled the circlet of pills. She stood alone in her loft, except for a small golden kitten she'd recently acquired who was curled up daintily on a pile of not very clean underclothes. Connie was dressed in underpants with a purple feather boa straggled round her neck. She was very hot and the boa trickled. She dragged it off her, flung it to the floor and trampled across it once or twice, before sitting and then lying on her back.

Eyes closed, she pictured cool green wetness and, for the first time, it seemed desirable. She thought of sweet clear air, the smell of peat smoke, sunset burning the edges of dark clouds and sunrise splitting apart early-morning mists, of rain that came unexpectedly and soothed the skin and the mind. Languidly, she reached for a book given to her by Merlin.

> This great purple butterfly
> In the prison of my hands,
> Has a learning in his eye
> Not a poor fool understands . . .

She put the book down on the floor and placed the rather too full circlet of pills on top of it. She was clear now how it had happened and all that remained was to decide what to do about it.

Unlike many of Chicago's young, Fay's brother, Daniel, had no ambition to live in New York. Fay got him there under false pretences, writing just before her rift with Connie, 'I have the most beautiful girl in the world for you. She's Irish, very wacky and out of your age range, but at least you can look and learn.'

It was strange to have a proprietorial arm on a virile male. Fay thought of all the cadavers she'd carved up, all the sick people she'd cared for over the years and couldn't believe she'd done it without a man at her side, or in her heart. And how strange that these thoughts should come to her because of a visit from her brother. There had been men in her flat, men in her bed, but none with whom she had the rights of intimacy. Perhaps, after all, I want to have a man in my life, thought Fay, amazing herself enough to smile.

'I wish I could be a tourist with you.'

'But surgery would fall apart without you.'

'One corner of it. But I've wangled cover from six, touch wood. I'll give you the downtown tour.'

'Downtown beer and bagels is all I'll be good for by then.'

'It'll be cooler on the river. Take the trip to the Statue of Liberty. You pass Ellis Island on the way and you can imagine all those Jewish boys waiting to be signed up for the land of opportunity.'

They had reached the hospital and she was able to consider full frontal this all-American brother of hers, who bore not a shadow across his face. Wryly, she wondered if she could find a man like that.

That evening Fay and Daniel sat in a bar on Eighth Street drinking beer while Daniel described his girlfriend, Lee. 'She's so great, so warm. I've never seen Lee give anyone a bad time.'

'What's her surname?'

'Samuelson. I guess we'll end up getting married. If the war's still on.'

On cue, the level of the noise on the street rose dramatically and a banner blocked the evening light.

'What do I see?' commented Daniel, without enthusiasm.

They went to the window and watched the theatre of protest, the cheerful costuming, the mothers and babies, the angry draft-dodgers, the crippled veterans.

'Balloons, banners and, soon enough, batons,' murmured Fay. The mood changed. The batons came out as the flag was set up, stars and stripes held aloft, petrol poured, firelighters thrown at it. Then came the sound of sirens, overwhelming the shouting, the rage, the flames. A crowd of protesters fled into the bar, men and women wearing bandanas and flared trousers as if they were going to a fancy-dress party. One, too slow, was hoisted backwards on to the street and whacked over the head, then kicked in his groin. The policeman's righteous anger blazed higher as the flag lay black and sodden. Some of the protesters were exhilarated, triumphing over fear, others, the professionals, counted the success and failure.

The street in front of them began to empty, the scene chased further along.

'Let's go.' Fay felt claustrophobic. How could you spectate at a scene like that? What else could you do?

'In case they guess you're a doctor?' Somewhere in the corner of the bar, a man's arm dangled limply.

'He'll find his way to the hospital.'

They went out and the warmth of the street was gentle and dusky, a new crowd collecting by a cinema, as if the demonstration had never been. Just as she was thinking how strange it all was, Fay spotted Connie, white-clad, dangling something in or near the last remaining policeman's car.

'Let's eat!' she led Daniel hurriedly away.

Nina and Connie were having tea at the Tate. Connie had announced she was too jet-lagged to look at any pictures, which suited Nina perfectly. She had already spent nearly an hour sitting in front of the Rothkos and nothing could top that experience.

'How long are you in England?' she asked. Connie's arrival had been unexpected – not that anything could be expected about her. Nina thought that Connie's usual ebullience had been dented by something or other and wondered vaguely how Fay could be so unforgiving of someone so obviously vulnerable.

'I'm delivering in person my piece on finding my brother. The American papers were too close for comfort.'

'You really like him, don't you?'

Connie fiddled about with the sugar bowl, making little white cascades with the spoon. 'Oh, sure. Sure. He's husky and handsome. His politics stink, I have to say. But I really like Shirley. She's the most maternal woman I've ever met.' She stuck the spoon upright into the bowl and looked so hard over Nina's left shoulder that she was almost tempted to turn round. 'You know they've decided to adopt a baby.'

'Heavens! Aren't they too old?'

'Apparently not. They've got one in mind.' Now she was pouring sugar over the table.

'From one of those dreadful orphanages in Ireland you told me about?'

Connie looked up at Nina, her eyes, Nina thought a little jealously, more glistening pools than ever. 'They're not so bad. You know I like to make a good story: the nuns call the babies God's cherubs.'

'But what about their mothers? You told me they were used like skivvies, treated like sinners, punished—' Nina broke off, wondering why she should feel the need to resurrect one of Connie's self-justifying anti-Irish stories.

Connie swept the sugar off the table on to the floor. 'For whatever reason, they're getting one from America. I expect it's easier that way . . .' Connie's voice trailed away as she frowned at her toasted muffin.

Nina guessed she had something more to say but it was not her way to question so she filled in the time by describing Helen's prowess as a rider. 'This summer she won eleven rosettes. Now she wants me to buy her a pony. My mother goes to watch her at all the shows. Sometimes I think she's more her mother than I am.' Why was she saying such things to Connie who had never shown the slightest interest in her home life? She began on a new tune: 'And how are the married man and the killer?'

'In fine fettle, I believe.' Once more Connie started her sugar cascades. 'One dropped me when he discovered a friend of his was my brother and I dropped the other when he killed my kitten.'

'Connie! You don't mean literally?'

'I do, more's the pity for little Goldilocks. He was explaining to me about the windpipe, you know, how the air goes in and out and he took up Goldilocks as a teaching aid.'

'Well, that's terrible.'

'I thought you'd be pleased.'

'I mean about the kitten.'

'Yes. I shan't get another. Her poor little body reminded me of all the kittens my da drowned back home. Threw their wee bodies out into the peat bog. I had plans to bury Goldilocks in Central Park but events overtook me.'

'Events?'

'A protest march, actually. In general, I've given them up but this one fitted my mood.' She paused. 'Serge was there.'

Nina felt herself blushing like a child. A thick warmth of memory. Yet her voice was cool enough. 'How is he?'

'Unchanged. Good. As saintly as ever.' Connie seemed to gain a little more energy and, to Nina's relief, pushed away the sugar bowl.

'Yes, I suppose that's right. A man of principle. That describes Serge.' She wondered if William was a man of principle too. Just different principles. But now Connie had launched into one of her stories.

'Truth to tell, it was all rather too dramatic. Like a few other protesters, these days, they'd hit on the idea of burning the American flag.' Connie described, with a curiously detached air, the collecting crowd, the protestors and counter-protesters, her sort of friend Allen Ginsberg, like another kind of saint, so loving and all-embracing, the speeches, sloganising, yells, songs, skirmishes, journalists and finally police, batons out, arrest ... 'So you see why I never buried poor Goldilocks. I flung her through the window of a police car, in the end. So her life, or rather her death, served in the cause of peace, quite apart from finally ridding me of Trig.'

'Weren't you terrified the police would catch you?'

'There was no one in the car. They were all beating hell out of my friends. But it's heartening to think they came back to a dead cat, although I fear they may not have treated her body with proper respect.'

Connie seemed cheered by this sad story but Nina, nevertheless, was struck by the calm way in which she unfolded the drama, as if she had other more important things on her mind. 'I saw Fay,' added Connie.

Perhaps that was it. Fay. 'You're speaking again?'

'Oh, no. Fay has cast me off. I saw her watching the protest march with a man. Young, large. Arm in arm. Perhaps she has a secret boyfriend.'

'I'm sure Fay would tell us,' said Nina, thinking at once that she had no idea what Fay would tell them. 'They're closing the café,' she added.

'So they are. Shall we look at the Rothkos?'

Startled, Nina began to blush, as she had at the name of her lover. 'Much too late now, I'm afraid.'

The next day, on the aeroplane to Ireland, Connie wondered why she hadn't told Nina about the baby or Trigear's ridiculous reaction. Her breasts were already bigger, apparently. Tender. She had protested at the roughness of his mouth and he had become so proprietorial that she had found herself telling him the truth. Doubtless a bottle of wine had helped. She had laughed at his hands on her windpipe so he had turned to poor little Goldilocks.

She had planned on going to see her parents in Mayo. She took the bus from the airport to Dublin and felt her soul rejuvenate, or so she told herself. The city amazed her. O'Connell Street had ambitions to become Fifth Avenue. It was raining, which pleased her, and soon she found her way to the river and watched the autumn gnats dancing among the raindrops. She remembered the good times, Billy Ferguson's chocolate kisses, which maybe had inspired her towards America, and she wondered why she had never tried to find him. But these nostalgic ideas were less vigorous than she expected so she started walking towards her sister's house.

She was very wet now. Her hair, which had grown long recently, dripped down her back and across her collar-bones, her shoes were sodden and she began to amuse herself by splashing deliberately through puddles. If Eileen repudiated her, she decided, the best procedure would be to gather her dollars about her (now a soaking wedge in her pocket) and proceed to the Shelbourne Hotel to drown her sorrows with the posh folk.

On the other hand – she hesitated at a crossing, noting inconsequentially how melodious was the sound of Irish voices about her – she could go and have a Paddy's whiskey first of all, to settle herself down, set herself up, to celebrate her return to the Old Country.

Her sister's house hadn't changed. Peering through the window, Connie was startled to find how exactly she remembered the emerald furnishing, the brown patterned carpet, the table with its heavy glass bowl, the holy picture of a female saint (not the Virgin Mary, she thought), the mantel with ornamental animals of uncertain origin.

'Will I be giving you a leg up?' asked a male voice close behind her.

'You think I'm an intruder? It's a misunderstanding for which you cannot be blamed.' Connie swung round to confront a young man with what she hoped looked like dignity. 'I am a relative,' she added, capitulating to his suspicious expression.

'You'll be looking for my mother, then?'

'I will indeed.'

'Well, you won't find her here. She's out at the Marian Hall with our Rose and little Bobbie. I can direct you if it's your will.'

Connie considered how her will felt about confronting her sister in the midst of holy works and decided that there was certainly a better course of action. Besides, the whiskey had sunk from her head to her bladder and she was in imminent need of relieving herself.

'I couldn't wait for her here, could I? To be frank and fearless, I came from England this morning and from the States not too long before that and I have a crying need for a period of quietness. Furthermore, I've still got clothes on me damp from the morning's weather.'

'You'd better come in, then. You know something? You've quite a look of my mother.' He unlocked the door and ushered her in.

Connie fell asleep, head on a chair-back as green as an Irish field. She was woken by a hand on her arm.

'You're Auntie Connie.'

Connie opened her eyes and smiled at the youth. She remembered him now and how she'd geed him up as a little boy. Paddy was his name but not his nature. He'd always been inclined to stodginess. She found his friendly recognition had started a warm glow round her midriff while the sleep had knocked away the effects of the whiskey. 'So how many are you children now? Over the dozen?'

Paddy ducked his head. 'Mam wasn't too well after wee Bobbie. We're just the eight. Will you be resting the night here? You must have some stories to tell.' His look of longing increased Connie's sense of the benign.

'And how is it you have the house to yourself?'

'I'm on shifts. Terry'll be in just this minute, then Madeleine, Brid,

Michael. Mary will be back from school and Ma soon after to make our tea. There won't be much quiet for sleeping then.'

He had hardly finished speaking when the door banged open and a crowd of children swaggered in, two girls singing, two boys kicking a ball and behind them all, a child on either hand, a bag slung on her shoulder, Eileen.

'Here's Auntie Connie visiting!' shouted Paddy.

Eileen turned in the hallway and frowned into the lounge. Connie stood up and waved as if she were on the edge of a swimming-pool and about to jump in. And yet, although she liked the fun, she wanted the emotion, too, and needed to feel herself wrapped in her sister's embrace.

'Connie!' Eileen came towards her. With a shock of surprise, Connie saw how pretty she looked, that delicate skin which had never seen hard sun or air-conditioning, the soft, matronly contours, the dark hair, streaked with silver. How could she look like this with all these children, these succubi?

'I've been in America.' She made it sound as if she had been there for years and years. 'I'm just visiting.'

'You could have written.' Eileen came in and sat down, bags and children collected round her. It was a reproach, of course, but as Connie prepared to prevaricate, beat her breast, throw herself on her sister's mercy, she had another shock for she saw that her homecoming was not the biggest event in Eileen's life. She was distracted and she began to give commands to some of the children.

'I expect you want to know about Ma and Da and Michael?'

'Oh, yes. And you. You all.'

'I'm here in front of you. I am what you see.' She patted the head of the smallest child, who put his thumb in his mouth and tried to climb on to her lap. She pushed him off kindly. 'I have eight of them – all, even the last little one, God bless him, healthy, good children. I have a husband who's been in work for all our marriage and gave up the drink four years ago now. I have some friends, I have the Church.' She interrupted herself to explain to a large daughter the whereabouts of some cold potatoes and mayonnaise. 'You'll be staying for tea?'

'Indeed, yes. I'm so glad for you.'

'I'm blessed. We'd be wise to go on through if we're to stop the children running wild, brave hearts that they are.'

The kitchen, like the lounge, was exactly as Connie remembered it. She said so to Eileen, who was removing her youngest girl's fingers from the jam pot. 'Rosie, will you stop behaving like a dirty old bluebottle? The same? Sure, Connie, you've lost your memory across the Atlantic. Just this six months we did over the whole lounge, new suite, the lot. Himself took a week off work to do the painting and lay the carpets. If you want to find things unchanged, you'll have to go find Ma and Da. They've got the electricity, true enough, but the thatch is still as filled with vermin as ever. Now, Bobbie, come and sit on my lap and help me spread the butter.'

'And are they still lamenting . . .' Connie began, with her eyes down, but then, as she looked up, and saw little Bobbie smiling between his mother's arms, she stopped abruptly. How had she failed to notice his narrow eyes, his paper skin, the broad flatness of his head?

'Lamenting your departure? Oh, Connie, tell that to your father confessor. They're well enough. I send some of the children to them now in the summer. Michael still hasn't found a wife but he's built himself a neat bungalow with his own hands. It has a silver gate and blue-painted lintels. Go see for yourself.'

Connie, never comfortable in the sidelines, felt a great sorrow, part self-pity, part shame. She had come to tell her sister about her baby, her pregnancy. But now, in the midst of this hard-working, happy family, with little Bobbie gaily squashing the butter with a spoon, she knew she could not speak. In the eyes of the world she might be a success but here, in this kitchen, she was merely a squalid fornicator. 'You have a truly gorgeous family, Eileen.'

'Oh, yes. I know.' Only then, Connie caught a gleam of steel, enough for her to stand, in preparation for leaving.

'Do you have a telephone?'

Connie rang Nina. 'How do you fancy a trip to Cork? I'm writing a grand piece on returning home.'

'But Cork isn't your home.'

Nina had been called from her studio by her mother to answer the telephone. She stood with a paintbrush loaded with a complicated mix of Prussian blue, Payne's grey and viridian green. It was, she recognised, a murky colour, even ugly, not successful at all, not what she had meant but – she nudged a bit of it on to a finger – she had no idea how to make anything better. As Connie continued to lure her to Cork, Nina realised suddenly that up till now it had all been a game, her recently established art classes in Hastings worse than useless. If she were serious, she must study properly, which almost certainly meant living in London. She would be an art student, living in a rented room, following in the steps of Matisse. She felt her heart bound joyously at the prospect. How ridiculous and how even more ridiculous that she was absolutely certain it would happen! 'Yes, I'll come to Cork,' she told Connie. Such a leap of the imagination was nothing compared to the leap she had just taken.

Connie had taken for granted Nina's arrival. She had booked them into the same room in a hotel and, on Sunday morning, led her to a bar sheltering beneath one of the many spires in Cork. It was Sunday and church bells had been ringing for hours. Nina could see how pleased Connie was with herself and noticed how, as if better to enjoy the sounds of Ireland, she shut her eyes. It was Nina therefore, not Connie, who saw a tall man approaching.

'May I introduce myself? I am Orlando Partridge.' He waved a glass mug. The name was enough to catch Connie's attention but then she shut her eyes again for a second as if in rejection. 'Constance O'Malley,' said Orlando Partridge, with what seemed to Nina an odd formality. 'I recognised you at once. I have read a piece or two of yours and I wondered then, with an Irish name like yours, that our paths had not crossed.'

Nina watched this strange apparition curiously. He had protuberant green eyes, now intensely staring, a magnificent nose, chestnut curls and he was rather bowed and slender in the way young men are, although he was not young. She wondered, slightly bitterly, why Connie had summoned her when her path was so crossed with adoring men.

'I am, of course, neither beast nor fowl,' continued Mr Partridge, whose lips were red and lightly tinged with Guinness froth. 'I am that wicked species known as Anglo-Irish.'

He was also, Nina could see only too obviously, Connie's type, which made it mysterious that she sipped her own Guinness silently with black-lashed eyes downcast. She is just so beautiful, thought Nina despairingly. 'Well, I'm Anglo and Connie's Irish,' she tried, since, after all, Mr Partridge was her sort of person, an Irish landowner's son and poet, living in some romantic and decrepit house, doubtless not unlike her own. He had no mother, he was telling Connie, ignoring her remark. But Connie evinced no interest beyond ordering another drink. 'And my father used to be interested in shooting and cattle-markets but now spends his days disturbing the daughters of Lir.'

'King Lear?' asked Connie, her attention momentarily caught.

'Sure, you're no more Irish than I'm English!'

'You mean the swans, the princesses who were bewitched and turned into swans.' Connie looked dreamily into her glass. 'They came to Mayo in the end, you know.'

'I know.' For a second Connie turned her blue eyes upon him. 'Although if we talk of history now, it's another story. My father is a direct descendant of the men who put Irish like you into coffin ships and sent them to their death on the Atlantic. He is cruel, stingy, snobbish and narrow-minded but he is my father and I love him. Do you think this could be a barrier to our friendship?'

Nina began to go off Orlando Partridge, then remembered that she did not want a man. She had an ex-husband, two children, a mother and a passion. Oh, my God! Painting. Orlando Partridge, happening to turn towards her at that moment, caught a gleam of glory and changed tack sharply. 'Where in England do you inhabit?'

'Inhabit. Inhabit,' murmured Connie.

In a flash he was back to Connie again. 'You know the line from Milton, perhaps?' He was about to elucidate when, without warning, Connie stood and walked briskly out of the bar. He, too, stood as if to follow then sat back in the chair opposite Nina.

He looked at her straight, his bulbous green eyes blinking. 'You will say I'm ridiculous, but I shall marry your friend. She hasn't realised it. This is unimportant. You are my witness.' He hesitated. 'Why did she run away?'

Nina decided to assume he was sincere. Indeed, she believed it. 'I don't know. Maybe she's gone to church.'

'Of course. I saw it in her eye. That Sunday-morning look. All Catholics wear it, however slight their belief. I wear it myself on occasion.'

'You're Catholic?'

'My mother, rest in peace. Will you forgive me?' He rose and left the bar.

With a beat of delight Nina remembered she had brought sketch-book and pencil with her. She gazed round the darkish room and saw a series of challenging shapes and tones. Breughel faces, she thought. She forgot Connie, except in a glancing sort of way to decide that there must be a limit to friendship.

The church was whitewashed and filled with vulgar statuary, Connie estimated mostly female: St Veronica, with handkerchief, the Virgin Mary, all in blue with a starry diadem, St Elizabeth, Mary's more homely cousin, St Anne, Mary's mother. Such women, such pressure, such coy matriarchs. So were these tears of misery or tears of homecoming? And why was she here in Cork and not in County Mayo with her family? At least there was no mass in progress, no ghostly voice of conscience, no false benediction.

'Am I intruding on your solitude? Am I stepping between you and your maker?'

Connie turned and looked blindly at this strange man who perched at her shoulder. 'Why have you followed me here?'

'I wish to make an impression on you. I wish you to remember me.' He was ridiculously serious but Connie did not notice him enough to mock. 'I have written out my name and telephone number for you. Some time you will wish to call me but please overlook my father's telephone manner if he should happen to answer. His aim is to stop the ringing without having a conversation. He doesn't understand that he only pays if he makes the call. In his case frugality is not a virtue.'

'Virtue,' repeated Connie, taking the scrap of paper. 'I'm sorry. Did you want something?' She was gentle, a soft churchy voice, because the glowing curls on his head were turned into a halo by a phalanx of candles behind, lighting the altar of Christ the Redeemer. She would remember him.

Nina and Connie lay side by side in their parallel beds, whispering into the darkness. Their words ran parallel, too, as neither felt brave enough to confront the other with what was important. Soon they fell asleep.

The men came in an hour or so later. They banged into furniture, chinked glasses and settled in to talk. Nina thought at first that they were inside their room, too uninterested or too drunk to notice that two women were asleep in the beds. 'Connie?'

'Yes?'

'Can you hear?'

'Are they real? I thought they were the voices of my father and Michael.'

'They're in the next-door room. The walls must be very thin. Can you understand what they're saying?'

'I can give them words.'

The words, a continuous flow, interspersed with chinking, were incomprehensible yet loud enough to give a sense of character.

'There is an older one and a younger,' Nina whispered. 'But why do they talk so much at this hour?'

'We're in Ireland.'

After a while they both dozed, waking now and again to hear the voices continuing with exactly the same intonation. Only at dawn, when the first birds were piping out the night, did they become silent.

At breakfast Connie, pushing thick rashers of bacon round her plate, announced, 'I shall not go home on this visit, I think.'

'I'm sorry,' said Nina. Surely Connie had already decided that when she summoned her. Or had she been planning to take her to Mayo? 'I would come and support you.'

Connie looked horrified. 'No. No. At least I saw my sister. She will pass on the word.'

'But won't that seem even more cutting?'

'Perhaps. I have to go back to America. Kevin is expecting me.' Connie gave Nina a strange, grave, assessing look.

'What is it? What's the matter?'

'Nothing's the matter. I think I've caught a cold.'

But something *was* wrong. Nina watched as Connie delved in her pocket for a handkerchief but instead produced a crumpled piece of paper. She looked at it in surprise. 'I wonder who's writing poetry to me now. Listen:

> "Unwearied still, lover by lover,
> They paddle in the cold
> Companionable streams or climb the air;
> Their hearts have not grown old;
> Passion or conquest, wander where they will,
> Attend upon them still." '

'I think it's Yeats,' said Nina.

'Oh, well. If he can't even compose for himself . . .' Connie dropped the paper on the floor.

'So you do know who it's from.'

1970

William came to Nina and wept. They met for lunch in his club where he looked strong and confident and ordered a good bottle of burgundy, of which he drank the majority. Nina found herself looking at the two of them from the outside. She was struck by the comfort and security of the scene: their own healthy, prosperous, well-dressed appearance, their civilised manner of conversing with smiles in appropriate places, the large table with immaculate cloth and elaborate place-settings, the waiter who managed to be both servile and superior, the larger surroundings of the elegant room, which had too much plasterwork to be tasteful but just avoided being vulgar and was filled with substantial couples like themselves. The only problem was that, from her point of view, it was a complete charade.

'I would prefer Jamie to go to Eton.'

'But why ever Eton? It's not as if you went there yourself.' For a moment they looked at each other, startled. The stridency of Nina's voice stayed between them. She had never spoken like that before, not even during the previous year when they had both been consulting lawyers. They had met politely, talked about the children. Yet now she had scorned him at high volume in his own club where women were only tolerated on sufferance, blasted his pride as if he were a fool, an idiot, a child. So he began to weep. Tears started in his blue eyes, tipped over the edges of the lower lids.

Horrified and mesmerised, Nina watched, lips compressed tightly however, for she would not say, 'I'm sorry.' Instead she gazed beyond him at the white-veiled windows and was reminded of that honeymoon hotel in Hastings.

'I shall have to find another wife.' The words, in contradiction of his tears, were produced with a kind of satisfaction, even a sort of bullying. Nina wondered how it was possible for him to feel tragic and vengeful at the same time but, on balance, was cheered by the confidence shown in his future. 'I shall love you for ever,' he continued, even more confusingly. 'You are the love of my life, which is blighted now and – er – for ever, but I need a wife.'

'Any old wife?' Nina felt like asking but desisted, managing instead a dismissive, 'Yes. You do.' She noticed that the tears were no longer brimming and those that remained were brushed away briskly with his napkin.

'You may be surprised to hear that I have someone in mind.'

Nina was very surprised indeed. Their divorce could not be finalised for over a year.

'You may have heard that Dr Nairn had a heart-attack.'

Nina had not heard. She felt a sharp pain of nostalgia. All those years ago in Malaya Dr Nairn had taken her seriously. He had sent her to help that young soldier in his hospital bed who'd had his leg blown off. 'He seemed indestructible, although I suppose he was quite old.'

'Sixty-five. Anyway, you remember him. And his wife, Felicity.' His voice had become grave.

Nina made the effort to remember Felicity. 'Her eyes were different colours. She was a brilliant tennis player.'

William hesitated, as if disapproving of this judgement. 'Felicity is a very vulnerable woman.'

'I am sure. Being widowed.' Nina hastened to dispatch her image of the wiry tennis champion, the tough supporter of army ways. 'I've lost touch with my army friends.'

'She talks of you fondly.'

'Oh, good,' said Nina vaguely, because she had begun to think about Serge and how their love affair in New York had done so much to help her, their talks about the war, about soldiers, eventually about her feelings for William, and even about her father. 'What did you say?' Perhaps she had heard but needed the words repeated, pompous as they were.

'I have asked Felicity to be my bride.'

He really had said just that. 'I'm so glad, William, so happy for you.' And why did she now have tears in her eyes?

Connie stood naked in the bathroom (daffodil yellow carpet and drapes to the floor) and admired the egg-roundness of her belly. She imagined the baby curled up in her soft water-bed and how she would swim out with her flower face gazing at the world. Making a gargoyle's face in the mirror, Connie stepped into the bath.

This had been forbidden by Shirley after a pathetically anxious midwife had advised that if the cervix was dilating soapy water might enter and cause infection. 'You cannot gamble with life', Shirley had insisted. Rebelliously, Connie emptied half a bottle of purple bubble bath into the water, then lay back luxuriously. The steamy, sweet-smelling vapours made her feel ridiculously sleepy for first thing in the morning. All this pampering would end soon enough and she'd be back in the real world.

Connie stood slowly, feeling rather dizzy, watching the glistening bubbles slide off her smooth body, felt the water gliding down her legs and then felt rather more water than was likely. Bending a little, she saw two dots of red fall and rest on the white crests of the bubbles. 'And now the waters will break,' said Connie, and smiled a dreamy smile of satisfaction.

'It's crucifying,' whispered Connie, then bit back the word so hard that blood came to her lips. Her body had been taken away from her and,

113

although she had offered it up freely in the interests of a happy future for all, now she felt she should have chosen an easier form of death.

Shaved, drugged, naked, legs strapped up and apart, a wedge between her lips, agonised, reduced and powerless. The light was harsh, giving no indication of night or day. Sounds had receded as if her ears were blocked. The fiery torture was worse, she thought, than any suffered by the saints, including St Glyceria, AD 177, who was hung by her hair, beaten with iron rods, put in an oven and finally exposed to wild beasts.

'Two fingers dilated,' rasped her torturer. How could women submit themselves to such cruel humiliation over and over again? For a child. Was that the answer? The sweet, flattened face of her nephew Bobbie fixed itself in her head. For a child like herself who was up and gone the moment she got the chance. For a man? Could that be it? Did Eileen joyously present husband Terry, weak and second rate as he was, with the seed of his loins? Did her ma feel such love for her grim, sunken father that she wanted to share with him the act of creation? It was impossible, impossible. 'Ah!' Somewhere, someone screamed.

'Hold back, young lady,' a cool voice commanded. 'Keep your pushing for later. Now we're trying to turn her.'

'Ah!' Another cry from that remote person. But now she could feel her own limbs shaking and a violent wave of nausea.

'Look out!' cried the ugly, despotic man who had taken control of her body. Nina had two children. Nina, so quiet, so calm. Nina, who had cast William out of her life. William had given her two children. Was that not the correct phrase? Given. God gives and God takes away.

'Ah!' That scream. Rick's baby would have been dark and pale and composed. Rick's baby would not have tortured her like this. But then Hubert's – oh, Hubert's . . . But that was gone, spiked out through his baby heart.

'It's dropping . . .' Dropping? What was dropping? Why could she not be part of all this? Why was she cast out from her own birth? Correction: her baby's birth. Correction: Shirley's baby's birth . . .

Suddenly she was moving. Lights broke over her into darkness, a turbulence seemed to have grown around her, noise, spinning movement, eclipses of light and sound. There were people all around, pressing her for something she could not give. And then there was blackness.

'She was stuck, you see.' There was Shirley, tears watering her usually immaculate face.

'Connie, you're both grand. Can you hear me, Connie? The baby's grand. She's an O'Malley all right. Her hair's as red-black as a beech after dark.' Was that Kevin, emotion returning him the Irish gift of the gab?

Connie wanted to mock him but he sat beyond her blackness.

'We're going now but we'll be back in the morning.'

Thankfully, she could drift back into peacefulness.

'There she is now. Open your eyes and you'll see your beautiful baby right in front of you.'

Who had come in the night to command her like the devil? Why should she open her eyes and see what God had given and soon would take away?

Something soft and pliant was laid on her breast. Connie thought about cruelty first and then about curiosity. Curiosity was a sure sign that life was in her body yet. Connie opened her eyes.

The baby, coiled across her bosom, like a giant brooch, snuggled on top of her.

'Are you planning to breastfeed her?'

Unable to move, Connie could only shut her eyes again and turn her face sideways. Did the nurse not know what happy future was ordained for this baby? She had been assured by Kevin it was all posted up: a week's stay in the hospital but minimum contact. Was this minimum contact?

'You'll feel better in the morning,' said the nurse, lifting the baby away. 'A Caesar after a drawn-out delivery is always the worst.'

Connie lay in the darkness feeling her stomach, the sharp prickle of gut stitches, a long line of barbed wire from navel to pubic hair, if there had been hair.

She reached out for the telephone. Who to ring? Whether to despair or rage? And the baby's pale face, rosebud mouth, veined temples, quiet eyelids, dark fluffy hair like bird's feathers. How could she ever forget that? There was no one to ring. Kevin and Shirley had captured her and now there was nothing to be done but regain her health and will. Connie picked up the telephone again.

Nina got out of bed only after it was clear that the ringing would not stop. It was six o'clock on an ice-cold January morning and she and her mother were economising on heating. She stood in the dark hall with her eiderdown wrapped round her.

'I've had a baby girl. I wanted you to know. Only you. When I'm well again, I shall return to England. The baby is to be called Kathleen and she is not mine in truth but the prized possession of Kevin and Shirley.'

Nina heard Connie begin to weep, tears so mournful that, all across the Atlantic, they impelled sympathetic tears in Nina's eyes, horrified and almost disbelieving as she was. So this was why Connie had seemed so strange and depressed last year. Too many questions caused her to dare none.

'Oh, Connie . . .' But should she say, 'I'm so sorry,' as seemed to be the case from Connie's point of view, or should she try congratulations? Connie a mother! It seemed impossible. Five years had passed since they had met in hospital. That breakdown had been after an abortion.

'When was the baby born, dear, dear Connie?' A neutral question, loaded with affection.

'Yesterday.' The lamenting, almost keening, continued, until the note altered and a clearer voice, more recognisably Connie's, emerged. 'They strapped me down, rendered me powerless, and cut out the child from my body. It was an obscene experience. Obscene.'

'Childbirth is pretty horrid,' began Nina obligingly, though in fact she had happy memories of her experience in the compound hospital outside Malacca. At that stage, the two babies, so nice and well-bred, had seemed to be the summit of her life's ambition, which was to be a good wife and please William. It was easy to see that things might look a little different to Connie, if even half of what she said was true. Where – or who, indeed – was the father? And had she meant that it was to be adopted by her American brother?

'I didn't expect to be marked for life,' continued Connie, anger rising above misery. 'What man will look at me now? With the mark of Cain, a zipper right down my middle, screaming out for all the world to know, "She's a sinful, fallen woman, who has a baby outside the Holy Sacrament of Marriage." My life is utterly changed. I have been used, abused, despoiled. I never want to see another man in my life.'

More continued in this vein until Nina's feet, as cold as fish on ice, led her to the smallest of protests. 'Did you not choose anything for yourself, Connie?'

'Choose? Of course I chose. But only as a woman can choose, which is no choice at all. I came from a patriarchal church to a patriarchal society where all the best choices have been taken long ago by men, leaving only motherhood . . .'

'Is the baby all right?' Nina interrupted the flow.

'They tell me so.' Switching moods at once, Connie began to weep even more plaintively than before.

'You should sleep,' advised Nina, whose feet had gone numb. Yet what was lack of feet compared to what Connie faced? 'Shall I fly over? I could, you know. I wish you'd told me. I wish—'

Connie cut her off. 'You're such a friend. It's women who count. I see that now. Don't fly over. But if I could come to you as soon as I'm well again. Stay, perhaps? Just while I find myself somewhere to live . . .'

'Of course. My mother and I and the children . . .'

'Your mother, your children . . .' Connie began to sob once more, before breaking off again to whisper, 'At least the baby's alive.'

Nina drove Jamie to school. He was looking more and more like William. It would not be long, she thought, before he would be the same age as William had been when she had first met him. With a strange, empty-hearted gasp, she realised that one day Jamie would be an adult, responsible to himself and not to her. But hardly had the gasp puffed out its message before she recalled her mother, still there, still her mother as she was her daughter.

'I forgot to tell you there's the school photograph today,' said Jamie, 'and we're all supposed to wear white shirts.'

'Oh, darling.' Nina weighed the importance of this message. Colour was very important to her but how serious was Jamie's grey shirt in comparison to the recommended white? It was not, she decided, a question of colour at all but of Jamie's feelings.

'Do you want to go back? I'm sure Granny's got a white shirt somewhere.' She glanced sideways at his face, the self-important anxiety so reminiscent of William suddenly cracking into a smile that reminded her of no one.

'Just remembered. The photo's tomorrow!'

Nina laughed. 'You were teasing.'

'It could have been today.'

They drove on. The boys' preparatory school that Jamie attended as a day boy was six miles down country roads. Often Nina wished he weekly boarded there like the majority of other boys, but this morning she needed an antidote to Connie's night-time confessions. Here was a happy, healthy son.

'Felicity's sons are jolly clever,'

Where had Jamie met Felicity's sons? 'I didn't know you'd met them.'

'Dad told me. Dad says they're frightfully clever and super at games. He says I'll really like them.'

As he paused with an interrogative air, Nina adopted a magisterial tone. 'They are very much older, of course, but that doesn't mean you won't get on. Perhaps they will give you good advice, like older brothers do.'

'I'm hoping to go to Eton,' said Jamie, even more seriously.

'Well, darling, that's quite an ambition.' Again Nina glanced sideways.

The invitation was printed on thick white card, ornamented with an elegant silver stork carrying a cradle tied to its beak by a real pink ribbon. A pink satin ribbon. Fay looked at it and thought how happy such a sight would make her mother. The card said: 'Shirley Jean Smith O'Malley and Kevin Patrick Toussaint O'Malley take pleasure in announcing the arrival of Kathleen Mary Smith O'Malley and invite you to her baptism on March 10th 1970.'

So they did adopt. Fay clocked it casually because she had set aside a morning to keep abreast of the medical journals, and 'births' or even 'arrivals', were not high on her agenda while Connie was still right off it. She flung the card in her new basket, 'Pending, pending, pending'. But as she flung, a smaller card emerged: 'Dearest Fay, I would be so grateful if we could go together. C.'

Fay rang Nina: 'Connie's trying to get me to this christening thing of her brother's despite the fact I haven't spoken to her for months. In fact, I plan never to speak to her again.'

'Fay, you have to go.'

'My own brother, however, is causing my mother anguish . . . What?'

'You have to go.'

Fay was silent. Nina never told people what they should or shouldn't do. What was this? A conspiracy to bring her back together with Connie? 'Look. I'm not being plain enough. I can't go to Connie's adopted niece's baptism in Washington.'

'She isn't her niece.' Nina found her hand was sweating on the telephone. 'She's her daughter.'

Connie, very thin, dressed in black, met Fay at Kennedy airport for the flight to Washington. Fay, who had just had another call from her mother about Daniel's determination to go to Vietnam and who had worked till midnight the day before, had accepted her role as needed friend in adverse circumstances but felt Connie must come out to her. Perhaps even apologise.

'I'm so very sorry,' Connie whispered, eyes downcast. All round them large, loud people bullied and celebrated.

Fay, shocked by her appearance, began to accept and forgive the past when Connie, green as an adder, repeated, 'I'm so very sorry, but I'm afraid I'm going to vomit,' and disappeared in search of a lavatory.

She came back soon and took Fay's hand confidingly. 'Do you mind if we don't go, after all? Please. Dear Fay. You're so very good to have come. Please may we just sit in your nice apartment?'

When they arrived at Fay's apartment, her answering-machine was blinking accusingly. 'Do answer it,' whispered this sadly shriven Connie. 'Do you mind if I lie on your bed?'

'No. No. Be my guest.'

Fay picked up her message. 'This is your mother speaking. You've got to talk sense into Daniel, Fay. There's people dying over there and I mean Americans. He thinks it's some fraternity party, all the brothers doing their thing under a sunny sky. He's dropping out of graduate school, Fay, to go and be killed. It's Lee, you don't need me to tell you. They've split. Hardly married and they've split . . .' The tape continued, her mother sounding more despairing as she talked her son into a coffin and closed the lid. Eventually, there was no more room on the machine.

Fay dialled. 'Mother . . .'

'Oh, Fay, Fay. You've got to talk to him . . .'

'Mother . . .' It was no good. She rehearsed the dialogue: 'He's grown now. Makes his own decisions . . . He's your brother, Fay. He's a baby . . . I have a friend staying . . . He's your brother, Fay . . . I have to operate on a little girl tomorrow . . . This is a matter of life and death, Fay . . .'

'OK, Mother. I'm coming.'

Connie, eyes closed, lay on the bed. Fay came in and sat beside her. 'Sorry.'

Outside the sky was blue. It would be cherry-blossom time in Washington again. 'I'm sorry.' Connie put out her hand.

Even that was beautiful, Fay thought. She looked at her own, scrubbed daily, and reminded herself of their skill. 'It's my brother.'

'So I gathered. I'm sorry.' Fay thought Connie had said sorry more often that day than during her entire life. 'Do you mind if I stay here just tonight? It would help me. I'm flying to England tomorrow. I shan't come back.'

Fay decided not to address the last piece of information. 'Yes. Of course you can stay over. There're clean towels in the cupboard.'

Connie smiled slightly. 'Dear Fay. But you're right, there's no need to talk. I'd be as successful an unmarried mother as I would a surgeon. I wouldn't answer any questions you might think of asking. Except just one thing. The baby wasn't Trig's. There you are, I said the word "baby".' Slowly, she began to cry again.

So Fay flew to Chicago instead of Washington and found when she got to her mother's apartment that she still had Kathleen Mary Smith O'Malley's baptismal present in her bag.

'What's that?' Her mother's magpie eye caught the pink and silver gift wrapping.

'I should have been going to a baptism in Washington.'

'You stood them up! After buying a high-class gift like that!'

'It's only a mug, Mother.'

'A mug! You're introducing a mug into Washington high society . . .'

Fay hugged her mother and said she'd better go straight off to find Daniel, in the borrowed car made available. Though she'd been travelling just about all day, she took some pleasure in her strength and capability, which made the unknown car no problem and map-reading a positive pleasure.

Daniel's room was small and very neat. What is it about Daniel and me that makes us tidy our lives away into drawers, cupboards and even cartons? she wondered, noticing one in the corner. She went over and pulled it open. Books. Old, dusty books, some with ornately engraved covers, others worn paperbacks. She picked one out. Louis MacNeice. Poetry. Lines highlighted:

> Nightmare leaves fatigue
> We envy men of action
> Who sleep and wake, murder and intrigue
> Without being doubtful, without being haunted.

'Fay?' Why did she feel guilty as she swivelled to greet him? A sister and a spy. 'I know why you've come but you won't change my mind. I suspect you haven't noticed how old I am.'

'Do I get a cup of coffee?'

'Coming up.' Competent as ever, he made her a good cup and they both sat. Outside, a group of students shouted with the freedom of much younger kids.

'I didn't know you read poetry.'

'That's no reason not to fight. The truth is, I need a fresh start.'

'The truth is, you only have a year to go and you're right out of it. For God's sake, Daniel, things can't be as bad as all that.'

'Look, Fay, I'm not laying it on you. But between you and Vietnam, I don't seem to have made one decision for myself. If I'd been drafted straight after college, I'd be through it by now. So what do I do? Graduate school in a subject I don't care for, marriage to a girl who doesn't really care for me. I feel like my whole youth has been dominated by avoidance, avoiding the draft. I never thought of myself as a weak character but I guess I am. I know so. The truth is, I've always wanted to do my bit for America. You remember Uncle Larry? Of course you remember Uncle Larry. But you wouldn't remember his war stories because you weren't around. He only told me, the little all America boy. I was proud to hear how he'd fought for his new country . . .'

'But Daniel, World War II is another life time, we've had Korea since then and Vietnam can't be compared in any way . . .' Fay gabbled in her determination to put a stop to her brother's hideous wrong-headedness. She could feel her mouth frenziedly twitching in and out. 'Don't you see, you're right out of line. I mean, just no one with your educational background, your opportunities, thinks they should be going to Vietnam—'

'Untrue.' Daniel interrupted in his firm steady voice. 'I know plenty of people who believe in the Domino theory. Who believe we're holding the line here. They may not be much in evidence on the campus.'

'Regular soldiers believe in it. That's what they're paid for. The uneducated might as well believe it if they're being shipped off into the jungle—'

'And that's another thing. You lot. You intellectuals—'

'You're an intellectual!'

'Bullshit. Your friends who argue about civil rights but are quite happy to send the poor, the black, the uneducated to fight their war . . . Every day there're protests here, looking after number one and letting others do the dirty work.'

'No one's happy about that! We want to stop the war for everybody. I know what you're saying. The system's unfair but that's no reason to go and get yourself killed.'

'Who's talking about getting killed?'

'Or maimed.'

'Here we go again. You know I'm the rational one here.'

'Don't you see? How you feel now is about your personal situation. Your present unhappiness. About Lee. It has nothing to do with the war at all. It has nothing to do with principles. All your high-mindedness is just a cover . . .'

Daniel stood up. 'I hate this sort of argument. Why don't you go back to what you're good at, saving babies, and leave me alone?' He turned back. 'You could find yourself a man of your own.'

For health reasons, Fay took an early morning walk every day. Often protesters left over from the night before were huddled in doorways, bundled in layers of material with sleeping-bags as pillows. Every time she saw them her stomach wrenched with conflict. She tried to make it rational: on one hand, she despised these people who never did a day's work, had no idea about responsibility, about regularity, discipline; on the other hand, she ached to be with them, to scream and cry and throw bombs at every reservist officer's training building on every campus, particularly in Chicago. The thought of Daniel was with her every moment of the day, even during the most intricate operation. She began to read reports of the war with the same concentration she had used to reserve for medical journals. And Daniel hadn't even left the US. 'I am going crazy,' she told herself, and briefly found an outlet for her intensity in several nights of desperate sex with a fellow doctor.

They were getting up together, bleary, sweaty, about to shower, when the radio reported a riot at Kent State University, which had ended with five students being killed by the National Guard firing a volley of shots into the crowd. Fay sat back on the bed, tangled herself in the sheets. Her fellow doctor continued towards the bathroom.

'Nixon got it right,' he said, over his shoulder. 'Bums. That's all they are. They think it's fine for all the violence to go one way. Now they've learnt different.' He shut the bathroom door without caring to discover her reaction. He presumed it mirrored his own.

Serge and Fay kept in touch, although she seldom went to Judson. 'There's a big march on Washington May ninth,' he called to tell her. 'It's been declared a day of protest. My brief is to call up folk who no one could describe as bums and hippies.'

'OK,' agreed Fay. She would do it for Daniel. She would wear her doctor's overalls and make a placard saying: 'We save bums, not kill them.'

Fay stayed overnight with Shirley and Kevin. She didn't explain why she was in Washington and Shirley, still overwhelmed by the baby – Kathleen was now an alluring four months old – didn't enquire. Kevin was away. Fay, watching Shirley bathe Kathleen, thought America was undergoing a kind of civil war in which, up till now, the bloodshed had taken place in another country. 'Look at this,' said Shirley, putting the naked baby on the carpet. 'See? She's sitting up on her own.'

'That's great,' said Fay admiringly, trying to disguise how out of tune she was with this proud-mother act. Kathleen was a sweet child, with Connie's striking colouring of dark hair and blue eyes. The still unknown father must have looked pretty similar.

After eating it was still warm enough to sit in the garden and since Kevin was out and Shirley clearly longed to go to bed, Fay announced she would go for a walk.

'Take my car. The keys are on the console.'

Fay drove towards the White House. She felt filled with emotion as if Daniel's determination to be, in his terms, a patriot, had connected her for the first time to this vast country where her family had made their home. Now she had to define her own terms and what better place to do it than within walking distance of the Capitol. I suppose we are making history, she told herself, to raise her spirits as she parked carefully. At the very least we are exerting our rights as citizens. She noticed a placard leaning against a fence: 'I don't give a damn for Uncle Sam, I'm not going to Vietnam.' We are learning confrontational politics, she thought, most unwillingly in my case, because I want to do my job and not think about such things. She was walking now, the night air balmy, the groups of protesters growing, some gathered round a singer with a guitar – 'Where have all the flowers gone . . .' Now and again there was a soldier, sometimes smartly turned out in dress uniform, sometimes in combats.

Television reports from Vietnam had made combat uniform part of everyday life. She supposed that once Daniel went overseas – it was still an incredible idea – she would become addicted to the television news, like all the other relatives, like most of America. Except her. She had been too busy being a doctor.

Fay walked. She wanted to be part of this protest, to feel herself supported by shared attitudes, to cheer derisively as they did when police cars trawled by them, but she was too old, too serious, too conflicted. She thought she had always felt herself alone since she was a very little girl. It had got worse as she grew older and noticed her mother was a fool. It was no accident, she thought, that her two closest friends lived abroad – an English woman with whom she had almost nothing in common and an Irish woman who, at least half of the time, she didn't even like.

She overheard a snatch of conversation: 'This kid, he was so goddam excited. He saw his dad on the TV. Next morning they get the knock on the door.'

Fay shivered and thought that she had wanted Daniel as a comrade. She had needed him but he hadn't needed her. She was beginning to feel like a ghost, walking invisible among so many people, but she didn't like to go back, to risk a meeting, perhaps an argument with Kevin, who was profiting from this unstoppable war machine.

Fay continued on, and the white buildings of Washington had never looked more romantic, their tops touched by moonlight streaming from a gentle black sky. She reached the Lincoln Memorial. Several other groups were there already, planning to spend the night. She stood among them, staring upwards, invisible.

The face was familiar. He appeared suddenly among them, at first only remarkable for a self-consciousness and valeted cleanliness. The word 'President' took several minutes to surface. He approached a couple of boys who were too bewildered to speak. He seemed to be lecturing them. Other protesters joined the group. They were all quiet and polite, as if this soft night was an off-duty time for anger.

Nixon, pudgy face trying to fix itself into lines of high moral earnestness, began to talk about the Second World War, about how at the time he had admired Chamberlain but afterwards he had recognised Churchill's greatness. His audience listened respectfully. Fay could hear only a little of what he was saying and moved closer.

'I know that probably most of you think that I'm a son-of-a-bitch but I want you to know that I understand how you feel . . .' Fay heard the words with a sense of disbelief then hatred. This man, who was in command of the biggest army in the world, which for the last five years had caused the deaths of forty thousand young American soldiers and partly caused the deaths of hundreds of thousands of Vietnamese, was standing out here in the moonlight by the Lincoln Memorial asking to be loved. It was disgusting.

She wanted an abusive reaction. But, as if it were in a dream or nightmare, no one raised their voice or even showed any evidence of shock. A young man muttered, 'I hope you realise that we are willing to die for what we believe in.'

This merited a lecture on spiritual hunger – Fay drew closer as the crowd grew behind her – 'which all of us have and which, of course, has been the great mystery of life from the beginning of time.'

Fay pushed out of the circle. This is an example of democratic freedom of speech, she tried to calm herself, freedom for the President as much as for the humblest citizen. Then she thought of the students killed and wounded at Kent State and it didn't feel like democracy any more. It felt like madness.

Connie took sick the moment she entered Nina's home, sick enough to stay in bed and not to eat or talk. 'I am having a diplomatic breakdown,' she told Nina, before she stopped talking, 'but do not lament beyond reason. It is not like before when we three met in hospital. Did I tell you that Fay and I are friends again? That time my sickness arose out of a bad conscience but this time my conscience is clear enough. It's only my body aches for its child. It will pass, as things of the body do.'

Nina talked over Connie's situation with her mother and they considered calling in a doctor. 'I'm pretty certain she is not suffering from a physical pain – at least, she didn't even mention the Caesarean. And if Dr Roly comes, she'll bedazzle him with words and her beauty, and he will be of no use at all.'

'Dr Roly is perfectly sensible,' suggested Veronica, 'and has no need for dazzle.' But Nina knew he would not suit and might make things worse.

'All she needs is peace for her soul.'

'For her soul?'

'Don't question it.'

Nina did lament for her friend but not beyond reason because her soul (although she did not quite believe in such a concept) was bound up in the pagan energy of the spring. In a few days' time, she would think about nothing but painting. As a preliminary to life as a student in London, for which she had applied to start in the autumn, she had signed up for a series of life classes.

As if to fix it in reality, she kept a diary:

Day one.
We're in a barn in the middle of a web of lanes overflowing with cow parsley. The hills rise up in gentle patchwork, edged by the herringbone of May, still white. The barn, perhaps more shed, is painted in natural reds and ochres, sage green. One room has a large table with

Madras cotton tablecloth in pale checks. Cow parsley, forget-me-nots, buttercups, ragged robin erupt from a vase on the table, bringing the outside in.

We are looked after by a pair of sisters, straight out of Augustus John's notebook. Long boyish necks, small oval heads, they are both tall in long full skirts, widely belted, plain dark blue and red, with white blouses.

Our first model, Harry, is a black Rasta from Notting Hill, very handsome, with hugely developed pectorals and a hand-span waist. He is married to a very blonde wife with an olive-skinned, black-eyed baby.

My fellow students are disappointing, except for the man, Leo, who immediately launches into two dazzling oil paintings of Harry. The others, well, the nice, deaf one, the Cheshire-set one, the smart Home Counties, the sharp-nosed getting over a breakdown, are nothing, in short, to do with painting. Dull people, dull pictures.

On the drive back, exhausted, despairing. Look out at the vanishing countryside and wonder what is the point of struggling to produce art when Nature does it so effortlessly. I guess it is Nature who will be both my principal competitor and principal subject.

Day two.
It is strange to look so intently at a naked man. Extraordinary how quickly one gets used to it. At first comparisons with William and Serge – the only men I have seen naked – but v. soon become detached from sexual response. Looking, analysing, shape and form. Black skin already nearer to 'art' with the beautiful smooth uniformity of ebony. How can the pale races ever have convinced themselves they were superior in looks? It is strange at the end of the day, when his wife arrives with their honey-coloured baby, to think of him as the project of Harry's seed, ejected from that much stared at and measured organ, and now cradled, the baby I mean, in his mother's arms. I think how William and I made babies without any understanding or forethought.

Oh, I was such a child when I married! I never loved William sexually the way I loved Serge whom I hardly knew at all. I haven't touched a man since Serge. Am I turning into an old maid?

Day three.
Connie in bed as usual when I leave. My mother has already left with Jamie. I notice neither of them fully, although I hug them gratefully

for being happy together. Principles of composition. Diagrams. Vanishing points. Picture plane. 'Through a glass darkly.' Followed by a measured drawing. Holding up the pencil against the head first as the measure for the rest of the body, moving downwards, torso, penis, legs, feet. Using a plumb line made of a length of black cotton attached to a tube of paint. I need years and years of this.

I cannot talk all evening. Sit with Jamie while he has his bath. His body is very beautiful but he is beginning to be shy about his nakedness. He won't let me dry him and talks a lot about 'going to visit Dad and Felicity'. I ask him if he'd let me draw him sometime and he, knowing just what I mean, says, 'In my uniform.'

Connie brighter. She says she is going to look for a flat in London after the summer. Maybe we will share. I don't want to think about anything except painting.

Day four.
Oil. My God. Three colours only. Orange. Blue. White. A new model. Clarissa. Tall, beautiful, white globular breasts, small waist, wide hips, strong legs. A naked Matisse. Impossible. Two of our number refuse to use oil paint and set off on their usual competent water-colours. Wonder why they are here. Wonder why I am here. We are learning about cold and warm colours. Tone. About the drama of contrast. I'm happy.

In the evening I paint. My studio is a challenge and a refuge. It is always cold which helps deter visitors. Connie comes and watches. She says nothing, except to admire the blue clematis dangling over the window. I think she is jealous that I have a passion and the means to follow it. Then she says she has become vegetarian and has made a macaroni cheese. Jamie comes in and says can he have bacon instead. I stop painting.

Day five.
I am very tired. I did not sleep. My period has started heavily. I feel surprised each month that my body still functions that way. It is raining. The white flowers of the cow parsley lie all around the stems. They do not look so white any more. They look like sago. We are drawing again. This is where I have most to learn. I am happy.

In the evening my mother tells me to go to bed. I hear Jamie laughing from his bedroom. I think about Helen. And then I consider what painting means to me, but like love, it is not open to analysis. I place a print of one of Rothko's paintings from the Tate in front of my eyes and eventually sleep.

Connie sat in the garden with a stack of books and a cigarette packet at her elbow. She wore a large, battered straw hat. Veronica sat nearby doing cross-stitch in a complicated design of flowers. The school holidays had begun and the ten year old Helen lay on a rug on her stomach, making an attempt at reading *Pride and Prejudice*. No one knew where Nina was, although it was obvious she would be sketching or painting. Painting had made her elusive.

'Aren't those books hard work?' asked Veronica. She put down her tapestry and crouched beside the pile. *The Feminine Mystique, Sex and the Single Girl, Sexual Politics, Patriarchal Attitudes, The Second Sex, The Woman's Room, A Room of Your Own.* She read out the titles then smiled at Connie. 'I see you've turned against men.'

'You're a wicked lady,' said Connie, who had begun to appreciate Veronica, in particular the cool, undemanding Englishness of her. 'This is not a personal matter, it's a matter of principle.'

'I am not at all sure you would recognise a principle, my dear, unless, that is, you invented it yourself.' Veronica returned to her deck-chair and took up her tapestry.

'You're in the right to think I'm learning to understand the principle of principles. But you're wrong to think it's beyond me.'

'I wish you two would stop talking,' complained Helen. 'You did promise we'd all be quiet.'

'Sorry.' Connie picked a daisy head and flicked it at Helen, who rolled over and failed to disguise her adoring look.

'So I suppose you're going to become one of those feminists,' said Helen, shutting her book.

Connie smiled. 'There's no question of becoming, my darling child, I *am* one, by force of circumstances or God's will or whatever you please. I'm just catching up on the paperwork so I can launch my views, properly substantiated, on the world. Unlike the fate I predict for you, books and I parted company before I reached the age of reason.'

'Are you sure you've reached it yet?' cried Helen, daring in her flirtatiousness.

'You're so clever, the little folk will come and steal you away in the night.'

'I expect you're going to burn your bra, too, like in America.'

'That's only for those who can afford more than one.'

'I would have thought, Connie,' Veronica put down her tapestry again, 'you would be better advised to study your sad country's situation and present that to the world.'

Connie pushed up the brim of her hat to get a better look at Veronica. Criticism was not her usual style. 'I don't need to read about Ireland. The history's bred in my bones. It was in the slump of my father's shoulders, my mother's prayers to the Blessed Virgin, in the names of my brothers and sisters who are no more than that now to my ma and da. It's in my sister Eileen's eyes when she looks with pride at her eight, gobbling their sliced white bread and beans. It's in my brother Kevin when ... when—' She broke off abruptly and, with surprising force, hurled *Patriarchal Attitudes* to the grass. With unsteady hands she pulled out a cigarette.

'My dear Connie,' said Veronica, while Helen rushed to pick up the book, 'those are library books.'

'Yes. Yes. I'm sorry. It was just the devil having his way with me, a weak and feeble woman, which is not what I planned to say at all. What I planned to say, and you listen, Helen, and stop smoothing that book's plumage as if it were a lame seagull, is that for too long Ireland's affairs have been run by the truly weaker sex, by the brave heroes, by the braggarts and cowards, by Kevin Barry and even the great and holy de Valera. It's the man with the gun who looks to the woman with the baby.' Again Connie broke off but now she merely smiled absentmindedly at Helen. 'Why don't you go for a ride? Girls your age need plenty of exercise. I used to get it carrying water back from the well.'

Helen looked as startled as if Connie had revealed she'd been a cannibal in her youth. But Connie wouldn't continue. Instead, she gathered her books and went to lie in the cool of her bedroom where she hailed a line of hardworking woodlice with medieval litanies: 'O Gate of Heaven: O Golden Casket: O Couch of Love and Mercy: O Temple of Divinity: O Beauty of Virgins: O Mistress of the Tribes: O Fountain of the Gardens ...' Here she interrupted herself to pick up one of the woodlice, which immediately curled into a hard little ball in her palm.

Soothed, she tipped it out of the window into the brilliant sun and lay down on the bed.

Fay wrote to Daniel once a fortnight. She was not certain if he relished this sisterly concern since he answered irregularly. His letters described the beauty of the countryside, the dawn over paddyfields, the water-buffalo lumbering through marshy rivers. Sometimes Fay wondered if he did it to mock her concern. Occasionally, he wrote about his

companions, their weird sense of humour, their ignorance or knowledge: 'Mike knows the whole of British history like it was the football
scores. I told him you were the girl for him. Expect him to drop in
sometime.' He cannot expect me to believe he's on a golden vacation,
Fay thought, and she became convinced that he was in a city
somewhere, answering yes and no to some half-witted general. That
would make him safer.

Mike never did look her up. Missing, she presumed, or dead.

She'd had a letter from Nina at the start of her first term in a London
college of art: 'We're sharing a flat in London. Connie and myself, as if
we were students. But, of course, I *am* a student. We're starting over,
isn't that what you'd say, starting over . . .'

Fay wrote to Daniel about the political situation, about their
mother's health, about the tough and terrifying grind of being a
paediatric surgeon, about the amount of women students who were
now coming to her for help, about the days she thought she couldn't
get out of bed. When she wrote to Nina she told her about her own
new apartment, which was on the fifteenth floor of one of the named
buildings on the east side of Manhattan. The doormen addressed her
with proper respect. 'Have a good day, Dr Blass,' when she passed in or
out. Once a week she went to concerts or the theatre. Even though she
wasn't at the top of her field, she earned so much and worked so hard
that she couldn't manage to spend half her money. She was looking
into ways of saving, bonds and suchlike, but she didn't bother to write
Nina about that. She wondered if all her story of hard-earned success
made any real impression on Nina who had never earned a cent. And
why did she want to impress anyway? Surely the poor little Jewish girl
from Chicago had disappeared long ago.

My mother's staying

she wrote, or rather typed, handwriting being kind of antediluvian.

Yesterday, guess what, we went shopping. I felt fifteen going on five. I
insisted on buying her a heavy silk scarf. She kept asking if I could
afford it, so in the end I was pissed off and told her my salary. I
thought she'd be the first death in a pastry shop on 72nd Street. We
were eating Riga tarts and surrounded by East European intellectuals
with numbers on their arms so I guess she'd have died happy. By
mutual agreement, we never talked of Daniel. Who says life's about
change . . .

*

The flat smelt acrid but not too disagreeable. 'I think it's the glue,' said Nina, pleased to have located the smell as issuing from the furniture restorer's on the first floor. The flat was on the second and third. The 'restored' furniture, which seemed to be built from scratch, was then sold on the ground floor, which was a quite grand antiques shop.

'They're all fakes,' hissed Connie, peering at the glowing tables and chairs.

'Fakes to whom?' enquired Nina. 'The buyers don't want their antiques to be old for then they might have defacing scratches or stains or scars . . .'

'Like me,' giggled Connie, lolloping about. They had been to the pub to celebrate their sharing this new home. The house was mid-nineteenth century, in a quiet street between Baker Street and Edgware Road. Nearby a church clock struck the hours. Now it struck eight.

'The purchasers wish them to look old or, to be more precise, "antique" which to them is a style not a definition of age,' Nina said, following Connie upstairs. It was strange to be a weekday student again when she was thirty, had two children, a house and a widowed mother. If anything, she was the antique.

At least she didn't have to share a bedroom with Connie, who was back in frantic mode, although confiding in Nina that her personal life was over and now she was going to dedicate herself to her career. 'If ever my determination fails I need only look at the mark of Cain across my stomach . . .'

On Fridays Nina planned to go back to Sussex where she could see the children if they were home and paint in her studio. It all seemed so utterly amazingly what she wanted that she expected the skies to open and shoot her down. For the first time in thirty years she was being totally selfish. Correction: the second time. The first was when she had left William. And yet how happy she was to slide down the slippery slope! How little she cared about anything or anyone but her painting. It was shameful. Bent over her block of paper, her newly bought pencils and charcoal, Nina flushed with the shame and joy of it. Was this her mark of Cain? This passionate need to make lines and colour? She could not think so. And, if it was, she didn't care. This was her time of life and she would do with it as she pleased.

'You look as if you're in love.' Connie, sleepily in bed, waved her goodbye on the first morning. Nina had been up since six. It was a dewy early-autumn morning. As she looked at the streets, at the brick buildings with shops below and the cars still parked for the night, she pictured her own garden with the grass silver-streaked, the roses drooping heavily, the jasmine shoots spiking up through late-blooming clematis, the apples letting go of the branches, falling and rolling. This would be her subject, but first she had to learn and learn as a starving person needs to eat and eat.

Connie sat on the floor with the telephone, a pile of paper and numbers. She had already rung ten editors. She had offered them articles on Vietnam, women's rights, and the Irish question. They would be personal articles, she had assured them, written from the woman's point of view, and she would drop in a couple of her American articles to give them a taster. Connie was not dissatisfied to find that her journalistic career in England had disappeared without trace. She was in the mood to start afresh. Perhaps she would change her name to Glenda Rudd.

1971

Connie lay on the old spongy sofa and listened to Helen playing the piano. After ten months living with Nina in London, and weekends and holidays in Sussex, Nina was like her sister; Veronica, Helen and Jamie were her family. Crossly, she shook her head. Of course, she didn't believe in such a ridiculous concept as 'family'. After a while she forgot it was Helen and just listened to the music. It was a piece she recognised which, since she was uneducated musically, meant either that it was very famous or that it had been used for a hymn. The room was lit only by the lamp over the piano, which cast a golden glow over the girl's pale face and bony shoulders.

'That was gorgeous, Helen! You have the gift.' Connie plunged forward: she wanted to hug the clever girl.

But Helen looked at her coolly, as if the music, far from softening her heart, had hardened it. 'I was just planning to give it up.'

'But, Helen, you're a grand player.'

'Mummy doesn't care. It's Granny who's the problem. She imagines me taking off from where she stopped.'

'But why not?' Connie found herself on the point of telling the parable of the talents.

'I want to be in the real world, not the arts, painting, music.' She looked severely at Connie. 'I want to have the sort of job men take for granted. I want a career.'

Connie went back to her sofa. They all had their place in this old room: Veronica on an upright wing-chair by a lamp, Nina (when she cared to join them) as close to the largest window as possible, Helen usually on the floor or a stool. She herself inhabited this sofa. It had such depths that once, so Veronica had told her, a whole family of mice had lived in it undetected for several months.

The dimness of the room made the garden seemed lighter by comparison, and she could make out leaves, hedges, shrubs and flowers, all coloured blue by the July twilight. She remembered that somewhere out there Nina was sitting, painting. And here was her daughter, still a child, quoting feminism with a practical application. It's a new generation, thought Connie, and smiled smugly into the darkness.

Nina came back to the acrid-smelling flat and found a note on her bed. She frowned. It had been written with one of her favourite crayons, the point now broken: 'I'll be back late. Turn on the TV if you want to catch me.'

The television had arrived a couple of weeks ago. Nina was already clear that she hated its intrusive energy but Connie watched it whenever she was in the flat. Grudgingly, Nina went to turn it on. The black and white image of an excited woman gesticulating wildly made her recoil until she recognised the exuberant black curls.

'A woman is a woman, not a wife, a mother or a whore!'

'Surely a man can be a man, but equally a father, a husband, and a – a . . .' The reasonable male interviewer, pallid with glasses and a bow-tie, searched for the appropriate word.

'Male prostitute. Try pronouncing it. I dare you. The point I'm striving for here is that the female attracts an extra label as if she doesn't exist simply as a woman. Worse still, she is sad appendage to a man, a woe-man . . .'

What utter rubbish, thought Nina, but at the same time she admired Connie's confidence and her volubility. She looked stunning, if crazy. Her Irish accent, spiked with American and English, gave her added magnetism.

'My dearest fellow, women haven't helped their case by wanting men to look after them. If a man dare open a door for me, I'd raise my hand to his face.'

'And what about money?' enquired the reasonable interviewer. 'Would you let a man buy you a meal, champagne, flowers?'

'Most certainly not! As long as we women are prepared to let ourselves be looked after by men, men can use it as an excuse not to give us our rights. Do you remember the story of Cinderella?'

'Of course.'

'As long as women believe that if they do their hair prettily, apply the right makeup and smile their please and thank you, their lives will be transformed by a handsome prince, as long as they expect help to come from the outside, enter Fairy Godmother, then they will never make any real headway in becoming independent beings, the equal if not superior, given their child-bearing powers, of any male in the world. Women are not going to have their chains taken off them, they have to break free from them.'

'You're not putting the blame on men, then?'

'Of course I blame men. I abhor the male sex.' Here, Connie gave a ravishing smile to her interviewer. 'Men are weak, bullying and hypocritical. But women, being the stronger, more talented sex, have to take some of the blame for creating these monsters. That's why I say that women have to sort themselves out first or they'll go on being subjugated for ever. That is exactly what my book, *Say No To Sex* is all about. The first step for a woman to gain her self-respect is to stop thinking of herself as a sex object for a man. Sexual politics can't get more important than that. Fucking is a political act.'

As Connie, showing a generous portion of thigh, spoke this shocking, forbidden word on screen, the camera, which had been in close-up, gave a compulsive shudder before abruptly cutting to the interviewer. His eyes revolved widely, and for a moment or two he appeared incapable of speech, before stammeringly he introduced a new item. Connie did not appear again. Nina wondered what fate was held in store for those who so abused the airwaves. Arrest, imprisonment or an old-fashioned dressing-down, a wigging from one of those weak, bullying and hypocritical men she had described?

Three hours later, long after Nina had gone to bed, Connie appeared. She carried a half-empty bottle of champagne, which she plonked down beside Nina's bed. 'I've arrived, Nina! Can you hear me? I've arrived.'

'I waited up for ages,' mumbled Nina, producing peals of laughter from Connie.

'I don't mean that sort of arrival. I mean me as a feminist, me as an activist, me as a household word, me as a best-selling author. One "fuck" – only the word, you understand – and I've got them crawling all over me.'

'But, Connie, you never swear. You told me that ever since one of your nuns told you "bloody" meant "by Our Lady", swear words stick in your throat.'

'My darling Nina, I would never swear in passing but this was for a purpose. You should bear in mind that Our Blessed Lady was one of the early feminists, as were many of our holy saints. Have you ever considered properly the issue of virginity in relation to women's rights? I bet you haven't. We all know about Queen Elizabeth the First, the Virgin Queen, ruling without a man to make a muddle, but how about St Pelega of Tarsus, virgin and martyr, AD 304, who preferred being roasted to death inside a red-hot brazen bull rather than submit to the advances of the Emperor Diocletian? Or St Amalburga, who clung to the altar so that King Pepin broke her arm, or St Regina, who when she refused the wicked Pepin was locked in a dungeon, tortured and finally beheaded. These heroic women knew that the moment they submitted to a man, they would become powerless. *Say No To Sex* will have at least one chapter on the early Church. You should know the cult of the Virgin Mary has been much misunderstood.'

Nina, who had been drifting asleep during the description of religious atrocities, became more awake. 'But you haven't written a book, have you?'

Connie paused from swigging at the bottle to have another good laugh. 'Certainly, I haven't written it yet as a book *per se*, but in terms of the articles I've already written, I've got enough words to fill several books.'

Connie turned away then. She did not want her triumph or, perhaps, her sense of triumph, reduced by Nina. But she gave her a kiss all the same, remarking kindly that she was a fool not to take champagne when offered by a fellow woman. She went to her own room, which was so filled with clothes and books and other stranger possessions (like the plaster cast of Trigear's erect penis, which she had once found arousing and now found ridiculous) that her bed, anyway small, (a camp-bed bought second-hand from a Boy Scouts' shop) was not immediately obvious. Flinging objects behind her, she dived into her sleeping-bag. She lay for a minute or two, enjoying the peace, but soon it became dull and she reached for a book. Rejecting for once *The Lives of the Saints*, she turned to *The Mill on The Floss*. Her excitement in the story had been heightened by Nina informing her that George Eliot had been a woman. An interest in self-education was new to Connie and that in itself was exciting. She had redirected her boundless energy from men, sex and herself to women, success and herself.

An hour or two later Connie was out of bed again. The mirror was small, decorated with enamel gilt and glass. Connie moved it down her naked body until she reached her stomach where she held it steady for some time. The zipper scar was pale now but still clearly defined. A photographer using careful lighting would have no problem making a clearly recognisable image of this sign of women's degradation by men. Such a mark of Cain would make a perfect dust-jacket. It was a nice oblong shape too. On the whole, however, she felt it should be an anonymous contribution to the presentation of her book. She lowered the mirror and ran her fingertips over the inch width of the scar, allowing herself to remember for a moment the sensation of the baby's smooth head pressing against her skin from within.

Nina came back to the flat at night so exhausted and exhilarated that she seldom felt like doing more than making soup and reading. Since there was no central heating and the weather seemed fixed in autumn days of turbulent and icy winds, which winnowed easily through the ill-fitting windows, she often got into bed. She had made no effort to make friends in London and, knowing any visitor would be for Connie, ignored faraway banging on the street door. It was, therefore, a considerable shock to hear heavy footfalls inside the flat, soon advancing from living room to kitchen to the stairs leading up to where she sat tugging the bedclothes under her chin.

'Who is it?' called Nina.

A very large man appeared, bronzed face, massive shoulders on which the epaulettes of a pale mackintosh stretched tenaciously. Nina knew she had seen him before.

'Trigear. Is Connie around?' The voice was American, the name memorable.

Trigear! Nina's head resounded with the insults that his name had collected from Connie in the last couple of years, although in a sense the details of his failures were hardly relevant since he failed the fundamental test by being a man. 'I'm afraid she's not in.' There seemed no point in querying the mode of entrance from such a man, even if her prone posture had not made aggression difficult. On the other hand, she had no intention of standing in front of him in socks, pants and one of Jamie's rugger shirts. 'I'm Nina,' she said. 'We met in New York.'

'I've been away since then.' The smile that accompanied this information gave Nina the creeps.

'She won't be back this evening.' Lies have never been my thing, thought Nina, as she heard the door slam downstairs and Connie's voice sing out, 'Daily, daily, sing to Mary, Oh my heart, her praise sing!'

Trigear turned silently and went to meet her.

Connie saw him like a well-clothed statue above her on the stairs. For a shameful second, she was on the verge of throwing herself into his arms, crying joyfully, like a child to her daddy, 'Trig! Trig!' She imagined leading his giant paws to her breasts, pulling them down over her body ... It was an ancient reflex, visiting her at the end of a hard day's grafting and discarded before Trigear had caught more than the tiniest flash of quickly doused welcome in her beautiful eyes.

'Trigear,' said Connie haughtily. 'I didn't know you found victims in London.'

Trigear laughed, the laugh of a man who is mystified by his goddess and cannot speak.

Connie stood, icy draughts zipping around her like bolts of lightning. Trigear stared, and eventually managed a few words. 'I've missed you. You're an extraordinary woman.'

'Well, I'm obliged to tell you that I cannot say I have missed you, except in the sense that I've noticed your absence with pleasure – no, that is too strong, with relief.'

Trigear appeared not to take in the meaning of her words. 'I had to see you,' he pronounced weightily. 'I came to London to see you.'

'I won't ask how you tracked me down, knowing you have your ways and means, but you have made a wasted journey. I have forsworn men. Not only you but all men. Your body has as much interest for me as a block of stone and, since your mind was never of the slightest interest to me, we now have absolutely nothing in common.'

'Connie!' He came down and put a hand on her arm, as a huge mastiff pleads for the love of its master.

'I am not saying that you wouldn't be attractive to others, but for us the story has ended. It ended badly, you may recall. I am now a feminist. I think of man as the oppressor. I think of sex as the method of oppression. I'm writing a book about it. There is nothing here for you. It's best you leave.'

Instead, Trigear took a step forward. 'You had the baby, did you?'

Connie's goddess-like righteousness fell apart and she collapsed into a chair. 'If you insist so rudely and since I shall never see you again, you might as well know that I did have the baby, who has been adopted and gone out of my life for ever.'

'Mine? Mine?' Trigear loomed over her.

'Of course it wasn't yours. Your memory or conceit is distorted. I told you the truth at the time, which led to your cat-strangling antics. You were playing on your killing-fields somewhere at the time of the conception, which was virtually immaculate anyway. Oh, do stop being so dramatic, Trig, it's giving me a headache.'

Trigear sat down at the table. He clasped his hands in front of him. 'I'm truly sorry for you.'

'You are *so* irritating.' Connie looked at him properly for the first time and allowed herself to remember how happy he had made her, even if it had only been in an impurely physical way. 'Please take yourself away, dear Trig.' Standing again, she tried to pull him to his feet.

Trigear, rocklike, seemed not to notice this. He spoke in mourning tones: 'You were the last girl I'd expect to become a dyke.'

Exasperated at his misunderstanding, Connie temporarily forgot the solidarity of sisterhood. 'You've got it quite wrong! Think of me as a virgin and martyr or perhaps a vestal virgin. Sex is right off the agenda. Male, female and/or buffalo!'

'I thought you were the real thing,' continued Trigear, presumably not finding it easy to recast Connie as a virgin. 'Goddammit, I love you!'

Connie sat down again and put her head in her hands. 'Dear Trig. Be cool. You're not my real thing. Nor am I yours. Our lives were briefly entwined. There is more than a continent of differences between us. We met, we parted. Actually, you departed. So, please go! Budge from my kitchen table. And pray to St Joseph, the patron saint of good husbands, that you pick better next time.' She paused. 'Or maybe it's St Anne . . .'

'I see you want nothing more to do with me. You give me words when I want your cunt. You are my woman.' Trigear rose to his feet at last, dignified, with faint echoes of the Samoan chief. Determined not to take him seriously, Connie performed a few ballet exercises in a casual *demi-pointe* fashion.

'Goodbye, Connie. One thing more . . .'

'Oh, Trig . . .'

'If you ever need me, call this number.' He handed her a card then descended out of the flat, out of her life.

'Did you hear that? How could I ever?' Screeching and gasping, Connie flew upwards to Nina. 'Why did you not stop me?'

'We did try,' protested Nina mildly.

'And yet there was something almost noble about him as he left.'

'Like a gorilla is noble,' suggested Nina, and they both began laughing hysterically.

'He might have turned nasty,' gasped Connie.

'Crunched you up in those great jaws.'

'And how unlike him to give me a card.' Connie stopped laughing and read, 'Violetta Sugden, pianoforte renovator and tuner', which started them off again.

Nina stared into the windows of London picture galleries as a child stares into a sweet-shop. She seldom penetrated inside, but stood noting the pictures chosen for the window, catching an indication of those behind. Occasionally, the door was open, with people inside, glass in hand, and also talking and laughing on the pavement, as if the paintings were not essential. At these openings Nina, a large quiet woman, with her pale, broad-eyed face and brown hair smoothed back into a plait, slid unremarked into the gallery. On proper inspection, however, the paintings often turned out to be disappointing, facile and fashionable abstractions that seemed to reflect nothing but a talent for juxtaposing shapes and colour.

'Nothing to learn here.' Nina was not aware of having spoken aloud until a man at her elbow laughed and retaliated.

'This is an art gallery, you know, not a school.'

'But surely the only point of looking at a picture is to learn something from it.'

The man, to Nina, was frighteningly smart and handsome, but for some reason she continued talking as if he were one of her fellow students. It was the sort of theoretical discussion she liked. 'In fact, I expect to learn something from everything I look at – really look at, I mean – otherwise it's a waste of time. With this painting, for example, I ask myself whether I would get more from the red and black of a hot sunset under a raincloud.'

'And you wouldn't?'

'I'm afraid not.' Suddenly Nina felt self-conscious. She was a gate-crasher dressed in a dirty smock, wearing sandals with a basket over her arm from which a loaf of bread and a bottle of milk stuck out. Quite possibly, after a long, intense day painting, she smelt of body odour. 'I should be off.'

'Having found the pictures wanting. That's not fair. Shouldn't you listen to my side of the story?' He was her height, narrow, thirtyish, fair wavy hair nearly to his shoulders as was fashionable, a neat straight nose, continuation of his forehead, wide full lips, light brown eyes. Why did she inspect him so closely?

Nina felt the weakness of physical desire. She was not used to the sensation and felt flustered. As she turned to escape, the man picked up a glass from a passing tray and passed it to her. She took it gratefully, gulped with downcast eyes.

'You see, I'm the boss here, the owner, you might say, and I like that picture very much. I would much rather see it than your dreary sky and, with any luck, enough people will feel the same tonight to keep me in business whether they learn something or not.'

Nina held her glass aloft, courage returning. 'I was speaking only for myself. As a matter of fact I thought I was speaking to myself.'

He laughed again. 'Look, I'll show you my favourite picture. Perhaps I can persuade you to rethink.' He took her arm, propelled her between the guests and placed her in front of a big yellow and blue abstraction.

'The problem,' said Nina after a while, 'is that it's not Rothko, which, I think, is the problem with the red and black one too.'

This time there was no laugh. 'Of course they aren't Rothkos. Who said they were? This is a small gallery specialising in young, not very well-known contemporary paintings. I suppose if I had a hanging of tables with still lives and elaborate wallpaper, you'd criticise it as not being Matisse.'

'I might.' Nina was cautious. She saw that other people, glamorous people, were queuing to talk to this man and she was beginning to feel trapped. 'Thank you. Now I have to go.'

'I hope you've written your name in our book.' The man sounded quite irritable now. 'It's just behind you.'

The conversation pursued her as she walked slowly along the pavements, breathing in air with as much relief as she had gulped the wine. She had talked, in the gallery, as if she despised the paintings hanging on the wall. And yet she herself painted far less well. Did that mean she thought it only worth painting if you expected to become a Matisse or a Rothko? Was any lesser ambition some form of self-indulgent therapy? Yet how could she have such confidence in her own talent? It was impossible. Miserably, Nina waited a long while at a bus stop and then began to walk again. She would write to Fay.

Fay took the bundle of mail proffered by her doorman with a weary gesture.

'There're overdoing these circulars, Doctor,' he sympathised. 'Want me to drop them down the chute?'

But Fay had spotted Nina's handwriting and passed hurriedly up to the elevator. At least that was something to look forward to, after a day when the air-conditioning had broken in her office, management had tried to question some of her charges at the same time as introducing a heavier workload, and one of her new young women doctors had had a nervous breakdown. Kicking off her shoes in her large, airy apartment, she cut open the letter with a paper knife and began to read.

'Dearest Fay, I feel ashamed that I write to you far too often with my problems . . .' Fay was immediately surprised by this supposition that seemed utterly false. It was always a matter of guessing between the lines, which flowed in mellifluous repetition of painting, children, the countryside and Connie's latest escapades.

> . . . I only met him once and we immediately talked with an intensity that I haven't experienced since I met Serge. But, of course, it's nothing whatever to do with sex. I don't feel like that sort of thing any more. It's just that our conversation made me feel absurd, like an overgrown schoolgirl, with high-falutin ideas about ART – the sort that comes in capitals – Oh, Fay, how can I paint, feeling like this?'

Fay read the rest of the letter but she had made up her mind already. She sat down immediately at her typewriter.

> Dearest Nina,
> Methinks the lady protests too much. Stay cool and don't mix up fast heartbeats with whatever's going on with your painting . . . separate, individuate, prioritise . . . Finally, get tough with yourself! How about I come over for a visit?'

Nina took off the washing-up gloves and hung them neatly over the side of the sink. A few glistening bubbles dropped from the tips. She then lined up all the washing-up implements with perfect precision and finally rinsed her own hands before drying them methodically on a paper towel. She knew this was all a carefully worked-out plan to defeat the ghost of the person who washed obsessively.

'Why aren't you painting?' Her mother had been watching her.

She did not wish to tell her mother that, since her conversation in

141

the gallery, she had lost her nerve. Washing-up was now fraught with danger. Ironing or talking to the children, who were on half-term, calmed her a little. Helen's views, her precocious knowledge and confidence, both relieved her defeatism (at least she had produced a clever child) and also reinforced her humility. It could not be called a sense of failure because her painting, until she had had her fatal conversation, had not depended on or looked towards the hope of success. Nor had she been competitive. She had painted – or learnt how to paint – only because it was the most exciting occupation in the world. Even now her face flushed at the thought of picking up a brush loaded with Prussian blue: a cello colour, she thought. But the meeting in the gallery, her ridiculous hot and floral appearance, as she saw it now, her pompous pronouncements about art, ART, had made her self-conscious and therefore able to see how impossible it was that she, a soldier's wife, mother of two, irrevocably part of middle-class England, should feel herself a painter in any sense at all that was worthwhile. Fay's answer to her letter, received that morning, with its easy assumptions, had only thrown her into more of a muddle.

'I haven't felt quite like it,' muttered Nina, and burst into tears.

Veronica said nothing, did not move forward. In fact, she turned away and for some reason Nina thought she was going to play the piano. Instead she announced abruptly, 'I can see Helen trying to catch Prince without success. We'd better take some sugar lumps.'

Wiping her eyes, Nina followed her mother. Outside wood pigeons were calling energetically, the lawn, which had never had a last cut, had grown far too long but glistened a spectacular green. A rose bush, grown wild, was covered with scarlet hips.

'And it's all paid for by William!' cried Nina despairingly. 'Where am I, me, myself?'

Veronica stopped and looked round at her daughter. 'Heavens! Six o'clock in the evening and still so light. We mustn't forget the clocks go back tonight.'

As Veronica went ahead, calling to Helen, admonishing the pony, who had cantered to the far end of the field where he stood warily swishing his tail, Nina stayed where her mother's words had caught her, under a stalwart apple tree she had known since a child. It was bent now, weathered into grainy knots and carbuncles. Most of the leaves had fallen but the apples, an exuberant excess from such an old tree, still clung tenaciously, round and red. She had often sketched and painted it before, never with the slightest degree of success. It always remained obstinately outside her paper or canvas.

Nina took a few steps backwards better to take in the tree's form and detail. What was it Fay had said? 'Get tough with yourself!' It was such an un-English way of putting it and she found herself smiling despite her misery. Fay certainly followed her own advice, stomping through life as if she were a samurai. She looked back at the tree again. The sky was purple-blue behind it. She imagined the roots of the tree striking down deep into the earth on which she stood. She circled a little, moved forward a few paces, back a few paces, then turned suddenly and raced back into the house. She re-emerged carrying her sketch-book and a small mat.

Nina sat on the mat while the damp encircled her, misting the darkening air and turning the tree into a black silhouette. The garden grew quiet as the birds went home to roost and the wind came to stir the trees. Occasionally, a car passed in the lane beyond but Nina did not notice. Finally, she was on the last page of her pad, in the last glimmer of light.

Fay arrived in Sussex on a windy November day when the leafless trees were whipping the sky. It was nearly four years since she had seen Nina. They had written letters to each other as if to anonymous confidantes. It was a shock to be faced with the corporeal identity. Fay was surprised by Nina's reduced size and yet conversely by her physical weight. She had begun to cast her as a piece of romantic England, charming but not quite real, but here was an almost beautiful woman, tall with an oval face, long chestnut hair loosely piled on the back of her head. She wore a heavy sweater and a red skirt belted at the waist. Yes, she was almost beautiful. She was also almost, but not quite, formidable because of her unselfconsciousness, her lack of interest, as Fay assumed because that was the message of her manner, in herself.

'Oh, Fay! How lovely to see you! How elegant you look.' They hugged on the small station where a jungle of elder trees sheltered them from the wind. Fay knew she looked smart and successful, with her dark suit, fine nylons and good shoes. Nina was wearing socks and sandals. As Nina led Fay towards the car, she began to apologise for the rubbish inside.

'Oh, please,' protested Fay, settling happily among the bottles of turpentine and old rags, 'this is my vacation from sterile swabs. Think of me as a deprived inner-city child. What I need is a course in mud pies.'

Gradually the shock of their differences faded and they remembered it was the same differences, however exaggerated now, that had made them interesting to each other. Nina allowed Fay a short visit to her studio. She would not turn round the canvases leaning with their faces to the wall but she permitted Fay to view the recently finished canvas on her easel. It was a landscape centred on an old apple tree.

Fay, looking at Nina's face, red and pale by turns, felt the weight of a proper comment. Was it possible she could get away with saying nothing? No. Nina's expression of awful trepidation made it clear she was to speak and on her words would hang future brushstrokes.

'It's the old apple tree in the garden,' Nina murmured. 'I paint it a lot at the moment. I don't know why. I suppose I'll go on till I'm satisfied.' She moved forward with humbly bent shoulders, as if to remove the canvas.

'Oh, don't take it!' cried Fay. 'I'm sorry I haven't said anything. It's just that as I stood here I found myself quite overwhelmed. You see, I hadn't realised – this sounds so rude but you know how it is with friends – I just hadn't taken in that you were a real painter!' By now they were standing close to each other, Fay with one arm outstretched, Nina with a hand on her canvas.

Fay's emotional words astonished herself as much as Nina. As she looked carefully at the painting, Fay had seen that Nina had a true talent. Now Fay noticed tears in her friend's eyes. Obviously intending to hide them, Nina gave a wild laugh and spun round, collapsing in the pink armchair.

'Oh, Fay, I'm so pleased.' Inevitably, she began to study the painting from this lower angle.

'So am I for you,' said Fay, smug in having felt and expressed just what could most help her friend.

Fay told Nina about her constant anxiety over Daniel, caught in the dregs, as she saw it, of an unjust war. 'Did you ever discuss Vietnam with William?' she asked, as they sat up late after dinner. William, Serge. Whenever the men in Nina's life were mentioned, she took on a hunted, harassed look.

'William was never in discussing mode with me. Perhaps he's changed with his new wife.'

Fay thought that Nina's badly disguised lack of interest in world politics made it likely that she wasn't much of a one for discussion mode either. Impulsively – perhaps it was the unaccustomed effect of lavishly dispensed sherry – Fay found herself crying out, 'You don't know what it's like to get up each day knowing that what you do is really important!' She didn't mean to imply that what Nina did was unimportant – at least she thought she didn't – but she could hear it sounded like that.

'It must be just so hard,' responded Nina humbly. 'I do so admire you.'

But Fay caught a glinting hardness in Nina's eye, and tried to backtrack. 'I must sound very conceited—'

'No. No,' Nina interrupted her. She changed the subject. 'Did Connie write to you about Trig turning up?'

Immediately Fay leant forward with an expectant air. 'Connie never tells me anything . . .'

The next day Connie came down in person. 'I'm just so old,' she shouted, looking at Fay who was attempting to check the Vietnam news via the *Daily Telegraph*, 'but nothing like as old as you, darling Fay. How can you be reading the kind of newspaper that only Veronica finds welcoming?' Throwing herself on to the sofa, she displayed to advantage her legs encased in pink and purple striped tights below a skirt measured in inches.

Her arrival, Fay thought, immediately changed the atmosphere in the house. She admitted to a kind of jealousy that Connie was so at home there now, livening up Veronica with her silly jokes, and treating Nina with the affectionate disregard of a sister. She even had her own bedroom, a squalid place that smelt of incense. She's a cuckoo, thought Fay unkindly.

But after lunch, in that same cold dining room where they had first come together – six years ago now – Nina announced she was going to her studio to paint and Connie and Fay should go for a walk. It seemed like a command.

It was again a clear windy day and they decided to take the walk across the fields that led to the wood.

'We won't go into it.' Connie gave a skip. 'Certainly not look for the ancient yew. Not without Nina.'

Fay smiled at the memory of that absurd first visit. They walked for a while before she felt the silence become oppressive. 'Nina says Trig tracked you down.'

'Trig?' Connie seemed hardly to recognise the name.

'Your lover,' suggested Fay, drily.

'Don't be mean, Fay.' Connie gave another little skip and looked as if she wanted to whirl her arms too. But then she settled on a seriously questioning look. 'How are you, dearest Fay? I do miss America, you know.' She paused and, to Fay's surprise, seemed determined to listen.

So Fay talked, not quite as she had to Nina because she could never trust Connie fully, but she told her about Daniel, and Connie, with the occasional sympathetic interjection, continued to listen.

They had crossed several fields by now and were considering turning round. Connie had picked up a stick, which she was swishing at the grass. 'Have you been to Washington?' she muttered.

At once Fay understood and was amazed she'd been so slow – so self-centred, she had to admit. Connie's baby. That was why she had been questioning her. Perhaps even why Nina sent them out on the walk. Connie knew she had struck up a friendship with Shirley and wanted a report.

'Yes. I've been to Washington a couple of times.' She hesitated. 'Kathleen is fine.' She tried to imagine what words would give least pain but it seemed she had already said enough. Connie had started for home, calling over her shoulder, 'Thank you, Fay, my darling. You are always so kind.'

Fay followed slowly, thinking she was not kind at all.

They arrived back at the house to find a huge tea of scones and cake laid out in the kitchen. Fay, leaning against the warmth of the Aga, cup of tea in hand, found herself the target of all kinds of love and attention from Nina, Connie and Veronica.

'You look tired,' said Veronica, patting a seat beside her. And it was true. She did feel tired, absolutely to the bone.

'You work far too hard,' said Nina severely. 'For the next five days you're to rest and let us look after you.'

'You need fattening up,' contributed Connie, liberally spreading jam on a scone before handing it over.

Fay thought that if her mother had dared behave like this she would have been furious but in this cool, comfortable home, with the ragged garden banging against the windows, she could allow herself, just for the five days left of her visit, to relax.

Nina, returning to the flat, tired and wet, hardly listened to Connie's unlikely welcome: 'A very flash sort of man came visiting. He said his name was Hector Pijane. Not you at all, to my way of thinking. But when I tried to warn him off, he became sharp and told me to mind my own corner – or words to that effect. What have you been doing, Nina, to deserve such a shark?'

Nina did not have visitors. She looked at Connie's costume of merry-widow corset topped by a feather boa. 'Did you greet him dressed like that?'

'As a matter of fact I did. I was able to explain to him that we were a strictly feminist household and that he must draw no male-chauvinist assumptions from my cleavage.'

'And did he?' Nina sat on the chair in her living room and pulled off her wet boots.

'He was admirably self-restrained. However, he promised to return.' There was a banging from downstairs. 'Ah, that must be him now.'

Hector Pijane sat on a chair in the living room – the only chair – while Nina wavered about looking for something to offer him and Connie, propped against a beanbag, assumed an aggressive expression above her boa and enquired whether art was any longer necessary.

'It has never been necessary,' replied Hector, tapping the shiny, slightly painted tip of his boots, 'because it is fundamental.'

Nina, overhearing this and despairing of finding anything liquid in the house other than sourish milk (Connie disposed of all alcohol on a first come, then finish basis), felt like going to bed. However, as this thought appeared she caught Connie's eye.

'Do sit down, Nina. I must go and finish my article on the male obsession with penile dimensions. So gorgeous to make your acquaintance.'

Feeling prim, Nina replaced Connie on the beanbag.

'Wherever do you paint?' asked Hector, in neutral tones.

'At college. At home in the country. I have a studio there.'

'A country girl. I see. That explains it.'

'What?'

'One: your absence when I first tried to look you up. Two: your freshness.'

Nina tried not to show her confusion. She tugged her full skirt over her knees. She was thirty-one with a long life of experience behind her. How could anyone be 'fresh', as he put it, with an ex-husband and two children. 'I'm sorry you didn't get me.'

'Spiritually fresh, you understand. How is your painting?'

'I'm still learning.' She looked at him warily. She did not talk about her painting, least of all to flash gallery owners, and she remembered how she had lost her nerve after their last conversation.

'I really came to invite you to an opening. Look.' He held out a card to her. 'Matisse engravings. It's amazing how cheap they are.'

Nina knew she would go, not because of the engravings but because she wanted to see Hector again. 'I'm having a terrible time with life drawing at the moment.' She spoke severely.

'Perhaps I should read you Matisse's thoughts on the subject. I've printed it on the programme.'

'Please do.' Hector began to read and Nina, although listening hard with one part of her brain, realised in a dreamy other part that it was his voice she found most attractive. Deep ochre with shades of purple and gold.

Hector was coming to the end of his reading: '. . . a rapid rendering of a landscape represents only one moment of its existence. I prefer, by insisting on its essential character, to risk losing charm in order to obtain greater stability.'

'Well, that's it, isn't it, really?' Nina roused herself. 'You have to find the esssential character. Whether it's a woman or a tree.'

'Otherwise it's doomed to one moment of existence.'

'Quite.'

Soon afterwards Hector left.

'You're like two old witches at a coven, going on about your painting,' grumbled Connie, who'd taken time out of writing her latest provocative article to listen on the stairs.

Nina laughed without answering.

'I predict this smooth-talking, deep-voiced shark will only bring you unhappiness.'

'Just because you're making a living out of the theory that men are the root of all evil, there's no need to do a Cassandra on my future. He's a gallery owner. You should be telling me to cultivate him.' She turned away from Connie's ironical stare.

1972

Connie had never liked the Underground. The darkness beyond its window-panes, as if fierce hands had pulled down black-out blinds, filled her with unease. She felt forced to fix her attention on the interior, the advertisements, the metal bars, the swinging leather holding-straps, the carpeted seat coverings and, inevitably, her fellow passengers.

It was thus one morning, restless as always, she fixed on a young girl. This girl, golden frizzy hair, pale shrewish face with a wide unpainted mouth, seemed filled with irrepressible delight. Like Connie, her crossed foot twirled in the air, her hand touched her hair, patted her cheek, tucked itself under her hip. The other hand held a book, which she was reading with joyous concentration. Unfortunately for Connie's curiosity, the girl's fingers, spread wide and protectively, obscured the title.

What could be in so small a book that could bring such happiness to its reader? In the moment she looked down contemplatively at her empty lap – she never had the patience to read on a journey – the girl was on her feet, face glowing, book was clasped to her bosom.

Connie jumped up, took up position near her. The fingers shifted and the title was revealed: *Penance In the Light of Christ's Crucifixion*, read Connie, mouthing the words in her astonishment. Lest there be any mistake, Christ, head crowned with wicked thorns, heart bleeding, was painted on the cover. The train came to a station, the doors opened and the girl, still looking as if she had a song in her heart, stepped out briskly.

Connie followed. She touched the girl's arm. 'Excuse me. Would you mind ... I saw the cover of your book ... your ecstasy ...' The word did not seem too great. The girl turned, transfiguration lessening. Duty and politeness took its place. She had not heard Connie's plea but felt the pulling arm, saw the urgent, enquiring face. 'Yes?'

'Penance,' said Connie. 'How can penance make you so, so radiantly happy?'

The girl looked taken aback. 'I'm in a hurry.'

'But it's important – I need ...'

The girl relented, the glow returned. She thrust the book towards Connie. 'Here. Take it. I can easily get another. It's the answer to everything!' Giving Connie a brilliant smile, she hurried away into the crowds.

Too impatient to wait, Connie sat on a bench in the station. It was Baker Street. Brick archways gave some seclusion from the home-going crowds. The light was dim and suggestive. She could have been sitting in a church. Connie shivered and opened the first page.

Nina looked up at the apple tree, then below it. Waves of apples, golden and red, lay all around it, half hidden in the bright green blades of grass. Some had rolled and fallen further, some dropped from the furthest branches and perched glowing on the path.

She said, very seriously, to Hector who stood at her side, wearing a wide-brimmed Panama hat. 'I've heard every one of these drop.'

He didn't understand at first. But she insisted. 'That's what I've been doing all summer. Sitting here, trying to paint this tree. They're Beauty of Bath. Ripen early. Drop early. When I started it was covered with greenish apples, hardly visible among the leaves, then they began to turn green and yellow, then green and yellow and red, then yellow and red, and then they began to drop off the tree. They make a terrific plopping noise, particularly when they hit the path.'

'Shouldn't you have picked them up?'

Nina looked surprised. 'Why?'

'To eat them. Or something. Make cider. Whatever people do with apples.'

'I see.' They were both serious, standing slightly too far apart. 'I didn't think of that. I mean, I did eat a few. But one person can't make much of an inroad on a whole tree. They don't last, you see. My father used to make me pick them up in a wheelbarrow so the gardener could mow.' She frowned. 'Look, do you mind if I finish what I was going to say? It's about my painting.'

'Oh, please.' He spread his hands.

They both paused, stood staring pensively at the tree. Then Nina turned and started walking back towards the house.

'What's the matter?'

'Nothing. I just don't think we'll get on.'

He caught her up. She had moved swiftly. 'We don't have to get on. I've come to see your paintings.' He sounded irritable.

'Sorry. I'm so sorry.' Nervously, Nina undid and did up a button on her blouse. 'It was rude of me.'

Without speaking, Hector took Nina's hand and pressed it to his full lips. Nina looked up for a moment, just in time to see an apple above their heads break loose from the tree. She leant forward and her lips met Hector's. She felt the apple graze her back before it fell on to the path.

Nina never understood what Hector saw in her large, ungainly self. It was true they talked about art for hours, lying together in post-coital comfort. To be honest, she talked mostly while he listened, grunting the odd agreement. Sometimes she thought sex with Hector led up to that moment, although when she had not seen him for a while, her body fired up with longing. His eyes were pale brown and nearly yellow, the colour of a cat's. His shoulders were straight and broad, his hips narrow, his legs long. His boyish perfection reminded her of Bernini's statue of David.

Connie, watching Nina prepare to meet him, shook a ladle at her like a warning finger. She had taken to making pots of soups filled with indeterminate vegetables. 'You're punishing yourself with Hector.'

'Why ever should I do that?' Nina stopped pushing hairpins into her coil of hair, which had grown very long and heavy.

'Guilt over William, maybe. You have to be ashamed at going with such an arrogant shit.'

Nina smiled at the thought of how the tables had turned and replied mildly, 'I can see all his faults as well as you. He's conceited, self-centred and narrow-minded as well as being an intellectual and social snob. He's also lazy, mean, jealous and untrustworthy.' She found herself, after all, surprised at quite such a long list of faults. She thought of adding, 'Also he makes me happy.' But Connie no longer believed in the importance of happiness so it would be a waste of breath. He made her happy because he stroked her body and made her comfortable and easy with herself and because he took her painting seriously. What a heady combination! Perhaps she loved him – with all his faults. 'I'm so happy!' she cried, throwing caution to the winds. And received the expected disapproving frown from Connie.

'Love is a seeking after what is essentially unobtainable. But it helps if you have a good man.'

Nina became more involved. 'Good men! Guilt. You're talking as if Trigear had never existed.'

'*Touché*, sweetheart. But over two years of celibacy gives me the right to advise. Remember, *Say No To Sex*.' Connie's book, published earlier that year, lay on the table. She made a kissing motion as Nina went out smiling.

She thought, as she went down the dark stairs and into the sharp-aired streets, that Connie had hit on the crux of the matter: she and Hector had very good sex. That was what held them together. She walked more quickly, stifling in the movement and urgency of her desire the knowledge that she was as mistrustful about her own feelings for him as she was about his for her.

Fay always got up very early in the morning, particularly in the summer. She liked watching the sun light up the water-towers on the roofs around her. It had become her favourite time for writing to Nina.

NY, August 1972

Dearest Nina,

You believe you are in love with this Hector, but you do not seem to like him one little bit. Under separate cover, I am sending you a medical book on human sexuality. Try reading a little each day. This is no time to be a romantic. The world has turned a little and we can see things more clearly than that. The body needs servicing like any other machine, certainly, but as for love, it can only arise between the greatest of friends. I am also sending you a book about ancient Greece. I suspect old-fashioned concepts of married love will only continue among a small minority of people too scared to admit the truth . . .

Nina, for once sharing supper with Connie, showed her the letter. 'Do you think this is a lesbian overture?'

'Gay, please, Nina. Actually I don't.' She read the rest of the letter. 'She's shit-scared for Daniel. I read a desperate woman here. We must invite her for another heartening trip to this country of peace. Incidentally, I haven't seen Hector for a week or two.'

'Oh, Connie. You know Hector and I don't tie each other to a regular commitment.' Even to herself, this sounded unconvincing. Hector was only interested in the occasional fuck. Was that the truth? 'As long as he doesn't renege on his promise of a show next year.' This voice had a bolder sound.

'Hear, hear,' agreed Connie. 'And a hey-nonny-no.'

Having bounded up to her room, Connie collapsed luxuriously on the bed and took an envelope from her pocket. The letters had started arriving after the publication of her book. They had come through her publisher and from a man with the absurd name of Orlando Partridge, who reminded her that they had met a few years ago one Sunday in Cork. The first letter contained an acrostic on her name:

> Cursed be
> Orlando Partridge
> Never to see
> Never to touch
> Illuminosa O'Malley
> Exoticissima Connie

How could she resist such an approach? Although she seldom scribbled more than a short note to him, she began to look forward to his fervent letters. She even read his announcement that they were made for each other and it was only a matter of time before she realised this, with a tolerant lack of belief. He was clearly unlike any normal male and, besides, he lived in Ireland where she had absolutely no intention of visiting. He was her pen-friend and admirer, secret even from Nina.

Today there were three pages of writing, including a long folk tale about an Irish druid and a butterfly which proved the existence of the soul.

Nina was spending the autumn half-term at Lymhurst. Day after day of low mist, made up of millions of droplets of rain, which made her think of a scarf knitted of water, swaddled the countryside. Nothing had a distinct outline, the colours still remaining in the garden, mauve for the Michaelmas daisies, cream for the late roses, even the gaudy yellow of the Black-eyed Susans, blurred into a hazy depressed stillness. There was no wind, which was why the mist would not move. The topmost leaves of the tallest trees did not stir, except occasionally to disgorge a sodden and dispirited leaf, which dropped on to the road where it soon became a shiny spot, a rusty fault on the wet Tarmac.

Nature is standing still, thought Nina, who was taking a walk one afternoon, just as I am. She hadn't heard from Hector for weeks. And I cannot lift my paintbrush in anger. As if to prove her point, she stopped her brisk, mechanical walking and planted her feet firmly, stared downwards, hands in her pockets, shoulders hunched, head bowed. She dared fate to move her on.

The frog was completely black, as black as a shadow, spreadeagled neatly on the road, squashed flat, perfect in every respect although indisputably dead.

Nina stared at it for a long time. Clearly, it could only be Fate's messenger. There was no other explanation for why she should have come to a halt just there. But what did it mean? A squashed frog? There were no entrails to read, perhaps twitched out by some greedy scavenger. It was a frog's carcass, empty. It was, she could hardly avoid realising, the embodiment of her own view of itself. But it was also ridiculous, one of the most ridiculous sights she had even seen. A flattened frog. As if it had lain down in front of a steam-roller. Could a frog commit suicide?

With abrupt energy, Nina resumed her walk back to the house, dashed into the kitchen where she found a fire shovel. She was anxious about whether the frog would still be there – Fate's messenger might have been consumed back in the world beyond – but it was, blacker than ever in the dimming light. She slid the shovel carefully under it.

'What you got there?' The boy had come unnoticed, his peaky face curious above his bulky anorak, a stick in his hands.

'A dead frog,' said Nina, stifling a childish voice that cried, 'It's mine. Finders keepers!' She held the shovel closer as the boy poked out his stick.

'What you going to do with it? I've got a penknife if you want to cut it.'

'No! No thank you,' she added appeasingly, because the boy, too, might be a messenger from Fate. 'I'm taking it home to study.' She emphasised the last word, which she felt might discourage further interest.

'I study worms by cutting them in half and then in half again and then again. They stop wriggling off if you get them small enough.'

'I'm sure they do.' Nina began to edge away.

'I won't touch it,' said the boy, reading her thoughts. 'I can get plenty of live frogs from the pond and they're much more fun to study. You should see them hop. Till I get my knife.'

'Much more fun,' repeated Nina, repressing a shudder. 'Goodbye, then.'

He let her go and soon she heard the sound of a tree being beaten by a stick. Turning her head, she saw he was gathering conkers from their prickly shells.

She hurried back to the house and into her studio where she arranged the frog on a square of white board. Excitedly she squeezed out new paint and put a fresh canvas on her easel. She stood staring at the frog, heart thudding.

Nina became aware of the telephone ringing. 'Hello.'

'May I speak to Nina Purcell?'

He had not recognised her voice because she was working, which made her another person.

'It's me, Hector.' Her calmness was extraordinary and gave her a lightness of being that made her smile. She did not need him.

He was explaining now that he had been away, seeing a new young painter. She noticed, even through her lightness, that he emphasised the 'young'. As if such a thing could hurt her.

'Hello. Are you there?'

'Yes. I'm here. Sorry. I'm painting.'

There was a pause. She could hear him take in the words. There. He had an excuse now to ring off or at least to put them back on an official basis. She was giving him a chance to disown her because now she felt strong. Her eyes flicked back to the canvas and then to the frog.

'Can you talk about it?' He was tentative.

She felt even more powerful. 'No. I don't think I do want to talk about it.'

A pause. 'Nina . . .'

'Yes.' The word was an abstraction, without even a whiff of invitation.

'Shall I come to see . . . you?'

He was not wholehearted but she didn't care.

'I'll be working. Don't come for two or three weeks. Not till I have something to show you.'

He was disappointed. Now she knew he had been planning to come. Perhaps tonight. They could have locked the door on the studio and filled the rooom with their love-making, made her body rosy and warm. But then he would have gone, his pale eyes shifting from her gaze, his hands patting back his long hair.

'I'll telephone you,' she said. This was good. She had learnt something at least from Fay and Connie's admonitions. *Keep the cards in your hands. Play the cards yourself.*

'If that's how you want it.' He was beginning to sound impatient. 'I suppose you might answer the phone if I rang to ask how you were getting on?'

'I might. If I haven't taken it off the hook.' She was being too daring. She reminded herself that it had been over three weeks during which he had felt no need to telephone. 'I'm not going anywhere,' she compromised, with a kind of relenting, immediately regretted: 'But I must go now!' She put down the telephone and unplugged it from the wall.

A few days later she received a letter from Fay: 'Last week I went up to spend the weekend with Shirley in Washington. Of course we passed the entire visit with Kathleen. Do you think I should tell Connie about it? She's quite a character, exactly like Connie to look at which, fortunately, is exactly like Kevin . . .'

Nina wrote back: 'Don't tell Connie. She's unhinged enough already.' She put down the pen and looked at the words. Was Connie more unhinged than usual? And, if so, in what way? She had been so taken up with her own affairs that she had hardly noticed Connie recently. And, of course, that was what was so strange. Normally, in whatever state of exhilaration or misery, Connie impressed herself on all around her. But recently she had been silent, unobtrusive, secretive.

Father O'Donald looked different. He had lost some hair so the redness no longer flew over him like a halo; his expression, although fond and welcoming seemed wary. Perhaps he was always like this, thought Connie, and I have forgotten it or did not care to notice. She had gone to find him in his office in Archbishop's House, an imposing building next to the huge Victorian cathedral with its tall Italianate tower.

'Well, you are grand,' said Connie.

'It's true my circumstances are grand. We're not given the choice, you know.'

'An assistant to an archbishop amid smart red bricks and curlicues. I fear you will hardly have time for a humble sinner like me. I brought you a present of my book.'

'Ah, the book!' The priest leant forward to a tea tray between them. 'You'll have a cup and a biscuit, perhaps?'

'Thank you.' The book with its outrageous cover of her stitched-up stomach lay beside her in a brown paper bag. She imagined it steamed slightly, like pornography.

'I imagine it is your book you've come to talk about. I read it with interest, of course.'

'You've read it!' She had hesitated for months before daring to approach him. Now she found he had already read it and seemed to be looking at her with an expression she did not remember, mildness disguising a fervent desire for debate.

'Naturally I would read it. Four chapters on feminism in the New Testament, it's part of my job to read such things. After all, it had a lot of media attention, serialisation in a . . .' he hesitated '. . . serious Sunday paper. Leaders in the two Catholic weeklies. I myself was asked to review it for a Catholic broadsheet.'

'Oh, yes. I see.' Now she felt ridiculous with her brown paper bag and took out the book, turning it face down.

'I'm glad, Connie, you are searching for a voice. You've got a powerful soul. May I ask you something?'

'Yes. Please do, Father.' Father. There was a word she hadn't pronounced for a year or two. Where was her brash confidence that laid down rules of conduct in interviews on radio shows or with television talking heads?

'Why did you not think of discussing your ideas with me before you wrote the book?'

His question confused her. The answer, she supposed, was that she had considered the book too shocking for a priest to be involved with. The language of violence, of sex, which she had employed, was designed to make the world sit up and take note, which was not to say that she didn't believe her thesis or want to deny her rage. And then there was her perception of a priest as part of an organised church, with beliefs laid out for him to follow and no room for doubt or deviation. The one true Church. She may have written admiringly of feminism in the New Testament but that did not mean she equally admired the Church headed by the Pope in Rome. On the contrary. As far as she could see, there had been very little feminism since AD 33. She decided to be honest.

'I never considered talking to you. I suppose I thought a priest, even a priest like you, could not be open-minded. Remember where I grew up,'

'I grew up there too. I would not have told you what to write. It's your book. It's your life. Did I ever tell you how to live your life?' He looked at his watch, suggesting other appointments. 'Now, what did you want from me? Will you let me give you a blessing or must you strike out, always alone?'

Connie felt tears surge into her eyes. How could he say the very thing that would make her saddest? So, it had to be a confession. Of course, that was why she had come, the book merely an excuse. She looked him in the face, although she saw nothing. 'In 1970, Father, I had a child, a daughter. She's adopted now by my eldest brother and his wife who live in Washington. She's called Kathleen and she will grow up without knowing of my existence. In case you wonder, the father was nothing to me.'

Surprised, Connie found she was kneeling at the side of the table. Bowing her head, she let the tears fall. She felt as if she were praying for something, although she didn't know what.

The priest leant forward and touched her head so lightly she could scarcely feel it and yet its impression remained, soothing the screwed-up tightness. He spoke softly, the traditional words of forgiveness, words she had not heard for nearly half her lifetime.

It was always a mysterious plan, billed as a family Christmas. Veronica rang Nina in London to apologise. 'William sounded so desperate, Felicity in England with the baby, her boys coming home from school, William in Belfast till just before. I could hardly not invite him. At least it means we'll have Helen and Jamie with us.'

'Mummy, have you never realised that William makes me feel crazy? It's not his fault. It's just a fact.'

'All that's a long time ago. Anyway, you can go away and paint.'

'I shall invite Connie.'

'Of course you will, darling. I never thought otherwise.'

'And Fay. I know her brother's on leave so perhaps we'll invite him too.'

'We can open up the attic!'

'And Hector.'

'Doesn't Hector have family?'

Nina smiled, pleased to have caught out her mother: she did not like Hector. And who could blame her? When they were together, which was only occasionally these days, she thought he was what she wanted but when he went away she was relieved until – after a week or two – she or her traitorous body, certainly not her soul, longed for him again. 'Hector is a loner,' she announced, although the truth was that he hated being alone, which was probably why he was so faithless.

'It's a long time since I've brought out so many leaves for the table,' said Veronica. 'We'll be thirteen if you count the baby, so perhaps we won't.'

Jamie came with Nina to cut holly. 'I like cutting things,' he said at her look of surprise. So she gave him the clippers. There were three bushes in the garden, all heavily decorated with berries. In half an hour they had plenty of boughs collected into a sack.

'It's going to be a cold winter,' said Nina. She waited hopefully for Jamie to ask the reason why. 'You can tell by the amount of berries,' she continued. 'Nature provides extra for the birds when she's planning to lay on the frost and ice.'

'We have ice on the inside of our windows at school,' said Jamie, snipping off more boughs, although Nina had told him there were enough.

'But you've always liked your school?' It was a tentative question because for the last couple of years Jamie had perfected a technique of not hearing anything he didn't want to answer. It had become so pronounced recently that Nina wondered, guiltily, if he suspected she did not want to hear his answers and particularly not if they hinted at anything less than perfect happiness.

'It's all right.' He paused. 'Mummy?'

'Yes?' She bent to look closer and saw afresh his neat tweed jacket,

158

his viyella shirt, his well-cut hair, his serious, almost adult expression, and she was smitten with love. 'Yes, darling?'

'When's Daddy coming?' He shut his clippers and stared earnestly at his shoes.

Nina recalled the reason they were out of sympathy, but her love, not dependent on understanding or even ordinary affection, remained undimmed. She guessed it would always be like this; they would always be aliens to each other but, at least, she could love him. 'They're coming around teatime. All together, I think.' Her love spurred her on to greater daring. 'Felicity was a friend of mine, you know. In Malaya when you were little. Before Daddy and I divorced. I think she's very nice.'

Despite his continued downcast gaze Nina could see the red rolling up Jamie's cheek and neck. Had she transgressed the subtle rules laid down for conversation between mother and son? Was she not allowed to like her replacement? Suddenly she wished Hector was not coming, his adult maleness nothing like so alluring as her son's peach-like cheek. How would Jamie deal with *him*?

'I like Felicity. She's very nice,' muttered Jamie, as if Nina had not just said the same.

'Good. Good.' Nina wanted to hug him now but, clearly, he did not want to be hugged. He wanted to be reunited with maleness, with William, with his brothers, his step-brothers, Lyndon and Robert. He did not wish to know about his mother's feelings for his stepmother.

'Let's take the holly in,' she said. 'And don't forget there's the Christmas tree to decorate.'

Fay hugged Daniel. They were meeting at Heathrow airport. She had flown in from New York, he from Vietnam by way of Bangkok. They reeled back a little after hugging, from tiredness more than anything else. They decided coffee was needed and sat at a table under brilliant green plastic vines. Fay felt herself sighing inwardly with the relief of his presence. It turned into a collapsed, giggling feeling, as if she were high.

'So you've kidnapped me,' said Daniel, joking, 'and at last I meet the women in your life. Do you remember when you tried to set me up with Connie? When was it? 'Sixty-nine, 'seventy?'

Fay did remember. As it turned out she had not been speaking to Connie at the time, angry about her treatment of Merlin de Witt. 'You did kind of see her then. We took refuge from a demonstration in a bar, maybe you recall it? When it was over Connie was on the street outside dumping her dead cat in a police car.'

'Sounds my sort of girl.'

'Not any more. You'll see. She's London's leading feminist – well, one of them. She wrote a best-seller called *Say No To Sex*.'

'Phew! I can't wait to meet her.' Daniel put his head in his hands. Fay noticed with affection that his thick hair was sun-bleached blond on top. 'And what about the other one? Nina.'

'Oh, I couldn't try to describe Nina. She's a painter, I guess. You'll like her house. Her mother. The whole set-up's kind of English. Wait and see.'

'So this is Daniel. A walking, talking Daniel! I've heard so much about you.' Connie thought, My God, he's a soldier. She knew his history, of course, Fay's anguish at his decision, but she had not thought of the physical reality, of this large young man – he seemed to be about twice the size of his sister – who had chosen to line up behind an unjust war. Here Connie, who had just been writing an article on the subject in which she posited an army of women, recalled the Christian definition of a just war: 'A war that had to have a reasonable chance of success.' Even the bloodthirsty priests of Mayo would have been able to see that this squalid morass of failure that was the Vietnam war could never now progress to that. They were dealing with unjustified disaster and, if Daniel were not Fay's brother, she would have taken him to task on that. But he was and she couldn't.

'Come in, please, to my humble pad.' Connie, who had wound the ubiquitous feather boa over her sensible sweater (the flat was cold), took a step back, which was up the stairs. Definitely she could not attack this young beloved brother who had come on leave from a jungle hell-hole. 'Come in! Come in! This is a global centre. May I hug you, Daniel? Or maybe the kiss of peace would be more appropriate?' He was a soldier. His body filled with tension, his head set on his shoulders like a wedge, his fear of breaking down putting him on the edge of madness – or so Connie decided. 'I have nourishing soup,' she cried. Only then she thought to look at Fay and see how it was going with her.

Fay suddenly felt she was skidding and her arm through Daniel's was for her own support. It's only jet-lag, she told herself. This transitional period in London, with Connie looking like a cross between a Barbie doll and a high-school teacher, was unimagined. While climbing up the grubby staircase, she considered how Connie would mature, trying briefly and unsuccessfully to imagine her old.

'The soup is made from lentils with an injection of the drained blood of oxen. Although a vegetarian myself, I cannot force my beliefs on others.' They were in the kitchen, bags dropped off Daniel's broad shoulders to the floor.

Fay stared at him admiringly. He looked well, sunburnt, clean, like a sportsman. She had talked to him about drugs before he went, and he had listened for a while before interrupting her good-humouredly, 'Dr Blass, you're making out like I'm some skinny redneck, fresh out of south Georgia or someplace. How about this? I do not go beyond the odd joint. OK?' On his last leave he had reassured her further: 'I'm not in the field. They think too highly of my brain for that. You see in front of you valuable army property.'

'And when will the war be over?' asked Connie, in a conversational tone. 'I dreamed it *was* over,' she added, as if that were more important than the reality.

And yet, thought Fay, the reality is so unbelievable, that we're still out there, still bombing, killing, being killed, that perhaps her dream should be taken seriously.

'You can bet your life it'll be over this time next year,' said Daniel.

'Your life,' said Connie, pouring a violent purple soup.

'I beg your pardon?'

'You're betting your life, I'm not betting mine.'

Fay frowned irritably. This was Daniel's leave, a time of respite. Why was Connie taking this confrontational pose? When did Connie not take a confrontational pose? Particularly when an attractive man was involved. But surely that was all in the past as she'd just told Daniel. Yet at this moment it was hard not to see flirtation and entrapment in every line of her body, in every caustic question.

'You have never been to London, England,' she was saying now, 'where there's a statue of a conquering male on every street corner. Queen Victoria's the nearest they get to a woman. If we have time, I shall take you on a trawl.'

'We will not have time,' Fay interrupted, seeing her brother's face begin to show that hypnotised-rabbit look that had categorised all Connie's admirers.

'Post-Christmas,' suggested Daniel. 'Then I'll set my watch to tourist time.'

The truth, thought Fay, which should have been evident to her at once, is that Daniel is Connie's type. Not that he's a killer like Trigear was but, just at the moment, he is in a dangerous situation, a dangerous and very masculine situation. Connie has not changed at all, whatever she may declare.

'Would you like a rest, Fay,' suggested Connie, in a kindly manner. 'before we set off for Sussex?'

'I'm acclimatised to long hours, but I don't know about Daniel.'

When Daniel had gone upstairs, Connie put her arm round Fay's shoulders. 'How's the matters of life and death?'

'Tense. There's a new fashion for suing the doctor if the outcome isn't a hundred per cent.'

'But only God can tell the future.'

'We're learning not to take on high-risk cases.'

'You mean you won't take a chance.'

'That's the theory. But I take a chance every time I pick up a knife. I used to encourage optimism in my patients, in their families, but now I talk about risk. It's becoming a different atmosphere, Connie.' Fay thought that talking to Connie was a risk too, but was determined to treat her like an adult.

'I'm sorry, when you've worked so hard to get where you are.'

Fay smiled ironically. She had worked hard to get where she was but she had also followed a vocation to save lives. And yet. Was it the changed situation that was undermining her confidence? Or was it something in herself? Where was the comforting old thing called job satisfaction? Why did she feel so tense all the time? Fay sighed.

When she looked up she saw that Connie had put her forearms on the table and rested her head on them. Her voice was muffled. 'Have you seen Shirley?'

Fay liked Shirley. She even forgave Kevin for his hawkish attitude to the war. Perhaps she liked them because they were rich and kind, and even the spare room was filled with flowers. Perhaps she was tired.

'Yes. I've been in Washington two or three times and dropped in on Shirley. Your brother is in good shape, better still that he's close but not too close to the Republican camp. Kevin's a winner, I guess. Yes, yes.' She paused unconsciously. 'I have seen Kathleen . . .' She paused again as Connie gave a little bleat. 'She is a beautiful little girl. Dark hair, blue eyes, dainty . . .'

'Dainty! Dainty as in odious, spoilt, prim, child of Mary?'

'Sssh. She's dainty as in petite—'

'Petite!' shrieked Connie. 'Petite as in refined, girlish, self-conscious, lisping . . .'

Fay saw Connie was hating her for having seen her daughter. 'She's a pretty little girl, Connie. Started at pre-school. Speaks well for her age. Has everything she wants. Shirley adores her. That's all I can tell you. Sorry.'

Connie went up to the bedroom and sat near to the sprawling figure of Daniel. She wanted someone to hug but she had eschewed that sort of thing, hadn't she? So she pinched his arm instead. He had taken off his shoes, which lay like bricks. His eyes were covered with a black mask, his arms behind his head.

'Are you awake or dreaming? I don't expect your dreams are too nice.'

'I've taken out my contact lenses,' said Daniel, pulling up the mask and fumbling on the floor with one hand. 'I'm just about blind.'

'That's true. But I don't think a bit of old plastic will help.' She came even closer to him, inhaled his masculine smell.

'I beg your pardon.' Daniel sat up. His hair was so streaky blond it made Connie want to cry. 'Here you are.' She leant forward and handed him the lens container. 'And here you are again.' She kissed him gently on the mouth. She couldn't remember how long it was since she'd kissed a man on the lips.

'There's a car coming up the drive!' shouted Jamie inadvertently kicking holly along the hall floor. 'I bet it's Daddy!'

Nina fled to the two bedrooms on the top floor of the house. She could hardly remember these ever being used. They sat under sloping roofs and smelt musty despite windows forced open and a bowl of home-made pot-pourri on each bedside table. Jamie had already colonised one room, his clothes laid out neatly, surprising in a ten-year-old. On the table beside the pot-pourri was a small silver cup he had won for swimming the previous term.

The second room was bigger with two beds. A book had been placed on the table between them and Nina half recognised its faded green cover. She picked it up and saw that indeed it was the book on trees she had found for Connie and Fay on their first visit. As she flicked through, admiring the engravings, a piece of paper fell out, with just a few lines of writing: 'I will never be as unhappy as I am now. I am writing this down and putting it in this book so that when I find it again, many years later, I will remember and be glad.'

How extraordinary to read such words! And more extraordinary to have quite forgotten writing them. Certainly that had been a very low time, separated from William, in thrall to the terrifying compulsion to wash. She had found the book in the potting-shed, she remembered, mildewed and smelling of sprouting onions and soft apples. She must have written the note then. She looked at it again and realised, with a shock, that it was not her writing but her mother's.

She went to the window in trepidation, looked down. It wasn't William who'd arrived but Connie, with Fay and Daniel.

A log-fire blazed, the lights on the Christmas tree flashed, the faded wallpaper was garlanded with paper chains and stuck with holly. Daniel sat nearest the fire, his sunburnt face reflecting a ruddy glow. He answered Jamie's awestruck questions about jungles and helicopters, although he insisted it was years since he'd been anywhere near such dangerous playthings. 'I'd be as easily spooked as you.' Eventually Jamie followed Veronica to choose a stocking.

'Fools rush in,' apologised Nina.

'Let's declare this house a war-free zone.' Fay wore her doctor's look, Nina noted, which allowed for no compromise.

It struck Nina that Hector, when he arrived the next day, would be perfectly capable of sporting the T-shirt fashionable among his set, 'It takes a gook to kill a gook.' Hector, thought Nina, should stick to art. But this confident assessment was quickly undermined by the nagging doubt that had surfaced periodically ever since her visit to New York in 1967, that her own art suffered from a lack of political context. That she herself (and how could she be separated from her art?) would have painted apple trees in the Garden of Eden or on a battlefield with precisely the same perception. That meaning, in an important sense, would always elude her paintings because she, the painter, understood nothing.

'Whatever's the matter, Nina?' Fay came and sat beside her on the sofa. 'You're squeezing up your face like you're chewing on a really sour lemon.'

'Sorry. Sorry. Oh, Fay, I'm so glad you've come. You're the only one of us who really knows what you're doing.'

'Hey, come on. I just do what needs to be done. There's no call for knowing.'

'What's happening in Vietnam? When will the war end?'

Fay looked surprised at this question. 'Have we lost the war-free zone so quickly? Nixon's trying to bomb us into peace. Since December eighteenth they've been dropped on roads round Hanoi and Haiphong. He's ordered a ceasefire for Christmas Day but doubtless he'll be at it again the day after.'

Nina had heard this news on the radio, seen it in the newspapers, but it had not translated into any reality she could understand.

'Have you seen Serge lately?' she asked. Serge had taken a personal attitude to Vietnam and made it central to his life.

'Serge is still at Judson,' Fay said, 'I don't think he knows whether he's a political animal or a creative one.'

That was the nub of it, thought Nina. The way Fay was dividing the two. 'Why shouldn't he be both?'

'I mean he might go into politics or he might opt for directing theatre.'

Nina was disappointed. 'You're thinking in career terms.'

'Don't we all? I'm a doctor. A professional. When I talk about the war I'm airing my rights as a citizen but it's not like I'm a politician. You're a painter. That's your profession. When you explain Cézanne to me, I listen.'

Nina felt helpless. Fay was wrong, she was quite certain of it, but she had no way of expressing why. It was something to do with the whole concept of 'the professional'. She had only become a professional when she sold a painting but her views on Cézanne were just as good before.

'But you believe,' Nina tried again, 'that your view on how to end the war in Vietnam is less likely to be right than Kissinger's?'

'I could say it's all about knowledge. Doctors base their confidence on superior knowledge. I don't know what Kissinger has been up to, popping in and out of Hanoi, Saigon, Moscow. I guess he must have collected all kinds of information I don't have access to. Maybe, with hindsight, I'll say they've done as well as they could, given the cards on the table. Maybe Serge and the rest should leave it to the professionals . . .'

'My problem,' Nina looked at Fay with bitter appeal, 'is I always think other people know best.'

'That's not the way it looked from the outside. When can I see your paintings?'

Nina's expression changed at once. It was as if the mention of her paintings wiped out their entire conversation. 'Tomorrow. When it's light.'

'I shan't ask about Hector,' said Fay, smiling.

'No. Much better not.' Nina tried to return the smile and then became serious. 'What I was trying to say earlier is that I regret my non-involvement in world affairs. Oh dear. How pompous that sounds.'

'We have to lead our own lives,' said Fay. 'The trick is to find out what that is.'

Fay was happy to see that Nina looked relieved at this as if some burden had been lifted. She wished she could explain her own present confusion, her ambiguities about her priorities, her sudden, hopefully ridiculous, sense of a life wasted. 'My analyst tells me that all my problems are linked to one,' she said, in an ironic tone. The analyst was new in her life. 'I can't bring myself to love my mother.'

'Connie's adopted mine for the same reason.' Nina didn't look as if she took this subject at all seriously. 'I've no doubt there's plenty of mummy love left for you. Anyway, from what you've told me, your mother doesn't sound very lovable.'

'Daniel manages to love her.' With a bitter expression, Fay turned to look at Daniel and Connie and their young acolyte, Helen. They had unearthed some old board game, which they were playing with great intensity.

'Everybody knows daughters have problems with their mothers!' Nina spoke airily. 'I'm just lucky that my roots are so acceptable.' She swept her arm around the old, wide room, the upholstered chairs, the bookcases with undusted books, the pictures, one slightly askew and showing a clean patch on the wall behind.

'Don't apologise,' Fay said. 'Just invite me to stay often.'

William, Felicity and their baby arrived an hour before dinner. The baby, violently pink with a large head and little hair, seemed identical to Jamie at the same age. Nina, expressing admiration, thought it strange that William's genes should flatten and demolish her own and Felicity's. William was not, after all, a strong character, at least if the basic attribute of a strong character was the ability to stand alone. He could not survive without a woman. Now he had Felicity. Nina felt a surge of thankfulness at being let off the hook.

The baby took so much attention with his pressing needs that it was only at dinner that the party began to integrate.

Helen had made place cards. On some she had drawn an appropriate emblem. Nina had a paintbrush, Connie a pen, Fay a knife, Veronica a spoon; William and Daniel each had a gun.

Nina looked at them with horror, not least at their place on either side of her. But it was too late for change.

'Do sit down,' she invited everybody. 'Mother's overseeing Mrs Bundy in the kitchen but she'll be through in a moment.'

Fay, sitting on the other side of William, began to talk about London, and Felicity, on the other side of Daniel, took up the same theme. Suddenly Nina understood that no one would talk about anything important. There was too much at stake, so many possibilities for disagreement that they cancelled each other out. This was Christmas Eve in a family home, hosted by a middle-class widowed English woman who had brought them all together and prepared every comfort with an understanding that the strictest code of behaviour would be followed. She had followed this code all her life, even when most threatened, with her husband ill and in love with another woman. She pictured the scribbled note in that old damp-mottled book. She had not spoken out then and she expected no one to speak out now. Wearing a long black velvet dress, Veronica entered the room and took her place at the other end of the table.

'I'm so pleased to see you.' Nina bent graciously towards William with almost the first words she'd said to him since his arrival. With any luck it would be their most intimate exchange until his departure.

Fay enjoyed talking to William. She had never met him before and knew him only as the man who had driven Nina into obsessional behaviour. But this handsome very English man seemed to possess all the best qualities. He was modest, sensible and charming. They did not, of course, talk about Northern Ireland, neither of them wanted that, but she could imagine he was a concerned and responsible officer, liked and respected by his subordinates.

'It's quite something to have a new baby,' he was saying now, with a look of unassumed happiness and pride. Fay wanted to ask how old he was: he looked very young. 'The main problem,' he continued, 'is to find quarters big enough for all five children.' He paused and gave her a steady look. 'That's why we're here now. To be all together.'

'Yes. Of course.' Fay was even more impressed by this paterfamilias attitude and tried and failed to remember just what it was about him that had so destroyed Nina. She looked across at Daniel and, seeing him vivaciously entertained by Felicity, allowed herself to relax into a sleepily jet-lagged sense of a benign world.

The house, Connie thought, heaved and bulged and breathed heavily with the thirteen persons sleeping inside its elderly walls. She crept down the wooden stairs, crossed the hallway where moonlight came through a landing window and opened the door to the dining room. Sometimes a glass of whiskey was the only answer although, under the circumstances, it was easier to take the bottle.

The stairs creaked with familiar friendliness as she made her way up again and it struck her forcefully that there was one thing she would prefer to a bottle of booze. Setting down the whiskey, she slid into Daniel's bedroom. He was sleeping in Jamie's small bed in a twitchy sort of way, arms flung out so they almost touched the floor, head flung back, an occasional snort, and once he murmured, although she could not hear the words. She crouched beside him and put her hand on his forehead. He sat up at once, throwing off her hand but in another second had focused on her face.

'Hi, Connie.'

'Happy Christmas.'

He kissed her at once.

'This has nothing to do with my views on war or men,' Connie explained mildly between their kissing. 'You're my Christmas present to myself.'

'You couldn't make a better choice.' Daniel lifted off her T-shirt, which was all she wore. He was already naked.

It was very dark in the little room and their love-making was entirely by feel. It was only when Daniel's fingers touched Connie's stomach that she flinched away and he didn't persist, as if she had a right to privacy about the ridges etched in her skin. She suspected that he had learnt a good deal about wounds over the past three years.

Afterwards, Connie rolled herself into the eiderdown and on to the floor. She lay there beside him feeling happy, waiting for guilt that didn't come. In the early morning, Daniel rolled himself down to join her and they made love again, so tenderly that Connie found tears running down her cheeks. How could strangers give each other such happiness? She had forgotten about sex and loving.

'It's the first time I've made love for years,' she whispered to him, although she didn't expect him to believe her.

Nina had already told Fay that Hector was a very bad driver, which was one of the few things they had in common. On Christmas Day Fay watched from the living-room window as he drove too fast into the driveway, winging William's hired car.

The two men stood together peering at it with Connie leaning out from her bedroom shouting encouragements. Nina said feebly, 'At least it looks as if it'll still go.'

Hector did not apologise for long. 'That's what they're used to, these hired cars. Give them a kick and they move all the faster.'

'I believe it is insured for accidents,' conceded William stiffly.

Helen, as if taking sides, came out and stood by her father.

Hector went over and took Nina's arm. 'Do I get a cup of coffee or is that withheld as punishment?'

'Come and have some coffee all of you.' Veronica appeared on cue at the front door.

Fay, now pretending to read, saw them pass by and thought, How bizarre that Nina, so apparently calm, should be the centre of such emotional drama. And then she thought how she really did admire William, all the more on this bright morning. She watched him cross back again and go outside, and then Daniel appeared hurrying after him. 'We're going for a walk!' He waved at her cheerfully but did not come over. A moment or two later, Hector went by, turning up his collar over his long hair.

'What are you smiling at?' Connie, still not dressed, feet bare, black hair wild, padded softly into the room.

'Not telling.'

'So the men have gone out killing.' Connie settled down. Her body was filled with forgotten comforts. She thought: I made love last night with a good man, neither married nor despised, a man whom I like and who likes me. This is a first. Briefly, she considered her last letter from Orlando Partridge, as always both comic and supplicatory. Was there room in her life for a man now?

'Walking,' said Fay briefly. 'The men are out walking. Did you see a gun?'

Connie bent forward to whisper, 'What odds William and Hector come to blows? I bet William's the sort of man who hates letting a woman go even after he's chosen another.'

'No fighting in an English country house.'

Nina came in with a mug of coffee. She stood at the door with a shifty expression. 'Would you like me to show you my paintings?'

'On condition I can read you the opening line of my new book, Sixteen and Under Sex.' Connie wound her robe more tightly and prepared to follow Nina.

Fay stood up and took them on either arm. 'Next time you're both in New York, I'll invite you to watch the maestro surgeon perform an emergency appendectomy on a three-year-old.'

As they opened the door to the cold morning air, Connie, shivering and hugging her bare skin, felt young and silly and pleased with the secrets she was keeping to herself.

1973

Fay sat down without taking off her operation clothes – her hat, gloves, coat, even the mask still dangled round her neck. She tried to tell herself that this was the first child she'd lost on the operating table, that her record was the best in the hospital, that parents sent their children to her because she was so good. But her brain refused to accept the information. It told her that her incompetence had killed that three-year-old boy – Luke, he was called – with a white mother and a black father. A beautiful golden boy, with dark brown eyes and reddish-gold curls. He had been in her care; she had told them to trust her. She had not told them of the enormous risk because she had not wanted to think of it herself.

She accused herself of two wrongs: the wrong of allowing herself to love the little boy in an unprofessional way and the wrong of allowing this love to obscure the true odds of his pulling through, and then, worst of all, allowing the parents to have too much hope. That was arrogance of a cruel and dangerous sort. She was a very good surgeon but she was not God.

Fay got to her feet slowly. Now she must face the parents: Peggy with her flowing yellow hair and hippie's brown face, and Royston, a human-rights lawyer. Maybe he'd sue her, she thought miserably. Maybe they'd be angry.

But, of course, they were not and, in some extraordinary way, it was they who comforted Fay. 'He'd been ill for so long,' said Peggy, tears rolling down her face. 'We nearly ducked out of the operation. Somehow we knew he was not meant to live. But in the end we were weak and couldn't resist grabbing at the chance, however small.'

'We said our goodbyes,' added Royston. 'He was happy when he went under. I promised him a football match.'

'We're believers,' said Peggy. 'We believe he's doing whatever he likes most . . .'

'. . . and that's football,' put in Royston, not noticing he'd begun to cry too.

'Right now!' concluded Peggy, hugging her husband. 'So we're happy for him. Please don't reproach yourself.'

Half an hour later, Fay was sitting in her office doing the paperwork when her PA opened the door.

'My door's closed, Yoko. I'm working.' She frowned at the woman, who stood her ground, blinking in what looked like silent panic.

'Yes. I'm sorry. I . . .'

'What is it?' Fay saw she held a piece of fax paper in her hand. 'You've got a fax for me. Hand it over, then.'

Perhaps because of the morning's tragedy, Fay felt no warning intimation. She read the words as if they related to work, with hard, sharp energy.

Daniel had been killed in a helicopter accident. Fay's mind fled from the information, back to Luke's face in the operating theatre, his small body, his maleness, the pain she had felt at his death. She had thought that the limit of her capacity for pain. Just a few hours ago that death had seemed almost unbearable. And now it turned out to have been a dress rehearsal.

And then she thought it was not just Luke's death that had been a dress rehearsal but that everything in her life, her childhood, her university days, her work in the hospital, had been a preparation for this moment. She thought, knowing it made no sense and yet convinced of its rightness, that by working so hard to save lives she had kept Daniel alive, kept death at bay, but that the moment she had failed to save Luke and his heart stopped beating, and he lay, a small victim, on the operating table, then Daniel became vulnerable. She had lost her hold over death.

'I killed him,' Fay muttered, but loud enough for Yoko to hear. Yoko hurried over, put her arms round Fay's shoulders, hugged her. Fay seemed not to notice. 'My mother will blame me. And then she'll die.'

Yoko pleaded, 'Don't say such things. You're distraught.' Fay thought for a flash that Daniel's death had entered her on a long journey from which she might never return. She left her office, took the elevator and crossed the necessary corridors until she was in the street. Yoko stayed with her, walking crabwise in an effort to protect her. Fay walked along the crowded pavements. It was hot and she walked fast, her doctor's white coat making her particularly visible so that people stepped out of her way.

Fay's apartment block was on First Avenue, the canopy announcing itself among supermarkets, bars and small office blocks. A young doorman came out cheerily: 'Good afternoon, Doctor.'

Yoko had fallen behind but now she caught up anxiously. Fay fixed her hands in her overall pockets. 'I'm just dead tired,' she said, not seeming to hear her own words.

'I'll say you're not well,' began Yoko.

'Too right,' said the doorman. 'Take a few hours out. Put off your white coat.'

'I've left my keys behind.' Fay looked bewildered.

'No problem.' The doorman went to find a spare set.

Before he returned, Fay had taken off her coat, rolled it up and handed it to her assistant. 'You take it back. I won't be needing it.'

The doorman, who was new and curious, showed Fay into her flat. She noticed his narrow, clever face with hair too long for a doorman. 'You'll be OK,' she said, 'If they haven't got you now, you'll escape. Another month or two and it will be all over. It's just Daniel's misfortune.'

'Excuse me?'

'My brother's just had the misfortune to be killed in a helicopter crash in Vietnam. I guess the way things are going it will be the last helicopter crash in Vietnam.'

The doorman came right in. He took Fay's hand and led her to the bedroom. He took off her shoes and laid her tidily on the bed. He seemed to know exactly how to treat her and, grateful, she kept her eyes on his face.

'I don't want to be alone,' she heard herself saying, although what she meant was that she wanted this young doorman to stay with her. She needed a stranger. Only a stranger would understand.

He sat down on the bed. 'My name's Ted,' he said. 'I'll have to find another doorman for downstairs.' He went, and while he was away Fay put thinking on hold and lay with her face to the wall. She was hardly aware of his return, except that someone had put on the air-conditioning in the living room. The repetitive noise gradually stimulated her into some form of consciousness.

Ted came in as she fumbled for the telephone. She dialled her mother's number but realised, as it began to ring, that she could not speak. Ted took the receiver. 'I'm calling on behalf of Dr Blass. She'll be getting to the phone in an hour or so.'

'Say I'm looking for a flight,' whispered Fay.

So he did that and then stood looking down at her. 'There were people there. A young woman answered.'

'It's my mother's number. That's OK, then.'

'I'll be right next door.'

Fay lay on the bed, using all her energy not to think or feel. Some time passed. Music came from the living room, complicated harmonies. Fay realised she could still hear, which seemed very dangerous.

Ted appeared at the door. 'I've brought in my tape machine. You don't mind, do you? It's something I'm working on.'

Fay didn't try to understand. She was still trying to imitate death. It became dark outside. She went to the bathroom. Ted brought her a sandwich, which she didn't eat. The music next door became even more complicated, strings and percussion with the air-conditioning providing the rhythm. She got out of bed and went through. Her legs shook so much that she had to sit down abruptly. One small lamp showed Ted cross-legged in the corner of the sofa, scribbling.

'You're a student, are you?' She didn't mean it to be an accusation: a living draft-dodger.

'Yes, ma'am.'

Fay sat on the other end of the sofa. She had to speak after all. 'He wasn't a hero, my brother.' Ted said nothing. 'The telegram said he was killed instantly. And although they always write that, I guess it might be true with a helicopter crash.'

'I guess so.' He seemed more wary now that she was speaking or perhaps his mind was on his scribbles.

'What are you writing?' Why had she asked that? What did anything matter?

'Playing with music. When I'm not a doorman, I'm a student of music.'

'That's nice. Daniel could have been a lawyer by now.' How could she be talking like this?

'Yeah. I bet he was bright.'

'Why do you think that?' She sat on the other end of the sofa. She looked into his young man's face without a tear.

'With a sister like you. A doctor.'

Fay thought about that, about how all her hard work and ambition might have affected him. She'd got a head start on him, always five years ahead, and then the war came. 'He was married, you know. That is, he had been married. He married at your age.'

'Kids?'

'No kids. They split. You've heard about war marriages?'

Ted said nothing. He seemed good at that. He took off the music, turned off the air-conditioner and prepared to listen.

In the night silence, Fay realised that the air-conditioner had been like a helicopter in her head and now it had stopped. At last she began to cry. Ted brought her tissues. Then she began to talk again. Ted's face wore a settled-in expression as if there was no other call on him but this listening. On the other hand, he remained detached, a stranger.

The night passed slowly.

At six Ted stretched and said he'd better go off to do a bit of doorman duty. 'You sleep,' he said, 'and then I'll be back.'

So Fay, exhausted, went to sleep.

At eleven he came back with croissants and coffee from across the road. 'You'd better call your mother and catch that plane.'

To her surprise, Fay found she was strong enough to do that. She could even drink the coffee and pack a suitcase. She was glad all the same that her mother did not come to the phone. She was resting, which wasn't the same, Fay reminded herself, as being dead.

Connie made an appointment to see Father O'Donald. She began to shout the moment she arrived in the little room, the moment she spotted the crucifix with Christ and his agonised face. She thought she sounded as stupid as a dissatisfied shopper who had found a toaster defective. 'There's absolutely no way you can defend this God of yours! He's a disgrace! A charlatan! It would be much better if he'd never existed.'

The priest already knew why she had come and told her this was no time for a theological discussion. 'I'll tell you what,' he said, brightening, so that she realised how tired he had looked when she had made her storming entrance, 'let's go into the cathedral. The choir practises about now. We can say our prayers for the dead,' he pronounced the word with a steady confidence, 'to a background of heavenly singing.'

'Anyway, he was Jewish,' muttered Connie, 'and over Christmas we made the beast with two backs.' But that was a mistake because it started the tears again and the memories. When they had come back to town she had given Daniel the promised tour of feminist London and he had whispered to her, when Fay had turned aside, 'You're just a dream, do you know that?, a dream.' She'd loved that compliment.

The priest waited until she had composed herself then walked away briskly, over well-shined wooden floors until they entered the cathedral by a small door beside the altar. She followed him. What else could she do? The church was very dark, the huge undecorated heights of the ceiling rising into blackness, but every space was filled with singing. Father O'Donald led them to a front pew, Connie saw the choir high up behind the altar, several rows of young boys, backed by lines of men.

'Such a privilege,' murmured the priest. 'Does it sound like Fauré's Requiem?'

They sat together listening. Connie, who had begun to carry a little bottle of sherry with her, swigged at it absentmindedly. 'Blood of

Christ,' she riposted to the priest's mild look of interrogation. But the drinking was only reflex and not at all important. To prove this, she stowed the bottle under the pew and sat, like him, with arms folded.

After half an hour or so, she sensed he was planning to leave and could hardly deny him the truth.

'I am a believer now. Despite everything. Because of everything.' She looked at him to see how he was taking it. He was her friend. Christ's representative on earth. She even believed that. 'I suppose I always have been.'

He smiled, blessed her silently, seemed to be going and then turned back. 'Shall I say a mass for him, your friend Daniel, who died?'

'Do that, if you would, Father.'

After he'd gone Connie sat peacefully. The choir filed away, talking among themselves.

Connie shut her eyes firmly. Yet still I believe and still I worship my God and still I mourn Daniel who, in one way or another, I loved. Even though he was of the wrong, inferior gender.

Connie cried between her fingers and felt she was now strong enough to comfort Fay. She would go, with Nina, to her.

As she walked away down the great wide aisle of the cathedral, feeling thoroughly at home, she thought that one day, but not yet, she would tell Fay what her brother's death had meant to her.

At least she could write to Orlando Partridge. He would lacerate himself with ridiculous jealousy and understand everything.

It had been Connie's idea that they meet Fay in the Rainbow Room, sixty-five floors above the Rockefeller Plaza. 'It will give us perspective,' she informed Nina.

'Low moments in high places,' commented Nina abstractedly.

They sat together in a yellow cab, for Fay was to join them there. It was three months since Daniel's death but this was their first meeting. They arrived at the darkened room with its glittering sweep of sky and ordered a plate of shrimps and a bottle of Californian Chardonnay, although Nina insisted it would be inappropriate to start on them before Fay arrived.

'It would have been too dismal in her flat. Can you imagine?' said Connie, as time passed by and no Fay appeared.

Nina thought Connie's aim was to get as far away as possible from the Manhattan of her past. She walked round the circumference of the room, standing in front of the floor-to-ceiling windows where the black night was lit by stars to its crown and by man-made blocks, pyramids, arrows, garlands, whirls and arabesques below, the outline of a city that seemed to stretch as far down as the sky reached up. She returned to Connie, who raised a defiant glass. Nina was not amused. 'But a perspective on what? On death? The endless infinity of it is what I see, the bright uncaring dazzle of this world, which cannot possibly take note of an individual death. If I were Fay, I'd fly to the countryside, to the sympathetic softness of green leaves and grass.'

'You're such a romantic.' Connie sounded cross. 'Nature is far tougher than anything man can make. Indeed, you might well argue that man did make the Home Counties.'

'Don't let's argue. What if Fay should come in and find us?'

'We would stop.' Now Connie stood and marched the circumference of the room, although she looked scornfully, without stopping her progress, as if the magnificence of the view meant nothing to her.

Nina, eating the shrimps one by one, thought that this was the first time Connie had returned to America since the birth of her baby. The subject was never mentioned between them but it was easy to imagine how she felt. Perhaps she was wondering whether to go to Washington. Perhaps she had been invited.

Connie returned briefly. 'No sign of her?'

'I'm afraid not.' Connie picked up her glass and went away again. Nina finished the shrimps and started on the peanuts.

Connie poured more wine and sat down beside Nina. Tonight was one of those occasions when she longed to kick Nina, pummel her broad back. Even though she knew that Nina's outward calm was often completely at odds with whatever turbulent emotions she was experiencing, particularly when the odious Hector was involved, she still found it intensely irritating. How did Nina preserve such apparent tranquillity and why did she want to? Surely it was almost schizophrenic, thought Connie meanly, and then remembered Nina's washing disorder. No sign of that now, of course, but perhaps it lurked, a frailty of character.

'This waiting is terrible. I guess it was a bad idea of mine.'

'I don't know.'

'I don't know where you get your patience.' Connie fidgeted around the table, called for more wine and finally sat down. She was fighting the need to tell Nina about her night with Daniel. 'Have I told you,' she said, 'I've rejoined the Holy Mother Church?'

Nina looked at her blankly. It was a joke, of course, but what a time to spring it.

'I'm serious. I wanted you to know. Since Daniel's death. I went to see my dearest Father O'Donald and it started from there. Do you think I could mention it to Fay? I mean, I know she's not religious ...' Connie looked at Nina's continuing blankness and saw she wasn't religious either. Or perhaps it was all saved for her art. 'Well, forget it,' she said. 'I just wanted to say something consoling to Fay but I see now that as usual it's all about me.'

'Hi. Nina. Connie.' Nina and Connie stared at Fay and then at the man who stood at her side, holding her elbow in a quietly proprietorial way. 'This is Ted,' continued Fay, smiling at their surprised faces. 'He's a composer. Hey, don't I get a hug?'

Nina and Connie competed for the hug, shook Ted's hand.

Ted asked, 'What are we drinking?' Fay gave her credit card to the waiter.

'It's all on me,' she said. 'I can't tell you how I appreciate you both coming over. It means a lot to me. The Christmas we were all together was the last time I saw Daniel.' Fay looked at Ted. She had rehearsed this little homily beforehand in case they should misunderstand Ted's presence and feel she had no need of them. But now it seemed to have produced a sense of formality, which had silenced even Connie. She felt impelled to continue with all the things she had to say. 'I am going to change direction in my career. I'm going to leave the hospital and surgery as soon as I can set up my own practice as a radiologist.' She paused and again glanced towards Ted. 'Oh, and you might want to know that Ted has moved in with me.'

Now Connie burst into laughter. 'I guess this is the most positive wake I've ever been to!'

'I guess it is. And it's no disrespect to Daniel, whom I think of every moment of the day, to say it's all due to him.'

Ted seemed unfazed by the situation. 'Would you mind,' he suggested, 'if we left this glamorous place in the clouds and went down to somewhere with its feet on the ground? The honest truth is, I have an aversion to heights amounting to vertigo.'

'Ted, my dear,' cried Fay, 'why ever didn't you tell me?'

So they left the stars and found an Italian restaurant on 48th and 3rd, which Ted said reminded him of his months in Naples. Again Fay exclaimed with surprise and, in order to show off what she did know about him, she told Nina and Connie, who failed to hide their extreme curiosity, that Ted was working as a doorman at night to support himself at the Juilliard School of Music during the day.

'You mean you're a student!' exclaimed Nina. 'I feel so old I could die.'

'But Fay told me you're an art student yourself.'

'I'm a mature student, which is something quite different altogether.'

'I don't think you're mature in any way,' objected Connie.

'Well, anyway, Ted's the most mature person I've ever met, said Fay.

'Just think,' said Connie, 'at the ripe old age of thirty-three the iron maiden has fallen in love. Is he Jewish, do you think?'

'I've no idea.' Nina had been wondering the same thing herself. 'If it comes to that, I don't even know whether it matters to Fay one way or the other. I liked him.'

'So did I. I shall ask her,' promised Connie. But in the end she never did because it really didn't seem to matter. Nor, she now saw, would she ever tell her about Daniel.

The bridle path went across uplands, steep slopes with bracken and ragwort, mown fields, wide green spaces with views all around. It was the middle of August now, the cornfields mostly harvested, or being harvested. Nina walked and thought of Hector who had still failed to fix a date for a show. He was just a liar. A charming lover and a charming liar.

Nina climbed over a stile from a path bordering a wood to a huge field, stretching like a plateau, hardly sloping at all, across twenty or more acres. Towards one end was a ramshackle shed. The sun was hot in a clear sky and she tied her sweater round her waist. She was surprised to find how much weight she'd lost in the last obsessive working months: the arms of the sweater reached easily round and tied with long flapping ends. The warmth, the regular beat of her walking, was soothing and by the time she reached the shed, the constant anxiety from which she had been suffering the last week (made all the more frightening in case it should lead her back into the obsessional world of ritual) had disappeared. She rested her back against a more substantial part of the shed and shut her eyes.

A faint disturbance caused her to open them and she saw, directly in front of her, heading her way across the field, an aeroplane, not flying but moving smoothly along the grass. It stopped quite abruptly within a few feet of where she stood and a man jumped out, unclasping a leather helmet in a way she remembered from war films. He had a ruddy, good-humoured face, white hair and bright blue eyes.

'Do you mind helping me push her in?'

Nina tried not to look as stupid as she felt. 'In here?'

'It's my hangar. Well, my son's, to be exact. But I try to keep her exercised while he's away. You have to for the licence.'

Together they pushed the plane into its home and when it was neatly stowed, the pilot produced a motorcycle from a corner.

Nina had a wild desire to giggle. 'Do you keep that exercised too?'

He laughed. 'Want a lift?'

'No. No. Thank you. I'm walking. Tell me one thing. How did you get so close to me without my hearing?'

'I always glide in,' he said, matter-of-factly.

They parted, he roaring off, trailing clouds of blue smoke, she to continue into the next field with a lightheartedness that verged on hysteria. It was too delicious a feeling to analyse, perhaps too fragile, but she knew it had something to do with the utter unexpectedness of the aeroplane's appearance, with its prosaic guardian. It was a ridiculous vision that recalled all the random hilarity of life. If you could be on nodding terms with an aeroplane in a field less than an hour's walk from your home, what strange events could be, if not expected, not unexpected? She completed her walk with a sense of inward laughter. Her vivacity lightened the lugubrious heaviness of approaching autumn, tinted the leaves and the grass to an almost spring-like tone. If the partridge who stalked the shrubbery with crimson-coloured legs had spoken, she would not have been surprised.

The feeling was still with her when the postman jumped off his bicycle bearing his afternoon delivery: one letter. What, that morning, would have filled her with passionate elation was hardly a surprise now.

'I have a slot in the spring,' Hector Pijane wrote. 'Will you be able to get enough pictures together by then?'

1974

Hector had chosen a dress for Nina to wear at her opening. It was not exactly mini but far shorter than anything she had ever worn. He made her get out of his bed where they lay naked together to try it on. Nina felt undignified, she would not swing round or model it the way she guessed he wanted.

'You see, you've got splendid legs,' said Hector, languidly, lying back with his arms above his head.

Nina sat down so that all he could see was her back. She summoned the spirit of Connie to her side. 'I am a painter not a whore!' she wanted to cry, but before she could speak she felt his hands slip through the unzipped opening of the dress until they reached her breasts. She shivered violently and said nothing.

So the dress remained, a blue-green shimmer, sleeveless, out of which Nina's smooth, well-shaped limbs protruded like a doll's from a party dress. Nina wore it for Hector and tried hard not to feel it a badge of servitude.

The gallery was not yet full. Hector told her she was already a success because a big article had appeared about her in one of the glossies. He did not seem to worry that the article had been written by Connie. 'Life is about chance,' he had said, adding with a wink, 'It's not what you know but who you know.'

Helen said – sharp, not so little Helen, who had been allowed out of school for the occasion, 'Oh, Mummy, they're beautiful!' She stood in the middle of the empty gallery, apparently basking in the pictures, revolving slowly from one to the other.

Nina watched her with a strange mix of emotions. 'But, darling, you've seen them all before.' She hesitated. Perhaps she hadn't. Sometimes she forgot her own secrecy, her need to separate herself. At any rate, Helen had not heard her remark or at least did not react.

'They look wonderful hung,' said Veronica, in more neutral tones.

That was it, thought Nina, the hanging, the *vernissage*, they must be finished if they were hanging around the walls like this on public display, framed, cast off. No more dabs, no more scraping off, no more painting over the corner that filled her with dismay. This was it, this was what she had created: sixteen paintings of an apple tree, ten paintings of a dead frog and eight of a field – or, rather, a small portion of a field. Thirty-four paintings and I am thirty-four years old.

'Champagne for you, darling.' Hector came whispering in her ear, glass in his hand. Why, oh, why did she still have (or not have) Hector? 'Wine for the punters.' Hector looked like a modern angel, shiny waves of hair, a wide-shouldered, narrow-hipped, flared-trousered white suit. The place, she knew, would soon be full of his lovers, he had told her so, told her not to be concerned, they were all very ex.

Nina had wondered at his conceit, that he should think his sexual prowess would be of any interest to her when her pictures were being shown to the world. And yet when he had left her to welcome those arriving, she found herself childishly estimating who of these slim and glamorous young swingers Hector had taken to bed. She gulped her champagne and took Helen by the hand. 'Do you mind if we stand outside?'

Helen did mind. 'But I want to watch people looking at your paintings.'

Nina took her mother's arm then, but Veronica, although saying nothing, seemed resistant. It appeared that she, too, was determined to stand among her daughter's critics.

Nina went out on to the pavement, attempting to look invisible. One of her teachers from college, an old man, bent and greying in the service of art, though dressed in the traditionally romantic uniform of flowing necktie and pouchy jacket, put his arm round Nina, who jumped as if she really did believe in her invisibility. This was Hector's world.

'Agony. Agony,' sympathised the greybeard. 'I have red spots in my pocket if things become too desperate.'

'Red spots?' Confusion spread through Nina's assumed blankness. Was he ill?

'Stickers to indicate sales. I always do it for my friends. Gets things going. Success begets success.'

'But, then, surely a real buyer thinks they're sold.'

'A mistake has been made, you say. Easy enough. Peel them off in a trice. Besides, best to put them on the least good. Tricks of the trade. Not that you'll have any need I'm sure.' Patting her on the back, the elderly painter bounced into the gallery, leaving Nina consumed by new anguish. What if none of her pictures sold? How could she have been so naïve not to have focused on this aspect before, fearful only of reactions from the art world, of notices favourable or unfavourable, of entering the public domain? But now she saw she was to be judged by financial success.

'Sold anything yet?' It was true, then. The first person to ask her anything asked her this. The art world seemed filled with such energetic people, who made her feel absurdly immobile and tongue-tied.

'I'm afraid I don't know.'

'I like them, incidentally, particularly the apple tree. It is an apple tree, I assume?'

Surprised by the question, Nina nodded.

'I thought so. Well, you're very brave, then. Neither pop nor abstract nor even expressionist but something in between. Well, well. I shall come back another time when I can have a calmer look.'

'Thank you.' Nina watched his retreat down the pavement until he was crossed by William advancing purposefully. Who had invited him? Helen? Certainly Helen. Nina realised that this longed-for day was actually a nightmare. She began to shake and saw, with some relief, Felicity at William's elbow. Felicity turned him into a human being, made it absolutely clear he was only one woman's husband.

'I hope you don't mind us coming.' Felicity kissed Nina. 'We were just so curious we couldn't resist. Lyndon's come too. You know he's doing an art course?'

Curiosity seemed all too true a reason for their visit, as if they had heard she had turned into a monster with a second head and wished to inspect it, while William's continuing silence (probably ordained by Felicity so he wouldn't put a foot in it) gave an increased weight to his presence. She always forgot his extreme good looks, which seemed to increase as he grew older. Perhaps it was remarkable that she had never found him sexy. Or was she misremembering the past?

Shaking, Nina pointed to the gallery door, and in turning herself into a signpost gained a little courage. 'Do go in. I'm just getting a little air.' Resolutely, she avoided the appeal in William's blue eyes as he passed her. Why did he always do that to her? Felicity squeezed her arm reassuringly as they went.

'Sweet Jesus! And where do you think you're off to? By Jesus, you're running away!' Connie's voice, fake Irish at top pitch, reached Nina before she saw her, and not only her but Fay.

They came together, kissed, hugged. 'Oh, Fay. You're so amazing. I never expected—'

'Hold on a minute. Did you expect me to leave you to the mercy of this Irish desperado here or, worse still, to Hector? What sort of friend would I be?'

'Don't. Please. The whole place is awash with his sexy young girls. But how could you leave Ted?'

'Remember, I'm a retired surgeon now,' said Fay, not answering the question but with a smile that gave the answer more certainly than any words.

'Don't you think she looks a mite smug?' said Connie. 'Come on! I hear there's a passable show on in this gallery!'

1975

Connie had a letter from Orlando Partridge with a greater note of urgency than usual:

> Not a day passes when I do not think of you. I am now more businessman than poet. Please take pity and come on a visit. Even my father is eager to meet you. My friend, Brendan, at the Lir Arms, who I may have mentioned before, recommends the following poem as one of my best:
>
> > Orlando Partridge
> > Bottles water
> > From his spring.
> > But however much money
> > He makes, it never takes
> > Away his sadness
> > Because he thinks
> > Only of Connie O'Malley

For a disconcerting moment, the poem reminded Connie of the grotesque tortures of the ancient Hubert with his 'fine fettle kettle'. But then she looked at the word 'businessman' and took heart. She knew already that Orlando was selling bottled spring water, an idea so filled with images of grace and rebirth that she could hardly believe he had not made it up especially to win her. He had written, with childlike glee, that he was ahead of the game, with few takers, but soon he would rival Perrier.

Connie flew to Dublin and took a taxi to Lir. Since it was April it was still light when she arrived, but a wild wind rocked the sign of the Lir Arms on which were painted a quantity of swans who seemed about to take flight. As Connie stood watching them, an old man stumbled out. 'You're wise to watch them,' he said. 'There's many a day I've had to pull my hat down over my nose or they'd have the eyes out of my head.' Bent double, he hurried away.

Connie did not laugh but went quickly inside. She was a stranger to Westmeath, the lush green of the fields she had passed through unknown to her, the glimpse of silken smooth lake. She had grown up in a harsher land where the grass was bedded in rock not soil, where the

183

presence of the ocean, unseen though it was, gave the wind and rains a salty scorching quality.

'Is there a Brendan here?' Connie was conscious as she entered the bar, with its dark beams, thick smoky atmosphere and all-male clientele, that her accent reflected her long absence from Ireland, a good deal of English plus a little American. Her enquiry, directed to the young man pulling the Guinness, was met by complete silence. Connie realised she had forgotten the shyness of the rural Irish, the reserve that was the opposite side of the famous gift of the gab. Her question had been just too crudely intrusive. She moved from doorway to bar, parting the dozen or so drinkers as if she were the plague.

After a short pause, the young man leant forward, confidentially. 'I'm himself.'

'You're Brendan?'

'That's right.' He lowered his voice further for there was still total silence in the room behind them: 'And you must be Connie O'Malley.'

'I am that!' cried Connie, before lowering her own voice, 'And can you direct me to him?' She found herself unable to pronounce his name.'

'I can. Although, to be sure, he could be in at any time.'

'No, no. I wish to seek him out.' Connie knew she was living a fairy story, and for the story to unravel properly she needed to follow the thread to the end. So Brendan gave her instructions. 'And I can leave my case here?'

The wild night suited Connie. She unbound her long hair, and let it fly out. The wind was not cold or rain-bearing. She turned left across the grassy square and found the narrow road that led into the dark countryside. The wind blew from behind, pushing her forward. The stars and a bright half-moon lit her way enough for her to see the hedge bordering a field on her right. Only one car passed, reminding her that Ireland, even in this prosperous central area, was nothing like as developed as England.

So Connie dashed forward, the words of 'Danny Boy' in her head, looking for lights and the two carved-stone bottles that Brendan had described as indications of Orlando Partridge's driveway. She must also be prepared for barking dogs but not be affeared because, although wolfhounds, they were as gentle as lambs.

The bottles were obvious, set like lampstands with bright bulbs at the top. Expecting a dilapidated castle, Connie was surprised to find a short, newly tarmacked drive and at the end a modern bungalow, light glaring from its broad windows. She rang the bell, which played a short snatch of 'Danny Boy'. It was fate.

Orlando Partridge opened the door. He wore a suit that was rather too small for him and smoked a cigar. They both stared. Orlando took out the cigar and threw it past Connie to the grass beyond.

'My darling.' He held open his arms.

Sighing, Connie entered them. He smelt of cigar, sweat, peat and bacon. 'This is grand,' she said, gasping.

'You are grand! Now I shall look after you for ever. Come and share my supper. It is Mrs Murphy's soda bread, bacon from Mr Murphy's pig, named Kathleen—'

'Not Kathleen,' protested Connie, removing herself from his grasp. 'And do you have a tot of whiskey?'

'A tot! I have a gallon.'

It was nervousness that sat them on either side of the ugly modern hearth (though it did burn peat), with a glass on the arm of their chairs and the wolfhounds, Sodom and Gomorrah, at their feet.

'You find me in a bungalow,' began Orlando, scanning Connie's face, 'because I am a little richer and can afford to live a life independent of my father and the ruinous pile he inhabits.'

Connie listened as he told her more about his new world. He laid himself at her feet and she listened, eyes on his face except when she stared into her glass and took another hefty gulp. Learning was hard work. It would have been easier to fall into his arms as she had used to do with men she loved, and then there was the question of when her turn would come. He knew so little of her. He reached the end (she assumed) of his early narrative, which included the death of his mother on his tenth birthday, a long retelling of the story of Lir, which had occurred on the very lake where his family home was situated, and the inspiration that had driven him to start bottling Lir water. Although, of course, it came from a spring. 'A holy spring.' He rubbed his rather protuberant eyes, which were already pink and becoming pinker. 'Mrs Murphy's daughter, Aisling, had a bad case of chicken-pox, spots like the plague all across her face and upper body.' He paused. 'Did you know, my dove, my treasure, that the reason the Duke of Wellington fell out of love with his fiancée, Kitty Pakenham, who lived not many miles from here, was that she suffered from smallpox while he was slashing the enemy at Torres Vedras and was disfigured?' He paused again.

'Would you love me if I were disfigured?' Connie raised her head.

185

He stood up then. 'As Oscar Wilde answered in a court of law, "True art can never be obscene," so you, my darling, can never be disfigured.'

'Thank you,' said Connie wearily. 'I left my case at the Lir Arms. I think, I think . . .'

'You are worn out. Major decisions don't half take it out of one.' Tenderly, he lifted her up, took her to a large bedroom, papered incongruously with a pattern of elves and fairies. Otherwise it was Spartan, the bed neatly made, and this, above all, gave her hope. His words might be rambling but his habits were neat. Two people with the habits of gypsies would be out of the question. 'I will make you a sandwich, and if you need the bathroom, it is adjoining. You will rest while I fetch your things. Sodom and Gomorrah will accompany me. Remember, we have time.' Kissing her cheek, he retreated to the kitchen. When he returned with the sandwich, Connie had fallen asleep and didn't hear the front door open and close.

At dawn, Connie woke to rain scattering over glass, to wind flapping curtains, to the steady breathing of someone at her side. She knew the room was light but she kept her eyes closed with contradictory emotions of delight and terror. She and Orlando Partridge had slept together all night long like children. She put out her hand. Yes, it was him, naked. 'Orlando.' This was the first time she had pronounced his name. It felt absurd and made her want to giggle. He turned to her and put an arm over her waist. It was heavier than she would have expected and held her comfortably.

'Good morning.' His voice was sleepy but conversational. She opened her eyes and saw his curls, his face, eyes still closed.

'Darling.'

'Yes.' He opened his eyes briefly, before shutting them again, as if dazed. 'Is it tea you're wanting?'

Could it be that she had got the wrong end of the stick and he did not desire her body but merely wished to look after her as an ornament? For once, she regretted her beauty. Doubt, in Connie's case, always led to confrontation. 'Darling, I want to tell you something, show you something.'

'Yes. Yes.' He seemed abstracted, although now fully awake. Without warning he got out of bed, and walked naked out of the room.

Connie thought how beautiful he looked – he was beautiful in his unselfconsciousness – but he had left her and she felt tears ready to roll. He put his head round the door. The dogs, who had been shut away during the night, jostled at his feet.

'I had planned for so long, so very many nearly unending years, how to wake you on our first morning but I never thought I would oversleep.' A moment later she heard the sound of a cello, Bach or something earlier. She lay back and listened and thought that, however much Orlando Partridge loved her, it was clear that he was determined to take control. She smiled.

He returned, still naked, clasping his bow to his chest. 'I am your cello, you are my bow.'

'I hope you've got a sense of humour,' said Connie, but only with the intention to amuse. She knew he had a sense of humour and everything else she wanted. 'And now can we make love?'

It turned out that they could although, as Orlando pointed out, making love with someone you wished to spend the rest of your life with was a very different matter from anything of that nature that might have gone before and care and consideration were the watchwords, so that the beast would not lose sight of the man – or vice versa.

'I love you!' cried Connie, giggling weakly.

'That is the main point,' agreed Orlando seriously.

'Bewitched, bothered and bewildered,' sang Connie, stumping down a grassy track, a stream on one side, a wood on the other and the dogs foraging beside them. She stopped and listened. 'Jesus and Mary, a cuckoo.'

Orlando took her arm. 'We have everything here. Everything you could want.' He dropped her arm and pulled a cigar from his pocket, gave it a quick glance and then flung it into a thicket.

'That was a good cigar.'

'I only smoked them because I didn't have you. You are my only love. As I was saying, I wish to provide you with your every heart's desire.'

'I was impressed by the boots,' admitted Connie, looking at her feet. She would not tell him he had chosen boots too small for her, boots for a fairy, boots for a child. She had not told him either about Kathleen, although he had touched her scar wonderingly. For a while a horror had taken hold of her, not that she had had one child but that maybe she could not have another. It had passed now as they marched out into the countryside.

'You have to see my work,' he told her, like a boy proud of himself. And it seemed odd to her that his work was down this mossy path but no odder or more wonderful than everything else.

The house stood just above the shoreline of the lake, a great granite building, silhouetted against the waters, which merged slowly with the sky, white-tipped waves rippling into the edges like an inland sea. To their left a newly built road cut through the soft green land, a ribbon of wood and, nearer the lake's edge, marshland dotted with reeds and wild flowers and shrubs.

'The spring is about a hundred yards from the house. I make my workers park their cars the other side of the wood and walk,' said Orlando, with a mixture of pride and apology, 'but of course the lorries have to come down.'

Oh dear, thought Connie, is this not a blot, a sore, a desecration of the landscape? Is not Orlando Partridge at odds with nature? But just before this became too awful to contemplate, she remembered why she had fled her home in County Mayo. There it had been nature winning the battle against man, reducing her father to silent, sodden defeat, her mother to bitter frustration. There had been love, too, but that only survived despite nature's harsh dictatorship.

'I think it's a gorgeous sight!' cried Connie.

'And we employ men and women, incidentally, who've never been employed before. The day we opened, the bishop came to bless us and priests of both denominations—' He broke off suddenly not, as Connie first thought, to see her reaction to this startling triumph of ecumenicalism but to point at a figure splashing in the lake.

'My father.'

'Your father!'

They were near enough now to see white hair floating on the waves, wiry arms performing an energetic crawl.

'He swims every day. He is seventy-eight but will live for a century, I expect. He used to be too old to be my father and now he is too young.'

Connie squeezed Orlando's arm comfortingly. 'Sure you're the most generous man I've ever had the acquaintance of.'

He looked at her without understanding.

They took out an old row-boat on the lake and when they reached Mr Partridge, Orlando raised an oar, quivering in the air, drops flying away, and shouted, 'Father, this is Connie!'

And Connie sat upright in the stern thinking, This is one man I'm not going to charm, seduce or otherwise beguile. He will be my father-in-law and he can take me or leave me.

'Good morning,' gulped Mr Partridge, treading water. Connie realised that Orlando, not quite so generous, was glad to be performing this introduction from on high with baton aloft.

'Good morning,' replied Connie, and she bit back the voice that would have cried, 'I admire you so for swimming in that ice-cold water.' A smile would suffice. So they rowed on, and round a curl in the shoreline they found a group of swans, so white and wild and beautiful that they were inspired to lay down the oars and let the boat drift as they clasped their arms tight round each other.

On the shoreline, the wolfhounds galloped up and down barking as if they feared they would go the way of the cigar.

Connie wrote to Nina:

Darling, dearest Nina, Orlando and I are to be married on June 21st (the longest day). It is a miracle. I am applying to the Pope for it to be officially recognised as such. Please come. You cannot have forgotten him. We met him on our visit to Cork. Dear Father O'Donald, even though he's so grand now, is presiding and darling Orlando is receiving a crash course in Catholicism from Father Murphy, the priest here in Lir who approves of everything about him, except that he bottles water not whiskey. Tell me, what is this phantom of delight that has taken hold of me? Love and love again. I have enough love now to fill the world. I am exhaling love.

And to Fay:

My darling, like you, I am to be married. Who would have thought we would both be so old-fashioned? I am abandoning my book about sex and the under-sixteens – such a dull subject – to write either about Maria Edgeworth, a nineteenth-century Irish novelist, a true feminist, or about Blessed Oliver Plunkett, whose name was borrowed by my aunt, the holy nun and martyr ... I have one request of you, dearest Fay ...

'Is Connie serious?' Fay had called Nina from New York.

'As far as Connie can be serious.' Nina rethought. Was this the sour taste of jealousy in her mouth? 'Of course she's serious.'

'And she assumed I'm marrying Ted. But I don't expect I shall. I'm not at all sure that I believe in marriage and I certainly don't believe in giving up my name for someone else's.'

'But you will go to Connie's wedding?' Nina could not control the wistfulness in her voice.

'We want to but whether we can is another matter.' Nina noticed the confident 'we'. 'If only to meet her parents and whatever other family she chooses to invite. I must admit I am curious to see this Irish bog family she so despises. Incidentally, I have been delegated to take the news to Kevin and Shirley.'

'Ah. But surely they won't come to the wedding?'

'I guess not.' There was a pause.

'How are your offices, consulting rooms, clients coming along?' asked Nina, who was feeling an offputting briskness in Fay's tone. Probably she was phoning from her office.

'Good to all three. If I were a businessman, I'd say I'd picked a growth market. Nobody wants their X-rays read in some hospital annexe. I give them personalised treatment.

Nina thought she sounded like a businessman and waited to be asked about her painting, about her mother, about her children but, most of all, about Hector. The absent Hector.

'I'll let you know our plans as soon as possible,' said Fay.

Fay took Ted with her to Washington.

'Heavens, it's cherry-blossom time yet again!' she exclaimed, as their taxi took them past the white monuments to Georgetown.

Kevin, successful in all political situations, had extended his business interests even further since Nixon's resignation. Now he seemed to own a good chunk of Virginia. Mysteriously Ted, the doorman and music student, got on extremely well with Kevin. Ted explained that powerful men driven by ambition always liked him because they sensed he posed no threat. Fay wondered if that was why she liked him too. No, on the whole, she thought it was his reserve she liked. In many ways, he was still the stranger. She had nearly said to Nina, 'I couldn't take a stranger's name.'

'I have a surprise for you.' Shirley opened the door herself. She looked as near dishevelled as was possible, given her expensive clothes. 'I hope it won't upset you. I hope, on the contrary, you'll share my excitement.'

Fay followed her into the hall, Ted close behind. She realised how much she distrusted surprises. She had come here to talk about Connie, not to receive surprises. She thought she'd never received a good surprise in her life. She grabbed Ted's arm and suspected that his presence in her life was sapping her bravery. They went upstairs to the nursery, which struck Fay as odd since Kathleen was now over five.

Shirley opened the door and began to talk very fast. 'She's a Vietnam orphan, as you can probably guess. The old story, soldier father comes back home, mother dies, child abandoned. Tara, well, she was called Ba then, had just been picked up from the streets when we found her. She's actually three, although she looks half that age. Kathleen's already taught her some words, haven't you, darling? Kathleen's the best teacher any sister could have.'

The two girls sat together on the floor dressing a very large black doll. 'Skirt,' announced Kathleen, proving her mother's point.

'Skirt,' repeated Tara, and both little girls smiled proudly.

'Excuse me a moment, I need the bathroom,' said Fay.

'That's Auntie Fay,' she heard Kathleen say as she fled.

Tara couldn't be Daniel's child. That was perfectly obvious because she would have been born two years before his death and Daniel would have made proper provision. He had been that sort of person. Hadn't he? The child looked hardly western, just a heavier set to her face and more open eyes. But her hair was black, her eyes plum-coloured, no Aryan blondness anywhere. She could have been Daniel's daughter, her skin as pale. Fay began to cry and, having begun, could not stop.

Ted knocked on the door. 'We're all going for a walk. We'll go slow to give you time to catch up.'

Gradually, Fay recovered and found, as her face stiffened with drying salt tears, that instead of the miserable waste of Daniel's death she was thinking of the two little girls, of Ted's kind message. She pulled a strip of lavatory paper to blow her nose and rose to follow the rest of them.

Fay walked arm in arm with Shirley. As Ted went ahead with the children, she told Shirley about Connie's marriage.

'The O'Malleys are a strange clan,' Shirley told her. 'When you think what they've come from, a little hut in a bog in the middle of nowhere, I suppose it's not surprising. There's one sister who seems OK, although she's got far too many children for even my Catholic tastes. We've been corresponding a little, although of course I would never tell her about Kathleen. Then there's the drunk in the north of England. Somewhere, the one who's disappeared – Kevin seems quite vague about his name, beyond saying he used to want to be a priest. And Kevin himself isn't exactly straightforward.' Fay saw she was the sort of wife who believed the marriage vows included a one hundred per cent non-critical clause and looked away tactfully. The object of her visit had been achieved. She could tell Connie at her wedding that Kathleen would not be coming to her wedding.

Nina received a telephone call from Ireland. 'I need you. I can't see them on my own. I'm terrified. You understand . . .' Nina recognised Connie's pleading passion from crisis points over the years.

She remonstrated, although she knew it was hopeless, 'Surely you should see your parents for the first time in nearly twenty years with Orlando. Your future husband.'

'In the world of my dreams, I should. But it would be an Old Testament disaster. Darling, Orlando's a Protestant.'

'But he isn't. He's converted. You told me.'

'Conversion!' Connie gave a wild cackle. 'Don't you remember my brother Kevin's experience? No further contact because he'd married a Protestant. And she converted too. To people like my family, once a Protestant always a Protestant. Furthermore, all Anglo-Irish are Protestants whatever they might believe. I must go back first as a pure Catholic virgin. Then I can introduce the subject of marriage *à la* Partridge.'

'Then why don't you take your sister?'

'My sister thinks I'm a whore!' Connie shrieked.

'But you liked her.'

'She sniffed out my pregnancy in the state of unwedness. Please come!'

It was early May. Nina could see her mother weeding in the garden, flinging great hanks of ground elder behind her, like a badger flings out earth and stone. She had hoped to paint until just before the wedding.

'I'm a Protestant.'

'At least you're a woman. On the other hand I could invite Fay. Jews are so far removed from my parents' life, they'd probably assume she's a direct descendant of Jesus.'

'OK. I'll come.' Nina couldn't help noticing that she had felt herself in competition with Fay for Connie's attention.

'Oh, my God! Oh, my God! Oh, my God!' Connie was ashen, dressed entirely in black.

'Anyone would think you were going to a funeral,' said Nina. She was driving Orlando's car, which at first had seemed unwilling to leave home, stalling at every crossing, but now had the bit between its teeth and only responded to the brake after prolonged pressure.

Nina found she was happy to be in Ireland. Orlando was eccentric but impressive, his father merely eccentric. Sympathetic though she was to Connie's almost catatonic state of terror as they drove towards County Mayo, her heart beat cheerily. Its refrain: 'To hell with Hector.'

She had said a truly final goodbye a few weeks earlier and found, to her surprise, that the pain she had expected had not materialised. Her mother, assessing the situation, commented smugly, 'I always knew you didn't love him.' Nina decided not to speak. How would she know whether she loved him or not?

Connie held a map but it trembled between her fingers. 'I should not need a map to find my home. It should be written on my heart!' she cried passionately, and unwound the window with the look of someone who planned to vomit out of it.

'Like Eleanor of Aquitaine,' agreed Nina hastily, hoping to divert her to the general.

'I don't know what Aquitaine's got to do with County Mayo,' said Connie irritably. But she withdrew her head and rolled up the window. It was raining, of course, the June landscape shining an electric green, the granite cottages, churches, ruins, darkened almost to black.

'What time are they expecting us?'

'My brother Michael wrote back. His hand was small and cramped. I expect he's left-handed or perhaps he's mentally retarded. Why else would he have stayed? Maybe he's holding my parents hostage. O Mother of Mercy, take pity on your humble servant!'

They continued to drive. The radio played one station only, which favoured Irish jigs. The rain thinned, which was just as well since the wiper in front of Nina was no longer working. Connie cheered up and announced it was time for lunch. Nina thought that translated as time for a drink and wondered whether a true friend would point out the dangers of reliance on alcohol. But Connie had drunk too much for as long as Nina had known her. Besides, she had Orlando to look after her now.

They drank Guinness in an empty bar, which could produce no food at all except, after much searching, a small packet of stale cheese biscuits. 'Guinness is a food,' announced Connie.

As they were leaving, the young barman ran after them with a tin of Spam, which he pushed through the window. 'That would be a culinary feast,' called Connie, 'if we had an opener.' But this seemed beyond her admirer.

'We're in a third-world country. Progress comes dropping slow. My dearest Orlando Partridge is the future. This Spam represents the past.' She hurled the tin out of the window. Nina, through the rear-view mirror, saw it explode and lie in two halves.

'A voice from the past!' cried Connie. They ate it greedily, using two stones as utensils while Connie, between mouthfuls, suggested that, owing to the high rainfall and low population, Ireland was the only

193

clean third-world country. The sun came out. Nina went to the car for her map and came back with her sketch-book. They had stopped about a hundred yards from an abandoned cottage. Nina sat on the remains of a wall while Connie settled into a window-ledge and fell asleep. The silence, apart from birds and insects, was absolute.

Nina found she was holding her breath. She knew that the sleeping Connie with the overgrown tumbling-down cottage was the right subject for a new series of paintings. An urgent energy took hold of her because in a short time Connie would awake and demand to be carried on her way. Her apple-tree series had relied on a static and easily accessible subject, but here she must rely on the information that she could assimilate in a short space of time. She must record not only the sight but the sounds of bees, flies, butterflies, emerged in their masses after the long downpour and now celebrating the hot sun. Frantically, Nina drew. Just as frantically, she took notes.

Silence – no cars although only a few yards from the road. Very hot – although rain so heavy and so recent. Insects flying, crawling, hovering, sucking, sipping. Air buzzing, humming, moving. Birds shrilling, carolling, piercing, darting, swooping, plunging, flirting. Leaves opening, standing up, draining, drying, shining, greening. Flowers brightening, brandishing yet delicate and detailed. Fuchsia. Buttercup. Sage. Nettle. Wild rose. Elder. Daisy. Dandelion. Cow parsley. Grass everywhere, long, flowering, sharp, whippy, flash. Sound incorporated into sight, rising outwards in a shimmering movement like a fountain or a spray. The ruins of the cottage both more solid than dazzling nature, but also, in its tumbledown state, far less. A comment on the passing things of man, his creations more vulnerable to time than a single red bell flower trembling on the fuchsia bush, which reproduces itself every year in effortless triumph. And yet, as if to contradict all this, there was Connie – behold Connie! Unbelievably beautiful, a modern fairytale princess with her white skin and her black dress. Tranquil, at home. Happy and glorious. Asleep. Zipper scar forgotten, awaiting her prince. Imprinting sophisticated hope on the ramshackle cottage behind her.

Nina scribbled, not worried if it was rubbish, became red from the piercing new sun and hardly noticed when Connie awoke and came towards her.

'On the road!' Nina cried affectionately, gathering papers, pencils, crayons. 'Or we'll be benighted.'

'It stays light for hours in June in the West of Ireland.' Connie smiled. Her sleep seemed to have calmed her and she showed no curiosity about how Nina had spent the time.

The countryside was bathed in a blue light. Nina switched on the car lights then switched them off again, preferring to drive without. The landscape was no longer lush and the abandoned cottages now stood among peat bog or barren rocky earth. The road had more pot-holes than ever and the wild flowers a pinched, careworn look. Connie had the same wan appearance and when she had asked to stop in a village Nina had assumed she was looking for a bar. Instead she had walked to a church. On her reappearance she had commented, 'To abandon your parents and your child takes some forgiving.'

The blueness, like a filter changing the tone of every colour, was a relief, a disguising veil of an unpaved track. At the start of it, Connie asked Nina to stop the car and was sick behind a gorse bush.

'I remember that gorse bush,' she said, returning. 'I used to try to sniff it. I thought it smelt like honey – not that I'd ever tasted honey. But now I think it smells like sex and, God knows, I've had enough of that.'

'Connie, you've come to tell them you're getting married.'

'What's certainly true is that you get pierced with whacking long thorns if you get too close.' She paused, stared ahead. 'There's Michael standing at the door!' Her voice had suddenly lifted as if the sight of her brother gave her hope. 'He's in his best clothes. Oh, Nina, please make it be all right!'

Connie walked boldly up to Michael. She walked like a scarlet woman dressed in black. He smiled at her, a bewildered, pleased smile. Connie thought all her prayers had been answered.

'We guessed you'd be coming,' said Michael solemnly.

'What?' Connie was surprised. She'd written, of course, but he seemed to mean something else.

'With Ma ill. She prayed to Our Lady of Knock.' It seemed someone else's prayers had been answered. 'She's inside now, awaiting your homecoming. Better than any doctor, she said.' Forgetting Nina, tactfully still in the car, Connie followed him in.

Her father stood just inside the door. He had seemed so old to her when a child that he seemed hardly more bent or withered now.

''Lo, Connie.' He looked down in that way she remembered, a way of avoiding the world, admitting defeat, the way that had made her

195

determined to leave lest she caught the habit. And yet, she thought, Michael – standing at her elbow – had looked her in the eye; he was straight enough. Perhaps there were changes. Certainly the house, although basically the same, was garishly lit with an overhead light.

'What's wrong with her? I didn't know.'

This seemed to silence her father who turned his back to lead through to the bedroom.

'It's her lungs,' said Michael. 'We believed Eileen had given you the information.'

'No. I didn't know.' They entered the bedroom. The curtains were different, bright pink and blue, there was a bit of carpet on the floor, a shiny yellow eiderdown on the bed.

'Connie, oh, Connie!' Connie knelt beside her mother, tiny, white frizzled hair, seamed grey face, and wept. They both wept. The men stood at the door, hands in their pockets, watching.

Nina, entering timidly, found Michael putting on the kettle. There was a new-looking electric ring and a sink with a new geyser above it.

'You're Connie's friend, then?' Michael was handy with the kettle.

'I drove her here. I'm English.'

'All the way from England?' He seemed to be ironic.

'I didn't drive all the way from England.' He didn't ask any more questions but concentrated on laying out tea on the table. After he'd boiled the water he put bacon and potatoes into a frying pan. Nina tried to help but he seemed self-sufficient. She remembered Connie's stories of the Irishman's reluctance to marry. 'It's a natural form of birth control,' she'd said, 'although more to do with shyness than anything.'

'Do you live here?'

'I've a fine bungalow in the village. But I'm here each day for the meal and the peat.'

Connie reappeared supporting her mother, who was wrapped in a heavy wool dressing-gown, probably a man's. 'This is my friend Nina,' she announced. 'You must love her, even though she's English. She's an artist, a painter. If you ask her nicely, she might sit you down for a likeness.'

'We're grateful to you for bringing her,' said Mrs O'Malley. Connie's abasement had vanished. She sat elbow to elbow with her mother and Nina recognised that, behind the sickness, Mrs O'Malley was strong after all.

'Bless us, O Lord, and these our gifts, and may the Lord make us truly thankful,' said Connie, smiling.

'Amen,' murmured Mrs O'Malley.

Nina thought that Connie's power of emotion, so often used in self-destructive ways, was now carrying her firmly forward.

Connie was filled with love. She felt her mother's love for her, an old woman's love that expected no change out of the world and would accept what was offered. Her brother accepted her, too, although in his case, he seemed to be dealing with her absence as if it had never happened. There was no curiosity in his manner. She had most dreaded meeting her father, awaiting the righteously pointing finger: 'Our Father, who art in heaven ... forgive us our trespasses ...' She had been prepared to be penitent, to try to win him round with her rediscovered Catholicism (although she had always felt his attitude more pagan than Christian, bred in the unforgiving nature of the land he worked). But this man, although his looks had not changed but merely become more exaggerated, seemed too shadowy to be angry. It crossed her mind that perhaps the obstinate rage she had recognised in him as a child served her own purpose by giving her an excuse to escape. She had wanted him to be angry: it was better than having a broken man as a father. But now she could love them all. Oh, Orlando Partridge, you have made this possible!

After supper, Michael brought out the whiskey bottle and they poured a celebratory tot, while Mr O'Malley, not quite changed, looked away. Even his wife sipped, raising spots of red to her cheeks.

'I am getting married,' Connie stood to make the announcement, 'to a man from Meath. He is called Orlando Partridge.'

'What sort of name is that?' The whiskey had made Michael more loquacious. ''Tis not an Irish name to be sure.'

'It is not, you are in the right. But it is the name for me. You may all come to our wedding and judge for yourself what sort of man he is.' Connie looked into her mother's face, and her mother put her wrinkled old hand over Connie's white one.

Nina, sipping her whiskey, felt like a witness at a contract as binding as marriage. She tried to remind herself of Connie's independence, her battling feminism but it seemed, for the moment at least, that Connie was determined to follow a very different kind of agenda.

Fay sent a wedding present to Connie with an apology for her absence; it was five years' subscription to the *New York Review of Books*, the book review section of the *New York Times* and *New York* magazine. 'DON'T FORGET US,' she typed in bold.

When they began to arrive a month or two after the wedding, Connie used them to line the wolfhounds' baskets; they had been banished to a cold and distant shed.

A few weeks later she informed Orlando that she had given up her book on Maria Edgeworth since she was part of the wicked Ascendancy, and was starting research on that Irish heroine, the Pirate Queen, Grany Imallye, or in other words Grace O'Malley, known in sixteenth-century English records as 'a most famous feminine sea captain' and, without doubt, her own glorious ancestor.

Orlando was encouraging, although honesty compelled him to remind her that he, himself, was part of the wicked Ascendancy.

The snow was falling so heavily, hardly a space between the flakes, that Nina wondered if William would get through to the house.

Jamie was asleep, snoring slightly, his face less flushed than before and his limbs relaxed. Nina watched him closely then turned to her mother, whose attention was on a piece of tapestry. Carefully, she pulled through a piece of cherry-coloured wool.

'I'm going outside for a moment.'

'You do that, darling. Wrap up warm.'

For a moment Nina stood at the doorway, letting the whiteness surround her. When she stepped out it was as if she stood on a new canvas with white paint falling all around her. She watched the flakes settle on her scarf and coat, which were brilliantly mismatched, orange and green, brown and red. She supposed, if she stood still long enough, the colours would be overpainted by white and she would disappear into the blank canvas.

My God! The thought struck her with full impact for the first time. Jamie might have died. He might have been wiped out altogether, his delicate boy's body reduced to nothing. She felt herself begin to shake as if the snow had penetrated through all her wrappings and surrounded her heart.

'Nina! Nina!'

She had shut her eyes, sunk back into the canvas. William was shaking and tugging at her arm. 'Please, Nina. How is he? Is he worse?'

She opened her eyes. He was ridiculous in his London off-duty army uniform, overcoat, brown trilby, snow shoes. 'Oh, William, oh, William, darling. He's all right! He's recovered. It really was pneumonia, not death at all!' In that moment as they hugged and comforted and celebrated, she felt more love for him than she had through their ten years of marriage. As they broke apart, laughing, crying, still arm in arm, she asked, 'But how ever did you arrive like that? Out of nowhere? Or did I miss the helicopter drop?'

'I stopped the car in the drive. I knew I'd never get down it. You should get it cleared, you know, or it will freeze hard.'

His voice, reproving, the voice of good sense and authority, immediately reminded Nina of how he always managed to squeeze the life out of her. But she would not let him douse her happiness so easily.

'And have you left Felicity freezing in the car?'

'Felicity is busy. She sends you her regards and best wishes for Jamie's swift recovery.' Again, that heavy hand of criticism.

'Well, her best wishes have been answered, thanks to glorious antibiotics.' Gaily, she led him in, smiled only a little falsely at him again as she felt his emotion in the old house. What, after all, could she accuse him of except being himself, which was not the person she wanted? With a mixture of shock and fear, she realised that his mere presence at her side, as they passed the cloakroom, had touched the anxious growth of whatever sent her to wash and wash and wash.

'Darling William.' She repeated the affectionate word to reinstate it as the truth. He would never be her husband again but as they stood on either side of their son's bed, they could be loving parents.

Connie watched the scar down her abdomen slowly grow pink and widen. She wanted to be filled with joy but a question grew more insistent: how could Orlando refrain from asking the history now?

'I've always wanted to walk the whole way round the lake.' It was winter, but an Irish winter, soft and mild. Orlando had a huge new order for his bottled water and had bought a new second-hand suit which, in its baggy comfort, made Connie feel like crying. The bungalow was too small for them and what would it be like for three? Connie spread her books on Grace O'Malley around an abandoned ice-cold room in the big house. The book would have to go on hold.

'I've never walked the lake's circumference.' Orlando stroked her naked arm meditatively. 'There's a fine old bar half-way round with ale like you've never tasted and a room at the back I shouldn't be surprised. We'll leave Sodom and Gomorrah to babysit my father. I could carry my cello on my back and serenade you after nightfall.'

'I just want to walk,' Connie had not felt much like drinking recently, which had only happened to her once before in her life.

Connie felt herself sucked down into the boggy ground as if the soil was only an unsteady disguise for the lake. She put her hand into Orlando's and their boots squelched in syncopation. How could he continue to worship the ground she walked on (and he did, oh, he did!) when he saw her past turn into a murky swamp? It was a murky swamp even to her, incomprehensible, inexplicable. Could she be both penitent and queen? She thought not. Why had he never sought explanation for the mark of Cain, the fucking zip fastening? Connie fixed her eyes on the plants at her feet writhing under her boots. Perhaps she would tell him the good news first. 'Do you know something incredible?'

'I know *someone* incredible.'

She had always fallen in love with men who flattered her. She supposed it was a weakness of character but, as usual, it gave her heart. 'You haven't guessed?'

'That we are to have a baby?'

She was surprised. So surprised that she stopped still and hit Orlando in the chest. 'Why did you say nothing?'

'I love you. You're my leader. I wanted to hear you tell me.'

'And now you do hear. Really, Orlando, how can you be so secretive?' Puffed up with righteous anger, she heard her own words and began to giggle. 'Oh, darling . . .'

'Well.' He looked at her with uncritical pride. 'Our baby. It's a miracle.'

'You're so Catholic, despite your late conversion.' Connie continued to giggle. 'If you fuck as often as we do . . .' She stopped. 'Make love.' But now she was becoming entangled and, as if motion would help, began to walk towards the lake's edge, her feet sucking in the soft wetness. Love-making could produce babies but so could another kind of sex. He followed her. They stopped again and stared at the expanse of water, a brackish mauve-brown at the edges, deep purple-black in the middle. The black smoothness of it made Connie impatient. 'You know I had a baby before,' she said. She moved even closer to the water so that puddles formed round her feet.

'I know that,' agreed Orlando gently.

'I could not talk of it.'

'You need not now.'

'She was a baby girl. She is a girl. Five years old now. Name, Kathleen. She was adopted at birth. She lives in America. I have no contact with her.'

Orlando moved forward to clasp her. 'That's enough. You don't have to tell me anything. I love you. I love everything about you, everything you've ever done.'

'I had an abortion once and I couldn't bear another, even though the man was nothing to me.' Connie was now in the lake proper, sloshing about, unaware of the absurdity, avoiding Orlando's arms.

'Darling, you don't have to drown although, of course, I'd swim across the lake to save you. Please, say no more. I know you had a baby. I've always known. Your beautiful sacrificial stomach. At first I felt sad about it. I debated whether to ask you. I admit it. It was a shock. Just for a short while. And then it became part of you.' Orlando was in the water too, his face pink with emotion, his arms held out towards her. 'And now we're to have our own baby.'

'Oh, my God.' Without warning, Connie lay down in the lake, the water lapped gently round her body, a few trickles crossed her face. Orlando looked at her for a second then lay down beside her. 'This is the happiest day of my life,' said Connie, taking his hand.

'I'd never have guessed the water would be so warm.'

'It must be another miracle,' murmured Connie.

'Unless it's because we took the precaution of keeping on our clothes.'

1977

There were peacock feathers in the mirror.

'It's bad luck to bring them in, I know,' Connie made a self-excusing face, 'but it's too sad to leave them lying about the lawn. Besides, Leonardo adores being tickled with them. I'm proud to say he's a very silly little boy.'

'Everything about this place is a joy,' said Nina. She saw that Connie was happier than she had ever been and was pleased. Leonardo – the name as near an anagram of Orlando as possible – was a plump little toddler, rather quiet but given to sudden wild giggles, suggesting some inner source of mirth.

Walking down the grassy path that led to the lake with Connie's son wobbling ahead, she thought of Jamie. She had given him all the space he needed and now he was doing his best to disown her. It was retribution, she supposed, for her disowning his father. She suspected that if she were not living with his grandmother, whom he loved, Jamie would choose never to see her. At school, forced to make introductions, he kept his head well down and pronounced 'mother' in such a way that it sounded like 'Maud'. She had once offered him the use of her Christian name, a helpfully distancing process, she had hoped, but he had spurned her irritably, 'Don't be so silly, Mum. You're not my sister!'

Connie interrupted her thoughts. 'How's your work? Another exhibition coming up?'

Connie has chosen Ireland and motherhood, thought Nina, over England and the media. We've done an unexpected role-reversal in the last several years, which makes us uneasy with each other. Now I'm the working woman. Automatically, she thought of Fay who had swapped a vocation for a job and said she was so much happier.

'I won't have another exhibition for at least a year,' she told Connie. It had been six months since her last, not at Hector's gallery. He had been offended, she was glad to recall. She had shown the series of paintings inspired by Connie, sleeping in front of the deserted cottage. She'd sold to two major galleries and her first gallery in America. 'I am slowing up. Sometimes I paint for eight hours a day and have not a satisfactory inch to show for it.' She watched Connie's face lighten a little. It was wise to emphasise her difficulties.

'I've taken up again my book on the admirable Grace O'Malley,' sighed Connie, 'but most of the papers are in London. Do you know she met Queen Elizabeth I as one powerful woman to another? They met at Greenwich in 1593, both elderly by then.' She stopped, as if discouraged by the image. 'Did I tell you we have a house party this weekend?'

'A house party!' Nina was horrified, which made her uncomfortably aware of how reclusive she had become. If she were honest there were only two people she liked even half as much as her own company: Helen and her mother.

'It's the holiday season!' Connie began to walk more briskly. She had glimpsed the sheen of the water between the trees, sniffed the sweet dryness of thyme and sage. 'It only rains once a day, and the lake is warm enough for a swim.'

'I haven't seen Orlando's father?' asked Nina, remembering.

'He's in the bungalow. He much prefers it. He really wants to live in a caravan, but we can't allow it or the Society for the Protection of Nasty Old Men would be on to us. With any luck, he'll die soon.'

'Connie!'

Connie skipped ahead. 'Don't worry,' she called over her shoulder, 'Leonardo goes down and watches children's television with him. He's happier than he's ever been.'

The principal component of the house-party turned out to be an old schoolfriend of Orlando's whom he continued to see because, according to Connie, he was 'so *real*, in other words, boring'. Orlando, on the other hand, informed Nina that he was very clever, although a big fish in a small pond, a solicitor in a country town. 'He works every day,' he added admiringly. Neither of them mentioned that his wife had died of cancer, for fear of suggesting this was a match-making exercise, which indeed it was. The other guests were Connie's sister, Eileen, her husband and their three youngest children.

Connie had lied about the rain. It had not rained for a week and squares of cornfields were dotted yellow among the green. Orlando, who was trying to buy more land with his bottling-factory proceeds, said that he was checking personally on the yield of each field then making an offer the owners couldn't refuse.

'They do refuse,' objected Connie.

'Only as a come-on.'

'You don't understand the Irish at all. They would sell their children before their land and many of them have.'

'Then how do you account for any exchange of ownership?'

'Alcohol, gambling, deceit.'

This argument was interrupted by the arrival of the noisy car and the solicitor – on a motorcycle. He was large for the rather small bike, and since he wore no helmet, his balding head was very obvious. He seemed exhilarated by his ride and hardly responded to introductions. In a moment he had one of Eileen's children on the back. Then Nina found her cumbrous self – she had put on weight again since Hector's departure – with her arms round this tree trunk of a man. They slithered along the grass path, on to the road that had been built for the bottling-factory workers and down to the wood where the last wild garlic plants swamped them in pungent aromas. Eventually, the bike shimmied on one slimy leaf too far and keeled over on its side.

Nina lay where she had fallen, uninjured but unwilling to move. A few yards away, Gus sat up, rubbing his head. His large hand with long slender fingers slid over his skin tenderly. Guiltily, Nina stopped looking. It had been a private gesture, which had led her to imagine other private gestures. The light had become very peculiar, the tree trunks around them a vivid green decorated with silver discs as if marked for some ancient ritual. At the end of the path a wet gleam spilled over from the lake. Nina stared and the air became filled with buzzings and murmurings.

'Sorry,' said Gus, in his very English voice. 'I got carried away. Sitting in an office most of my life leads me to underrate the dangers of freedom. You're not hurt, I trust?'

'Oh, no. Is your bike?'

'I'm an admirer of T. E. Lawrence, although I don't plan to kill myself as he did.'

'I'm so glad.' Nina paused, while he waited politely. He seemed a particularly polite sort of person, she thought, perhaps because, as a solicitor, he was used to listening to clients. 'I would like to stay here for a moment or two. Among these trees, I mean.' She found herself blushing at the oddity of her request but was too old to worry. 'I am a painter, you see, and I have an idea.' It sounded either pretentious or ridiculous but he continued to look serious.

'Understood. You'll follow at your convenience.'

As it turned out, following this gracious behaviour, Nina, sitting on the damp earth in breathless anticipation of great thoughts, found herself curiously unrapt. Maybe she had the whole scene already: the small motorcycle, the large man, the crash as they tumbled together on the mossy earth. The ritual signs on the trees. The wet exhalation from the lake. Besides, the dusk was turning to dark and a nasty assortment of midges was skirmishing around her face. Nina wound her way back through the trees, now more veined with purple than mystic green.

Connie stepped into the huge rusting bath under Orlando's admiring gaze. Pipes descending *en masse* from the room above gurgled and banged. 'He's not a crook, is he? Your friend Gus,' she asked over her shoulder. 'Nina has always been unlucky with men.'

'All women are unlucky with men until they find the right one.' Orlando, still clothed, stepped into the bath. A huge wave flung itself backwards and poured over the edge.

'I know you're tiring of me,' pouted Connie, as Orlando put one hand on one breast and the other between her legs.

'I am besotted. And I believe Leonardo is being entertained by his cousins.'

'But what about supper?'

'You have forgotten. My father is cooking his risotto, learnt at the hands of Mussolini himself.'

'Then we may relax.' Connie began to wrestle with the zipper of Orlando's sodden trousers. Water had become their secret aphrodisiac.

Downstairs in the drawing room, Nina was questioning Eileen about the O'Malley family and, in particular, Mrs O'Malley, whose health had so miraculously recovered since Connie's re-emergence and marriage. The men were next door in the billiard room, discussing the lamentable state of the baize. Nina found herself listening to the modulated tones of Gus. 'Mice, I'd say. Mice, abetted by man.'

'And moth,' added Eileen's husband, who didn't seem to have a name. 'I'd say there's the teeth of a moth to be detected here.'

'But do moth have teeth?'

'As a vampire has teeth, by the tone of your voice.'

Nina began to laugh until she spotted Eileen's expression. 'So we expect neither of them to live long,' Eileen continued gamely.

'And your brother Michael?' enquired Nina, to cover her confusion. Who was not expected to live long? And yet, despite her inattention, she admired Eileen, who seemed so sure of her place in the universe. She had brought her youngest child with her, he of the winning ways and cheerful lack of understanding. Perhaps it was he who was to die.

'Michael is his own man.'

'Oh, I thought he was close to your parents.'

'He has many friends.' This seemed to be an area that caused his sister pain – although why this should be so, Nina could not guess. Before she could persevere a drop of water, a quite hefty drop, splashed down on to her nose.

They both looked up and saw a crack in the ceiling from which a row of drops hung as pendulous as stalactites.

'Gus!' called Nina (she later wondered why), and Gus appeared at once, with a billiard cue held vertically like an upraised lance. 'The ceiling!'

'Ha! The important thing is to avoid a collapse. In an old house, the collapse of a ceiling can be fatal.'

Extending his arm with the billiard cue at the end – the children had appeared to watch the performance – he made three decisive holes. Water poured down, substantially wetting the upholstered chair Nina had been sitting on.

'Pee-pee!' rejoiced Eileen's youngest child, before being hushed.

The incident had enlivened everyone, including Orlando and Connie, who descended with wet hair and a smug expression. They did not volunteer any explanation, although Connie suggested they should tick off Orlando's father for having an accident. 'He's quite gaga enough to believe it.'

It struck Nina, who found Mr Partridge very agreeable if eccentric – he called her Major and winked leerily – that Connie's attitude of justified reprimand had its roots in the terrible Hubert. Not that she had ever met the old gorgon-poet but she knew that it was he who had planted the seed of Connie's breakdown. Even literally planted. He was Connie's personal icon of male aggression and Mr Partridge was too close for comfort. It was no good that he should entertain the children with rice-cooking lessons, no good that he could produce the perfect risotto or quote Homer in a sing-song bass. His irremediable link to Hubert doomed him to outer darkness. Nina wondered whether pointing out this connection would lead to conciliation but decided quickly that the long memories of old friends were seldom welcome.

Connie whispered to Orlando, 'Your old friend, Gus, is quite like you.'

'How should we be friends otherwise?' They were breakfasting on the terrace where ragged undergrowth had cast up the stones as if they were paper. Gus, Nina and Mr Partridge had already set off for the lake, despite Connie's admonition on the loads of pig shit that had recently defiled the shore. Gus seemed to think this impossible and cited all kinds of rules and regulations.

'This is Ireland,' Orlando had reminded him. 'Everybody has sympathy for the habits of pigs.'

'How lucky you no longer bottle water here.' Eileen had seemed truly shocked, catching her husband's arm.

'That water came from a holy spring,' Connie had explained, with a gesture resembling the sign of the cross. 'The pigs were right off limits.'

'But Nina and I are far better friends than you and Gus, and we are not at all alike,' continued Connie.

'That is because you are unique.'

'It is true,' mused Connie, accepting the compliment with a graceful smile, 'that Gus is boring whereas you are not at all. I suppose daily attendance in the office wreaks its vengeance. I'm glad you don't work hard, my darling.'

Orlando was injured at this. He reminded her of his status as respectable businessman, how he had given up being a poet for love of her and how he had constant conversations with the manager of Lir Water and chaired meetings once a month, quite apart from consulting on major decisions like whether to export to England first or Europe. 'We are in a growth industry and, with our entry to the European Common Market, we'll be perfectly placed to benefit.'

'Now you sound boring,' said Connie.

As they swam through murky waters, Gus and Nina, perhaps to divert themselves from suspicious freckled oozings adhering to the reeds, held an animated conversation, during which they tried to open their mouths as little as possible.

Gus confided in Nina about his wife's death. She had been a solicitor like him and they had set off each morning together, although working in different firms. They had never wanted children, he explained, but now he felt surprisingly sorry about the lack.

'I have two children,' said Nina, 'and a mother.'

'I hope she plays bridge and then I can introduce her to mine.'

'She plays the piano, I'm afraid.'

Nina saw that he was assuming they had a future together and swam away for several yards. At that distance she was able to enjoy the thought that he was incredibly unlike Hector.

'And you have an ex-husband, I believe.' His voice was quite strong enough to reach her.

Nina kicked a little in his direction. 'William is a soldier. We did not mix well. Now he has a wonderful wife.'

'Whom I presume you detest.'

Nina took a gulp of water in her surprise. Could he be so stupid? 'Not a bit.' She spat energetically. 'It was a great relief when he married her. However, I do suspect she has kidnapped my son.' As she spoke she marched with her legs and thrashed with her arms because it was the first time this thought had occurred to her: Felicity had kidnapped Jamie.

'The weeds are dragging you under!' cried Gus coming to her assistance with a strong steady breaststroke. His flesh was pink with a pale mottling of blue, except where it was enmired by who knew what.

Nina forgot about Jamie and let his large cool arms close round her neck. 'I'm perfectly all right,' she said comfortably, and found herself entertaining the idea that Hector had always been a spindly little wimp. 'Just look there!' she cried.

Far out in the lake, Mr Partridge sawed through the water while the white swans turned their necks askance.

1978

'You're so dreadfully out of touch, dearest Fay. You haven't met Connie's husband nor seen her wild little Irish son and now I'm getting married and you have no idea about that either. That is, about him. Gus. At very least, you must come to our wedding...'

Fay, shocked, put down the letter on her desk. She must be out of touch. Nina had referred in passing to a 'large bald solicitor' – those were the words, she believed – but there had been no indication that he was to be important in her life. Or had she not read the last few letters carefully enough, too busy – correction, happy, correction, fulfilled – to have noticed the details of Nina's love life? After Hector had left the scene she and Connie had breathed a mutual sigh of relief and assumed that Nina would save her passion for her art. Reluctantly, she picked up the letter again. But before she could continue reading her private line rang.

'Are you busy?'

'No. No.' It was Ted. He liked to know that he was not interrupting. 'I've two tickets for the Brendel concert...'

Fay listened to him extol this relatively new pianist's playing with pleasure, although she had no intention of joining him. She had late clients and was looking forward to an evening in. 'You go. You go for both of us.' There was no time now to continue with Nina's long letter. That was another reason to skip the concert. She could read the letter while he was out.

Fay sat in her light and airy flat with the sound of Manhattan traffic a pleasantly dramatic chorus below. She picked up Nina's letter, marked with inky smudges, she noted indulgently, although no paint:

As I told you already, Gus is an old friend of Orlando's – from prep school or somewhere – and he's Leonardo's godfather. The thing is, Gus said he wanted a white wedding because his first wife had been too sensible for such things. We had a bit of a row about it actually because it reminded me of my marriage to William, so I told him I was too sensible for orange blossom. But he said I couldn't be sensible because I'm an artist and insisted he was the sensible one because, as a solicitor, he's paid to give people good advice.

Then he said Leonardo would be very disappointed if he couldn't be a page boy in a kilt and a velvet jacket. And when I pointed out he wasn't Scottish, he said it was an Irish kilt. So I had to give way. And now we're having a full church wedding, well, to be exact, blessing, but it feels like a wedding, with plenty of help from his widowed mother, Geraldine, so you see you and Ted must come over and support me. The point about Gus is, that although terribly good-mannered and loving, he always gets his way.

With pages still to go, Fay abandoned the letter. It seemed to her perfectly obvious that Nina was making a terrible mistake and at some level even knew it. Apart from her brief fling with Serge, men had only brought misery into her life. Why should it be any different with this man 'who always gets his way'? Nina was happy as a painter. Was it too late to warn her? Unusually, Fay poured herself a whiskey and by the time she had finished it, acknowledged it was much too late. Nina had written to invite her to the wedding. No regrets allowed.

Nina, dazed in so many ways during the weeks before her wedding, was also surprised to see her mother apparently revelling in this traditional activity. She bought a hat with cherries tipping over the brim, which she explained reminded her of the forties. Nina thought that this was the period when her father had been shut away in a Japanese prisoner-of-war camp, a time when mother and daughter lived in the shadow of his probable starvation, torture and death.

The night before the celebration, which was taking place in the cathedral town where Gus had worked and lived, Helen came to her mother accusingly. She had easy access since, for some reason, they were sharing a bedroom. Nina, nervous, overfed – there had been already several celebratory meals – sat on the window-ledge trying to recapture amorous joy by sniffing the June roses climbing up the wall.

'I don't know why you can't just go to a register office. It is your second marriage. And, if it comes to that, if you wanted a husband, I can't think why you didn't stick to Daddy. He's much more interesting than Gus.'

'I thought you'd like Gus so much now you're planning to be a solicitor too.' Nina's voice was weak. She could see Helen had a valid point: William, now commanding his regiment, might seem more exciting than a country solicitor – unless you factored in her confirmed lack of sexual interest in William and her wild enjoyment of the same with Gus. Not the sort of information you shared with your daughter. 'I'm so sorry,' she murmured, in what she guessed but could not prevent was an irritating manner.

'Don't patronise me, Mother.' Helen had swapped 'Mummy' for 'Mother' recently.

'I wouldn't dream of it.' This was true. Looking at eighteen-year-old Helen, neat and pretty, fair and composed, sitting upright and self-righteous in her bed, she thought she had felt patronised by her daughter for the last year or so. Helen – much as she loved her – made her feel she should pull herself together and stop being a painter. And yet only a few years ago Helen had been so proud of her.

'Gus wanted a service and a party.' She decided to conciliate a little. 'I know it's a bit ridiculous but, remember, he is moving to live with us. He is starting his firm in a new town.' Nina felt herself becoming hot at the realisation of the depth of Gus's love that he, so regular and orderly, should make such a change. 'I expect the church is to please his mother. And do remember it is only a blessing.'

'Anyway, I'm not wearing that hat.'

Nina took this petulance as indication she had won the argument and closed the window on sweet smells, light breezes. 'I'm just going to say goodnight to Gus.'

There was no answer so Nina crept away. Perhaps Helen would sleep and dream happily of her own boyfriend, collected at a local tennis party. He looked very like William, in Nina's view. Stalwart and serious.

'I hoped you'd come down.' Gus grabbed hold of Nina and kissed her ear, her neck, put his hand on her breast. They felt like wicked children, sneaking sex behind the adults' backs. 'Let's go into the garden.'

Back among the roses, Nina forgot all the strangeness and concentrated on reaching under Gus's shirt, down his trousers, on undoing the buttons of her blouse so he could feel the swelling bulbs of her breasts, the waxy nipples.

'Oh, my God, Nina. We can't do it here.'

'Oh, yes. Oh, yes.' She guided his fingers under her skirt.

Above their heads a window opened abruptly. 'Mother, Jamie says there's a moth in his room and you know I *hate* moths.'

*

Ted had never been to England before. In fact, he gave the impression that he had never left Manhattan.

'It's so unreal,' he whispered to Fay at the wedding lunch.

'Unreal in what particular way?'

'The perfection.'

'I suppose you're referring to the medieval architecture of the church, the Gothic reredos, the Norman font? Or, on the other hand, you just might be reacting to the flowery hats, the braying voices, the thick ankles, the complacency and the charm of the English county classes.'

'What charm?' Ted smiled at Fay's mockery.

'The charm of a race who knows who it is and what it wants and works very hard to keep it that way. The charm of security.'

'But surely the freedom to change is one of the surest signs of security.'

'No one is free to change,' objected Fay. 'We're all programmed from cradle to grave.' She might have continued but they were interrupted by Nina. She was wearing a long green and white patterned dress and, to Fay's New York eyes, looked curiously like the trees she so often painted.

'I've changed Gus's placement for lunch,' Nina said, with a guilty look. 'I've put Helen between you two. I do hope you don't mind. You've each got a relatively un-awful person on the other side. It's just that she's in a dreadful sulk with me and she's always so admired you. I suppose I should be relieved she's not as bad as Jamie, who's convinced himself Felicity is his mother.'

'She's no problem.' Ted seemed much cheered at the prospect of a bad-tempered teenager. Lately he had begun teaching music and Fay had noticed he had the highest regard for his most recalcitrant pupils. Suddenly, with a ridiculous quivering terror that she hoped could be blamed on jet-lag, she wondered why Ted had chosen her for his partner. Or had she chosen him? Perhaps, she thought, with off-the-wall dread, he had only been drawn to her because of her breakdown after Daniel's death. Perhaps even now he was looking for a more neurotic replacement, although her shrink had made it fairly clear she was as neurotic as anyone. Perhaps he wanted a younger, feistier, more demanding, less reserved . . . Perhaps he would fall for Helen. She was very attractive, fair, like William, but with a hard angularity quite unlike either of her parents. She must pull herself together and listen to poor Nina. Gus, in the flesh, had given her no more cause for rejoicing than he had on the page.

'At least you don't have to make a speech like poor Gus,' Nina continued anxiously. 'He's convinced he has to make jokes and you know how jokes depend on a sense of timing.' She hurried away again, leaving Fay with the sense that Gus had failed yet another vital test. What did Nina see in him? As Fay walked with Ted through the marquee, knowing no one and free to stay apart, she put a better spin on their relationship. In truth, she had never tried to hold him since she had no desire for marriage. He lived with her because it was convenient to them both. They liked each other's company. Fay looked at him now, his long, bony face topped by the absurd crew-cut he'd recently affected, and told herself theirs was the perfect friendship, a perfect love affair, uncomplicated by too much passion.

Helen challenged immediately. They sat at the top table, her mother opposite her, although, Fay assumed, not within hearing. 'She doesn't care about him at all. No more than she cared about my father. All she cares about is her painting.'

Ted leant close to her. 'Is that wrong?'

'What do you mean?'

'I thought your generation put personal fulfilment above everything.'

'You're not much older than me.'

'Thank you, ma'am, but you didn't answer my question so I'll give you another. Why do you think your mother's marrying Gus?'

'How do I know? Comfort? Security? To show William she can get a husband? She hasn't told me.'

'So you don't think it's love?'

'Love! Who cares about love?'

Fay took over. 'Excuse me. But I understood you were accusing Nina of not loving Gus enough or at least much less than her painting, but now you're saying love is unimportant. I'm muddled, Helen.'

'So am I!' Helen's neat and pretty Englishness dissolved and, stumbling to her feet, she dashed from the tent.

Nina saw her, half stood and sank back again as her mother moved with more conviction. Gus took her hand. 'What I like about Helen is her determination not to take attention from you on your happy day.'

'Never mind.' Nina resorted to vagueness. She tried to remember why she had ever consented to this hideously public wedding. It was to please someone but she could no longer remember who. The best she could say about it was that William had stayed away. To compose herself she pictured the house in France where she and Gus were to spend their honeymoon. It was small, built in the steep, chestnut-covered hills of the Ardèche. It had two bedrooms, a living room with a large wood-burning fire and a terrace overlooking the valley. At the bottom, a wide, slow river flowed over smooth, oyster grey stones. Gus would read while she sketched. Perhaps she would even paint. Hardly knowing what she was doing, Nina took from the coils of her hair the tasteful flower arrangement placed there by her mother-in-law's hairdresser and laid it on the table.

Seeing this as a sign to speed up the proceedings, Gus tapped the side of his glass and cried, in his good round baritone, 'Speeches! Ladies and gentlemen!'

He interrupted Fay and Ted, who were agreeing that Helen's behaviour was entirely due to the virgin's unacknowledged sexual jealousy of her mother. 'Just look at Gus,' said Ted vulgarly. 'He may not be beautiful but there's no denying he's a sexual male.'

'And the best thing of all,' added Fay, trying to look on the bright side, 'is that he's not Hector.'

Considering Nina had fallen for Gus in Ireland, it was perhaps not surprising that she had misunderstood his nature. For example, she had no idea how interested he was in politics and football. In October they drove to visit his mother. Gus liked the radio playing. He pretended he was willing to turn it off but actually he wasn't. It was just a part of breathing as far as he was concerned. Once Nina had established this, she grew accustomed to news on the hour, football results and *The Archers*. *The Archers* she was perhaps less keen on after he had admitted that it had been a particular favourite of his late wife, Erica, but even that she grew to like, as she grew to like his hard, straight shoulders, the exact curve of his eyelashes and the way his hips slotted into his waist. He had become thinner since they had met and so had she. It was sex, they both agreed proudly.

These lazy thoughts were interrupted when Gus, turning up the radio, announced solemnly, 'This is an important moment for England.'

He expected a response but she didn't have an idea what he was talking about.

'The election. Callaghan. He is about to make the announcement. Everybody expects it. We can exert our democratic right to throw out a government that has allowed the unions to hold this country to ransom. At least you must have noticed the electricity strikes. Those things that turn your canvases to black.'

'Yes,' agreed Nina, as Big Ben struck six. She didn't mind him pointing out her ignorance – not much anyway – but she did mind his minding. Suddenly, as if her concentration had jolted it, the whole scene in front of her shifted with a shocking violence as each car seemed to lose its focus and jerk to right or left, as if the entire motorway had suffered a momentary breakdown of nerve.

'My God!' said Gus. 'Callaghan hasn't called an election after all.'

Nina realised that their own car had skipped a beat as hysterically as all the rest.

'You know what this means?' Gus turned down the radio. 'The end of socialism for a very, very long time.'

'I thought Callaghan didn't call an election.'

'Not now. He's missed the moment. But once he does, the Conservatives will be here for ever. I may be a socialist at heart but I know when the country needs a change.'

'I'm sorry,' said Nina dully. She thought she didn't care one bit and, in her heart of hearts, believed politics made no difference to anything that really mattered. What if there were electricity strikes? Didn't Giotto and Leonardo, Rubens and Constable paint before the invention of electricity?

'You're unreal!' His tone was cruel, choked with the wish to hurt.

She thought this was their first disagreement. It was about all kinds of things: about her refusal to allow his mother to move into her house, about his anxiety that the Sussex office looked like taking longer to establish than he had hoped, about his realisation that she did not want a baby with him, about the fact that he was over forty and getting older. There was another reason for his sharpness: separation. He was leaving her soon to visit a client in Barbados. They had never been apart since their marriage. He minded more than she did.

The motorbike had taken up much of Nina's studio for the past year. She had made Gus bring it in so that she could try to recapture their first meeting by the lake. She had never tried to draw such a large, inanimate object and found the proportions extremely difficult. Then Helen came up with an idea. 'Why don't you just stick the photograph on the canvas and be done with it?' She used her most scornful tones. Nina, in the spirit of self-mockery, followed her advice.

Then Gus came into her studio the night before his departure for Barbados. He was trying on a pair of shorts, which were too small, and a very garishly patterned shirt. He had come for advice but now he stared with a critical eye at the painting on her easel. Nina allowed herself to recognise for the first time that he might love her but he did not care about her paintings. Worse still, he judged them as if they were separate from her.

'Those shorts are ridiculous!' Attack seemed the best form of defence.

'They're my school rugby shorts. You see the house colours down the sides? Of course, I know nothing about art, but isn't that a bit on the nose, psychologically speaking? The motorcycle instead of the black stallion. The male rampant. I mean, would anyone really want to hang it in their living room?'

Nina understood he was hating her and sat down on the battered pink chair she used for contemplation of work in progress. 'Why don't you pose for me? I've never been too confident as a portraitist but I can hold a body line pretty well.'

'I'm packing, and you've already said I look ridiculous.'

'Stand over there,' commanded Nina, who had not meant this very moment but now felt challenged to a bad-tempered engagement. 'Yes. There.' Standing again, she picked up a large brush, loaded it with a mix of rose madder and zinc yellow, and began to paint Gus from top to toe, the colour sliding smoothly over the photograph of the bike. She became immediately absorbed by trying to catch the obdurate stance that Gus had taken up. Carefully she squeezed out a sausage of monestrial green for the shadows. She thought Gus looked more like a gangster than a country solicitor.

'What bit of me are you painting?'

'I'm moving down your body.'

'Tell me when you get to the bit that matters.'

Nina began to paint Gus's schoolboy shorts and soon saw that they were becoming even tighter. Deliberately, she continued, looking at him and his ever-bulging crotch then back teasingly at her canvas. Eventually she could continue the game no longer. Laying down her brush, she went over to take off his shorts. 'Oh, my darling, darling, darling,' mouthed Gus, as he lowered her to the floor.

In a voice filled with desperation, Nina spoke to Connie on the telephone. 'I am thirty-eight. I have two nearly grown-up children. I'm too old to have a baby. I am much, much too old to have a baby. I'm painting for an exhibition but no one takes my work seriously any more. Gus mows the lawn and expects me to do the weeding.' She gasped and whispered, 'He thinks my painting is a hobby.' For once Nina had the house to herself and she was crouched in the hallway, letting it all hang out. She had never done such a thing before and she panted and sighed with the unaccustomed sensations.

'But you do love him?' asked Connie.

'Oh, *please*!' It was all right for Connie, contented wife and mother. 'So you do?'

'That's not the issue.' Nina collapsed in a chair. Could no one understand? 'It's the principle.' There was a pause. Nina felt too exhausted and upset to attempt any more explanations. Perhaps Connie didn't believe in her painting either. Perhaps she should have persevered with Fay. But Fay had been at a conference in Seattle. At least Fay had taken the trouble to come to the wedding. She thought that Connie had always been selfish. And yet she found herself asking, as if her present despair could be forgotten in forward planning, 'Why don't you come and stay here for Christmas?'

'I need to be at Lir for Christmas. It could be my mother's last. And I *so* want Leonardo to spend his childhood Christmases here.'

'Then how about New Year?'

'Let's face it, Nina, I'm probably going to let you down. But I'll try for New Year.'

Bitterly, Nina remembered all the comfort she'd given Connie in her bad times.

Nina dragged and pushed and fought the motorcycle out of her studio. She faced to the wall all the canvases in which it featured and put a newly stretched, pristine white canvas on her easel. But she could see the bike from her window. It looked aggressively reproachful. She went into the kitchen where, since Helen had started university life in Bristol, – Jamie staying, as usual, with William, and Gus being in his office – her mother was all alone, reading in a comfortable way *Country Life*.

'It's impossible!' cried Nina. 'That motorbike weighs a ton. Is the key somewhere so I can ride it away and tip it over a cliff?'

'This isn't like you,' commented Veronica, obediently searching among jars and saucers in which odds and ends collected.

For a moment Nina thought angrily she was referring to her pregnancy until she recalled she hadn't informed her about it.

'Here we are!' exclaimed Veronica triumphantly. 'But shouldn't you have a special licence?'

'No, I should not!'

The bike shuddered and juddered as Nina set off precariously down the drive. Soon she was out on the road and heading for the Downs. The light around her was hard and bright, with sudden casts of black as clouds passed overhead. She realised that the exhilaration of discovering she actually knew how to ride this bike had led her out of her depth. There were other cars on this road who must soon report this wild, helmetless woman. Her original aim, undefined, was to ride it away and dump it, rid herself of its stupidly male presence. This kept her going until she saw a track leading off left. It was an unpaved route to the Downs, she remembered now, the way her mother and she had bicycled (at least, her mother had done the bicycling) on her fourth birthday during the war. When they had a kite and it rained. The day, as she learnt later, that the Normandy landings had begun. How odd that she had never been this way since. Nina let her strength lapse a little and the motorcycle, hitting a rut, a stone and a ditch, jumped and swivelled and shot its rider off before landing in an ungainly lump.

Nina lay where she had fallen. She felt entirely disconnected, the gap between her fourth birthday treat, the wilful kite and herself lying on the cold ground impossible to fill in. Perhaps she was concussed. Or perhaps she wanted to be concussed. She thought that the state in which she now found herself was very like the one that produced her best work. That sense of a dislocation out of time that she had felt when she had seen Connie asleep on her way to find her parents. That series of paintings had inspired her for some time. The trouble was she had felt it, too, or thought she had, when Gus and she had fallen off his hired bike in Ireland. What a mess! Nina lay back and waited for someone to find her. To pass the time, she looked with hatred and derision at the motorcycle, all askew.

Connie walked down the path to the lake reading a letter from Nina:

> Dearest Connie, I have lost the baby so you don't have to come for the New Year if it doesn't suit. I'm afraid I'm going through a bit of trauma. I do wonder if perhaps I am not good wife material. Gus is being wonderful, so is my mother. The worst thing would be if I started obsessively washing again. How about lighting a candle against that possibility? PS I should add, thank God for football and politics since darling Gus has as much interest and consolation for the present plight of dear England as he does misery for his dear wife's

indisposition. Are all men sustained by events outside their personal life?

Fay took the letter from the doorman. Connie's handwriting. Connie hardly ever wrote. It must be serious.

Fay, my dear heart – and Ted, because you're so caring – poor Nina has got herself in a serious mess. She thinks she's going mad again – not that she was ever mad, merely obsessional, which is quite different. I have promised to stay over New Year, but Orlando is terribly against it. I suppose a man can't help being jealous of his wife's old friends, close friends. Orlando insists that he had set aside the time for practising the cello that he's sadly neglected over the last few years. His duties with Lir Water are by no means so heavy that he could not practise most days if he cared to, but when I pointed this out, he became untypically stubborn. So this is an appeal, dearest couple. I don't even mention the responsibility of my parents, my father-in-law and Leonardo, who has become rather a handful recently.

Fay passed the letter to Ted. She had just arrived back from her consulting rooms. Despite slushy snow on the streets, and a gusty wind down the canyons, she had walked home and even run a little, wearing ear-muffs over her head and trainers on her feet. She had become concerned about a life spent in air-conditioning and had begun to run checks on colds and flu shared throughout the apartment building. Lately, she'd been pestering Ted, in his role as ex-doorman, to monitor the use of disinfectants in the air-conditioning system. 'It would be a blast of fresh air,' she suggested to Ted.

'You don't have to go to England for that.'

'Are you jealous too?' Fay smiled at the unlikely idea.

'We were there in the summer for the wedding.'

'This would be different. You could work. You might be inspired.'

Fay couldn't understand why Ted appeared to have so few ambitions for his music. If she pushed it, he insisted that his composition was right out of line with modern trends but that he got plenty of fulfilment from his teaching. She refused to believe him.

Ted stood up and, without answering, went to the bedroom.

Fay picked up the *New York Times Book Review*. She read about a new book called *Infancy, Its Place in Human Development*, which was described by the reviewer as 'a critical examination of the thick cord of connectivity that is assumed to bind early and late human experiences . . .'. She smiled ironically at a book called *A Britain That Works*. She noted a new Updike and supposed she might read, if she ever got time, Foucault's *The History of Sexuality* and Schlesinger's *Robert Kennedy and His Times*, except that she was perfectly certain she'd never make space enough for that. Then she got stuck into the extraordinary story of the Dionne quintuplets, born in 1934. When she next looked up, Ted was standing in front of her with a large backpack at his feet. Her first reaction was to the backpack: it was stained and frayed at the edges. And then it struck her that she did not know where Ted had been or, now – she looked up at him, suddenly wary – where he was going. 'Ted?'

'There's a student of mine called Miriam. I've decided to move in with her.' His voice was steady, almost matter-of-fact.

Fay looked down at her fingers. She had never seen such white fingers before and so many of them. She realised that her sight was being dissolved by tears. She felt white and glassy all through and imagined that she must look like a skeleton to Ted.

'She's a pianist and viola player.' Ted stopped and looked at her enquiringly. 'You're a brave lady.'

'Yes,' said Fay, stupidly. It was impossible to believe that Ted, only recently designated by Connie as 'caring', who had come into her life in just that role, could say those words. *You're a brave lady.* What did that mean? Tears, she noticed, were now pouring over her fingers. So much for bravery. He was saying something else but her ears did not want more pain.

'You'll find someone more like you. There's that Dr Fleishman.'

Even in her numbed mind, Fay remembered Paul Fleishman. She had been attracted to him. They had met at a conference in Seattle and swapped stories about their parents. Perhaps Ted had thought they went to bed together. They had met a couple of times in New York and once she had brought him back to the apartment where he had met Ted, who had been wearing a towel and headphones. Thinking he couldn't hear her, she'd laughed. 'Here's my toyboy.' Dr Fleishman, with his confidence and successful practice in ear, nose and throat, would have made a very suitable husband. Her mother would have loved him.

Fay wanted to say, 'I love you, darling,' but she couldn't, because it might not be true and because it was clearly too late. Ted had met Miriam.

'I'll come back when you're out for the rest of my stuff. Goodbye, Fay.' He was walking. Fay's skeleton sat on her chair watching him. As if in a nightmare, she could neither speak nor move. Then the door closed. Now she wanted to cry out, 'Is this the way you end five years?' but she couldn't even say that. Maybe he'd only ever been sorry for her. What answer could she make to Miriam, who was fifteen years younger and played piano and viola? 'You know, I loved going to concerts with you, even if I can't play an instrument,' Fay tried whispering to herself, but she knew it was a lie.

1979

'How does it feel to have two men in your life?' Fay and Nina were playing Scrabble together in front of the fire. Five minutes ago they stood together at the doorway and waved off Jamie, now taller than Nina, and Helen, both wearing evening dress, who were going to a New Year dance. It was held in one of the houses where Nina had been taught to perform the quickstep and the waltz as a child and she was feeling gently nostalgic. 'I guess I'm thinking of myself,' Fay added. 'Sorry.'

Nina studied her pieces. 'I've always liked Ted so much,' she said.

Fay watched her as Nina put down letter after letter. 'EVERGREEN. Well done! I know you and Connie have always thought that my career means more to me than anything else, than anyone else.' Fay put down SADLY and smiled.

'But we so admire you for it! And to do it as a woman and in New York. I think New York's a terrifying place. I tremble at the thought of it. I was offered a show there and I couldn't face it.'

'You never told me that! And what about Serge? I guess you enjoyed your trembling with him.'

'Serge helped me after William. Or was it during?' Nina smiled at Fay as if to say, What's the difference?

'Anyway, a show in New York would have been great. All my friends aren't doctors, you know.' Fay watched Nina add ING to PERTURB.

'Tell me about Ted. I really want to help, Fay.' Nina pushed away the pieces.

Fay felt some relief of the painful constriction that had held her tight since Ted's departure. She had worked since, grimly studying X-rays that all seemed to bode the worst. In her office, she was Dr Blass, talented at reading the runes, a brisk and efficient single woman with a business to run. Now, at last, she could be feeble, in mourning, inconsolable, confused, and thoroughly miserable. What a relief! Almost a luxury. She spoke hurriedly. 'He came into my life so suddenly. After Daniel's death. But perhaps I shouldn't begin there. Perhaps I should try to explain. You see, I don't think you understand what it's like in America at the moment.' She had not meant to sound lecturing. Rather, she wanted to pour out her grief.

'I'm sure I don't,' agreed Nina encouragingly.

'Feminism is taken much more seriously. In England it's more like a game. Look at the way Connie went in and out of the movement in the space of a few years.'

'Connie's Irish.'

'Excuse me! You're not being serious either!'

'Sorry.'

'What I want to say is that in England, feminism is skin deep, a pragmatic position to progress the advance in women's rights, initiated with Mrs Pankhurst or earlier. It's not about changing your whole sense of being, your approach not just to men but to yourself.'

'There are people like that here. Fay Weldon. Fay Weldon thinks having a man in her life incredibly important.'

Fay sat up energetically in her chair. 'The point I'm not making too well is that women in America, because of their serious approach, not only ask for a change in their own attitudes but in their men's as well.'

'But over here we're training men to do the washing-up. Gus has even started doing some shopping now and again and he's a very old-fashioned male.'

'I'm talking about something far deeper than that.'

'Surely there're few more important indications of a man's changing perceptions than his willingness to stick his hands into hot, greasy water?'

Fay looked down. She stroked her fingers slowly one by one. 'Ted, you see, to answer your original question, is a classic product of late-seventies feminism.' Even to herself this sounded sad. But how else could she explain Ted's desertion without screaming?

'Oh.' Nina pursed her lips.

'He's a strong-minded male who has no wish to play the stereotypi-cal leader, hunter and protector. On the other hand, he doesn't want to play the wimp wife. What he wants, what he demands, without saying a word, is equality.'

'Gosh!' exclaimed Nina. 'That's a big word.'

'Yes.' Fay, who had been leaning forward intensely, flopped backwards.

'So why did he leave?'

'Because I couldn't deal with it. Once he stopped leading me, as I recovered from Daniel's death and my career change, I started to lead him. One of us had to be boss, as I saw it. I just couldn't get hold of his kind of equality, so he's gone off with his Miriam who doubtless can.' Fay stopped talking and peered deep into the fire, wondering if this was the whole truth.

'I see,' said Nina, but Fay thought she looked doubtful. Nina had never been very good on theory. 'So is it the end between you and Ted? I mean, you always seemed so good together. If you don't mind, I'll say happy.'

'I was. He, it seems, wasn't.' Fay began to stroke her fingers again. It was oddly comforting.

'Dear Fay. You're having a horrible time.' Nina put her arms round Fay and hugged. At that moment Gus came into the room, holding a bottle of wine. He stopped as if surprised at the scene.

'Am I interrupting? Girl-type things.'

Fay caught Nina's eye, and Nina smiled wryly.

Connie received a letter from Nina, enclosing one from Fay. She waved both letters in the direction of Orlando, who was pulling burrs out of Gomorrah's tail. 'They're either tearstained or she's washing again.'

'Should you joke about your best friend's troubles?'

Connie laughed and began to read Nina's letter. After a bit she sighed, 'Oh, dearie, dearie me!' and began to read aloud: ' "She knows I've been unhappy after losing the baby, yet she chooses this moment to attack me. How can I help it if I was born into the English middle classes? Don't I deserve any respect? Doesn't my painting mean anything? There are some pretty knowledgeable people who actually consider me a good painter. They even think painting matters . . ." ' She put down Nina's letter and picked up the other. 'Whatever can Fay have written? Do you want this one too?'

'Fire ahead,' encouraged Orlando. 'It's not often I get the chance to eavesdrop on the intimate exchange between women.'

'No interruptions, then.' Connie came to sit close by Orlando and started to read: ' "Our conversation about feminism could have gone much further. On the flight back I was struck by the way we have always rigorously refrained from counting in the economic factor in our relationship. And, also, the question of class. Possibly out of a foolish kind of deference to Anglo-Saxon reticence or because our first meeting cast you in the role of patient to me as doctor, I've never confronted you with my background, born, if not in a ghetto, at least in very humble circumstances, the home of refugees who had nothing to rely upon but their wits. (If I were Connie, I would add 'faith' but, since I never discovered that mysterious commodity, we'll leave it at 'wits'.) I knew from childhood that, without working, I would be nothing. Male or female, the workplace with all the commitment and responsibility it demands, was a financial necessity. You like to admire me for my career but you leave out the all-important fact that I *had no choice*. You, on the other hand, were born into comfort, if not luxury. You had a choice. You could have done anything – you were backed by money and security. You chose to marry. You chose to divorce. Then you chose to paint, a vocation far removed from ordinary constraints. You chose to marry again but were unwilling to have another child. My aim in writing this, dearest Nina, is only to throw light on our differences, not to criticise—"'

'Wow!' interrupted Orlando.

'That's a Warhol response, God rest his soul. What do you really think?'

'That even best friends behave badly when they're unhappy.'

'Fay, you mean. Heavy, man.' Connie pouted mockingly. 'So you don't think Fay's got hold of the truth when she implies Nina's a spoilt, self-indulgent, middle-class—'

'Truth and friendship. Well, there's a theme. How about inventing Connie the peace-maker?'

'Wow!'

Gus and Nina lay in bed. Nina wished they could make love but knew it was impossible. Gus liked to sleep with the window wide open and a cold wind blew intermittently across her face. The touch of conscience, she thought uneasily, and then reminded herself it was Connie, not she, who believed in such things. 'You're either angry with me or you think I'm mad,' she whispered into the darkness. She knew Gus was awake because he wasn't snoring.

'You are not mad.'

'Then you're angry with me.'

'No, I'm not. I love you.'

'I promise you I only rode that bike because I couldn't work when it was there. It was nothing whatsoever to do with the baby.'

Gus didn't answer. The silence was very painful. Nina wanted to hold on to him but didn't dare. It was three months since her miscarriage but nothing was resolved between her and Gus. Could she have wanted to kill her own baby? Would Fay's shrink have uncovered the murderer in her?

'I am just very sad,' said Gus eventually. 'Doubtless I'll get over it. People do get over things.'

Nina felt the leaden weight of his gloom and accusation. Now she wished he was angry. The truth was, she felt enormous relief that she was no longer pregnant and, according to the doctor, unlikely to become so again. But how could she ever admit this to Gus, dear, kind, protective Gus, who had been so excited to have a child? This morning she had started a new painting and then, shocked at her carefree excitement, she had scraped off the paint and spent five minutes washing her hands.

'I don't think I ever told you . . .' began Gus. He leant up on his side as if he could see her in the darkness. Once again, Nina longed to be in his arms. 'Or perhaps you've forgotten. Erica couldn't have children. We made the best of it, of course, pretending she was too involved in her work. I suppose we even believed it was true by the end.'

'Well, then, you should have married some nice young girl!' Nina cried out. 'Why are you telling me this if you're not angry? Of course you're angry. You think I killed our baby.'

'Please, don't say that.' He sounded infinitely weary.

'I'm sorry.'

'I told you about Erica because I wanted you to know why I'm so unhappy. But that doesn't mean I'm angry with you. I've told you, I love you. I love Helen, and I would Jamie if he'd let me. I don't know how I ever persuaded such an extraordinary person as you to marry me. Don't talk wildly. You had a miscarriage. You were overwrought. You've got an artistic temperament.'

'Oh, God.' Nina rested her head on the pillow. 'You think I'm mad.'

'I think you get wound up inside yourself. You lose a sense of proportion. You need to get out in the world more, or at least take more notice of it. This washing is all part of that.'

Nina didn't want to be in Gus's arms any more. His accusation was the same as that made by Fay in her hurtful letter. She had a terrible sense of claustrophobia and felt a flush rising up her body. She told herself that he was speaking out of anger and unhappiness. He didn't mean to be cruel. He meant to help her. He loved her. She loved him and needed him. 'How could I make you happier?' She spoke so softly that he couldn't hear. He was a bit deaf in one ear.

'What? Sorry?'

'I want to make you happy. I love you, Gus.' Now he held her but her flush had subsided and she felt cold. He stroked her neck and arm, her breast. She moved away from him slightly.

'I only want to calm you.'

'Yes. Yes.' They lay together. Nina began to like his warm weight beside her and made more excuses for what he'd said. Probably she'd misread his intention altogether. He was so proud of her painting.

'Have you heard of a set-up called Southern Painting?' murmured Gus. 'A client of mine was telling me about it. Apparently they're looking for someone to run it. I mentioned you might be interested. I hope you don't mind. It would be paid. Two days a week. Get you out of yourself. Helping others, you know, that sort of thing. Nina, are you still awake?'

'Yes.'

'What do you think of my idea?' He sounded humble, anxiously keen to please. 'Their head office is in town. We could drive in together.'

'I promise to think about it.'

'I'm so very glad we've talked.' With sinking heart, Nina heard how even this small promise had raised his spirits. 'Incidentally, darling, have you noticed the polls are looking remarkably as if Mrs Thatcher will provide the Conservatives with a landslide?'

The O'Malley clan was gathering at Lir to celebrate Mrs O'Malley's birthday. For once the house was warm. Orlando had turned up the central heating, which dated back to 1880 and heaved huge amounts of rust-smelling warmth into every room. Connie's mother, who arrived in a belted coat with the air of someone who did not plan to take it off, turned puce and began to sweat.

'You'll have to disrobe,' commanded Connie, but her mother clutched it across her bosom.

'You'd think she was wearing a hair shirt.' Michael looked at his mother and then gave a guffaw – he had already helped himself to the whiskey. 'Am I not at least half-way in the right?'

Under the coat Mrs O'Malley sported a large picture of the Virgin Mary strapped crosswise across her chest, with some sort of package beneath it.

'You're shameless, Michael O'Malley!' she cried, with considerable energy, given she was terminally ill. 'And you, too, Constance, and Eileen. Laughing at Herself as if she were some silly pop star. I wear her likeness next to my skin with a sponge of holy water behind because she keeps me alive for you all.'

As she delivered this Act of Faith, Connie saw that her mother was enjoying her centre stage, and saw also that they had much in common. 'Oh, you're such a drama queen!' she said, too soft to be heard by any but her sister.

They were ranged, dozens of her relations, in the room they called the hall, although it was a sitting room and not outstandingly large. Eileen had all eight children with her, the two eldest married and with children of their own. Stranger still, given her irrevocable determination never to see him again, was her drunken brother Joe, on a visit from Warrington where he still lived and where Connie had first stayed on her arrival in England. He and Michael hardly spoke but watched each other warily as if the twenty-five years since they had last met had made them not only strangers but antagonists. On the other hand, if Michael reached for a whiskey on his arrival, Joe came already tanked up with a bottle in his pocket. My God, what a curse our parents – abstemious bloody bigots – have left us with, thought Connie, pouring herself a small glass of sherry. And thank you, Orlando, for making me sane about so many things. 'Now, Ma, if you don't sit down, you'll have a stroke and then you won't reach your eighty years and there'll be nothing the Blessed Virgin can do about it.'

'Eureka! Eureka, my dear ones!' Orlando entered the room, carrying a crate of Lir Water.

Connie laughed at his optimistic self-delusion. 'Do you think anyone here present will take a glass of water?'

But he was right. Her mother and Eileen drank it neat with expressions of rapture – so pure, so clear, so full of fizz and pop – Michael put it in his whiskey, and Mr Partridge used some to dab an imaginary spot from his blazer. 'It's like acid, this stuff,' he remarked, winking at his son. 'It takes the stain off in a moment then eats away the fabric.'

Michael took up the refrain: 'Just mind you don't let it fall on your skin or it'll be through to the bone before you can say "Glory Be".'

Connie took a closer look at Michael and wondered what had changed him from the taciturn, modest man he had been when she first returned to Ireland. Anyone who could meet her father-in-law on his own terms had a lot of confidence. 'Has Michael found a woman?' she whispered to Eileen.

'Cross your legs it is that.'

Connie looked at her sister and marvelled. How could a woman of fifty-odd, with a dull husband, eight children, one of whom would be her responsibility for ever, look as if she had just come from a beauty parlour! Was it faith? Her faith was extreme, certainly, and it seemed to her that this admirable sort of woman was peculiar to Ireland.

'Do you remember our aunt Annie?' asked Connie, suddenly interested. Where was this strength of belief that had gripped even herself, although rather late in the day? Somewhere, she suspected, there was a shared love of the theatrical.

'Auntie Annie, Sister Oliver to us,' said Eileen. 'Sister Oliver was in love with Dev, isn't that the story, Ma? Saw the big man passing in a crowd of men once and his eye-glasses fell on her. Literally, believe it if you will. They fell off his face and right on to this girl in her white dress and she saw his big brown Portuguese eyes staring down at her. And she was lost.'

'I don't quite see why losing her heart to de Valera meant she became a nun.'

'Because she couldn't have him, idiot!' Eileen pushed her sister affectionately. 'Jesus was next best and he had the big brown eyes too. Although some said she could never tell the two men apart.' Eileen raised her voice, 'Isn't that right, Mam? Auntie Annie became a bride of Christ because she couldn't have Dev?'

'To be sure she thought him a great man, as we all do, God rest his soul.'

'God rot his soul.' Michael's voice, his face hot and whiskey red – perhaps he had been competing with his brother – hit the room with a sepulchral thud.

'Now, Michael . . .' said Mrs O'Malley, with the air of someone who knew the form and could not alter it.

'Just tell me this, did he have the killing of Michael Collins or did he not?'

'He did not,' said Eileen firmly, but was ignored.

'First, he impugned Collins's reputation, sending him like the gombeen man to barter in England, and then he has him murdered and his men murdered and the spirit of Ireland shut up in a little box named Eamon de Valera. I say, God rot his soul and I drink to a united Ireland. And may the British drown in the blood of those they have killed.'

The woman looked at Nina, who seemed about to flee the office. 'Yes, it's me,' she said. 'Didn't your husband tell you my name?'

Nina recovered herself. She took off her gloves. It was March and so cold that her mother threw out scraps from their plates and the birds ate them like hungry dogs. What would Veronica think if she stepped into the shoes of this nice, pretty woman? 'He probably told me.' She started to shake the woman's hand then kissed her cheek instead. She thought, You can't be *so* surprised the second time you meet your father's mistress – particularly when she lives so close. 'Are you well?' she asked.

'Oh, yes.' Lisa sat at her desk, which might soon be Nina's. The office was on the first floor of a Georgian house. It was painted a friendly yellow and the windows let in generous amounts of light and noise from the high street. 'You'll have to be seen by our little board but they're terribly excited that a real painter – a famous painter – wants to head our amateur organisation. They can hardly believe it. Haven't you got a picture in the Tate?'

'Yes. The Tate own a picture but they only hung it briefly.'

'How disappointing!' Lisa looked sympathetic. 'Still, being bought is such an accolade. We did wonder how you could have time . . . ?' The question mark was delicately placed but Nina understood that there were those who were not so bowled over at her application.

'I'm hardly painting at the moment.' She applauded herself for saying this without bursting into tears. Indeed, she attempted an enthusiastic interviewee's smile.

'I expect you want to know what would be expected of you.' Lisa became more businesslike. 'I've prepared copies of all our courses and our accounts. A sound financial footing is the most important thing for any small organisation and that we do have.' Lisa was positively aglow as she stacked up papers and slid them inside a folder. 'I don't expect you've had much experience of this sort of thing but nor had I when I started. It's called fund-raising.' She gave a schoolgirlish giggle.

'I'm not sure I would be good at that.' It seemed time for a bit of honesty.

'Oh, well. It doesn't matter now. We're set up for years to come. Anyway, I won't be altogether relinquishing the reins. That is to say, you'll have them but you can pull me in when you want me.'

More honesty seemed necessary. 'I don't want to upset my mother. I live with her.'

All traces of girlhood vanished and Lisa turned a serious gaze between Nina and the window. 'Ah, that. Yes. You know I've married.'

Nina thought about this, whether it altered the situation. On the whole she felt it did not. 'It's probably best if I talk to my mother. She's very sensible.'

'She was always sensible.' Lisa looked embarrassed. 'Sorry. I shouldn't have said that. Anyway, it's all just a coincidence, isn't it? It doesn't have any meaning.'

'I don't know,' said Nina, standing. 'Perhaps I'd better go and think about it.'

'Don't forget the folder.'

Nina took the bulky folder and went downstairs. Half-way down, she realised she had left her gloves but felt too faint-hearted to retrieve them.

'I know Gus is very keen on you doing it,' said Veronica, snipping a few late snowdrops. 'It's supposed to be bad luck to bring snowdrops into the house,' she added.

'But what do you think?'

'The point about Gus is he is both a loving and a practical person. We must not discourage.'

Nina looked up at the sky and saw some snowflakes as flat and thin as tissue floating slowly down. She watched them dissolve at once on contact with the grass. The lawn was looking particularly well kept. Gus said you could tell the state of a man's soul from the state of his lawn.

'It's snowing,' said Veronica.

'Hardly.' But the flakes contradicted her and began to settle. Vaguely, Nina remembered that May afternoon when the grass had turned completely white. Surely it had caused her to make some decision but now she could not remember what.

Veronica put her arm through her daughter's. 'You know what? I don't even dream about your father any more, although I think about him kindly enough. You must do what you feel is right.'

'Oh, I'm just a big baby. You know how I've been lately.' Miserably, Nina noticed how her mother had not mentioned her painting as if it had no place in her decision.

'We're going to be sopping in another moment. Cheer up, darling.'

1980

Connie, contemplating the news of her mother's death in Mayo, at first allowed anger to engulf sadness. How dare she die alone! That is, without the prodigal daughter who loved her so much. She had not dressed, and sat amid the chaos of her bedroom with tears rolling down her face. Outside the window she could hear Leonardo playing with a puppy they had bought him. The sound of his voice, gently admonishing the creature for breaking off a lily, made her cry even more. Where was Orlando at her time of sorrow, she thought, with a new attempt at anger, before remembering she had forbidden him to follow her. Sitting at her dressing-table, she brushed out the curls of her long shiny hair while she stared at her pretty O'Malley face. At length she put down the brush and lowered her eyes. It was time to admit that her sorrow over her mother's death, although genuine enough, had stirred up a different pond.

Connie retrieved the telephone from under a pillow and dialled Fay's office. She saluted her with 'I hope everything is as good and secure for you as always, dear Fay.' Belatedly, she remembered Fay had lost her beloved Ted, although that was over a year ago now.

'I'm working. Can I call back?'

Ignoring this, Connie began the explanation of her mother's death, the family funeral in Mayo, the need to contact Kevin, who did not yet know and, although estranged, should be informed and perhaps even given the opportunity to attend the funeral – with his family. She gave particular emphasis to this last word. After a pause, Fay said, 'I'll tell Kevin and Shirley,' and put the phone down.

Gasping, Connie hung up. The echo of Fay's voice stayed with her and with it remembrance of Kathleen's half-Vietnamese sister. Somehow she had never entered the imaginary pictures Connie wove around her daughter. She realised she could not even remember the girl's name. I am a selfish person, she told herself, and that in its turn reminded her again of Fay's unhappiness – presumed unhappiness.

The flowers were waiting for Fay in her apartment. It was a huge bouquet filled with unlikely and not very harmonious colours plus some strange cactus-like protuberances. Fay stopped at the doorway and took a deep breath. She turned her back on the bouquet to drop her keys in the usual dish, to put down her mail in the usual place, and only then turned back. The bouquet came, she felt certain, from Ted. He would divine, as Connie hadn't, that she was at her lowest, that life seemed without point, and that because it was her birthday in two days' time, she was committed to visiting her mother, who was suffering from angina. She had forgotten to leave on the air-conditioning and the room was hot, so that all but the protuberances – perhaps more like lavatory brushes than cacti – were drooping. She hurried away to find a vase and water before reading the note inside its little envelope, pinned to the Cellophane.

Fay sat in her smartly carved armchair, flowers nicely in her eye-line, air-conditioning gently cooling, and read the note: 'Dearest Fay, you are a friend beyond my deserving. Love from us all at Lir, Connie.' Fay folded the card carefully and put it back in the envelope. After a while she got up to pour herself a large Scotch. She got up again to put the flowers in the trash can in the kitchen. She returned to the can and put the flowers back in the vase, although she left it in the kitchen, behind the door. She considered all the things she could and should do, including ringing Kevin O'Malley (or at least Shirley) and did none of them. The Scotch went down pretty quickly but she didn't even have the energy for a refill. No one at work would recognise me, she thought, and soon she began to remember how she had felt after Daniel's death and how Ted had come to her, like a guardian angel. She supposed she had never expected him to stay or she would have told him she loved him, which she never had. Or perhaps there was another reason. Perhaps she didn't love him at all. Perhaps she was as inhuman as people thought she was, except she wasn't. She tried to remember her analysis to Nina about the sexual-political agenda behind Ted's leaving her but the arguments eluded her. She wondered whether she might call Nina but knew that she had sent a letter to cause pain. She was on her own. As ever.

Fay closed her eyes to the semi-darkness. When she opened them again nothing had changed, except that it was darker and she felt able to pour herself another large Scotch. Idly she remembered, in another life, that morning to be precise, disapproving of a patient who had told her that Scotch was the only link between him and this world. She could still remember exactly what his X-ray had looked like. No great art needed to see what he was suffering from. Not used to much drink, she began to feel better or, at least, different. She even felt able to smile at her idiot misapprehension. Of course Ted would not get in touch.

Cool now or even cold, the white skin of her arms covered with goose-bumps, Fay stood, picked up her purse and left her apartment. The heat on the streets was still intense. She hurried along Third Avenue going uptown until she reached 58th then crossed to Madison. The elegant boutiques, antiques shops, antiquarian booksellers, restaurants slowed her. She wondered if this was what she wanted. She peered closely at a suit with pink velvet lapels and thought that her mother would have died for it, except that she was dying anyway, without it. Everyone was dying, let's be straight about it. All the same, if the shop had been open she would have plunged in and bought it for her mother there and then, but that was not an option so she moved on to a shoe shop where the heels were so slim and high that a circus artist might have balked. Connie used to wear shoes like that, thought Fay disjointedly, before progressing again. There was a whole avenue of high-class shopping opportunities to be studied and she had not yet admitted to herself that she had a destination. Instead, she began to consider the nature of acquisitiveness. Was she, Fay, out of tune with proper female instincts? Her mother had always thought so. Rocking a little in front of a window filled with huge gold and silver necklaces, Fay tried to understand why anyone should want to buy one. Maybe if a woman thought herself beautiful, it seemed an appropriate adornment, but she had always known she was not good-looking and had lost interest in the whole idea a long time ago. Fay began to walk again. Am I so plain? she wondered. Her skin was clear and smooth, her waist small, her eyes dark and large. She looked down to check what she was wearing: the same she always wore to work in summer, short dark skirt, sleeveless pale-coloured blouse, pearl studs. None of this mattered. Fay stopped abruptly and turned off Madison, going west, crossing Park, Fifth, Sixth and arriving at Seventh Avenue.

How did she know the address? She even knew her surname: Miriam Suarez, a viola player who had had the benefit of Ted's company for months now. She lived in an old block of flats without a porter. Fay rang her bell.

'Yes?' It was a very sleepy voice.

'This is Fay.'

'Fay? It's . . .' a pause '. . . two in the morning.'

'I want to see Ted.' A child's cry into the darkness.

'You're the brilliant doctor, aren't you?' The voice was hardly distorted at all, awake now, bell-like – perhaps she sang as well as played the viola, thought Fay hysterically – not bad-tempered anyway. 'Ted left six months ago.'

Fay took this in. 'I need to talk.'

The voice laughed. 'Come right up.'

The girl wore a T-shirt and her largeness reminded Fay of Nina. 'Don't worry,' she said, 'I'd only been in bed five minutes. I like the night, do you?'

Fay said, 'No,' and drank the bad wine Miriam offered her. Miriam was like Ted, she thought, easy and secretive at the same time. She asked no questions and, without Fay asking any either, wrote Ted's address on a piece of paper. 'It's only two blocks over,' she pointed out obligingly.

Ted lived in a brownstone. Top flat, small window. She knew he lived there because she could see him silhouetted against the light. He had never cared much about night or day either. Something made him look out (had she screamed?) and he saw her standing under the street-lamp. She watched him move away from the window. Soon he stood facing her on the pavement. Was his face judgemental or merely tired? None of that mattered. She was a woman with a mission. She wished she had brought the remains of the whiskey with her. The thing was to say what you felt.

'I need you dreadfully,' she told him. 'I love you. I can't live without you. I love you. I love you. I love you.' Tears poured down her cheeks.

Gravely, Ted took her in his arms and wiped away the tears.

The next day Fay telephoned Connie: 'Kevin and Shirley and Kathleen and Tara are all determined to come to your mother's funeral. Perhaps they have called you already?'

'Yes,' replied Connie, faintly.

'And, incidentally,' Fay continued, 'Ted and I are back together again, and it was all thanks to the flowers you sent me. They made me realise how much I needed him.'

'Good,' said Connie, in an even smaller voice. Fay realised that she was terrified at the prospect of meeting her daughter.

Michael O'Malley had moved back temporarily with his father. This left his house in the village empty. It was a bungalow, built by Michael himself, with a garden in front and a plastered brick wall painted silver and decorated with chips of coloured glass. The house itself was painted an ice blue with white and silver trimmings. Connie confided in Eileen that it was the only thing she liked about her brother. Eileen said that she'd better open her ears and be put right about Michael. She was not

233

wearing her Catholic, successful-mother-of-eight look, as Connie liked to describe it to Orlando.

The sisters who, despite their extreme similarity of feature, skin, hair and figure, managed to look as if they were no relation at all, were driving west for their mother's funeral. In the back of the car they had, squashed closely together, Leonardo and his puppy plus his three younger cousins. They were eating sweets and shouting jokes to each other from a joke book.

'What I'm telling you is not what I'd tell anyone else. Michael has dealings with them.'

'Them who?'

'Them who want a united Ireland. He has things hidden down in the farm. I don't want to know what.'

'What are you saying Eileen? Are you saying our brother is involved with the IRA? That he's hiding lumps of Semtex or whatever it is?'

'Ssh.' She was right. Connie had raised her voice in shocked disbelief. She couldn't imagine anything more wrong than aiding and abetting murderers of whatever political belief. She made no difference between either side. Five days ago, the day of her mother's death as it happened, a ten-year-old girl had come back from school to find her mother tied to a chair and shot to a bloody mess. IRA . . . INLA . . . UDA . . . What did that little girl know? Connie sank down in her seat. She wondered if Eileen had decided to introduce the subject under circumstances that made it impossible for her to scream and shout.

'You're living in Ireland now,' said Eileen. 'You know our history. You know what has been done to us.'

'But this is doing more to us,' hissed Connie, 'if the doing is murderous attacks on innocent people.'

'They call it war. Innocent people get hurt in a war.'

'Do you call it a war?'

'I do not. It's in the North, isn't it? Let them sort it out.'

'Well, thank God for at least some sanity. But I suppose you've never tried to dissuade Michael.'

'We've never talked of it. He's fifty years of age—'

'That makes it worse. No excuses.'

They had entered a small village where the traditional rows of low, whitewashed, thatched cottages were interspersed with smartly painted bungalows, reminding Connie of Michael's glittering wall. 'I suppose he's creamed off some of those American dollars for himself,' she said bitterly. 'He and Kevin should get on just fine.'

'If you're implying nationalism is a family trait, then you'd be right enough. It's our da who started Michael off. You remember how he used to sing those songs . . .'

'Once a year when he got drunk.'

'To be sure it wasn't all show. But our mother kept him in check. She took the spirit out of him.'

They reached the end of the village and were out in mile upon mile of peat land. Connie looked at the beauty of it, the purple and sage and silver of it, and was filled with sadness. She had come to live in an idyll, put herself in an ivory tower with Orlando holding the key. She had thought she was part of the true spirit of Ireland but now she saw that she had been merely hiding from the reality. Was even her mother at fault for denying her husband his patriotic manhood?

'Are you suggesting that a man has to assist in violence to prove his virility?'

'I know it half killed our father, giving it up.'

'Half killed isn't so bad.' Connie had an image of her father as he had been when she was a child, that grim, woebegone look of his, which had used to drive her mad, perhaps had driven her away. It was amazing that he had lived so long, outlived her spunky mother, and now, it seemed, he had passed on his frustrated bitterness to his son.

'At least Kevin and his family have chosen to reside at a distance,' said Eileen, probingly.

But Connie did not want to talk about Kevin and his family.

The American contingent arrived for the funeral at Knock airport. Connie felt very frail. She had never felt any age before but now she felt forty – which she was. Everybody else looked very young and strong to her, including her older sisters and brothers. Even her poor widowed father seemed to her sinewy and indestructible.

Kevin and Shirley walked across the airport Tarmac. Behind them came their daughters, half hidden, strung about with bags. The family waited in a crowd at the barrier, black-red hair through three generations. Eileen's youngest was making the crowing noise that indicated overexcitement. There was a priest too, and a girlfriend Michael had produced. She was young with a vixen's mask below orange hair and Connie did not trust her. She was too young for Michael in her skimpy jeans and looked like a city girl with a packet of cigarettes in her hand. Connie did not think, I was once like that, because she knew she never had been. At her most wild she had kept an innocent heart, hadn't she?

Mr O'Malley stood with a son on either side and watched the third, the forbidden one, approaching. Connie wondered if he might assume guilt for not allowing his eldest back till his mother was dead. But perhaps even that was not certain, for Mrs O'Malley had been the daily communicant, the haunter of priests, the sister of a holy nun. Maybe she was the one who had kept the American couple at bay. Although Kevin, too, was making his Irish roots clear by sporting a violently green jacket.

They came closer. For a second Connie had a clear image of her daughter. At the same moment Leonardo took his mother's hand. He was overexcited too, with so much family and the airport. He was a country boy, born in the Irish midlands, who had never been to an airport.

'Who are those girls?' he asked.

Connie looked down at him. He was wearing a T-short, also green, with LIR WATER printed across it. His not very clean dark curls hung down to his flushed cheeks. Could he who made everything right make this right too? 'I told you already. Your cousins from America.'

'They don't look like my cousins.'

Connie stared. A dark slim girl with a fairer girl. That must be Kathleen. Had she been fairer as a child. Or was it the American sun? And so tall for a ten-year-old? Oh, my God, it wasn't Kathleen! Kathleen had died and no one had told her! Panicked, Connie looked at Shirley and Kevin, only a few yards away now. They were hiding anxiety under smiles and there between them was Fay. Of course, she had persuaded Fay to come, too. Fay would have told her of any tragic death. She must calm herself. This large sun-tinged girl was Kathleen. Her daughter.

There was so many people, so much confusion, warmth, handshakes, kissings, excitement, that Connie had met Kathleen and introduced her to Leonardo without knowing what she was doing. She retained an image, however, of a confident American girl who did not expect life to hold secrets. She is not like me, thought Connie, as she put her arms round Fay, as she hung on and managed not to cry. Fay understood. Fay had come to support her. She must not cry, not that anyone would bother in all the commotion. Connie began to recover. As usual, Leonardo was right. Kathleen was not like any of their dark, white-skinned family. Fleetingly now, she pictured Merlin de Witt but he, too, was dark and narrow. Kathleen had transmogrified and become just the daughter for thrusting Washington parents. Perhaps I'm relieved, thought Connie, holding on tightly to Fay. Or perhaps I'm dreadfully sad.

Fay felt as if she were part of a circus, all of them playing absurd roles for no obvious audience. Small buses had been hired by Michael to supplement the cars available. They came from his local church and had pictures of the Virgin Mary painted on their sides. The Americans – herself, Kevin, Shirley, Kathleen and Tara – who had seemed perfectly ordinary when they had crossed the Tarmac at Washington airport, had now become caricatures of themselves. Kevin, with his absurd jacket, was playing the part of a powerful Kennedy-style clan leader. Shirley had become cheerleader, while her daughters became the two sides of the moon, light and dark, infinitely mysterious. Even she felt the alien touch of her Jewishness.

'You should have brought Ted,' said Connie suddenly, speaking over Leonardo's head – he was sitting on her lap.

'I couldn't bring Ted for the best of reasons. He's been commissioned to write a film score.'

'A film score! There's news! Sometimes this trying family I have here makes me forget the world outside.'

Fay, made more kindly by Connie's admiration for Ted, thought this might be true. As if this bus did not hold enough circus performers, the other included two satirical and probably drunken brothers, a dozen or more children (or so it seemed), some physically and mentally handicapped, and an old, clearly insane man wearing a deer-stalker. 'You seem to have it under perfect control.'

It was at this moment that their bus broke down. The leading bus, driven erratically and at speed by Joe, disappeared round a corner.

They clambered out. Orlando, perhaps out of nervousness, took Leonardo on his shoulders, although he was much too big for such patronage. Mr O'Malley sat on a large stone, which just might have been a Celtic cross, and Kevin took up position at his father's side, standing, arms folded. Nobody seemed to be much interested in putting the bus to rights, which Fay pointed out to Connie.

'Oh, I expect Michael will return soon enough. He works in a garage, you know.'

Fay began to feel slightly delirious. She recognised the out-of-control idiocy of the situation from her past. 'If Orlando gambols about like that, Leo's in grave danger of falling on to the Tarmac head first.'

'How lucky we have a doctor in our midst,' responded Connie. Kathleen and Tara were holding hands and dancing on the road. Fay

237

watched as Connie took them on either hand and, giving a sly look at Fay, began to teach them an Irish jig. 'Now you Americans must learn the story of the door at the crossroads . . .' Ah, we're back at the ancient yew, thought Fay.

Orlando slid his son into the midst of the dancers and came to Fay. He was not her type, she thought, too ungainly, eccentric, hairy, Irish, English, incomprehensible. His trousers, she noted, were done up with a tie and he seemed to be wearing a pyjama top. He took her arm.

'You were admiring my belt. It's the All-Ireland rugby tie, my most favoured possession. A united Ireland is a great ambition.'

'But you're Anglo-Irish.'

'I also play the cello. Your Ted's a musician, I know.'

'He's a composer.'

Fay found they were walking up and down the roadside. She felt exposed but, for some reason, also honoured. 'And you run a water-bottling plant.'

'The best of me aspires to play the cello, although the results are disappointing. I am not a good businessman but, thanks to the Common Market, on the way to becoming an uncommonly successful one. Ha! It is kind of you to come.'

They were now at some distance from the bus and Fay saw that this was the reason he had taken her arm and led her away. 'I'm glad to come. Connie and I are very old friends. We've an unspoken agreement that I keep an eye on Kathleen. She's a lovely girl.'

'Yes. Yes.' Orlando turned away as if shy.

'Well, I suppose she's glad to see Kathleen.'

'I can't say. It is hard. Tell me, do you think she's . . .' he paused '. . . well?' His expression was serious, anxious, as if prepared for the worst.

Fay only needed to be honest. 'I'd never have guessed she could be so happy.'

Orlando took her other arm, so they were face to face. She saw that his eyes were filling with tears. 'That's all I ever wanted.'

Kevin's family and Connie's had crammed themselves into the old O'Malley farmhouse. At five Connie crept into the living room to say farewell to her mother. She had only been there a few minutes murmuring a Hail Mary over the smoothly drawn face, when Kathleen entered, barefoot and shivering. 'I've never laid eyes on a dead person,' she said. As if that didn't sound quite right, she added, 'She is my grandmother, even if I am adopted.'

238

'She is,' agreed Connie impartially, still on her knees. Could she pretend her teeth were chattering because of the cold? But what about her hands, wavering around like a marionette's? She fixed them firmly together. 'Will you say a prayer along with me?'

'If you like.'

Kathleen knelt and Connie saw she had the O'Malley foot with the long second toe and the narrow heel. Her heart began to rush but she looked on her mother, on the face of death, and reminded herself that she had done well to give this mortal being life. 'What prayer do you like?'

'At my confirmation I heard a new one: Hail, Holy Queen, Mother of Mercy ... I can't remember more.'

Connie began to recite in the sing-song voice of childhood.

> 'Hail, Holy Queen, Mother of Mercy,
> Hail, our life, our sweetness and our hope,
> To thee do we cry, poor banished children of Eve ...'

And when Connie began to sob, Kathleen put her smooth sunburnt hand over hers and Connie thought, I don't deserve this, and cried even more.

Everybody agreed they were thankful for the rain at the funeral. 'Who would want sun on an open grave?' asked Connie, rhetorically.

'It would put a body in mind of hell flames,' agreed Eileen.

The sisters hung on to each other, dressed in the darkest of black. Fay had never seen Connie so Irish. The three brothers, in their new black suits and white shirts, which still showed creases from the packet, were silenced, it seemed, by their responsibility for carrying the coffin, with Eileen's eldest.

Suddenly Mr O'Malley spoke. 'I used to have four sons.' He looked about him searchingly. Finbar! Finbar, the son who had gone to England during the war. Connie, normally attuned for drama, attempted to repress critical thoughts of her father, who could not be satisfied with five children present and correct. The only comment was made by Michael in an undertone, hardly appropriate over his mother's corpse: 'The bastard traitor.' Further comment or consolation was interrupted by the arrival of the undertakers.

Fay watched this funeral with a sense of awe. It was the hugeness of Catholic belief that amazed her. She had assumed that priests still promised eternal peace in a heavenly kingdom but that hellfire had disappeared at the same time as Latin, and virgins and martyrs. But it was perfectly clear from the priest's address in the village church, and the contented atmosphere of his congregation, swelled beyond the family by neighbours and anyone who wanted to attend a mass, that here in this reclusive corner nothing had changed for hundreds of years.

An old woman had whispered in her ear as she came into the church, 'The good soul has passed on to revive her drooping spirit near the restful waters of the Promised Land,' adding in a hiss. 'She has avoided the flames!'

Mrs O'Malley was to join the holy saints in heaven, not because she was a good woman but because she had produced seven children – one dead (mentioned), one missing (unmentioned), and because she had attended mass at every opportunity. In other words, as Fay understood it with some indignation, her life had not existed outside the precepts of the Church. She began to understand Connie's escape from Ireland more easily and her return to Catholicism less easily.

Outside, in the graveyard, rain fell continuously. The grave-diggers stood nearby, leaning in familiar pose on their spades, and Eileen's youngest was hushed by his brothers and sisters. Connie cried, then Eileen and her children, soon joined by Kathleen and Tara. Fay was surprised by all these tears when heaven was so consolingly near at hand. She thought of Daniel's funeral, which was blackened by her conviction that his life was at an absolute end and, worse still, had been given in an unjustifiable war. But even then she had not cried. Perhaps if things are too bad, tears are too paltry a reaction. Or perhaps it was just her.

The wake was held at the O'Malley farm. Food, drink, chairs, tables had all been transported there. A shed to provide extension for the house had been cleaned and prepared. The whole village, using a variety of transport, including bicycles, horses and tractors, was coming. Fay began to feel very tired.

At about four the rain stopped and the startling beauty of the countryside, combined with the sudden warmth and the bottles of alcohol already consumed, turned cheerful Christian celebration into hilarity of a distinctly pagan sort. The priest, Father Walsh, presumably feeling he had done his duty in fine style, was in the forefront of this mood. 'Well, Mr O'Malley,' he said, 'what's this I hear about a missing son? Do you want me to put Mother Church on his case? There's dear Father Patrick in Kensington now who's a mastiff's nose for missing sons.'

As Mr O'Malley considered this offer, although the profundity of his silence had grown during the course of the day, another voice answered for him: 'We don't want disloyal bastards in this country.'

'Michael!' protested Connie. Joe, also nearby, rose up from his chair to face his brother.

'Fin ... did his duty as a brave man, a soldier ...' He paused and swayed, giving Michael time to intervene.

'A soldier! A British soldier, you mean, in an army of murderers. The devil's army! He lost his right to be an Irishman. I will not call such a man brother and nor should you.'

'But, Michael,' began Eileen, who had also appeared – all of a sudden the little room was very crowded, 'he was only a lad, barely seventeen, and the war was over a few months after he joined.'

But Michael looked at her with steely eyes, filled with hatred. 'Tell them, Da. Tell these foreigners what the British have done to our country. Give them a bit of a history lesson. Of 1798 and 1916. Of the battle of the Boyne and the million starved to death in the famine.' His voice had risen and all the syllables were filled with rage. 'Tell them how our grandfather lost his arm and how our great-grandfather lost his life. Tell them how Miriam Daly was tied to her chair before they pumped her full of British lead.'

Now Kevin stepped forward, and Fay, seeing his respectable, educated bulk, felt comfortably sure he would deal and placate.

'I'm an Irishman, as much as you are, Michael. My blood is the same as yours, my allegiance is as great.'

'You're a great big Yank, Kevin!' jeered Michael. 'All the Yank money in the world can't change that. All the sentimental Kennedy twaddle didn't make him Irish and it doesn't make you Irish. All you're good for is dollars. You made your choice forty years ago when I was not yet a man. There's no second chance for patriotism, no second best either. You've bought yourself an American wife and American children and you no longer know the Blarney Stone from a pot of piss, or the song of Kevin Barry from America the Brave! Sure you're not as shamed as those who sup with the enemy but don't stand there and tell me you're an Irishman!'

Fay noticed Connie look to her father, perhaps to stem Michael's invective. Amid a babble of voices, Connie went to him, leaning silent against the wall. It struck Fay that he had a peculiar expression on his face. As she touched him, he shifted and, like a plank unbalanced, fell directly to the floor.

'Oh, my God! Oh, my God!' Eileen set up the cry. 'Look what you've done, Michael! You've killed your own da with your wicked anger!' They all were on the floor around him then, advising, cajoling, condemning. Fay remembered she was a doctor. She knelt beside O'Malley.

'There's no pulse,' she pronounced. 'I'm so sorry. So very sorry.'

The priest remembered he was a priest and, with shaking hands and hardly audible voice, began to say the last rites. The confusion became greater because only those in the kitchen knew what had happened. In the next room someone was singing and out in the garden the children had started dancing again and no one had the heart to stop them.

Connie, a glass in one hand, the other clinging to Orlando, watched as Fay, Shirley and Eileen, plus several women from the village, tended her father's body. She looked at her brothers, at Michael, his blank, blind, cruel face, at Joe, his head filled with whiskey, at Kevin, feebly suffering – men who caused death but could not prevent it. She took another large gulp of whiskey, letting the warmth whirl around her head. 'I promise, I promise . . .' she began, in a loud unnatural voice '. . . I promise you, God, that I'm not going to leave it at this, all this pointless hatred and confusion. We women know much better than that. I'll make myself the centre of a sisterhood for peace and you men of violence can go crying for your whiskey,' here she took another gulp from her glass, 'and your loving because we'll be telling you about another way of living, which makes guns as much use for a fight as spoons . . .'

Connie was drunk. Her voice faded away as she studied her empty glass disappointedly. Fay, who had stuck to Lir Water, was the only person, apart from Orlando, who listened to this vow as if it might have some meaning.

The paintings were dreadful, so dreadful that Nina could not bear to look at them for more than a few seconds. One, which was slightly less bad than the others simply because the painter had used only two colours – a fairly pretty mauve and a pink – she managed to contemplate, murmuring, 'Charming,' and hating herself even for that. Lisa dragged her inexorably forward.

It was Southern Painting's summer show, the fruit of six months' work by its members. Nina was being walked through their paintings, displayed tastefully against olive-coloured hessian. She was expected to display admiration. Lisa, at her elbow, had all kinds of laudatory words: painterly, evocative, harmonious, sympathetic, luminous. Challenged into competition, Nina studied a still-life of a bowl of apples, clearly modelled after Cézanne, and whispered, as if inspired, 'She's handled the different planes remarkably well. Is she a student you admire?'

'He's a man. A vicar, actually.' Nina saw that she had not made a popular choice. 'He insists on copying masterpieces. That's all he does, copies masterpieces from books.'

'You like a little more originality in your students?'

Lisa seemed to think she was poking fun and frowned. 'Eventually. Once they have mastered the skills.'

Nina peered at the label by the picture. How much better to express what Cézanne was expressing, even if second-hand, than to search for some non-existent originality or even individuality of their own. 'And you think the Reverend Ormsby-Fish,' could that really be his name?, 'has sufficiently mastered the skills?'

'Well, you mentioned his mastery of planes.'

'What other experts does he copy?'

'Usually Van Gogh.'

'I see.' They moved on. Nina could see that it was absurd for an English vicar called Ormsby-Fish to try to express the individuality of a lunatic French genius. Subject matter. She must not allow herself to start on that. Already she could feel a feverish anxiety.

They were now standing in front of one of the many vases of flowers. 'Who arranged these?' she asked. 'Or perhaps we should consider first who picked them.'

'Come again?' Once more Lisa seemed nonplussed. 'I think we need a cup of coffee,' she suggested consolingly. They left the gallery, Nina walking away so quickly that Lisa was forced to run after her. 'Of course, it's much more fun when you have all the painters here. They're a lively bunch. I think it might be helpful if you pretended to be rather standoffish at the start. Some of them are voracious!' Lisa laughed and opened the door to her office, soon to be Nina's. The gallery was on the ground floor, the office above. Nina thought her own office was the best bit about this utterly inappropriate job that she had taken on, for reasons too complicated to define – except at dead of night when the owl woke her and gave permission for dark anxieties.

'I expect you know all about answering-machines.' Lisa flicked a switch on a coffee machine. There were so many other things Nina couldn't do that it seemed pointless to admit she had never worked an answering-machine. All she could do was paint and she couldn't do that now. She just managed not to burst into tears.

'Biscuit?' Even the biscuit tin was decorated with a bad painting, reminiscent of Renoir at his most senile. Nina took three chocolate bourbons as a punishment and a pleasure. She ate them quickly. She thought she might become very fat indeed to annoy Gus. My husband Gus, who only wants the best for me and whom I love dearly. Perhaps she would grow to love the paintings she had just viewed, buy them for a song and hang them all round their house.

'A message from the Reverend Ormsby-Fish,' Lisa winked at Nina. 'He's probably sensed your presence. His wife paints too and once had a picture in the Royal Academy summer exhibition. It was of two goldfish on a table. We were all very impressed.'

'It's very difficult to be accepted. Students run past with the paintings while the academicians drink Bovril laced with brandy. It's called beef tea. Or perhaps it's tea laced with whiskey. Anyway, the point is they're blind drunk.' Nina reached for two more biscuits.

'Oh, we're only a little impressed by her being accepted for the summer exhibition. Quite a few of our members manage that. What we admire is her ability to paint from the imagination.'

'But surely you said it was a picture of two goldfish on a table.'

Lisa laughed in a superior manner. 'No one would kill two goldfish, would they, particularly not someone called Ormsby-Fish?'

Nina tried to laugh at what was clearly a well-practised joke, but her heart was filled with bitterness. How easily she could kill a dozen goldfish if it would lead to a decent painting. She would kill ten poodles if her name were Poodle and twenty peacocks if her name were Peacock. 'I'd better be off,' she said, standing abruptly. 'I'm meeting Gus in his office.'

Nina ambled through the pleasant streets of this little town she had known all her life. She had not thought Lisa a silly woman before. When she had revealed her past, the love affair with her father, she had seemed dignified, romantic, quite likely passionate. Nina had been able to respect her and not become resentful. But the woman she had just seen was boring, wrong-headed, petty. Either she had been corrupted by her husband, whom Nina had never met, or by her day-to-day contact with bad art. With a row of lime green poplars against the blue sky, with a cat among grasses, with poppies and cornflowers in a field, with a thundercloud reflected in a lake, with a robin poised enquiringly, with an upturned boat among reeds, a bowl of oranges, cherries, pears, a vase of marigolds, daisies, primroses, sunsets, sunrises, tranquil afternoons on the lawn. Nature had a lot to answer for, thought Nina.

Oh, my God, my God. The biscuits lay heavy in her stomach and she could no longer stop the tears. Is there no way I can get out of this?

Fay read Nina's letter during a short break before she took off for the hospital where she was to give a now rare student lecture.

Dearest Fay, You would be amazed by me. I pen this sitting at my desk. My desk! On which there is proper office equipment, not perhaps as high-tech as you but we do have a word-processor and an answering-machine on which members leave strange appeals. Yesterday a Mrs Snape spoke on the subject of autumn leaves for the entire length of the tape. I believe it was an enquiry about the properties of Yellow Oxide (in my view a very dull colour) but I have learnt that the name 'answering-machine' is not a command and such calls can be ignored, particularly if quickly wiped. I am proficient at the wipe button. My members are a very committed, hard-working lot. They are part-time artists who give it full-time attention. None of them has any talent, which makes their determination all the more remarkable, possible admirable. Matisse once told an interviewer that, if he felt no emotion as he approached his studio, he saddled his horse and went for a ride instead. Unfortunately, they do not follow his example.

I am both executive director and occasional teacher. The worst part of my job and also the most important is the need to comment positively on paintings so excruciatingly bad that it takes a valiant effort not to shut my eyes. I have actually developed a stutter so that 'beautiful' comes out 'b-b-b-' – the painter, you understand is hanging on my words, 'b-b-breath-breath-taking' or whatever lying adjective I have chosen. Eventually, in despair, I explained the problem to darling Gus, who took it seriously enough to suggest an evening spent with Roget's Thesaurus. We ended up with a three-page list, which he had typed up in his office – I was not so good at typing then as I am now. I call it my testament and carry it everywhere. Let me give you a flavour: 'brutal, compelling, powerful, overwhelming', that's for a storm at sea, 'evocative, spiritual, inspirational', for a single rose in a vase. You get the point, avoid understatement. Remember, they may not be able to paint, but they sure know how to accept compliments. It is, of course, very good for my character. I have been too self-indulgent in the past, and I have made a friend. He's called Dudley Ormsby-Fish and he's a vicar. He really only paints to annoy his wife who does a line called 'Romantic Nooks' (honestly), which she sells at local craft fairs. I will not describe them to you, beyond saying that she has a stack of artificial flower garlands in her front hall to be used when a nook is not romantic enough. Actually, that's probably the best thing about her as it shows a practical streak.

My friend Dudley wears a Panama hat and, whenever possible, a 3-piece suit. He talks about his 'flockette' – they are not very numerous – and he uses Latin tags against himself: 'Dementia virtutis umbra'. Gus considers him ridiculous but that's because he's jealous, which really is ridiculous because I have put on so much weight recently that no man, except a loving husband or the King of Tonga, could possibly fancy me. This is mainly because the previous incumbent in my position (my father's mistress, but that's another story) always kept a biscuit tin on her desk – to offer to members who popped in for a chat. Well, I only have to look at a biscuit tin to put on a stone ...

At this point, Fay felt unhappy enough to put down the pages. She took a sip of freshly squeezed orange juice and decided she hardly recognised the person writing this strange letter, a cheerful, ironic voice that rang absolutely false. It was like, she decided, a letter written home from the war, a First World War front-line missive, where merry play is made of mud being good for the skin and the other chaps being great with the wisecracks: 'What moves when it's dead? A stiff in no man's land.' It reminded her, in short, of the letters Daniel had written her from Vietnam. Lies, all lies. And, although she had never found out what Daniel's lies were disguising, there was some hope she could with Nina. Whatever was wrong was clearly very wrong and why was 'darling Gus' part of the whole ghastly scene? Fay popped a couple of tablets – she had taken up Mexican yam recently – and read on:

My teaching duties – a once-a-week class during term-time – are more educational for me than my students, I do believe. Some of them have been taught for twenty years, of course, whereas I only went to college for three. At first they were a little overawed, but only by my reputation, not me. They knew that I had a big success a few years ago and sold paintings to important galleries (it seems unbelievable to me now) but none of them had seen any of my paintings and they soon forgot all about that and treated me like a very ignorant teacher – which I am. On the whole they tell me what to say: 'If I ground the vase with a dark shadow here, it will throw into relief the sheen on the holly berry' – they're all painting Christmas-orientated pictures at the moment. Personally, I've quite forgotten what being a painter is like. Only my mother seems to remember. She hung one of my unfinished pictures in the kitchen the other day. It gave me a tremendous surprise, like a ghost popping up across the cottage pie. I started to look for the right adjectives, 'mysterious', 'emotional', 'magnetic', before remembering I didn't have to bother. It was my picture. I could call it 'bad' if I liked. Actually, it was rather good. The person who had been me who had painted it knew what she was up to. All the same I asked my mother to take it down. It was a picture of Gus's motorbike in the wood near Connie's lake . . .

Connie is well, I gather, despite the farce of her mother's funeral, or maybe she made it seem like a farce to cheer me up – not that I need cheering up. I am very proud of being a working woman . . .

Again Fay put down the letter. She saw from the further two pages that Nina now embarked on news of Connie, Veronica, Gus, Helen and Jamie.

Later in the day, she showed the letter to Ted, who scanned it with the concentration usually reserved for sheet music. 'A *cri de coeur*, I'd say. She's obviously forgiven or forgotten the notorious letter when you demolished her.'

'That's ages ago. I suppose I just may have influenced her to become part of the workforce. How ever can I answer it?'

'Support. Encouragement. Gus is obviously the one managing operations. You can't cross him. At least she doesn't seem to be washing.'

'You mean she doesn't mention it.'

Ted began to hum, a habit he'd developed recently. Since his return to Fay, there had been two developments: he had been commissioned to write a piece of music for television and a piece for a film; and he had begun to hum. He hummed more or less whenever he wasn't talking, or so it seemed to Fay. She told herself it was like a cat purring. He stopped humming for a second. 'Is it conceivable your instincts are wrong and she really is enjoying job satisfaction for the first time in her life?'

'Are you saying that if you tell yourself you're happy then you are happy?'

'Nothing so profound. But if we can't help her, we may as well look on the bright side. Unless you are truly guilty.'

Fay tried to call Nina but Gus, at his desk, answered: 'I'll get the phone as near as I can to her. We've just installed a new long cord. She's in the garden scarifying the lawn.'

'Whatever's that?' Fay could hear Gus treading down the uncarpeted stairs.

Gus was serious. 'The scarifier churns up the moss, chucks it, making a terrible mess of the lawn, which we then reseed, roll, feed with a combination fertiliser, weed-killer and later apply sand . . .'

By now Fay could hear the faint squawk of birds and found it easy to picture the Sussex sky, the trees, the paddock, the wide, flat lawn.

'Where's Nina?' shouted Gus, in an aside to an unknown person (probably Veronica) who mumbled unintelligible – to Fay – information.

'Ha. Ha,' said a pleased-sounding Gus back on line. 'There she is scarifying like billy-oh.' Indeed, a noise of some vibrating machine became gradually louder.

'Nina!' called Gus, voice almost drowned by the moss-eating monster. 'It's your friend Fay.'

At this point Fay wondered whether Gus knew it was a transatlantic call – she had said nothing, assuming he did know – and, if he did, did this making-free with her telephone bill imply an instinctive revenge on herself too, the too close girlfriend? If not, it showed either a careless lack of thought or a careless attitude to money.

At last there came the faint sound of Nina's voice. 'Oh! No. Hold on.' There was a squeak, a pip and then silence. She had been cut off.

Fay sat back in her chair and began to laugh. Why it was so funny she did not know. Something about a grown woman spending the afternoon tearing moss out by its roots (if indeed moss has roots), something about the term 'scarifying the lawn', and then presumably, being Nina, she had pressed the wrong button. Really, it was all too much. Surely someone out scarifying the lawn could not be in misery?

After a moment or so she looked at her watch. Possibly her eight thirty a.m. patient was not going to show. She returned for a second to efficient contemplation of the X-rays, glowing like shadowy mountains, against her wall, and then, irresistibly, dialled England again. Gus answered immediately, with the voice of a man back at his desk, yet sounding more flustered. 'I'm so sorry, Fay. I'm afraid Nina cut you off. Scarifying tends to take over a person, takes their mind off the present, if you know what I mean . . .' His voice trailed away.

'Not to worry,' said Fay. 'I'll call her later.' Laughing again, she switched off the telephone.

*

Fay's decision to marry could not be directly attributed to the scarifier, she knew. It was not that the country scene, as received over the transatlantic telephone, convinced her of the joys of domesticity. It was nothing at all to do with Gus's willingness to take a convoluted walk into the garden. It reassured her about Nina's welfare but it would be impossible to find any point of comparison with her own life and aims. On the contrary, it was the absurdity of this dissimilarity that at first made her laugh and then led to an unexpected revolution.

Suddenly, everything that had seemed fixed, inevitable and binding seemed to change shape. Her Jewishness, her feelings towards her family, her guilt, her ambition, her fear of loving too greatly, which had always dominated every thought and every action, moved into different perspective. The solid wall over which she could, at best, peer on tiptoe, had, in the course of her laughter, dissolved into a pile of rubble, leaving her the freedom to step out and do as she pleased.

Later, when she attempted to explain this sensation to her shrink, she could do no better than to say it was a sense of the randomness of any one moment that had released her. It no longer seemed sensible to place such emphasis on anything. In which case she might as well step forward briskly into the unknown. Brave abandon replaced control. In the space of a few minutes what had seemed impossible became easy. That evening, she had gone with Ted to the Italian restaurant where they had entertained Nina and Connie seven years ago and there, over a strong martini, proposed to him.

He, more obedient than celebratory, made it clear that he did not trust her shining eyes and signalling hands. 'It's so truly obvious!' she cried.

'Isn't this your busy summer?' he reminded her. 'Radiology in the office, radiology in the hospital, lectures to mean-spirited students and something called vacation time. And that's leaving out your mother.'

'There are some things that won't wait.'

It was the change in their love-making that seemed to convince him. It began with the way she took off her clothes. Instead of removing them in an efficiently organised manner: jacket, shoes, tights, skirt, shirt, slip, brassière, pants, lifting them one from the other as you might several layers of packaging, she ignored their existence, kissing him with such passion that his strong musician's hands shook as they fumbled with zips and clasps. Often neither of them was completely naked before he must enter her and, before long, both their heads were spinning somewhere fifteen floors high. In those moments of coming together, her body, following the example of her head, became both weightless yet at the same gloriously sensitive so she, too, who had always been silent in their bed-time meetings, yodelled her pleasure.

Afterwards she resisted feelings of fear and shame, and they laughed together at the thought of the bad-tempered lawyer couple below them. 'Marriage is reputed to put the lid on fun sex, Dr Blass,' commented Ted, holding his hand against the softer part of her thigh – much, much softer than it had ever been before. 'The shape of the flesh,' he told her, 'is dictated by the set of the mind just as the mind controls movement. You might put that into a lecture.'

Much later in the night she was aware that he had left the bed and a faint sound of music came from beyond the door.

Why *had* Fay got married? Fay knew that Nina and Connie wondered this as they produced their congratulations. It seemed so out of character, so bold, such a disorganised and disorganising sort of thing to do so late in the day when she was such a *success*. Surely she believed that the silver-coated knight with the plumed helmet was long crushed under the heel of the machete-wielding huntress? Marriage – they thought they knew her well enough to state her view – was for the foolishly romantic Irish like Connie or the inadequately self-indulgent English like Nina. Fay's role was to be made of sterner stuff, always had been, always would (a touch of, if not anti, then *Semitism* came in here). She had entered the lists, refused to flutter her eyelashes, nor offered her handkerchief to wear in a knight's gauntlet, because she knew better. So they thought, she thought, because she was *going somewhere*.

'We're just so thrilled for you,' wrote Connie. 'We're so very happy for you,' faxed Nina. And Fay, knowing them well enough, knew what they were thinking and was very glad they had decided not to throw cold water. She had never felt so happy in her life. And she was still working.

1981

Nina immediately felt the coldness between her mother and her husband. They stood at either side of the fireplace, one holding tongs clasping a lump of coal, the other a log of wood, green-pickled with lichen. They had been arguing certainly and, since they had chosen silence at her entrance, they had been arguing about her. Nina felt enraged, exhausted and humiliated. Wasn't it enough that she had made such a success of Southern Painting that the members now saw her as one of them, which gave her a consoling cloak of invisibility? She had done as her husband and daughter had advised (Helen, she believed, was truly impressed by her efficiency with the typewriter, the answering-machine, the fax – perhaps one of these days they'd even have a computer). She was doing her duty, out of love (out of despair), but did that mean she must also be happy? For she knew it was her happiness that had caused the argument. Or, rather, her lack of it.

'Stop glaring at each other,' said Nina, in her new brisk and cheerful manner.

Obediently Gus flung the log on to the fire and Veronica opened the claws of the tong so that the coal dropped down and found a bed for itself in the embers. Nina watched abstractedly.

'I'm going to make tea,' said Veronica, leaving the room.

Gus took Nina's arm and they went together to the sofa. She felt like a sofa herself, so plump, malleable and unproductive. Unproductive, that is, in any way that she could truly admire and yet Gus loved her more and more and she loved him back. Her flesh now warmed to his touch. If it weren't for her mother, they would lie down now on the rug in front of the fire. Sex is such a consolation, she thought and, as so often, found herself resisting the urge to cry. Instead, she smiled and said to Gus, 'I had a really productive day.' How could she use the very word she had just discounted? 'Irene Vane joined the club and she's due to be Mayor of Brighton next year.'

'What a coup!' agreed Gus. 'Does that mean you're up to the two-hundred mark?'

'One short,' said Nina brightly, while thinking that this target of two hundred members was utterly ridiculous and, if she had any guts at all, instead of working for an increase she'd put her efforts into a reduction, signing up only those who could paint a picture worth viewing. This week, although it was February, her members had already begun work for the Easter exhibition with its usual quota of egg-yolk daffodils. 'I think the Easter exhibition will be our best ever,' she said glowingly. 'It may even go on a little tour.'

'Well done.'

Nina looked at Gus, at the face she loved so much, the warm-coloured skin, pale eyes, rim of hair, at the slightly too long sideburns, and felt the tearing and wrenching of guilt and cowardice. I tell you lies all the time, she thought, to make you think I'm a sensible, happy person, because if I showed you the hideous, miserable muddle that is me, you would have every reason to stop loving me.

'You do look serious,' said Gus. 'Shall we go to a film?'

'As long as it has a happy ending.'

'Impossible, these days.' And Gus meant nothing more than that.

The small, privately owned cinema in town was in danger of being axed and the owners had asked for local support so Nina was not surprised to see her painting vicar and his artistic wife. And it was Gus who suppressed a groan.

'Greetings Prof and Prof's husband.' Dudley Ormsby-Fish was always at his most jocular in the presence of his wife. Nina assumed it was done to irritate and tried not to laugh too much. 'And how many daffodils have we had in today?'

'If only tulips would flower before Easter,' sighed Pippa Ormsby-Fish. 'They're such a *historical* flower.'

'You're referring to the market in tulips bulbs in seventeenth-century Holland, I assume?' enquired Gus, who always knew everything about everything, which was part of the reason Nina loved him because he made up for her knowing nothing about anything.

'I am,' replied Pippa, batting her mascaraed eyelashes. 'I am not easily persuaded by history but in the case of a tulip bulb I could be.'

Together they moved into the cinema, hurrying because of the cold. Idly, a thought passed Nina by. Perhaps I could fall in love with someone else, however old and fat I seem. But this tart spice of wickedness was quickly replaced by the usual ache of despair. This, too, passed. The foyer was warm and Gus insisted on buying her popcorn. Everybody said *The French Lieutenant's Woman* was a tremendous film. Doubtless she would agree.

Connie watched Leonardo watching the mare being shod. It made her smile to see how like a miniature Orlando he was, with the same prominent nose and wide-spaced green eyes. His pony was tied to a rusty ring in the wall, waiting his turn. Every now and again, Leonardo made a half-hearted attempt at brushing off a bit of caked mud, but mostly he watched the blacksmith who was paring off a slice of hoof. 'Doesn't it hurt?' he asked eventually, pursing his mouth as if he could feel the pain.

'As much as it hurts you when your ma clips your toenails.'

The rain fell softly. The stables were semi-ruined, slate tiles fallen, broken or stacked, stone walls standing firm but windows broken or askew. Ivy crawled about the outer walls, and ragwort and nettles, grown extra tall in their search for light, reached out of the roofless rooms. Only the old tack room and hayloft above it stood sturdily weatherproof and this was where Leonardo often played, imagining, he had once explained to Connie, a group of playmates. He was an odd boy, she sometimes noticed. He was not yet six but seemed older, sociable when possible but not afraid of being alone.

'So how do you fill this great town you've got here?' she heard the blacksmith asking him. 'You've enough buildings to house half of Dublin.'

The question seemed to upset Leonardo as if it were a reproach. He walked to the stable door, half off its hinges, and kicked it two or three times before returning not to the blacksmith but to his mother. 'We could, couldn't we, have some poor children out here?'

'Well, that's a fine idea!' The blacksmith dropped the horse's hoof to the ground. 'Get them out here and the older fellows will rebuild the place. Give them a goalpost and a boat or two for the lake and they'll think themselves kings of creation. It's a grand boy you are for ideas!' He gave Leonardo a commendatory shove. 'And now with the good Lord on your side, you've only got your ma and pa to get round.' He gave a large wink in Connie's direction. 'And you'll not get your house burnt down by supporters of Bobby Sands.'

Fay stroked Ted's naked shoulder and arm, although she knew he wanted to sleep. He had just conducted one of his own compositions in a small theatre in the West Village and only six people had turned up to hear it. He had gone ahead all the same, but now he wanted to sleep, in black, silent oblivion, and wake up to a different day. He was like that, secret, uncommunicative and determined. Fay understood because she was like that too, but now she wanted to tell him something. She could hear her heart pounding excitedly in the stillness. This news could not wait another moment.

'Do you think I could ever be pregnant, Ted?' She waited anxiously. 'Yes.'

'Would you like it if I got pregnant, Ted?'

'Yes.' He seemed to fall asleep between each of her questions but his answers were clear enough.

'You don't think there are already too many children born?' She rolled over on to her elbow and leant over him. 'Or that there's too much cruelty and suffering?'

'Are we talking Daniel here?'

'No. Yes. No.' She never forgot about Daniel but that didn't mean she was always talking about him. Or perhaps Ted was right. 'Not just Daniel.' Lately Ted, who was so much younger than her, had begun to go bald. He had cut his hair short and grown a small beard. Fay could just see its outline in the darkness. He was moving towards her, fully awake now.

'Do I have a part in this?'

'I was afraid I couldn't have children.'

'Why?' He held her now, listening to what she had to say. No humming yet.

'Because I never got pregnant.'

'That's because you're an efficient woman.'

'Or because I didn't want a baby.'

They both slept naked. At first this had been difficult for Fay because she was reminded of white cadavers waiting for dissection. Now she loved lying with skin touching skin. Even if they didn't make love, she enjoyed this skin communication and, each night, was surprised to find she did.

Ted reached down and placed his hand on her small flat belly. He hummed a few delicate bars then whispered into her ear, 'Are you telling me, dear Doctor, I'm to become a father?'

'I guess I am.'

Ted became incredibly still as if he were holding his breath. Fay held hers too. 'Guess what,' he said eventually, 'I've just stopped believing "Ode to Joy" is corny.'

'Listen, Nina,' Connie shrieked down the telephone. 'Fay's going to have twins. Twin boys. She knows everything about them already. They're called Lex and Jim and they're going to be born on Fay's mother's birthday. Fay's just so controlling!'

Nina wrote to Connie: 'Fay has sent me a photograph of her twins inside her womb . . . She says because she is so old and a doctor, she has them monitored in every way possible without actually killing them.'

Fay stood in her office, gazing at the ultrasound negatives on her wall of light. This was her job, gazing at photographs to detect abnormalities. As she looked at her womb and at the two creatures curled up so neatly inside it, she was overcome with a great wave of terror, followed immediately by an equal rush of exhilaration. 'Oh, my God! Oh, my

God!' Strange words for an unbeliever, but what others were there? Trembling, she felt for her chair and sank into it.

Connie telephoned Nina: 'Do you think you can pray for people who don't believe in prayer? I do want Fay's birth to go well. Orlando says God will sort out such problems but I wouldn't want to insult Fay's lack of belief.'

Ted scrawled the same fax to Nina and Connie:

30 November 1981

Lex and Jim born a healthy 4.10 and 4.5 respectively STOP Fay had a Caesar but is in excellent shape STOP

There followed a line of music which neither Connie nor Nina could decipher but Veronica identified as from Beethoven's 'Ode to Joy'.

1984

Fay received a fax from Connie, headed 'Sisterhood for Peace':

VISITING BROTHER KEVIN VIA NEW YORK STOP MAKE THE TWINS READY FOR GODMOTHER CONSTANCE STOP

Fay hoped Connie wouldn't be in too ebullient mood. Lex and Jim had woken each other in the night and then woken her. She and Ted were planning to look at a house in Brooklyn, with a view to buying, when the housekeeper turned up. If she turned up. Carole was having trouble with her own children: a teenage daughter was pregnant and refusing to give the name of the father.

Fay sighed. One of the many problems of being an elderly mother was that she had lost the kind of youthful selfishness that protected her from sympathising with other people's troubles. Or perhaps it was because she was a doctor. She considered this and concluded that she hadn't been an essentially caring sort of doctor for some time, which brought her back to age. At forty-four she was ridiculously old to have three-year-old sons. Fay's heart lurched with maternal terror. It had done too much lurching. Luckily, Ted took a brisker attitude. Always secretive about himself, he had only recently revealed that he was one of eight children, growing up, till he was ten on a small farm. Ted's view was that children brought themselves up – particularly twins. There was a set of twins in his family, one living in Nova Scotia, one in India. When Fay had objected that children in Manhattan could not bring themselves up if survival to maturity was the objective, he suggested they moved to Brooklyn, a house near the university, where he already spent much of his time, teaching composition.

'Where's Ted?' asked Connie, as soon as she entered the apartment. It was a cold day, just before Christmas, and she had arrived bundled up in layers of woollen cardigans, apparently hand-knitted and, in places, even darned. 'My mother's,' she answered to Fay's stares. 'Where's Ted?' she repeated.

Fay had noticed this often since the birth of the boys. Friends who had never previously put Ted at the top of the agenda, now seemed compelled to question his whereabouts and general state of being while her own situation was, apparently, less interesting. It was difficult not to conclude that this was the effect of motherhood.

'How's Lex and Jim?' continued Connie, proving that Fay did not come even in second place. 'You understand that I refer to their spiritual well-being, knowing that you are only too capable of checking out their physical.'

Connie had elected herself the boys' godmother, a role she carried out by assiduously plying them with religious material, including prayer books, holy pictures, rosary beads and plastic images of the Virgin Mary containing holy water from Knock. All this despite Fay pointing out that she and Ted had no intention of imposing any religion, least of all Roman Catholicism, on their children. '*Ce n'importe pas,*' Connie had retorted gaily. 'I shall do it all myself with no help from you.'

'Lex and Jim have gone off with Carole – she's the housekeeper – to their play centre and Ted is in Brooklyn looking at houses.' In the end, Fay had felt too tired to go with him.

Connie finished unwrapping herself and turned her attention to Fay. 'You're coming with me to see Shirley, I trust?'

Fay had often noticed that people with a mission felt no hesitation in putting their own needs first. She supposed that in her obsessive years as a surgeon she had been the same. Now Connie stared at her, blue eyes wide, her still near-perfect skin rather flushed. Fay felt she herself looked twenty years older and could see her own thought reflected in Connie's expression.

With an effort she thought seriously about Connie's reasons for being here and remembered her years in New York when the Vietnam war was being fought and protested. Had this been an influence when she'd determined to start this Sisterhood for Peace? Most probably, although her principal involvement had been with men of violence, like the terrifying Trigear.

'I did write to you my reservations. Kevin makes money a lot more easily than he gives it away.'

Connie looked impatient. 'I know Kevin gives thousands of dollars to Sinn Fein, but that makes it all the more important to nobble Shirley. Look, Kevin is my brother!'

'Have a cup of coffee,' said Fay, instead of pointing out the obvious, that Michael was Connie's brother too. After an interval for motherhood, Connie's life had returned to being more dramatic than anyone else's, thought Fay. Or did she just present it that way?

Over coffee, they became more relaxed with each other. 'I guess you think my visit has something to do with Kathleen?' Connie said to Fay. She had certainly wondered. 'I want to tell you, dearest friend, who has seen me through so much, particularly in this area, that ever since my mother's funeral and my father's death, I have stopped thinking of Kathleen as my daughter.'

Fay, still fairly new to motherhood, tried to disguise her disbelief. No one could make this sort of rational judgement about their child, even if it might make life easier.

'At the funeral I saw Kathleen,' Connie spoke the name without hesitation, 'as this American girl, Shirley and Kevin's daughter, utterly unlike me or Eileen or her children or darling Leo. She was bigger, brown-skinned, fair – just as Kevin is not like us. She was cheerful but not witty. I had an emotional moment with her over my mother's coffin, when I suddenly became intimate with her, but as if she were my niece, never as my daughter. Look how easily I pronounce that word! Daughter, daughter, daughter. Not mine. When it was all over, I thought about it a little more and I realised I had been hanging on to the idea of her as *my* daughter as you cling to a lover long after you've fallen out of love. The reality goes further and further into the distance.'

Fay, who had never considered Connie had much of a grip on reality, gave up looking sympathetic. 'But she *is* your daughter.'

'Oh, Fay!' Connie pouted like a child. 'Of course she is. I'm just saying that is only the biological truth whereas the reality, the *emotional* reality, which is always more important than anything else, is that she is Kevin and Shirley's daughter.'

Fay thought that 'emotional reality' was probably a contradiction in terms but did not have the energy to argue the point. 'Do you mean you're never going to tell her you're her mother?'

'Joseph, Mary and Jesus, no!' Connie seemed so shocked at the idea that Fay decided it best not to run past her the modern thinking that made knowledge of its parents essential for a child's psychological well-being. Since Connie had never confided the name of Kathleen's father, there was certainly no point in raising the notion of a father's rights.

'In Ireland,' said Connie, warming to her theme, 'mothers have brought up their daughters' bastards as a matter of good practice. A child needs love, not a certificate of birth.'

Again, Fay let it go. 'I will come with you to Washington,' she changed the subject, 'but I'll be no help in persuading Shirley to support your sisterhood, and I doubt you'll have any success. Kevin throws a party on St Patrick's Day. He's growing shamrock in tubs on his patio.'

'I throw a party on St Patrick's Day and my whole garden's overgrown with shamrock. You take care or I'll elect you president of the New York branch!'

'Me? A Jew?'

Fay said it mockingly, but Connie looked surprised. 'Peace has no race or religion,' she said lightly. '*Paix, paz, pace, pais.*'

'I prefer *amor*, love, *amour, amore.*'

'How we both have changed! Anyway, it comes to the same thing. Dear heart, I'm glad you're coming along.'

Connie hadn't been in Washington since 1970 but when Fay tried to point out some of the changes she became impatient. 'I'm not here as a tourist,' she said. 'All history is a kind of tourism.'

'Except Irish history?' asked Fay.

'Perhaps I don't mean history, I mean the past. The kind of past that turns everything into cherry blossom. I hate cherry blossom.' It had been cherry-blossom time when she had gone with Merlin de Witt to that hotel.

They were in a taxi, and since it was December, there was no danger of seeing cherry blossom. Instead the trees were garlanded with silvery Christmas lights.

'I had wanted to show you the Vietnam Memorial. It's taken all this time to get one but there it is.'

'Oh, Fay, I'm so sorry.' Connie was instantly filled with remorse. Was she still the most self-centred person in the world?

They stopped the taxi near the Vietnam Memorial and Fay took Connie to show her the black granite walls. They began to walk slowly, searching for Daniel's name among the fifty-eight thousand inscribed there. It was very cold and soon drizzling rain gave the walls a more brilliant shine. Fay said apologetically, 'I wanted to come here with you before anyone, even before Ted, because you were with Daniel that Christmas night.'

'Yes. He's important to me.' Connie paused and laid her hand against the wet stone. What did Fay understand by 'with Daniel that Christmas night'? She had never told her about their love-making and Daniel had hardly had time. In fact, she had not even told Orlando, although she told him everything. After so many years – nearly a decade – it seemed silly to carry this sort of secret around when the telling might make Fay seem less alone in her mourning. Yet something held her back. After all, she would not want Fay to know before Orlando. 'I'm the right companion for this time of remembrance,' she said soberly, 'because I believe in life after death.'

'You're lucky.'

'It's hard work. I know it sounds unlikely but Daniel's death brought me back to the Church. It made me realise I couldn't survive on my own.'

Fay was amazed. 'You cared so much for him? But you hardly knew him!'

Connie looked at Fay's expression of surprise verging on indignation and wished that the rain wasn't crawling down her back and they were sitting in a nice bar with a glass in their hands. It was so difficult estimating the right thing to say with this terrible marble slab, too – she had begun to hate it now and longed for a cross, a graveyard, a promise of immortality. What should she say to Fay?

'We made love,' she said, her wide blue eyes staring earnestly at Fay's pinched face. 'He brought me back to life in a way. He was the first man after, after . . .' She let the sentence trail, not least because Fay had turned her back and walked several yards down the line. Perhaps she hadn't heard, thought Connie. The rain was enough to make anyone deaf.

Fay stared at the black marble. 'You had sex with my brother. The very last time I saw him. Couldn't you have let him alone?'

'We made love. Fay, please,' appealed Connie, in a faltering voice. It felt as if she were overacting, although she knew she was not.

'Love,' repeated Fay, in an expressionless voice.

'I didn't mean to upset you,' said Connie, in the same little voice. She

259

guessed it was irritating but couldn't find another. 'Are you very angry? I'm sorry. It just happened. It was wonderful. He was wonderful. Please, Fay, don't be angry.'

Fay seemed to be watching two people approaching at the other end of the memorial slab. They both held efficient-looking umbrellas. She turned to Connie. 'We haven't even got an umbrella between us.'

She's furious, thought Connie dismally. I come all the way to Washington with the terror of meeting my daughter in my heart, I come all the way to raise money against the murderous bastards who kill without a conscience, and what do I do but cause anguish. I am old, she thought. Anguish never worried me in my youth. What was there to do but soldier on with the truth? The truth was so cold. 'I didn't take him from you, Fay. It was only sex for him. It meant more for me. Just a happy accident. You mattered to him.'

Fay turned round. 'Yes.' She went closer to Connie, whose white skin had become luminous with the rain. She stared at her, sighing. 'You're so beautiful but I can't blame you for that.' Slowly she reached out her hand. 'I'm sorry I reacted as I did. You're the generous one, Connie. You have to forgive me. I never was very close to Daniel, if the truth be told. He didn't tell me what mattered to him, and about the one important thing, the war, we utterly disagreed. Let's look for his name together.'

'Sisters,' agreed Connie, eagerly. She thought how small and cold Fay's hand was.

Hand in hand, they walked along the streaming black walls and at last they found Daniel's name and Connie, never one to do things by halves, got down on her knees and recited a long series of prayers while Fay read and reread her brother's one-line memorial. Eventually Connie was silent and Fay gave her a hand up. 'I was picturing him as a young man and as a boy but images of Lex and Jim kept coming in. At least his name lives on. Although even that's spoiled because he was fighting in an unjust war.'

'It's impossible to understand,' said Connie, wiping mud off her knees. 'Death, I mean. As a Catholic, I should at least be able to accept it. But I can't even do that. I suppose that's why I started my organisation.'

They arrived at Shirley and Kevin's house exhausted. Fay realised that Connie had come all the way from Ireland to try to involve Shirley in her Sisterhood for Peace by sheer force of personality, and now she was paper pale and silenced by sadness. It had been selfish to take her to the memorial, even if she knew perfectly well that Kevin would never let his wife join this passionate sisterhood. He was passionate too. If the subtext to Connie's visit was an unadmitted wish to see Kathleen, then it looked as if she might be disappointed about that too for there was no sign of her or Tara.

'The girls are swimming.' Shirley seemed embarrassed, suggesting to Fay that this was not exactly the truth. She served them China tea and English muffins. As they talked of Fay's boys and Anna Quinlan's relationship with Ben Bradlee, Washington gossip that meant nothing to Connie, she began to recover.

'Dear Shirley,' she said, 'you know why I'm here not exactly behind Kevin's back.'

'I did write to stop you,' interrupted Shirley, which was news to Fay. 'It's not that Kevin isn't as desperate for peace as anyone else but he also feels desperate about the British occupying force and desperate that Ireland should be a united, independent country.'

'Desperate enough to kill?' began Connie, but then stopped abruptly. Fay guessed she was thinking about how well her brother had done out of the Vietnam war.

She listened politely, although with a somewhat faraway look on her face, as a horrified Shirley protested that Kevin would never condone any killing and that the money he raised was entirely to support the political struggle being fought by Sinn Fein.

To Fay's surprise, Connie did not put forward any further argument nor even try to explain that Sinn Fein could not be conveniently separated from the IRA. Eventually, there was a longish pause and Connie said, very carefully, looking at her finger, 'Just say to him, do not send money to Michael. If he sends money to Michael he may believe in peace, but he's putting guns into the hands of murderers.'

Fay thought Shirley gave a kind of gasp, as if such a sentence should not be pronounced in her pretty living room. But perhaps that was to do her an injustice. 'Kevin is away. I wrote you that, too. He's on a golfing vacation in Florida.'

Since Connie said nothing to this, Shirley made a sudden plunge for honesty. 'He can't understand what you're thinking of, Connie. "An O'Malley from Mayo siding with the enemy." That's how he talks of you.'

Connie sat up straighter. 'He's been out of Ireland too long. He hasn't been to the North.' Again Connie stopped. 'I'm sorry, Shirley. Fay was right. I should never have come.'

They left without seeing the girls. 'Do you think Kevin kept them from my polluting presence?' Connie asked Fay, in their taxi back to the airport. 'He certainly kept himself away.'

'I expect so.' It was time for Fay to hug Connie. Secretly, Fay did not believe that this Sisterhood for Peace could ever amount to much. 'You can't work only for an outcome,' Connie had said to Ted the evening before. 'You have to do what's right first and, if you're lucky, maybe the desired outcome will follow.'

'Peace,' Ted had said.

Connie had laughed. 'Something tiny like that.'

And Ted had said, 'Well, I guess you're an idealist.' To which Connie, looking extremely pleased, had agreed that idealism was certainly another big word she'd like to have in spitting distance.

I suppose the problem, thought Fay, as they reached JFK airport, is that I know too much about Connie to take her seriously, even when she takes herself seriously. And then she wondered whether Orlando felt the same. Or perhaps love changed the picture. Now she was able to love Connie for coming to the war memorial, for crying and praying with her there. Emotions, that was Connie's forte. She, Fay, was good at the other sort of thing.

Which reminded her: they were all out of cereal and juice; she must make time for some shopping on the way home.

The noises were of a person in distress. Helen. But Helen was never in distress. Nina, who was spending a night at the flat in London, got out of bed and pulled on her socks and a sweater. Was it the door that had given her the clue, the way it had been opened and closed?

'Mummy, go to bed.' Nina realised Helen always behaved as if she knew best. But her face was taut, skin as stretched as a ship's canvas.

'What's the matter?'

'Oh, nothing, Mummy. I told you, go to bed.'

'What time is it?' When had she become daughter to her daughter? Perhaps it had always been so after the very early years.

'Two, three. I don't know. Does it matter?' Helen sat down, looked at the floor. She was dressed all in black, except for her white shirt. Straight black shoulders, straight black skirt, black legs, shoes. Of course, it was her going-to-court dress. 'I'll tell you if you really want to know.' She glanced up. 'How old am I? Twenty-four. Four years older than when you married Daddy. On my way to becoming a criminal barrister. Proficient at exams. Anyway, I stood on a doorstep tonight with a man. The right amount older than me, bright, reasonably good-looking. We like each other. The doorstep leads to the house in which he has a top-floor flat. Great place. We'd been there before. Together. Until his duvet got too hot. We get on. Actually, he's great. So we stand on the doorstep, all ready for a repeat performance, and he has his key in the lock and I look up at the sky while I'm waiting, see the cool stars and the cold moon, and I suddenly understand that all I'm doing is going through the motions. I really have no feelings for this man – he's called Philip incidentally and earns a ridiculous amount in the City. A real Thatcher boy. He just happens to be there and sex seems an appropriate end to the evening. What's worse, I'm pretty certain he feels the same. We're like two automatons, programmed to meet, have dinner, mate, part, go to work.'

She stopped or paused, Nina didn't know which. It certainly seemed horribly cold-blooded. 'I don't quite understand . . .' she began feebly.

'Why I do it, you were going to say? I like Philip. Even after the moon frowned at me, I went up with him and we made perfectly satisfactory love. Friendly, sexy love. But now that feeling's come back again and I wonder what's the point of it all.'

'Of it all?' Nina remembered her worst months with William. It was the sort of question she'd asked herself then, until the pain grew too great and she took to washing obsessively instead. But Helen was not married to a man with whom she had nothing in common. She was a career girl, foot successfully placed on the first rungs of the legal ladder.

'Love. Sex. Other people. The point of work is perfectly clear.' She sounded impatient and Nina was able to recognise her again. 'And don't tell me I haven't met the right man.'

'Why ever should I do that? You're forgetting I'm the generation who destroyed the notion of a woman's need for the right man.'

'But you've only been happy since Gus appeared. When you see his bobble hat, you look like a romantic teenager.'

Nina considered this description, part rebuke, part compliment. Almost, but not quite, entirely wrong. She did not wish to be disloyal to Gus or to underestimate his part in her life, particularly to Helen who had never really seen the point of him (it struck her that this not seeing the point had been a consistent habit of Helen's). The kitchen clock began to tick loudly as Helen waited with the clever, expectant look that had made Nina nervous during her daughter's childhood.

The one thing she could not do was lay her own problems on Helen. If Helen felt she and Gus were filled with romantic love, then why should she be disabused? If she did not love Gus, there would be no problem. She reminded herself that this was Helen's story, not hers. She must try to make sense of what she didn't understand herself and sound like a helpful, strong mother.

'I was quite old when I met Gus and we have no children together.' She paused. 'And I have my work as you have yours.' What was it Helen wanted to hear? If she knew, she would say it. Perhaps she should be more daring. 'I must say, darling, it does seem pretty depressing to sleep with someone you don't care about a bit.'

At once, Helen was on her feet, all lassitude vanished. 'You don't understand a thing I was saying. Of course I feel something for Philip – in your terms, I probably even love him, whatever that may mean. Just don't worry. Let's go to bed. You look exhausted. Bed. Bed.' Her energetic command turned the word into a threat.

'Yes,' agreed Nina, humbly. 'As you know, I like Philip.'

'You haven't met Philip.'

'No. No. I'd better go to bed.' As she spoke, failing – she felt – as a mother, her eye fixed on the shadow of her daughter against the bright wall, the dark wall beyond, and she felt a forceful rush of excitement. Could this be a painting, contrasts with an absent figure? The shadow moved. It had been speaking. Her daughter. And she had missed the last sentence, quite possibly the sentence that would explain everything.

'Darling, darling,' she propelled herself into the space between light and dark, 'I'm so glad we've talked. So pleased, honoured . . .' How absurd she sounded, but what did it matter? Thank God, Helen was smiling and she dared to embrace her. The momentary rush that had been a painting passed and was erased.

1986

Connie sat in bed surrounded by newspapers. She'd organised a meeting in Dublin the evening before and only arrived back at the house at one. Then she'd needed a drink over the telling of stories. Now she was searching for reports. 'Blast them to hell for being lying, hypocritical men!' She flung the third newspaper to the floor.

'You made the RTE news, my darling,' Orlando, sitting on the edge of the bed, reminded her mildly. 'That's far more important than any paper.'

'Oh, yes! Oh, yes! Ten seconds featuring that mad woman . . .'

'That gorgeous woman . . .'

Connie looked out from her frenzy and saw Orlando lit in the brilliance of a recently rainy morning, his beloved face surrounded by a halo of silver curls. 'My God, Orlando, you've gone completely grey!' Stunned by this sudden revelation – when had it happened? Overnight when she was at the meeting? – Connie flung herself forward to assess the truth of the matter. As she did so, a sheet of newspaper clinging to the bed presented itself in close-up, and she found herself looking at a man's face that she more than half recognised. Putting this aside to be examined later, she continued her trajectory and reached Orlando. 'How dreadful for you, my dearest, to be getting old.' She caressed his face and, to show she didn't care, ran her fingers through his ageing locks.

'What does it matter,' replied Orlando, 'if I have you – not that I have much of you these days – and Leo, not that I have much of him these days?' Leonardo was now at a boarding-school near Dublin.

'Thou shalt not repine, I'm here now for the weekend.' They kissed but when Orlando laid a hand on Connie's breasts, she drew back. Whose was that face? The face of a politician side by side with the Prime Minister of Great Britain. She picked up the paper hurriedly and read the caption. 'Heavens, Orlando, my first lover, the one of whom I don't talk or think is under-secretary for Northern Ireland. Why did I not know this before?'

'Reshuffle,' said Orlando briefly. He wandered towards the window. 'I'm going down to the lake. Donal says my bullocks have escaped again.'

'You and your bullocks.' For a second Connie thought how nice it was that Orlando had recently acquired animals and land to keep him busy, and then returned to the paper. It was Rick sure enough, fatter, almost bald, heavily bespectacled – no wonder she had hardly recognised him. He must be nearly fifty but he looked more. Connie hung sideways out of bed so she could catch her reflection in the dressing-table mirror. Even after an exhausting week, a late night, too much to drink as usual, she still looked pretty good, pearly skin, clear features, hair the kind of red she'd decided on a few years ago so she could hardly remember her own hair colour. She'd invite herself to lunch at the House of Commons to see how the land lay. 'O Blessed Mary,' Connie slipped easily to her knees, 'give me the equivalent spiritual power of a vamp to convince this fairly powerful ex-lover that he has a duty to help. Amen.'

This method of prayer, or more correctly intercession, had become a habit with Connie over the last year and was a source of ribald comment from Orlando. 'You can't charm the Mother of God.'

Connie was unrepentant. 'She's a woman, isn't she, as well as all the rest?'

Raising herself from her knees, she returned to study Rick's photograph. Her first impression was confirmed: he had coarsened into a man she could never find even remotely attractive. That would make her task easier. Her letter would be formal: 'Dear Richard Wyberley, I am writing to you as chairperson of the Sisterhood for Peace Organisation founded by myself in 1980. First, may I congratulate you on your new appointment, etc., etc.' Only after her signature would she scribble in her own handwriting, 'We knew each other in another life . . .'

When she came to London Connie stayed at Nina's flat. It was the same flat they had shared twelve years before. It reminded Connie of how little the geography of Nina's life had altered once she divorced William. She still lived in the house in which she was born. In fact, the flat was mostly inhabited by Helen, who was a barrister. She had soon sorted out its raffish charm into a clean functional space, which Connie, incapable of producing such an atmosphere herself, rather admired.

'I always feel so calm here,' she said. She was less keen on the transformation of the two floors below them into a smart modern flat for a smart modern couple who left for work at the same time on smart modern bicycles. 'Where's the smell of glue?' she lamented. 'The sounds of antique furniture being knocked up overnight? This couple are like mice, scurrying and tapping and playing respectable classics at a respectable volume. You're too young, to know, Helen, but time is running away with us all. A week ago I noticed Orlando's hair is quite grey. I see your beloved mother no more than twice a year now. I hardly have time to get used to one year before the next is upon me. Soon I'll be in my grave.'

'Nonsense.' Helen laughed. That morning Connie was to meet the minister in the House of Commons. 'Do not wear that hat, Connie,' Helen advised her. 'Not for lunch in the House of Commons, preferably not anywhere.'

Although professing gratitude for this tip, Connie ignored it. How could anyone forced to wear black and white all day long retain any fashion sense? Besides, she hadn't confided in Helen the minister's previous role in her life. He had sung 'Sur les toits de Paris' in that little garret room and told her it was wine, women and song all weekend and he had been so carried away by his energetic love-making that he hadn't noticed her guilty lassitude. She had thought of Hubert while his son's hands squeezed and pummelled. And as she was dressing, preparing to take the ship back to London again, he had announced, in an unfamiliar tone, the sort of tone she imagined he used at work, 'I have written a letter to you. Read it on the ferry.' That had been cruel, if not as cruel as her.

Yes, a pink straw hat was perfect: it would separate her from the herd and soften any slight changes that time had wrought in her appearance. Her hair, for example, might not be quite the shade he remembered it. Connie never made the mistake of believing a high moral purpose wiped out less important concerns. She adored her pink hat chosen, with Orlando's approval, in one of the smartest shops on O'Connell Street. That very morning she had bought a new coral lipstick in the airport to match it.

Connie drew a pile of papers towards her. In it were documented all the latest outrages committed by the IRA and the UDA, and various satellite and independent voices. It was important to know such hideous facts in detail. What she wanted was the minister (he had almost stopped being Rick) to head a procession for peace she was organising on Christmas Eve.

Connie met Rick in the lobby of the House of Commons. She had been there before and felt comfortably excited by the round, domed hall, the marble floor, the Victorian paintings, the policemen, the attendants, the tourists, the visitors, the Members of Parliament, the latter just a little bit preoccupied with affairs of state. A woman would never be so pompous, she told herself, and just at that moment recognised a woman MP with exactly the same air of unctuously overcoming feelings of condescension as her male colleagues.

'Connie!' And there he was, not as fat and balding as his photograph, tall, vigorous and welcoming.

'Rick, hello – or is it Richard now?'

'Richard.' He tried to kiss her under the brim of her hat but his glasses took all the available space.

Connie managed to repress a mocking laugh. She must remember her serious mission. 'So you gave up the City,' she said, in conversational tones, as they walked towards the dining room.

'It gave me what I needed to become a politician.'

'Money, you mean?'

'Afraid so.' He was cheerful, bonhomous, but beneath his confidence she detected a note of anxiety, whether to her advantage or disadvantage she couldn't decide. They passed through tables to find their own and just for a second she was reminded of that Hastings dining room when she had first met Hubert, and Nina had been on her honeymoon. But then she concentrated instead on noting Richard's popularity as he stopped to receive congratulations on ministerial office.

Men are such show-offs, thought Connie, before deciding it was all for her benefit.

'Wine?' asked Richard.

'If you are.' He was. Unusual for a politician at lunchtime. Perhaps he really was nervous.

'I admire your work,' he told her, over the menu. 'Any protest organised from the South is very valuable.'

'I like to feel it's more positive than a protest.'

'Yes. Of course. The Scottish smoked salmon is good here.' He stopped.

Connie laughed. 'Let's call it Celtic.' They ordered.

'I had my secretary get the news clippings on you. You're married with a son called Leonardo. But it didn't tell me how you got into this.' He stopped short again.

'I can't answer you. It's private.' She could never tell anyone about Michael – until she told the British army but that she could never do. She rethought. *Not yet, anyway.* 'I'm trying to organise two processions for Christmas Eve, one starting in the North and one in the South, meeting for an ecumenical service as near the border as I can make it.'

'I shouldn't think you'll get many Protestants.'

'Women will come, whatever their religion.' Connie looked at this smooth face, which once had seemed to hold the answer to the meaning of life, and realised, first, that security considerations would make his attendance extremely unlikely, and second, that she no longer wanted him there. 'It's also a fund-raising exercise with the money going to victims of terrorism from Protestants and Catholics alike.'

'Obviously, you appreciate this government is working very hard for a new agreement. A ceasefire on both sides.'

'In the South most people are less aware of the troubles than you English. Of course we don't get bombed. I think it's fairly shameful. The North seems a long way to most of us – unless you happen to be smuggling petrol or alcohol.' Connie laughed. She realised she did not even want to talk about Ireland with Richard, no longer Rick. How could he understand? And anything he did know, he wouldn't be able to tell her.

'You haven't changed much.'

So now they were entering the personal. 'You have. Are you married too?'

'Yes. I have four children, a wife and a house in the country.'

'A big house?'

'Very. My wife likes riding. She's a JP and sits on all kinds of boards and trusts. Anything else you'd like to know?'

Connie thought about it. His tone was conciliatory, but not particularly emotional. She thought that ambition and success seemed to have flattened out any personal characteristics. She realised they had not yet started on their main course and, at heart, she was already very nearly bored. Orlando never never bored her. She leant a bit closer. 'Were you ever in love with me?'

Even this provoked little more than a bit of embarrassed blinking and a slight flush around the gills. He seemed to have grown fatter again. 'Surely you know that anyone who's ever met you falls in love with you.'

Connie felt livelier. She looked from under the pink brim of her hat, which seemed to have fallen rather lower, and imagined how her blue lagoon eyes would seem to him. 'I wasn't talking about *anyone*.' But the effect was too great. He might, she saw, become lugubrious or, more likely, absurd. She relented. 'Question number two. Are you hoping to become Prime Minister?'

'Surely anyone who becomes a politician is hoping to become Prime Minister.'

Connie remembered then that although Rick was the man she supposed herself to love, it was his father, the ghastly ancient poet, Hubert, who had most deeply attracted her imagination and, if she were perfectly honest, her body too, ogreish though he was. What, if anything, had this *Richard*, this would-be Prime Minister, ever known about anything? Connie realised she had been drinking too quickly, remembering too dramatically and not listening to her host's conversation. He'd probably always believed she was a bog-Irish whore. 'I'm so sorry,' she said, sounding a little too random to be convincing. She saw he was hurt. He pushed away his plate and smiled at a distant admirer. Then he took off his glasses and leant close across the table. To her horror, she saw there were tears in his eyes.

'I knew about you and my father. When you came to Paris. I knew already. He told me, of course. Boasted, I should say. I wrote that note to you, saying it was all over with us, out of self-defence. Do you understand what you did to me, Connie?'

Connie became distracted with this sudden turn of events. Could that really be the truth of it? Was she not the victim but the culprit? But of course she was. In her heart she had always known that; the Church had told her that. Taking off her hat in an unconscious bid for freedom from such mind-bending thoughts, she hung it on the back of her chair. It fell off immediately and was kicked along the floor by a passing waiter, who picked it up with obsequious irritation and handed it to Connie who put it back on her head, this time back to front. 'You knew everything!' she whispered. 'In Paris.'

'Yes.' The minister replaced his glasses. He composed himself. 'My father has a very destructive personality. Even now.'

'I'm sorry.' Connie sank back in her chair. What else could she say? 'I'm sorry,' she repeated. Yet, she thought, he hasn't mentioned my pregnancy. How odd! Then she thought, I suppose men don't care so much about such things. Not the sort of man he was, anyway. All that was her story, not his. She sat up straighter. 'I guess it's time for platitudes: it's all a very long time ago. We were very, very young.'

He did not smile. 'Of course my father hates me being a Conservative politician.'

Connie felt constricted by the heavy dining room, filled with people who believed politics was the way to deal with problems when anyone could see they created more than they solved. Under other circumstances, she would have picked an argument about the small minority of women MPs. She could guess his answer: *We are striving to attract more women of the right calibre.* After all, she could not escape the personal. She cupped her face in her hands and looked up. 'That Paris trip was doomed to be a disaster. Do you remember I arrived on a ship filled with drowned bodies? There was a fog and we picked them up off a Yugoslavian fishing boat.'

'I'd forgotten that.' He fiddled with his food before continuing, with that horrible pained look on his face once more, 'You didn't meet your husband for some time?'

So he wanted more of her life story. Connie, intent now on avoiding too much of the emotional past, decided to give him only the facts. 'No. My husband founded the Lir Water bottled-water company. We live on the edge of a lake. For the last three years we have used part of the house and the old stables for bringing children together from the different communities in Belfast and some from Dublin too. Just a kind of summer camp for a dozen kids but it makes me feel I'm helping a little.'

'I didn't know about that.'

'We don't publicise it much, in case of trouble. It's small-scale. Actually, it was my son's idea.'

To Connie's relief, Rick looked ministerial again. He clasped his hands together. 'If you ever have any need of extra funding, I might be able to point you in the right direction.'

So, after all, it was a business lunch. Connie felt more kindly towards him and, on a sudden impulse, decided to recognise the truth. 'We were never suited, of course. Your father did us both a favour. Take my hand for old times' sake.' She held out her hand across the table.

Rick started to stretch his towards her but progressed no further than his coffee cup before being interrupted by a private secretary. 'We're already late, Minister.'

Connie said her goodbyes with this man standing impatiently at his master's elbow. There was no handholding and no opportunity for a second kiss.

Nina had come up to London for a meeting at the Arts Council. She and Connie seldom saw each other now without husbands or children. That evening, they left Helen in the flat and found an Italian restaurant round the corner. 'It has to be very cheap,' Nina insisted, 'or I'll feel guilty Gus isn't with us.'

'Why? Is he your minder or something?' Connie's voice was disapproving.

'Sorry. I was just being feeble.' Nina felt herself frowning in self-disapproval. She didn't want Connie utterly to despise her.

'I'm getting old,' Connie said later. 'I've started talking about the past. Today at lunch.' Nina listened to Connie tell the story and her sense that she had loved the horrible father, not the pompous son.

'In my view, you loved neither.' Nina smiled. 'You were waiting till you found Orlando.'

'Darling, you're so right!'

Nina thought, We're too old to be having this sort of silly conversation and, as so often now, when she thought of anything at all personal, she felt like bursting into tears. 'My meeting with the Arts Council was quite successful, I think. The woman was nearly as large as me. It was a bonding factor.'

'You look lovely!' exclaimed Connie. But Nina knew she was lying and Connie's next remark proved it: 'Why don't you go on a diet?'

'I can't.' To demonstrate her point, Nina reached for another doughball and stuffed it into her mouth. 'Gus says he likes me big!'

'I'm not saying you don't look rather wonderful.' Honesty could not be stretched further than this. 'I'll never understand why you don't paint more.'

'Connie!' The words came out as a wail of despair. How could someone who had known her for so long toss off a comment like that?

'Sorry. I can't tell you how many tragedies I meet through the Sisterhood for Peace. I've probably become desensitised. Anyway, I blame Gus.'

'Gus is a tremendous support! I won't hear anything against Gus!'

'Methinks the lady protests too much.'

'Without Gus I'd curl up and die!'

'That's pathetic.' Connie stared at Nina. Nina stared back with drowning eyes but there was no way she could confide in Connie. For one thing, if anyone outside herself understood her black thoughts she'd be thrown straight into a mental hospital, and for another, Orlando and Connie had introduced her to Gus and, for a third, she loved him. She was the problem, never him. 'So was your lunch useful in any way?' she asked determinedly.

'Maybe.' Connie changed the subject. 'Tell me about Helen. You said she might marry.'

'Not immediately. I don't understand her at all. I just feel guilty. But, then, how can I help her if she doesn't tell me anything?'

'Why ever not? I've always found you very sympathetic.'

Nina smiled at Connie's self-centredness. For some reason it always cheered her up. 'I guess it's as simple as she's never forgiven me for leaving William. And I suppose that makes her nervous of marriage too.'

'My dearest Nina, you can't feel guilty about that. William made you mad.' Nina thought of saying that she didn't feel exactly sane now but that was far too difficult a scenario to entrust to Connie. 'I think that daughter of yours has her own problems. I'll invite her to Ireland and get it out of her. Trust your wise old friend, Connie.'

Again Nina smiled. 'Please do.'

Helen flew to Ireland for a holiday with Connie and Orlando. She arrived in a smart hired car and, after amusing Leonardo with stories of murderers and judges, took Connie into the garden and burst into tears. 'All I do is work.' She gulped.

'But it suits you.' Connie had never believed in overmuch sympathy for the young and strong. 'You're so competent.'

'Oh, my God, you sound like my mother.'

'Yes. Why aren't you talking to your mother?'

Helen stopped crying, but brushing too close to a wet laurel bush made rain tears fly across her body. She stopped to wipe them off. 'It's not that I'm not talking to her but when I do she's so distressed she stops listening.'

Connie laughed. 'She's always been hopeless at dealing with emotions. I guess it's the fault of that soldierly father who made her feel picking a flower was an act of rebellion. She thinks you're still angry about her dumping William. I told her that was rubbish.'

'Heavens!' exclaimed Helen. 'That's an age ago. I suppose Mum's messy approach to life gets to me sometimes. At least dumping Dad was an upfront thing to do.'

'So, if it isn't Nina's fault, what's the problem? How about Philip? You've been together for years now. You live together, don't you?'

'Yes.' Helen did not elaborate.

'Why not marry him? Have babies.'

'I work!' It was almost a shriek followed by more tears. They walked on, Helen swiping in an agitated manner at some flies, which had clustered over her head. 'Last year we had an abortion because we weren't ready to get married.'

Connie felt the temperature drop around her. She stopped still for a moment, shivering, then headed Helen off to a streak of sun she had spotted on the way to the lake. She must not judge, she told herself. It was an honour to be taken into Helen's confidence. 'You do love him?' she asked tentatively.

Helen seemed to be weighing up this word as they stood thankfully in the slant of sun. 'Yes,' she agreed finally. 'I think we can be happy together, but how can I ever be sure?'

'You can't.' Connie put her arm round Helen. She was much too thin: she could feel shoulder-blades like hard wings. It was unnatural, she thought, in the daughter of such sturdy parents. 'If I were you I'd take a chance.' She thought of all the chances she'd taken. 'How about Gus? He's a sensible fellow. Can't you talk to him?'

'He's having work problems. Anyway I'd never tell him about the abortion when I haven't even told Mum. She'd be terribly upset. I talk to Granny but she's from a whole other generation. I could never tell her either.'

Connie wished that Helen would stop talking about it. 'Did it not make you unhappy?' she asked bravely.

'Yes. But it was the right thing to do. I was in the middle of a big case.'

Connie became desperate to change the subject and began to feel near tears herself. 'We like to behave responsibly,' continued Helen, inexorable.

'Of course,' responded Connie humbly. How very, very irresponsible she had been! She tried to rally a little, remind herself she was a middle-aged woman giving advice. 'Personally, I'd recommend marriage.'

'You sound just like Granny. Did you know that Grandpa, that soldierly fellow you were describing, had a mistress for years? People make such muddles of their lives. I don't want to live in a muddle.' Again, Helen's eyes filled with tears.

'I'm afraid life tends to be rather a muddle, however much you try to shape it up.' Connie tried not to sound too sad because she didn't feel sad about this. This fact of life had always seemed evident to her and she was only amazed that, in the last years, she had found so much personal peace and happiness. She supposed that was the reason, aside from having a shameful brother like Michael, that she had started the Sisterhood of Peace. However, she could think of no way of conveying any of this to Helen. She would have to learn for herself. 'Darling Helen, you're such a good soul. Try to do what pleases you.'

'And Philip?' reproved Helen.

'Philip too,' agreed Connie.

'Well, Philip wanted to get married,' she burst out suddenly, smiling, 'so I expect we will!'

'Thank heavens!' cried Connie, giving up reining in her emotions, and laughing wildly.

Only afterwards Connie wondered if she had failed by offering no principles of morality for Helen to adhere to. Surely, as a Catholic, she believed in such things. She must remember to have one of her periodic telephone conversations with Father O'Donald and discuss the whole matter.

'How can I tell you love me if we don't make love?'

Gus made his depression clear despite the total darkness. Nina felt unhappy too – but not quite so unhappy. 'Can't we just be loving without actually making love?' They were lying in bed on a cool summer evening.

'Probably not.'

Nina turned on her side, away from him. How angry was she with him? Did she wish to blow apart her marriage? 'Darling?'

He turned at once, warmly expectant. Was it possible making love was so important?

'Darling Gus.' She stroked his cheek. She loved him. Why shouldn't they make love?

The next morning Nina got up early. Her feet were very heavy. Her whole body was heavy but her feet in particular. She did all the usual things – lavatory, teeth, breakfast. Then she drove off to Southern Painting. Gus was around doing some of these activities but she didn't really notice him. They did kiss briefly. Of course.

Nina and William met to discuss the financial arrangements for Helen's wedding. Nina was surprised to find the conversation filled with rancour. She had been so happy that Helen had made her decision, spurred on it seemed by her visit to Connie. Nina was lunching with William at his club in London and she remembered how he had cried long ago, sitting at the very same table. Now he was far from tears.

'You have had the use of Lymhurst ever since we parted,' he said severely. He was still handsome, although heavy and bullish. 'This represents an enormous sum. If I sold it, I could realise a considerable amount of capital. With five children to support, this would be very useful indeed.'

Nina thought she might be the one to cry this time. She made an effort not to whimper. 'I know the house is much too big for us but Gus does pay for the upkeep now. In fact, he was thinking about buying it from you.'

'No.'

'What?'

'The house is not for sale. It's for Jamie.'

Nina felt weak. Had he not just suggested selling the house? Anyway, why should Gus not leave Lymhurst to Jamie? She then remembered that three of William's step-sons and Helen were earning their own living. 'So you will contribute to the catering?' She tried to sound forceful. The wedding was, after all, the reason they were lunching.

'I suppose so.'

'And we'll do tent and flowers and transport.'

'Yes.' William leant back in his chair. Nina wondered whether she could leave now but there seemed something more on William's mind. He seemed mellower now as if his display of bad temper had soothed his spirits.

'I'm coming to the end of my second tour in Northern Ireland. Soon I'll be retiring. Tell me, do you see much of your friend Constance O'Malley?'

'Quite a bit,' said Nina warily, 'although of course she lives in Ireland.'

'Quite.' William looked a little confused. It was a look that he had carried through from childhood and always made Nina feel guiltily warm towards him. 'I admire what she's trying to do, you know. It won't come to anything but that's no reason not to try.'

'Connie's always determined.' Nina suddenly recalled Connie's visit to them in Germany when Helen and Jamie were little and how William had admired her then. 'You haven't met her, have you?' It was a suspicious question.

'No. No.' Clearly he still had something else to say. 'Felicity and I have grown to love Ireland.'

'It's such a beautiful country.'

'I've taken up fishing and Felicity is involved with a hospital project. Actually, we've bought a house in County Down. For when I retire.' He stopped, looking for a reaction.

'In the North, you mean. Will it be safe?' Nina was surprised, impressed.

'We're far off from any troubles. In the country. It's so peaceful. We've made many friends. Catholics and Protestants. I just wanted you to know.'

Nina saw he wanted her approbation and was happy to give it. How strange he seemed to her now, so much more sympathetic than she could have expected, all that early belligerence evaporated. As they parted, he took her hand. He spoke emotionally, 'Would you and Gus mind if I paid for the whole of Helen's wedding? I've only got one daughter, you know.' He paused and swallowed, frowning. 'And if you'd like Lymhurst, I'll make it over to you. It was always yours, really.'

The phone had rung while Fay was gazing at a new batch of X-rays pinned up to her wall. She couldn't remember if she had always hated this search to identify a tumour in a child's brain.

'Say again, Nina . . .'

The skeleton head was as beautiful as a seashell. She moved across to view a second angle and noticed her hand was holding the receiver too tight and had begun to sweat. She turned her back on the images and faced her desk.

'Sure I had the invitation. It sounds like a great marriage. I'm so happy for Helen. But, these days, with the boys needing so much support and Ted all over place . . .'

She'd turned back without planning it and caught the dark shadow out of the corner of her eye. Too bad. Just too bad.

'Of course I'll come over. It was just a momentary hesitation, stress-related.'

The boys were young and thin, the smallest perhaps only eight or ten. They wore anoraks and had the wild look of the chronically unsupervised. Connie, Orlando and Leonardo, passing through London on their way to Helen's wedding, each noticed them for different reasons. Connie instantly thought of her city kids back at Lir and hoped none of them would drown in the lake – one of her midnight fears – while she was away. Leonardo watched with the curiosity of a thirteen-year-old abroad and Orlando recognised what they were actually doing.

'Those boys are killing that tree!' His voice was choked with outrage. Before Connie could stop him, rehearse the dangers of inner-city crime, he had dashed across the road and was talking to the tallest boy, who held a brick. Connie, watching anxiously, saw that the boy continued to chip fiercely at the bark of the tree even as he listened. It was clear to her that this attention from a male stranger was extremely satisfactory to him and probably the reason he had attacked the unprotesting young tree in the first place. At length, he put the brick aside or, rather, dropped it on to a pile where it broke into fragments.

Orlando returned. Pleased with his intervention, he smiled at Connie and Leonardo. 'I explained to them that if they continued to hack at the bark until they had destroyed a circle round the trunk, the tree would die. I told them they would have a tree on their conscience. They seemed quite interested.' Orlando looked modest. 'You saw how he dropped the brick.'

'Oh, darling.' Unfortunately, Connie could see that the boy, having taken the precaution of pulling his hood over his head, had resumed his hacking at the tree with increased vigour.

'What do you mean?' Orlando turned round and, without pausing, bounded back across the street. All five boys saw him coming. The tree murderer stood, brick raised in anticipation of a throw, while two others picked up fragments of bricks.

'No, Orlando!' shouted Connie.

'No, Orlando!' mimicked the smallest boy. But it was too late. As Orlando grabbed an arm, the brick came down on his head followed by other well-aimed missiles, one cutting his face and others bouncing off his back. Leonardo, who had followed his father across the road, tried to grab one of the boys but they were all off at high speed. Two passers-by, a young man in shirtsleeves and an older man in a suit, shocked witnesses, gave chase. The boys were well ahead, streaking and dodging.

Connie knelt by Orlando. He was sitting holding his head and a second after she arrived, he shut his eyes and keeled over.

'I should have helped him,' said Leonardo, almost in tears.

'He isn't dead.' Connie's voice was firm, although she felt as if all the blood had drained from her body. 'Help me hold him, darling. Please, God, he's just concussed.'

A small crowd grew, among them a policeman. Connie, holding Orlando across her lap, whispered into his ear, 'You can't die before me. Just no chance of it. Understand?'

Helen took the telephone call, even though it was the morning of her wedding. Nina watched her standing, lean and neat in her jeans and T-shirt, and saw that she was struggling to accept some sort of shocking news. It was a heroic stance and Nina felt a long-forgotten urge to protect her.

'What is it, darling?'

Helen turned and immediately handed over the receiver. 'It's Connie. You speak to her.' She went over to the polished wooden stairs and sat down with her head between her knees. It was a dark morning with sun appearing infrequently between the clouds. Beyond the open door a large white marquee reflected an artificial brightness.

Nina put down the telephone and came to sit beside Helen. 'He'll be fine, Helen. It's just a bang on his head. They just took an X-ray as a precaution. The hospital is going to let him out soon. They won't even be late.'

'Oh, it's all so impossible!' Helen cried out vehemently.

'Whatever do you mean?' Nina's heart gave a nasty lurch.

'I've tried so hard to make things work but I can't any more. Everything's too horrible!'

Nina put her arm around Helen. She was glad to be big enough to impersonate a warm, cuddly, protective person. 'You're just exhausted.'

'But what's the point of it all? If some boys can throw bricks at Orlando and nearly kill him, what is the point?'

Nina thought of what Connie had described to her, a terrible desolation that Orlando could leave her, followed by a furious anger. 'You're in the crime business,' she said. 'Surely you know all about the wickedness of life.'

'Yes. I do.' Helen sounded even more despairing. 'I just wanted one carefree day. And I love Connie so much.'

'Connie's tough. Connie's a survivor. It's you I'm worried about.' Nina thought how odd that Helen's concern for Connie should bring them together like this. 'It's eleven o'clock. Coffee time. The caterers are in control. Let's take mugs and escape.'

Nina and Helen took refuge in the old potting shed. They pulled sacks on to a block of wood and sat companionably close in the earth-smelling darkness. For several seconds at a time Nina found her eyes were closed.

Helen talked. She talked about her childhood, what she could remember of Malaya, of Germany, of an English boarding-school, of her grandmother providing her with security, of her feelings for Jamie, for her father, of her determination to have a successful career, of Philip who was often so like her and then quite different.

'How different?' asked Nina. Grateful that she was left out of this history – a failed mother – she hardly spoke at all. But Philip's difference seemed important.

'Stronger,' said Helen, as if she were smiling.

Nina took a breath. 'Men aren't stronger, you know. I made that mistake.'

Helen laughed. 'He's not stronger because he's a man. In fact, I'm stronger in all the traditional male ways. I'm more ambitious, more controlled and controlling, more self-confident – well, to an outside observer, at least. No, he's stronger in quite female ways. The other Cs:

compromise, cooking and children. He loves children. And he has a fourth C. He's centred.'

As Helen carried on talking about Philip, Nina felt a profound sense of happiness. It seemed that Helen was, as she would have said, 'sorted', and that even the little breakdown on the stairs, which had precipitated this unlikely tryst, was positive rather than negative. When they had finished their coffee, they would return to the fray, perhaps even arm in arm. She must find a moment to tell Connie that Orlando's brush with martyrdom had not been in vain.

Connie felt glad that people continued to fall in love with her. It consoled her for that moment of agony when she held Orlando unconscious in her arms. He was her mast, her bulwark, the prow against which she bound herself. Connie's pictorial imagination became overwhelmed by emotion.

She was sitting in Helen's wedding marquee beside William, who was the last person from whom she expected admiration and yet he was breathing it all over her. Under pretext of more champagne, Connie gave a swift look at the table to check Orlando was stable and upright. He was, the plaster rakishly over the place were the doctor had cut his silver curls. Felicity was sitting beside him. Connie returned to paying William attention. Listening had never held much interest for her. It seemed a diversion, so often, from whatever was important. Occasionally she needed to hear answers to her questions. She had asked Orlando while they waited for the doctor whether he was contented with his bullocks. He had understood at once, and taken her hand. 'I'm contented enough, darling Constance O'Malley.'

'But you promise to tell me if the contentment factor should drop too low?' she had asked him anxiously.

He had laughed. 'You mean if the ratio of time spent in the company of my mad father, your drunken brother Joe and the bullocks rises to unacceptable levels above the time I spend with you?'

'Yes! Yes!' she had cried.

'I'll tell you,' he had answered seriously.

William would settle in Ireland, he was telling her. Northern Ireland, of course. She supposed he had grown used to living in a bit of England that was on foreign soil. She remembered her visit to Germany and how attractive he had seemed. And poor Nina in such a state. 'Is there any hope of a political settlement?' she asked.

William looked at her gravely. 'You saw pictures of the funeral of the three IRA men killed in Gibraltar. You know much more about Irish passions than I do. I'm just an army man. You'll have to ask the politicians about peace. The politicians or the others.' He stopped, with some sort of question in his voice.

'What do you mean, the others?' Really, she knew what he meant. The others. All the many others on both sides who had forgotten about peace. With a nasty lurch of her heart, Connie realised that he just might know about her brother Michael's involvement. *I'm just an army man.* She looked at the white marquee's garlanding of yellow and white flowers, at the young and merry faces around her. She had already thought about death too much for a day that was supposed to be filled with joy. Again she checked Orlando. Two days ago a little boy had his legs blown off while in his father's arms. Neither would survive.

'Why are you crying?'

'Nothing. Nothing. Orlando's accident.' Connie dashed away the tears. She could not slip on to her knees here.

Philip was making a speech. Fay looked at him with interest. It had been hard to travel from America when she felt so exhausted all the time. She was working four days a week. Ted was busy too, and the house in Brooklyn meant that she had to commute, making endless logistical problems with Lex and Jim. Only Nina's begging had brought her here, and now Nina glowed with health and happiness, pride in her daughter, her family. The effort had been unnecessary.

Fay returned her attention to Philip's speech and thought that the English young seemed to have more spirit than she had expected. 'I'm so sorry.' The strange vicar on her left had whispered something into her ear. His name card told her he was called, unbelievably, The Rev. Dudley Ormsby-Fish, which also rang a bell from Nina's letters. He was her friend in Southern Painting, Fay remembered. He considered himself an Errol Flynn lookalike, judging by the moustache, and a wit too as he quoted an unfunny Chesterton joke about too-long sermons. 'I think Philip's doing a great job,' said Fay firmly.

On her left sat Jamie. Fay liked him. He was straightforward, sensible, determined. It was a pity that he had decided to follow his father into the army. On the other hand, if there had to be armies in the world, then there should be a few good men in them. It was impossible now to avoid thinking of Daniel and she did not really try, lowering her eyes to allow a picture of her brother to emerge as she remembered him in Sussex more than fifteen years ago.

Fay opened her eyes again and looked across at Connie, as beautiful as ever, easily vamping William. She smiled at the thought of Connie going to Daniel's bed that Christmas Eve. Silly but true that it was now one of the main reasons for her continuing affection for Connie.

I wish I did not worry so much about Lex and Jim, Fay thought, as Ormsby-Fish tried and failed to amuse her with an anecdote about a life class where the model, a man, had found himself seized with uncontrollable lust for the prettiest student. 'Do you have children?' she asked.

'Not on me, thank the Lord.'

Turning away from this latest sally, Fay caught sight of Nina, the formidable height and width of her, the dangling earrings and embroidered jacket. If her style was slightly more arty than the other English country ladies, she still gave the same impression of confidence. The truth, Fay knew, was very different. Perhaps she was wrong not to take Nina's troubles more seriously.

After dinner there was dancing, with two smart young men to run the disco and strobe lighting criss-crossing the floor. Most of the older guests drifted back to the house where they could talk comfortably with a glass in their hand. But the Reverend Ormsby-Fish grabbed Nina round the waist, crying jovially, 'The priest in charge of the wedding has first call on the mother of the bride!'

Nina laughed at him. 'You've drunk far too much champagne to dance.'

'Nonsense. It's only smooching. I can hang on to you for support.'

And so he did. Nina, in an increasing euphoria (today was one day when she could leave her painting out of the equation), recognised that the growing hardness pressing at her was the Vicar's erection. It was not altogether unexpected. She knew he found her attractive and, although she quite often found him ridiculous, she had never denied to herself his sexiness. On the whole, however, she had considered he flirted primarily to exact vengeance on his wife. Nina moved her hips a little to make sure she was feeling what she thought she was feeling. She was.

'Don't spurn me,' pleaded the Vicar. 'Your American friend gave me a real pasting. That's why I had to hit the champers.'

'Fay's one of my oldest friends.'

'Does she ever laugh at your jokes?'

'I don't think I ever make jokes.' At which point the Reverend Ormsby-Fish lowered one of his hands until it touched her breast. Worse than that, she felt, all of a sudden, very responsive in a way she hadn't for ages.

'No,' she muttered.

'All right, how about a stroll in the garden?' He suddenly sounded very much less drunk.

Why did she go with him? It couldn't have been the old childish reason of not wanting to disappoint a man. Perhaps it was quite simply because she was filled with lust and her loyalty to Gus – in these hours of euphoria that had nothing to do with him – was not quite strong enough. Besides, the darkness of the garden would cloak her body, which she now considered fat and ugly.

No one noticed as they slipped out of a side flap and headed for the even greater darkness of the trees. The night was surprisingly warm, low cloud girding the stars, and the Vicar was already half out of his clothes, capering like a satyr behind the apple tree. But even this didn't deter Nina. She wanted to be taken by a man, feel his cock thick inside her and forget everything else. She did not feel like that with Gus any more.

They lay on the Vicar's jacket, the grass soft beneath them and he exclaimed at her magic white shining voluptuousness. It did not last long; they were both too eager. But afterwards Nina laughed and the Vicar said, in a very unpriestly way, 'You're the best fuck I've ever had.' And Nina felt satisfied with this because she was a good fuck, no one had ever complained on that front. 'Yes,' she said, smiling still. 'It was great fun.'

Regretfully, they rose, dressed carefully and passed each other as tidy. They had been away from the marquee for less than fifteen minutes.

The only person who spotted their sporting *sur l'herbe* was Connie, who had led Orlando, suffering from a headache, to bed and felt in need of some air.

Returning to the house, she asked herself how much she disapproved, good Catholic as she now was, and decided that some moral fibre had been left out of her nature. She felt no kind of condemnation at all but a warm sympathy that Nina should find a little light happiness. She supposed, on further reflection as she joined Gus and others in the drawing room, that this view could be intensified because she was angry with Gus.

'Hello, my darling Gus,' said Connie, opening her arms. 'We haven't talked at all, at all. Let us inhabit this sofa, just vacated, and you can fill me in on Sussex solicitors' gossip. Who, could you be advising me now, is sleeping with whom?'

Orlando periodically reminded Connie that one of her only weaknesses was an inability to safe-harbour a secret. Connie did manage not to inform Gus of his wife's infidelity but found it necessary to tell someone. Taking pity on Orlando, restlessly asleep, she led Fay into a corner of the drawing room. Unable to resist provocation, she whispered, 'Thank God for the jolly vicar. I saw him and Nina screwing under the apple tree.'

'Tell me you're joking. He's such a creep!'

Connie laughed. 'He's Nina's staff and support.'

'He makes the worst jokes. I had to sit beside him at dinner.'

'You were honoured.'

'A plague on the lot of you. I give up. I'm going to bed.'

Connie watched her go with some guilt. She should not have told her. Rebelling at such prissy good behaviour, she shimmied up to a surprised William and suggested they hit the dance floor.

When they got there, Connie immediately saw Nina demurely in the arms of her husband. How this transference had been effected she did not know but, to her eyes, Nina still had the afterglow of good sex.

'*Hola! Mein* host and hostess!' hailed Connie, and thought how difficult it was to reconcile the spirit and the flesh. This led her yet again to applaud her good luck in having found Orlando, and shiver, yet again, at what that cruelly thrown brick might have achieved.

Later in the night, when she sensed Orlando was awake, she told him, 'I could not manage without you!' She hugged him, stroked any part of his body she could find.

'Then you must give me more of your time.' The voice, though muffled, was clear.

'But, darling, do you not believe in what I'm doing?'

'Oh, yes. But you can do more with the city children in the stables and less with the grand ideas of peace.'

The night was still, starless and very dark. Connie was used to the noises of an old house in the country. She listened to the mice in the walls, the birds in the roof, the pipes as someone went to the bathroom, the creaks as they crossed uncarpeted floor. She heard the owl hoot and stop hooting, to be replaced by the early chorus of birds until they, too, fell silent and the sun slowly came up, bringing with it the more ordinary sounds of day.

'And there's Leo,' remarked Connie, as if their conversation had not been discontinued for several hours.

'So there is,' agreed Orlando mildly. 'He'd like more time too, I expect.'

'I think we should go to the sea,' Connie announced, the morning after the wedding. People seldom set off to the sea from Lymhurst, to look at it, perhaps, from a cliff top but not to visit it in the way Connie was insisting. A trip to a seaside town. Veronica would be allowed to stay behind with the excuse of watching the caterers clear up and leave, even perhaps supervise the marquee men dismantling.

Since William, Felicity and Jamie had already left, the party would consist of Nina, Gus, Fay, Connie, Orlando and Leonardo. Of these Orlando, though battered, had drunk nothing and was the most exuberant.

Connie, after a sleepless night, far too much champagne and a need to answer difficult questions, felt downcast. Could Orlando really want her to be the sort of wife who tended the garden and waited for him to come back from Lir Water, and Leonardo from school? For comfort, she grasped Leonardo's hand – he was sitting beside her in her car. But after a moment, he slid it away. *Et tu, Brute!* Surely they were both so proud of her?

The seaside town had an end-of-the-season feel. Half the small shops and kiosks, mainly selling rock or fish and chips, were already closed and, although it was a bright and breezy morning, the proprietor of the amusement park had not yet thought it worthwhile to unlock the painted horses or the sleek torpedoes.

Nina walked along the pebbly beach, between Connie and Fay, while Gus and Orlando strolled ahead, discussing, as Nina could hear quite clearly, the reasons why the Russians loved Mrs Thatcher. At the end of the sea a few boys were fishing, some families drinking tea from Thermos flasks. Nearer the centre of town, they could see more people, striped deck-chairs and even a parasol or two. So Nina suggested they turn in the other direction. Leonardo left them to dash at the sea in gladiatorial fashion.

They walked for some time in what seemed to Nina a not very companionable silence. She, of course, was trying to estimate the importance of what had happened under the apple tree the night before. She couldn't deny to herself the pleasure but had it *meant* anything? However hard she tried, she couldn't find an answer. It had happened, that was all she could understand, and for a little while she had been happy.

'Do you think he loves me?'

Nina and Fay stopped abruptly at Connie's wild cry. The question was absurd, of course. Everybody loved Connie. It might not always make her happy but it was one of those facts of life. Last night William could hardly take his eyes off her, and Jamie too, Nina thought. If she was referring to Orlando, who seemed to be in the direction of her gaze, then she was merely fishing (an echo of Ormsby-Fish stabbed Nina uncomfortably) because it was patently clear that Orlando doted unreservedly. Perhaps Connie was suffering from a lack of husbandly adulation, wondered Nina meanly. Looking again at the back silhouettes of the men, tramping solidly through the pebbles, about the same height and width under the now darkening sky, she flashingly considered the possibility that Connie was referring to Gus, that something had happened last night that had revealed his affection for her. In this sea-borne moment – the waves were breaking only a foot or two from where they walked – Nina considered Gus falling in love with someone else (not necessarily Connie) and discovered she did not really care. This was both frightening and releasing. She then considered, all in the same micro-second, whether she loved the Vicar and discovered with no trouble at all that she didn't. He merely cheered her up. She turned to Connie. 'Of course Orlando loves you. He couldn't help himself.'

'Thank you,' said Connie gratefully. 'I was afraid I put too much reliance on the bullocks.'

No one laughed. 'But I'm not sure it's the right question,' continued Nina.

'It certainly isn't!' Fay was suddenly loud with anger. A seagull made her even more emphatic by swooping low with a plaintive cry.

'What I was going to say,' interrupted Nina, because it seemed important, 'is that it is not so difficult to be loved, particularly for someone like you, Connie, but to love. I don't think I've ever loved anyone, not passionately, and I don't suppose I ever will.'

'Oh, really!' Fay stopped and spread her hands. 'It's a perfectly documented fact that everyone's programmed to love and be loved.'

Nina was surprised that Fay seemed so cross with her. 'You love Ted and the twins . . .'

'I'm a rational human being, Nina. A rational human being loves her children and their father!'

'Oh dear,' murmured Connie. She took Fay's arm as Nina moved away, closer to the noise of the breakers. Nina looked back and saw they were talking to each other. She felt excluded and guessed she was their subject. Next time she looked round, Fay had separated from Connie and was walking towards the yellow cliffs. But Connie still did not come to find her. Instead she went to join Orlando and Gus. Now walking behind them, Nina saw how Orlando held Connie's arm and they both laughed and joked.

Perhaps I'll own up to Gus about Fish, thought Nina desolately, before thinking she was far too cowardly.

That evening, Nina took Connie into the pantry where her mother had lined up home-made plum jam and green tomato chutney. 'I'm desperate, Connie. Fay's here for five days. What will I do with her when you go tomorrow? She seems cross with me all the time. Even Gus has noticed, and he didn't like her much in the first place.'

Connie held up a bottle against the light. It glowed a splendid red amber. She remembered how Nina used to be so excited by colour and felt sad. 'I told her about you dallying under the apple tree,' she said regretfully. 'She didn't approve.'

Nina blushed in fair imitation of the jam. 'Oh, Connie, how truly embarrassing! How could you? However did you know anyway?'

Connie laughed. 'Don't worry. I'm not a voyeur. I just got the drift and couldn't resist sharing it with Fay. I apologise unreservedly. It was not the act of a friend. Except Fay's a friend too, I suppose.'

'You know it was the first time?'

'You don't have to defend yourself to me.'

'I'm not. That's fact. And, although it made me feel good, I shan't indulge again.'

'Indulge?' Connie began laughing again. Nina saw that all her fears of not being loved were well gone. 'You indulge in chocolate, not in vicars.'

'Oh, I don't know. I expect vicars would be better for my figure, at least. So will Fay forgive me if I talk to her?'

'I should think so. Ask her about this new radiology machine she's testing, I can't remember what it's called – she loves talking about that. Be serious, that's the main thing. Come on, darling Nina, you're much closer to her than me. You know exactly what to say. The unfortunate thing was she'd already ticked off your randy vicar as the ultimate English bore.'

'She's quite right in a way.' Nina sighed and then smiled to herself. 'I don't think there's any way Fish can be presented as a serious person. It's just that in my black moments he makes me laugh. In fact his silliness, his terrible jokes make me feel sane, keep me from the lure of the taps . . .'

'You're not washing, are you?'

'Under control, but thank you for asking without looking as if the world might fall in. So you don't think I'm an idiot and a monster?'

'Idiot, yes. Monster, no. As far as I'm concerned you can use the apple tree nightly. I blame Gus.' As Nina was about to remonstrate, she carried on quickly, 'Now I know you're not washing, let's put in some help in the kitchen.'

Fay, loading the washing-machine, glanced at Veronica with total approval. Here was a woman widowed for twenty-odd years, who was utterly self-sufficient, clever, charming, self-effacing, an excellent mother and grandmother. It was so unfair that Nina should have her as well as everything else. At the moment Veronica was arguing the case for fighting the Falklands war. Although Fay had been against it at the time, she was almost tempted now to be persuaded just so that they could be on the same side. 'But what if Jamie had been old enough to fight there?'

'He wasn't, but he's chosen to be a soldier.' She paused and touched Fay's shoulder. 'I'm so glad you're still a friend of Nina's. Nina's never found life easy and now she's crucified herself to this dreadful Southern Painting. I daren't say a thing but perhaps you could?'

Fay closed the washing-machine carefully. 'You can't tell a forty-eight-year-old woman what to do with her life.' She felt her face becoming rigid.

'Of course she wasn't at all happy with William, but I don't think she's any better off with Gus. What do you think?'

Fay was spared the need to answer by the re-entry of Connie and Nina. A spark of jealousy was lit. Did they have to look so confederate? Suddenly, for whatever reason, perhaps Veronica's words, perhaps Nina's obvious nervousness, the picture turned round and, for the first time, since arriving in Sussex, she had a confident sense of herself and an accurate assessment of Nina. This large, talented, unhappy woman is my friend, she thought and, catching Nina's eye, surprised her with a wide smile.

'Chess?' responded Nina immediately, which was very nice of her because Fay always beat her.

'How about a walk in the garden instead?'

It was dark but still warm, the grass flattened and reproachful from being under the marquee. Nina turned her eyes from the apple tree and led Fay to a bench at the other side of the house.

'Dearest Nina,' began Fay, 'I apologise that I've been so grouchy. Put it down to overwork, being an elderly mother and having a husband whose chosen profession takes him out of the home just when he might be useful. That was a lovely wedding. Helen was a terrific bride, Philip looks like a winner, and Jamie is the handsomest boy I've seen for a decade even if he does look just like his father. I guess I've always been jealous of you.'

'Oh, Fay!' Nina began to cry, huge wrenching tears that shook and distorted her whole torso.

'Hey, did I say something mean?' Fay could think of nothing better to do than carry on talking. 'This was the happy-making speech, not the dissolve-into-misery one. I haven't even started on your terrible vicar yet. That's when you cry.'

'I'm sorry.' Nina snuffled and lurched. 'I'm just a bit emotional at the moment and I'm so pleased you don't hate me.'

'Why ever would I hate you?'

'Because I'm such a pathetic human being, that's why.' Nina found a handkerchief and began to wipe her face and blow her nose. 'I know that's what you really think and you're quite right. I think it myself.'

'So what do you want to do about it?'

'You know what I want to do about it. Throw up Southern Painting and lock myself in my studio for a year.' Nina sat up straighter and turned to Fay. 'Oh, Fay. Why ever did I marry Gus? If only he beat me or something. If only it wasn't so comfortable here. If only he understood about my painting. If only I didn't love him!' She stopped and began to smooth out her handkerchief. They were near enough to the house to be lit by upper windows, casting down shadows from their double silhouettes.

'Love? You could have fooled me.'

'I do! I do. I couldn't bear it if he stopped loving me.' Nina held up the handkerchief, red dotted with white.

'Sorry, I couldn't quite hear that.'

A few days after Helen's wedding, Lisa came into Nina's office to share a cup of coffee and a biscuit. She had often done this over the years, offering advice based on her time in the controlling seat, but it was only recently Nina had realised these visits made her profoundly uneasy.

'You've become such an efficient administrator,' Lisa was saying now, 'but some of the members do complain you're not always there for them . . .'

Lately, Nina had begun to think there was something strange in her continual obeisance to Lisa when she was no longer any real help and, if anything, undermined the new initiatives she was instigating. It was

Connie who gave her the clue when she casually mentioned Lisa's dismissal of her plan for a new branch in Totnes. 'Lisa!' she had exclaimed. 'Isn't that your father's lover?' Nina had forgotten she had confided this bit of information. 'You don't want to take any nonsense from a whore like that!' Connie had laughed, as if she were joking. But when Nina considered her remark later, she realised that, in the usual contradictory way she led her life, she was tolerating Lisa's interference, even bowing to her opinions when she most disagreed, because she did not want to seem to blame her. She had felt emotionally involved in her love of her father. But that Lisa had disappeared long ago: in her place was this bossy, managing, ageing person, married to another man for more years than she had known Nina's father. Why did she not get shot of her?

'I do apologise, Lisa, but I'm afraid I'm going to kick you out of the office. I've a load of work to get through.'

Lisa stared. Her face registered shock, annoyance, acceptance. 'I'll be off, then.'

Was it that easy? Lisa left the office, shutting the door behind her. Nina looked at her desk in a new light, slightly fearful (it was all her own – what a coward she was!) and with new energy. The telephone rang. It was the Reverend Dudley Ormsby-Fish.

'I'm celebrating,' exulted Nina. 'I've just seen off Lisa.'

'About time too. Shall we have lunch?'

'Oh, no,' said Nina, with as much ease as she had seen off Lisa. 'You know we can't do that. Not after what happened at Helen's wedding. In fact, we can scarcely talk to each other any more.'

'I thought we'd talk more.' He sounded hurt and definitely unapologetic, let alone guilty.

'I want to put it down to champagne.' Nina felt herself becoming more and more like a headmistress and didn't care. 'For God's sake, Fish, you're a priest!'

'If you're going to bring that into it . . .'

'Yes, I am.' Nina put down the telephone.

Nina sat in the garden with Gus. It was a warm afternoon about a week after the wedding and she had made sure the apple tree was out of sight. Gus was half asleep. Since his business had not been going so well he had developed a tendency to sleep in comfortable chairs. The organising Nina who ran Southern Painting was irritated by it but the sad self sympathised and might have done the same.

'Gus.' She had to say it twice before he awoke, eyes on the newspaper as if he'd never stopped reading.

'How lucky we are not to have been born in Bangladesh.' He read out loud a report of the devastating floods, as if to reinforce his knowledge of the world.

'Gus, shall we talk?'

There was a longish pause. Gus folded his paper and, after some consideration, put the pages on the chair and sat on them. 'Those must be the most frightening words in any marriage,' he said. 'Shall we talk? Shall we bring oxygen to secrets? Shall we see how strong we are? Look, Nina, I know what you have to tell me. I'm trying hard not to lose my respect for you. I'm trying not to think you ridiculous at best, contemptible at worst. I'm attempting not to make it serious.'

Nina's spirits became very low and with them dropped her energy level. She could not even ask him how he knew. She wanted to say, 'But it *is* serious. Fish may not be serious but the reasons I lay with him under an apple tree are very serious. That is what we have to talk about.' But she could see that he was not going to let her progress beyond the guilty party. Forgiveness was all she could ask for, all he was prepared to discuss.

'And on such a happy day!' said Gus.

'I'm so sorry. So sorry.' Despairingly, Nina went and crouched beside his knees. 'It meant nothing.' She should have said, '*He* meant nothing' but *it* meant – means – a lot. But she seemed helpless to play anything but the abject penitent.

'He's so absurd!' Gus became angrier.

'That's what Fay said.' Nina hated her small, sad voice. She remembered what else Fay had said. She wouldn't like to see her crawling at Gus's knees.

'You mean Fay knew?'

'I thought she must have told you.'

'I suppose everybody knew except me!'

Nina looked at Gus's red, furious face and felt a great sense of unreality. Surely he must know that all this was totally unimportant. That the only thing that mattered to her, her painting, had been taken from her, that he had engineered it *for her own good*. Had he said that or had she imagined it? They should be discussing whether it was still worth their living together. Whether they still loved each other. But she was too frightened and she did love him. 'I love you, Gus.' Why couldn't she tell she hated him too? That was almost equally true. How could such complicated feelings live together? And there he was, still fuming about poor Fish. 'But you did know.'

'What can you mean?'

'You said everybody knew except me, I mean you.'

'I didn't *know*. I just had a strange feeling. Then I asked Connie.'

'You asked Connie?'

'On the way to the airport. She was in the front of the car with me. Orlando and Leo were talking in the back.'

'She never told me!'

'You haven't seen her. She was very fierce. She said I didn't deserve you and it was no wonder you fancied someone as dreadful as Fish – although fun. She said that, fun!' Gus seemed as scandalised by this as anything else. 'She said that she regretted introducing us and that I was an utter bore and, worse than that, a bully.' Gus paused. 'If it hadn't been Connie talking, I'd have been quite upset.'

Nina who, during the first part of this description, had believed that the moment of truth had come after all saw it disappear again. Gus, it seemed, did not take Connie seriously. Perhaps he could never take any woman seriously.

Gus laid his hand on Nina's head. She felt like a huge Labrador. She had used to love his touch. Not so long ago, their bodies had made love with great confidence and pleasure. When had it stopped? The night of the wedding, when she had wanted Fish so much, it had felt like years but now, she had to admit, it was more like months. Their bodies had gone on performing long after their minds were disengaged.

'I shall probably take early retirement.'

'What?' Nina stood up, went back to her own chair and looked at him with a shocked expression.

'It needs a younger man to run the firm. I'm nearly sixty. I shall sell it to Gerald. He's keen.' He could not look at her directly.

'But what will you do all day?' Nina began to be horrified. Was it he, not she, who was having a hard time? Was it he, not she, who would stay at home in this house and garden? Perhaps he would take over her old studio and begin to paint. Maybe he would turn into a woman! She realised she was hysterical. At least William, she thought wildly, had never stopped working.

Gus got up, and came over to her. 'It's just wonderful you've grown to like your job so much!' Nina gave a half shriek, half laugh. 'I know it's a shock. And it won't happen for at least a year. Probably longer. But I wanted you to know first.' He put his arms around her shoulders.

'I want to be here for you, Nina. I love you far more than I did when we first met. If I've been preoccupied recently, not given you enough attention, then please forgive me.'

'You've forgiven me?' Nina felt bewildered. The scenario had shifted to his point of view so thoroughly she could hardly remember her own.

'Of course I forgive you. I want us to start afresh.' He kissed her then, pulling her to her feet so that they could hold each other. Nina found that her heart beat with such a mixture of relief and despair that she could do nothing else but kiss him back.

1990

Fay's mother had died several months after the twins were born. There was no time for grieving, beyond being sorry that they would have no grandmother. She had said the day before her death, 'You were always twice as clever as anyone else's daughter, Dr Fay, and now you have proved it all over again.' It was almost a witticism. So, at the end, she had brought pleasure. But as the years passed and the babies grew into little boys, Fay suffered a painful sense of failure.

She had not only failed to love her mother, for which her shrink said she should forgive herself since love would not always be commanded, but she had failed to talk to her. *She had never found out her story.* She had never even asked her for it. This failure gradually became near obsessional, a sense that by not knowing her mother she had lost something for herself and for her boys. She suspected that at the root of these feelings was her grandmother, the old lady who had survived Auschwitz and never talked about it. She pictured often the moment in the kitchen when she had seen the numbers tattooed on her grandmother's arm, so that it came to have hardly more reality than a dream or a childish invention.

Then one evening, Ted announced, 'Someone called David Blass introduced himself to me today. He's a session player. Plays the fiddle. He said he's a cousin of yours. Why don't you get together? He still lives in Chicago most of the time.'

'He must be Uncle Larry's son. I'd forgotten all about him. He wasn't at my mother's funeral.'

Fay invited David to lunch and he was indeed Uncle Larry's son and he hadn't been at his aunt's funeral because he was playing Tchaikovsky in Europe. On the other hand, as he pointed out agreeably, she had not attended her uncle Larry's funeral, not so long ago.

'As a family we're not very good at living,' joked David.

'Or, to put it another way,' said Fay, 'we're not very good at living as a family.'

They were eating in a small kosher restaurant because Fay remembered nothing about her cousin and wanted to be safe.

After he'd laughed at her joke, David became very serious. He was narrow and dark, very like her, Fay suspected, and not at all like Daniel, which was a relief. 'I was sorry to miss your mother's funeral. At one time I saw a lot of her. She came to call on my father often when I was still living at home. After our grandmother died. I used to listen in to their conversations. I was always so curious but they never answered direct questions. They used to say, "The past is all bad. What does a young man like you want with the past? Go on and make yourself a good future."'

'But you overheard?' Fay felt hot and breathless, guilty also, like an eavesdropper.

'They were sadder than gypsies playing Paganini.'

Fay wanted to cry out, 'But my mother wasn't sad. She was a tough, feisty woman. And your father, too, better at cracking jokes than a Greek with a pile of plates.' But she restrained herself. This was listening time.

'Our grandmother had told them everything. All the horrors about what happened to her and her family and her friends. A young boy, that's how he was described, *like an angel*, was hanged in Auschwitz – that little tragedy stayed with me for days, months. He had committed some pathetic act of rebellion and they were all forced to watch him as he danced on the end of a rope for far too long because he was so light. Strange how such an image gave me nightmares when so many worse things happened. Or just as bad, as grotesque. Our parents lived all the time with this knowledge of evil, because she didn't want them to forget. They couldn't stop her. How do you contradict the wishes of a woman who had seen husband, sister, brother-in-law, nephews, nieces, friends, neighbours all wiped out? But they did commit one fairly serious act of rebellion.'

'They never talked about it to us.'

'Check. They didn't want us to be part of it, to carry the burden of guilt they carried. They wanted us to be free, like American kids.'

'But that's not true!' Fay noticed she had shouted and lowered her voice. 'They may not have told us the details but it was in the air we breathed. The nightmare that we had all escaped. It was far worse because it was never discussed!'

David looked sombrely at her. 'Nothing could be worse than the reality. Until a few years ago, I only knew what everyone knew, then I began collecting books about the Holocaust. I could hardly bear to understand what I was reading. Your mother lived with someone who was evidence of its truth. How do you think it was living with a mother who had numbers on her arm? Even the death of your brother can have been no surprise to her. I expect she encouraged you to get out?'

'I fought to get out!' Again, she was shouting.

'Oh, I'm sorry. I'm making assumptions. Anyway, she was proud of you.'

'Oh, yes.' Why was she saying this bitterly? 'We never got on. She drove me crazy. She wanted me to be a well-groomed wife and bring up children who prayed on Fridays.'

'Are you sure?'

'That's how it felt.'

'Well, maybe she was torn. I only got the proud-of-you bit. Did she object when you married a gentile?'

'She was old by then. We hardly saw each other. She lived long enough to be proud of her grandsons.'

David sat back. He seemed to feel the subject was exhausted and perhaps it was. What had he told her? That her mother's life had been swamped by her own mother's terrible history. That she had heroically refrained from passing on the burden. Was it possible that the mother she remembered – fussy, grasping, silly, material through and through – was also this other woman who had tried, heroically, to protect her daughter? Failing totally in the process, of course, but maybe that could not be blamed on her.

'One thing more,' said David. 'I wondered whether to tell you. You may know already. When your mother and my father left Poland, she was already in love with my father's best friend. They were hardly more than children, but she had an adult love. That's how she put it. This friend died in Auschwitz. They often talked of it because our grandmother met him there.' He gave her an ironic smile. 'It was a small world for Jews at that time. He was helpful to her, caught typhus and was sent to the gas chamber.'

'She never told me anything,' said Fay. 'Nothing. There were things I knew. I knew my father was not what she wanted. She made as if he didn't exist and then he obliged her by dying.'

Now it was enough. They ate their food – David commented in an amused voice that he hadn't eaten kosher for a decade or more. They began to talk again, mostly of Ted's music.

'He's my hero,' David said. 'I only recently caught on he was your husband.'

Fay thought he was keen to elect heroes but was only a little surprised. Ted was becoming famous. She, on the other hand, was becoming more and more a full-time mother. Soon she would only work three days a week and then two and one day perhaps she'd stop altogether.

Ted listened to Fay's stories told to him in the darkness. They made love and afterwards he stroked her, smiling and whispering, 'Do you think we've made triplets this time?'

'Like grandmothers make babies.' Fay was shocked by the sour note in her voice after such beautiful love-making, and wound herself closer to Ted as if in contradiction. She was lithe and young and the eight years' difference in their ages was nothing. But the truth was, she did feel old, more so because of her young children. Worse than this, she had begun to worry about her death, noticing that Ted, although loving his sons, took no responsibility for their existence, agreeing with all her plans for their upbringing and education. Sometimes she felt it was her bad luck that now he had so many commissions he could hardly handle them. A lot of his work was for films, and often he travelled to the west coast and sometimes was away for weeks.

'I love you, Ted.'

He had fallen asleep but woke again, humming a little. 'I love you. You are my half-diminished seventh chord.' He hummed again and fell asleep. He never snored, too thin, too musical. Fay lay awake, listening to his quiet breathing, and wondered why Lex and Jim had inherited none of his musical talent. She pictured them bowing away at rosewood violins. Gradually this image of two little Corellis was overtaken by a small figure dancing at the end of a rope. *Like an angel.* In an effort to banish him, she directed her thoughts to her mother and tried, and failed again, to turn her into a hero.

'Mum,' exhorted Leonardo, clutching Connie's arm as if she might escape him, 'I want you to come and see what Eric's done now.' Eric was an American ex-medical student, enrolled by Fay and paid for by Kevin O'Malley, who was director of the city-children project, established in the Lir stables. It was now a year-round venture with forty children from the South and North of Ireland resident at any one time. Since Eric's arrival, there were constant new projects. This time it was an indoor riding school. 'We can jump and do dressage. We'll have contestants at the Dublin Horse Show yet.'

'That's grand,' agreed Connie. 'Now give me time to find some boots.'

They walked together through the garden, where the overflowing fuchsia spread across unkempt beds, and beech hedges, surprisingly well clipped – it must have been a project for the stables, thought Connie – were interspersed with tall urns filled with catmint and falling roses. Leonardo was determined to enthuse his mother but she, as usual, was too enthralled by his presence to listen to his actual words. In the last few months he had grown several inches taller than her, which made her both admiring and fearful. How would he, with his extraordinary high-minded soul, deal with manhood thrust so unceremoniously upon him? Even his beloved face, she thought, had changed almost entirely, the elegant little nose elongating, the fine brows thickening, the mouth taking a more decisive line. How she wished she had some experience of being a man so she could know how all these changes *felt*.

'You are so beautiful, Leo!' she cried, causing him to laugh, frown and confront her firmly.

'I shall berate you, Mother, if you ever let such words escape your mouth again, particularly when it proves you haven't listened to a word I said.'

'Berate? There's a word. A humble *mea culpa*.' I must not flirt with my son, Connie admonished herself.

The stables were no longer luxuriant with rampant vegetation but still preserved a shambolic romanticism, despite Eric's efforts. A city boy, Eric was somewhat in awe of nature and failed to take up arms with the rigour of a countryman. A sycamore tree had been allowed to remain in the middle of one building and a huge ash almost blocked the entrance to another. Under the ash she spotted her brother Joe being lectured good-humouredly by Eric. He was attempting to enlist Joe as the builder he had once been and Joe was equally determined not to shorten by a single minute his hours at the Lir Arms.

'I'll catch up with you later!' Eric told Joe, and came over to them. He treated Connie with deference, which she tried not to enjoy. 'You'll be wanting to see the school?'

Connie noticed with satisfaction that he was beginning to use Irish inflections. All he needed was an Irish girlfriend and he'd never leave them for America. The school was simply built out of the remains of a great old barn and struts with corrugated roofing. The ground was covered with wood chippings. 'All made by ourselves,' explained Joe proudly.

'But where've you hidden the children?' asked Connie, surprised at the lack of activity.

'They're at the lake. Did you not get an invitation? We're staging a regatta for the children who are leaving. There's swimming races, boat races . . .'

'But surely it's too cold?' It was July but it had been raining off and on for weeks.

'Eric's conned some American company out of wet suits,' explained Leonardo excitedly. 'That's what I was telling you when you weren't listening. You've got to come and see.'

Connie allowed herself to be persuaded. Orlando had driven to visit his father who, at the age of ninety-five, had finally agreed to live in a home run by patient nuns who laughed at his more outrageous remarks and allowed him a bottle of whiskey in his bedside table. When he became too rude they pinned his arms by his sides and tucked his bed so tight he couldn't move a muscle. Leonardo discovered this punishment one afternoon but failed to move either of his parents to complain. 'It's never too late to learn good manners,' Connie had commented complacently.

They walked towards the lake, along a rutted track, wide enough for a tractor or car. Since her work with the Sisterhood for Peace, Connie could not look at it without being reminded of all the quiet tracks and secret lanes used as access to IRA hiding places for arms-caches or the corpses of disloyal members. She still saw the beauty of Ireland, but pockmarked with black sores where evil had taken hold. After nearly ten years of organising rallies, writing reports and even a book with a collection of essays from prominent women on both sides of the border, she had handed over a lot of the work to her sister. Eileen was a better organiser than she, being used to running eight children, and less emotional. Besides, she was married to a real Irishman.

Ever since Helen's wedding, Connie had been careful to leave Orlando on his own as little as possible. 'One night a month is the uppermost limit of my tolerance for separation,' she had told him and stuck to it. 'I shall gradually become an *éminence grise.*'

'Impossible that you should ever become *grise*, my dearest.'

The lake, also under Eric's direction, had been cleaned up at the edges, a couple of natural inlets turned into neat harbours and several boat-houses and sheds constructed.

'So here they all are!' exclaimed Connie, her view suddenly filled with children, all, it seemed, decisively engaged at shoreline or on the water. Many wore yellow life-jackets, brilliant against the soft greens and greys of the landscape and the lake. A whistle blew and a dozen or more children raced across to a row of canoes and lifted them above their heads. 'It's a miracle.' She wondered whether, without listening to the accent, you could tell which child came from Dublin and which from Belfast.

'And where did the canoes come from?'

'Philadelphia,' said Eric, looking as smug as a truly modest person can. 'Kevin gave us an introduction.'

'Another American gift.' Connie walked a little way from the regatta and nearer the edge of the water. No pig shit now. A recently arrived sun was gently lowering, reflecting warmth over the scene. She realised it was almost ten years since her parents' deaths and Eileen's remarks about Michael, which had prompted everything she had tried to do. She had initially wanted the American link to be important but, after her visit to Shirley when she had turned down the appeal to start an American branch, Connie had more or less given up trying. It had been too painful to think that Kevin's misguided patriotism, in some dreadful kind of competition with Michael, was probably supplying the kind of cowardly men she most despised.

But here, in front of her, was evidence of a channel of Kevin's donation to Ireland that was as positive and strong as anything she could have imagined.

'Doesn't he want to see it?'

'What?'

'Kevin. Doesn't he want to see his philanthropy in action?'

'We invite him. And Fay, of course. She persuaded Ted to give a concert in Manhattan for us.'

'I'd forgotten.' Connie thought she hadn't seen Fay since Helen's wedding and felt guilty. 'Yes. It's wonderful what Fay does too.'

'But they won't come, either of them. Fay's got her boys and her work, and Kevin says photographs give him the same kick.'

After supper, Connie uncovered a piece of Lir Water notepaper headed by a swan, wings outstretched, and wrote to Fay. 'Dearest Fay, I feel like a world has grown between us – at least I did till today when I went down to the stables. Two years since we met! Leo as tall as a tree – well, maybe a sapling – and Lex and Jim must be . . .' She paused, failing to remember their ages '. . . eleven or twelve, perhaps? But this afternoon I was down at the stables, first time for a while and Eric showed me the new canoes and the wet suits and so much else, all due to you or Kevin, the American connection as I'm beginning to think of it. And I remembered how desperately I had wanted to break the American dollars feeding the murderers over here, of one side if not the other (including, of course, my own brother), and I never managed that but instead I have a counter-flow, all good. So, my old dear friend' – she looked up, aware of being watched, and there stood Leonardo with intense thoughts in his head that she couldn't hope to understand.

'Darling?'

'Who are you writing to?'

'Fay. You remember Fay?'

'She's Jewish, isn't she?'

'I don't know.' Connie felt foolish. Of course she knew. It was just something she never thought about. It would seem vaguely insulting to categorise her in any way. 'Yes, I suppose she is, not as a religion, as a race.'

'Yes. I've been reading *The Diary of Anne Frank*. It's so horrible what was done to the Jews.'

'Well, yes.' Connie began to doodle on her notepaper. 'I don't believe Fay thinks about it much.'

'Doesn't she? I would if I were Jewish.'

'Well, I don't think she feels particularly Jewish. At least, she never talks about it.'

'Perhaps you don't want to hear.' Leonardo's green eyes stared at her.

'Leo!' She was shocked by this near accusation.

'Sorry.'

Connie returned to her letter. On impulse, she wrote, 'Orlando and I would love to invite ourselves for a visit for a few days. Perhaps we'll bring Leo too.' She put down her pen, conscious that Leonardo was still fidgeting nearby. 'Do you want to talk, darling?' She stood up and went over to the sofa she liked most, which was covered with worn yellow damask. Leonardo sat beside her with his hands on his angular knees. Connie supposed he wanted to talk about sex and wondered why he had not approached Orlando.

'I'm thinking about becoming a priest.'

'You're much too young! You're only fourteen.' She had reacted instantly out of a kind of terror.

'Fifteen. And that's not too young to think.' He was almost casual now he had got the words out.

Connie tried to joke: 'I'm surprised you don't want to be a rabbi.'

'There's so much cruelty in the world.' He was dignified.

'Oh dear.' Connie put her hand on the place beside her and Leonardo sat down. She must be serious. 'Certainly you're not too young to think. I expect I'm too old.'

'Mother.'

'Is that what you call me now?' She tried to say it gaily but it came out sad.

'I do like sports too.'

'I know. I know. You forget I have an old friend who is a priest. I am not as shocked as I seem.'

'You seem very shocked indeed. And yet I thought you'd noticed I was a little different.'

'I thought that was because you were my son.' Again it didn't come out with quite the insouciance she would have liked. 'I would be a daily communicant if it fitted in with my schedule.'

At last Leonardo smiled. 'I'm fifteen years old,' he said, 'and it feels like I've hit on the right future for me.'

'Well,' said Connie, 'I expect you're praying for me.'

'And Dada.'

'Have you told him? He would never be a daily communicant. Really he's not a believer at all. At least, he believed in me.'

At that moment Orlando came into the room. Connie was filled with a warm rush of confidence.

'What are you two plotting?' He had decided to give away some of the books in the house and carried a tall pile. As he stood still, his new dog, an enthusiastic cocker spaniel, pushed him from behind and the books toppled out of his grip on to the floor.

Leonardo crouched down to pick them up and Orlando took his place beside Connie. 'Any effort to create order in this house results in more chaos.'

'Leo's thinking of becoming a priest,' said Connie.

Leonardo made a footstool of the books and placed Connie's feet upon them. 'I'm only thinking about it,' he said.

'The Catholic Church in Ireland has a lot to answer for.' Orlando gazed at his son. 'I can tell you things laid at the door of priests that would give you sleepless nights.'

'But lots has changed, Dada, though lots more needs changing.'

Connie listened to her husband and son. She had no wish to join their discussion. She noticed one foot was resting on her book, whose cover was the close-up photograph of her Caesarean scar. Surreptitiously she removed it from the pile and slid it under the sofa. Not that she was altogether ashamed of her past, but sometimes it came as a bit of a surprise.

In the end, Connie took only Leonardo to see Fay in New York. Orlando said he had a board meeting to decide whether Lir Water should be sold and make them rich. 'Imagine,' he said, 'we could employ two gardeners and a housekeeper. We could cut the hedges and Hoover the floors. We could build a gazebo and mend all the broken furniture. We could buy silver that isn't brass and hang curtains that are not in tatters. We could buy a bed without springs poking through and replace the carpets where the mushrooms grow.' Running out of ideas, he had looked for enthusiasm from Connie, but was not surprised to find little.

'I suppose we could drink champagne for breakfast,' she said eventually, before rousing herself a little to add, 'The stables need a new roof on the riding school.'

Connie found the Brooklyn house large and very orderly and was amused that Leonardo was so clearly delighted by it. He had never seen clean, white space before. The basement, heavily soundproofed, was dedicated to Ted's music, the first floor to general living, the second to adult bedrooms and the top to Lex and Jim. Leonardo was to sleep with them there.

'I hope the kids will get on,' said Fay, rather anxiously to Connie on the evening of their arrival. 'Lex is going through an independent phase and Jim can't be separated from his computer.'

'Oh, don't give it a thought,' replied Connie. 'It must be such a relief to find you can tell them apart.' She had come as a good Samaritan to cheer Fay along and had perfect confidence that Leonardo was equal to anything. Had he not recited Yeats to her as they stood queuing at Dublin airport and, at Kennedy, sprung a line or two of Ted Hughes. 'Leo's very independent, too.' She had decided, on Leonardo's forceful wish, not to mention his priestly ambitions but, as they sat cosily on Fay's bed, the subject was temptingly near the front of her mind. 'Truth to tell, he's going through a religious phase.'

'Is that right?' exclaimed Fay, looking even more bowed with anxieties, which, in the event, turned out to be well founded.

'Just because Fay is one of my two bosom friends,' as Connie remarked to Nina later, 'that's no reason why my son has to like her sons. On the other hand, there's no reason why they should hate each other.'

They did hate each other. One night in the same room was enough to prove this. Leonardo told Connie: 'They have no conversation. They play computer games, watch television and talk about films and places and people I don't know. They are patronising because I live on a tiny island and they live in a huge continent. The age gap is the width of the Atlantic. If I spend time in their company, I'll go mad.'

'That doesn't sound very priestly.' This conversation was being whispered in Connie's bedroom. They had both woken early owing to the time change. 'They must have some good qualities.'

'They're good-natured, I suppose. But I don't want to see New York through their eyes.'

'We'll go out ourselves then, right now.' Connie put her white feet out of bed. They seemed smaller, somehow. Could this be the shrivelling of old age? 'And I will show you my old haunts before breakfast. Scribble a note, my darling.'

'*Eheu*,' wrote Leo, in his monk-taught italic. 'Mater and I are investigating her juvenilia in rosy-fingered dawn. Back soon.'

Lex and Jim showed Fay this note as confirmation of their heartfelt view. 'He's crazy, Mom, not dangerous, but not human either.'

Fay felt sad. It was terrible that Connie's beauty combined with Orlando's eccentric but charming personality had produced such an odd son. According to Lex, he had sniffed and snored all night, talked to himself on occasions and been quite incapable of a normal conversation. Jim had added that he was wearing bathing trunks instead of underpants, that he did not use a deodorant and he had brought no toothpaste. 'He is like an overgrown child.' They both agreed and, although promising to show him the Manhattan sights, were extremely reluctant to release him on their friends – particularly girls. 'Honestly, Mom, he comes on like a sex maniac.'

'That's just plain silly,' protested Fay.

'That's what all the sex maniacs say. He blushed, Mom, blushed bright red, when Jim said "shit". I tell you, he's weird.'

'Hey, come on. I'm on his side. I don't like those words.' Nevertheless Fay suspected her bright, city-wise ten-year-olds had a point. She tried to turn it into a joke. 'He's clever, anyway. Sex maniacs are never clever.'

'Don't you believe it.' Neither boy would be convinced. 'No one's clever who lays it on so heavy. How long's he staying? He's got to go before we take off for the beach. Can you imagine him in the sun?'

*

Connie decided she was not cut out to be a good Samaritan. And on the whole she estimated Fay to be in good shape. She hadn't seen how she was round Ted because Ted was in Germany conducting something or other, but she seemed to get herself off to work on time, spoke kindly of the world and thought her children were terrific.

'I guess we'll have to go to Washington,' Connie told Leonardo, 'so you can meet your uncle Kevin and cousin Kathleen. I'll track down Fay in her office. But first we'll go downtown to visit Serge. You'll like Serge. He's very high-minded.'

Nina was sitting in her office piling up a new batch of membership forms for Southern Painting when the phone rang. It took her a moment to grasp that this was Connie ringing from Fay's office in New York.

'It's so weird here,' she said. 'Fay has a whole wall of lights where she puts up her horrid X-rays. Death comes in black and white. Spooky, man.'

'Fay, I'm in my office too, in a meeting.'

'Southern Painting has meetings you don't want to break up?'

'Just for a minute or two, then.'

'I rang because Leo and I looked up your old flame, Serge, and it's just so scary because he hasn't changed at all. As thoroughly good as ever, although he does have a wife in the country and three children . . . or was it six? A lot of kids anyway. Leo has gone off with him to help feed the noble poor in a soup kitchen. Erase. In a spaghetti kitchen. Imagine, Nina, if you'd stuck with him you, too, could have had six children.'

'How's Fay?'

After Connie had rung off, Nina took a moment or two to run through her memories of Serge. She was disappointed to find that the warm sexuality they had enjoyed together had now faded behind her sense of her own misdirection. Why had Connie felt the need to resurrect such a reproachful ghost?

Connie sat at Fay's desk and admired the orderly procession of paper-clips, scissors, pens, pencils, cards, staplers, rubbers and Sellotape. She thought idly that, in this computer age, they had the ornate and indulgent air of jewellery. The telephone rang.

'This is Dr Fay Blass's line,' she said, pressing the button for the speaker so that she could have both hands free.

'Listen,' said Orlando, 'don't speak, just listen.'

'I am listening.'

'No, you're not, you're speaking.'

At first all she could hear was the gushing interference of an open line. So she listened harder. Then the meaningless noise changed shape and formed itself into crashing waves of sound. She felt certain she was hearing the ocean, tumbling against a rocky shore. She pictured the dark sky, the black water, the white crests, the wild birds rising from the jagged cliffs.

'What do you think?'

He always knew about her. At any moment, separated by thousands of miles he knew, better than anyone, what she needed.

'How did you do it? A shell placed to my ear. The roar of the sea captured inside. Magic. Virtual reality?'

'Not at all.' He sounded very pleased with himself, his English accent with the Irish softening. 'You know me. Reality or nothing.'

'Then what?'

'Listen again.'

Once more the roaring gigantism of ocean waves came close to her ear and then receded.

'Guessed now? No. Yes, surely.'

'I can't be so stupid?'

'Of course you can, my darling. My tape-recorder and I stood on the edge of the Atlantic at the black cliffs of Moher, next stop America. That's what you're hearing.'

She didn't want him to say anything more. It was all in the vast surge forward of the water. She wasn't even prepared to joke about it. She put down the telephone. Had Orlando guessed she would go to find Kathleen?

When Fay returned to her office – she had a migraine or something worse coming on – she found a necklace made of paper-clips sitting in the middle of her desk.

'Who was here, Maria?' she asked wearily, although she guessed the answer.

'Constance O'Malley.' Clearly the girl had been impressed by Connie and could have reported every detail. Seeing Fay's strained face, she confined herself to the essentials. 'She made a call and then rushed off. She said she had to meet her son and that I was to tell you they were going to Washington.'

Fay went back to her office and sat down carefully. Stress. Fatigue. Sickness. She dangled Connie's necklace from her fingers. She dialled a number. 'I'd like to make an appointment with Dr Windlass.' Checking was always a fine idea. 'Yeah. I'll take the cancellation.' Sooner was better than later. Maybe.

Leonardo had bought a pile of magazines in New York, which he read intensively on the train to Washington.

'I hardly call that priestly reading,' said Connie, pretending to be bored with the *Times* and the view of cold rain from the window.

'I'm not going to be the sort of priest who cuts out the world.'

Connie thought about this. Maybe this was a note to her. Maybe he already knew about Kathleen, who was twenty, in her second year of college. Her two children were becoming close in age – twenty and fifteen, soon they'd be in the same age group. And yet an age had passed between the two births.

'Those two adopted daughters,' began Leonardo, reading her mind, 'will they be there? I suppose they can't be as bad as Lex and Jim.'

As usual, Connie had forgotten all about Tara. 'Kevin didn't say. He's obsessing about retiring to Ireland, God preserve us.' Kevin had moved out of Georgetown and into the suburbs of Washington.

Shirley stood at the door. 'I'm so happy to see you both. Such a very long time. And Leo. What a giant! You'll be able to entertain Kathleen. She's broken her leg skiing. She needs so much entertaining.'

Talking, she led them inside. Connie noticed her own legs were behaving in a very odd way. If she hadn't been wearing boots to the knee, she feared they might have dissolved under her.

'Coffee?' said Shirley, leading them into the kitchen. 'I've made it fresh.'

In Kevin's semi-retirement, they had become less grand. No maids, a house with little swagging, fewer ruches. 'Go on, Leo. You be the advance guard to Kathleen.'

Sitting quietly opposite Shirley, Connie's legs recovered. 'So how are the girls?' she asked. 'Apart from the leg.'

'I wanted this opportunity to talk with you alone.'

'Oh, Blessed Virgin, that sounds serious!' Connie tried to laugh.

Shirley winced and continued, 'Kathleen has been asking about her birth mother. It's quite natural. I'm only surprised she's taken so long.'

'What did you say?' whispered Connie. She could hear voices upstairs. Why ever had she taken it into her head to come to Washington?

'We told her it had been a private arrangement and that we didn't have permission to tell her the name of her mother.'

'So what did she say?' She was fighting the wish to make the sign of the cross, to ward off evil spirits.

'She broke her leg.' Shirley, usually competent, was beginning to sound helpless.

'I don't feel as if she's my daughter. I was another woman, then. I feel as if you're her mother.'

'She does look so like you!' Shirley burst out and looked as if she might cry. 'And the trouble is that when Kevin visited her in hospital, I believe he dropped a hint, something about her mother being Irish. He's so proud of that.'

'You're her mother,' cried Connie. 'She's much more like you than me. She's an all-American girl!'

'She's changed. And then there's Tara trying to find her father. At least she has the good sense not to want to trail off to Vietnam. But with Kevin planning to buy your family house from Michael – not that Michael actually owns it – and Kathleen so unsettled . . .' Now Shirley did cry, the small squeezed-out tears of someone who was unaccustomed to letting go.

'You don't want her to know the truth, do you?'

'I just want to do the right thing.'

'Well, you don't have permission from the birth mother. Tell Kevin to keep his big mouth shut or I'll get Michael to kill him.'

Shirley managed a smile at Connie's fierceness. 'Go up and talk to her. You'll see the change.'

Kathleen lay on a bed in a small, newly painted room. Leonardo sprawled nearby in his ungainly, charming manner – charming to Connie, at least, who was avoiding looking at Kathleen.

'Hi, Aunt Connie. Aren't I just the biggest fool?'

She had to look at her then and saw at once that Shirley was absolutely right: the fairish sturdy American girl had transmogrified into a white-skinned, fine-boned Irish girl with masses of red-black hair and big blue eyes.

'Leo's been telling tales on Fay's terrible twins,' continued Kathleen. 'He says they play computer games all night long.'

'Leo's turn for coffee,' said Connie, heart thudding. She took her place in his chair.

Kathleen twisted her hair into a rope on her shoulder. 'May I ask you something?'

Connie felt her heart turned to an engine so powerful that she was amazed it didn't propel her off the chair. Perhaps she could become invisible and float above Kathleen like a guardian angel. 'Of course.'

'It's very difficult and you must promise not to say a word to Mum. It's just a suspicion I have.'

'A suspicion?' Here we go.

'About my mother. My birth mother.'

Connie found herself panting and thought that if it went on like this she'd have a heart-attack. 'You want to know her identity?'

'I think I've guessed.' She stopped. They stared at each other. 'I hope you won't be offended, being Dad's sister . . .'

Pause. Pant. Tempted to take the initiative, Connie gave a quickly muffled shriek and just managed to hold firm. Worse still, she was fighting an urge to cry, 'Darling!' clasping Kathleen to her bosom.

'You see, I look just like an O'Malley. When I came to Ireland and saw you all, Uncle Michael, Uncle Joe, Eileen, you . . .'

'Me?' A squeak.

'I've worked it out that Dad must be my natural father and my mother must be someone he had a fling with. That's why they won't tell me. What do you think?' She was eager now that she had got it out.

Connie leant back in her chair. No daughter today. No daughter, period. Somehow she had to speak. 'It could be true,' she said, very slowly. 'As they say in the papers, I can't confirm or deny.'

There was a silence. Clearly Kathleen took this as confirmation. 'I will never say anything to Mum and Dad. If they want to tell me they will.'

'Yes,' agreed Connie. She fixed herself in an upright position and forced a playful smile. 'You're a very sensible woman except when you're on the ski slopes.'

Connie and Leonardo sat on the train taking them back to New York. Leonardo had picked up a new load of magazines in Washington. These had the faces of politicians on the covers. He spoke casually, above a grinning President Bush. 'Do you know, it's so weird, but Kathleen's the spitting image of you, give or take a decade or three?'

As he finished his sentence, and looked for a reaction, Connie felt tears brimming in her eyes. 'I'm sorry, darling. I . . .' She put her hands over her face.

'Are you crying? Why are you crying?'

Fay, standing at her office window, looked down at the street. It was six o'clock in the evening, a lively, bright spring evening in Manhattan when all the glass high-rises jostle to preen their reflections in their fellows across the way and, down in the crowded streets, people push and shout and hustle, but are good-tempered enough to keep their elbows to themselves as they wait for the lights to change.

Fay stepped back and shut the blinds. She lit up the banks of screens on the back wall and for a moment felt herself bathed in the glow, but it was a cold, uncomforting light. She reached for the envelope on her desk and took out the X-rays – one for each screen. The nurse had asked, 'Why six?' and she had answered, 'Because I have six screens,' before adding, 'We'll do a tomogram also, so I can get the fullest amount of information.'

She put them up, one by one, muting the white light on her poor suffering breast. Despite all this careful checking, she had no doubt about the cancer. And there it was, an area of lesion, micro-calcifications, clear enough for a student to detect. Different angles, depths, same lesion. Involuntarily, she put her hand to her breast and felt the lump. Working in radiology had been her way of keeping death and illness at a distance. Up till now.

The telephone rang once, twice and the answering-machine had picked it up before she remembered her assistant had left already.

'Fay. Call me at home. Or, better still, come home in person. We can beat it, darling. Don't take it as punishment.'

She flicked a switch on the telephone. 'How did you know the tests were positive?'

'Don't forget I'm tuned in to the music of the spheres.' She could hear him strike several chords on the piano. He must be sitting in his music room, holding the portable phone in one hand. She decided not to ask what he meant by punishment.

Nina sat in front of the Rothkos as she still did whenever she was in London. They filled her with a kind of nostalgic melancholy, a meditative calm in which all the dreary Southern Painting efforts were swept away. Her eye was restored to balance and when, after an hour or so sitting in front of them, she returned to the embankment and walked back to the Underground station, with the river slow and oily on her right, her head was filled with good clean lines and colours. London itself seemed to change shape.

Sometimes – for an hour or more – she would sit on a bench and allow herself to enjoy this sensation, a distant echo of what she had felt before starting a new series of paintings. Once or twice she found she was forming up the line of the river, the buildings on its southern bank and the bridge into a canvas-shaped rectangle. Old habits die hard. After a while, the river and its surroundings reverted to their more usual form and she walked briskly to the Underground.

Fay looked at her watch. Why was Nina taking so long to answer? She had timed the call carefully, ten o'clock New York time, five o'clock Sussex time, when Nina came back from Southern Painting. The most necessary loyalty of a friend is to be there when wanted.

'Hello.'

'Nina, where have you been?'

'But the phone only rang a few times.'

Could this be true? Fay looked at her watch again but without enlightenment. The urgency of her need may have turned seconds into minutes.

'What did they find?' asked Nina, sounding anxious.

'Oh, that's not why I'm calling.'

'Now, Fay, I know you're a doctor and all that, but we've all been very worried.'

Fay noted that Nina still could not pronounce the word 'cancer' and said, in kindly tones, 'I guess it's not great news. They've found a few malignant cells but they'll cut out cleanly enough. I won't die on you, I promise.'

'But Fay, that's awful!' Fay heard Nina whisper to someone, Veronica presumably, 'Fay's tests were positive.'

'I heard that,' said Fay, thinking that, even to her mother, Nina could not pronounce the death word. Perhaps, after all, she was not the right friend to invite on the mission she had in mind. Perhaps she should have called Connie, who was brave and outspoken and able to talk about passion and misery. But Connie was a Catholic. 'The point is, Nina, I need a companion for a trip to Poland.'

'Poland!' Nina floundered. 'You want me . . .' She hesitated.

'The point is, I want to go to Auschwitz,' explained Fay, with a kind of quiet politeness because she did not want this word of horror to explode Nina into fragments.

'Auschwitz,' repeated Nina nervously. 'I see.'

Of course she could not *see* anything, Fay had not expected it. But she would explain how they would go together and Ted would look after the children, and before she went she would have the operation followed by three weeks of treatment and then, after she had got back her strength, they would make this trip. A little break. And if she needed more treatment when she got back, that would be OK too. They would not go for long. She couldn't stand to go for long.

'As you know, my grandmother survived Auschwitz but many of my relations did not. It has become necessary for me to go.'

'I see.' Nina sounded desperately panicked. 'Of course I'll come,' she continued more bravely. 'I'm honoured you've asked me.' Her voice was firmer now.

Fay, standing in her apartment, thought that this was the first stage in her journey completed and let out her breath. She allowed her ears, closed to anything but Nina's answer, to open again and hear a police siren on the streets outside and then a muffled cry of triumph from one of the boys – Jim, she guessed, solving some problem posed by his computer. She turned and went through to him.

Immediately Nina telephoned Connie. Helen was staying and Nina had taken her month-old baby on her lap as if for protection. The baby was a boy called Will and looked, to Nina's eyes, exactly like Jamie had at the same age. Nina told Connie about the cancer and Fay's request for her company on a visit to the concentration camp where her grandmother had been held.

'There's so much cruelty,' said Connie, before adding, 'We never did find out whether Ted was Jewish. I suppose we decided it was unimportant.'

'I'm terrified of Auschwitz. I shake even at the thought of it.' Nina held the baby closer, a small sleeping lump of contentment. Did she really have to put herself through the horror of such a visit?

'You'll survive.' Connie seemed to smother a hysterical giggle. 'Sorry.'

'Fay says she may need no chemotherapy at all. Being a doctor herself, I guess she'll make certain they snip out just the right amount.'

'No pound of flesh,' agreed Connie. Nina was reminded that Connie could not remain serious for a moment. She'd once said that if you allowed tragedy to overwhelm comedy, that was the final defeat. 'Guess where I've just come back from?'

'I can't.' Reluctantly, Nina allowed Helen to lift the baby from her arms. She wanted to appeal, 'I'm a grandmother, now.'

'Staying with William. We stood in rivers together. He held my hand and told me he loved me. Should I take him seriously?'

'Of course not!' Nina's explosion startled Will, who wailed indignantly.

Connie began to laugh. 'I was only joking.'

'What?' shouted Nina.

'They have a delightful slate-roofed house and Felicity cooks roast leg of lamb with rosemary when she has time to spare from running the village. Anyway, it's quite an agreeable place to stay when I have to be in the North.'

'That was Helen's baby crying, since you haven't asked.'

'Don't make me feel old. But give her my love. Nina?'

'Yes?'

'Are you sure you wouldn't have been better off with William?'

'Yes. Thank you, Connie, for your attention.'

'Not really.' She sighed. 'He's so manly. Do you think I'll always crave attention?'

'Yes,' said Nina crossly. 'And thank you for being so helpful about Auschwitz.'

The aeroplane's air-conditioning was not yet working. They had already sat on the runway for three-quarters of an hour. Nina felt the sweat gather round her too-tight waistband and in her shoes. She envied Fay her slim coolness. But that seemed an inappropriate thought under the circumstances. She was reading a guidebook to Krakow but that, too, seemed inappropriate. Krakow had not been flattened into rubble like Warsaw because the Nazis had made it their headquarters. Now it was a tourist destination. They would take a taxi from it over the seventy kilometres to Auschwitz and Birkenau. Birkenau was their real destination, where Fay's grandmother had survived and four million had not. It was indexed in her guidebook under Oswiecim, the nearest village. Nina did not know what she felt about anything and took consolation in the conviction that it was not her that mattered anyway, only Fay.

She glanced nervously at Fay sitting beside her. She saw that her black hair had grey in it but that her skin was hardly lined and she seemed calm. Deciding on honesty, she said, 'I'm terrified.'

'About what?'

'That I'll let you down in some way. Not understand.'

'That doesn't matter. I'm just paying homage, that's all. I hated it all so much, all the Jewishness, when I was a child. I'm doing a little bit of penance, recognition. But I don't expect it to change my life. I'm not religious, not like Connie, and I'm not planning to dash off to Israel. Ted would hate that.'

Nina plunged in: 'Is Ted Jewish?'

Fay seemed surprised. 'Not that I know of. Why?'

Confused, Nina found herself blushing. 'Just curiosity.'

'Quite. Well, if you want to know, it wasn't of any importance to me whether I married a Jew or not.'

Nina felt reproved, which Fay noticed. Not everything could be explained. 'Let's have some wine,' she suggested.

The train from Warsaw to Krakow passed through long flat fields singed by the sun. It had become very hot. Inside, groups of boys smoked and drank beer. They were on some religious outing, it seemed. Their laughter was a relief compared to the dour silence of the older people in the carriage. Warsaw, too, had been a dour city; the gay fancy dress of the rebuilt old city seemed to Fay like dancing on the grave. The ghetto area, its outline defined by Communist-built residential blocks, seemed a wasteland still, despite the heavy stone memorials. She was glad of these youthful enthusiasts, born twenty years or more after the war's end. Let their elders disapprove. Fay looked at the face of a pursed and moustachioed old woman whose skin folded like a scarf around her neck, and reminded herself that this could have been her grandmother. Except she, judging by the cross between the folds, was a Catholic.

Will I become angry? she wondered. Not sad, not the quiet memorial I promised Nina, but filled with hatred and righteous anger? But then, she smiled wryly to herself: The only anger I have a right to feel, is against myself because I disliked my grandmother so much. Or what she stood for.

I am OK, so far, thought Fay, and smiled at Nina, who was staring out of the window. How right she had been to bring her along! She'll be protected from too much suffering by many generations of security on an island. Her eyes reflect the woods and fields of Sussex. That is not to say she's insensitive or does not know how to be unhappy, her breakdown in her first marriage is evidence enough of that, but at heart she's strong, almost impervious. Moved by these thoughts, Fay touched Nina's hand. 'Thank you for coming.'

*

It was still hot. The arched iron gates with their infamous message, 'Work brings freedom' – what blacksmith was employed to make them? wondered Fay – stood behind them. They walked together, not talking, past rows of brick-built blocks. Each block had a small flight of stone steps leading up to it. Bravely, they entered one door and then another. After they had been in four blocks, Nina sat on one of the steps and put her head in her hands. Fay sat down beside her, concerned. But she did not want to be concerned about Nina. 'We can wait here as long as you like,' she said. But she meant, Not for ever. I need you.

'It's not . . . It's not . . .' Nina looked at Fay. 'I'm so sorry.' She wiped her sweating hands on her skirt. 'It's ridiculous of me, so English. But these blocks make me think of my father. I don't know why I didn't make the connection before. You know my father spent three years in a prisoner-of-war camp.' She stopped. Fay was looking at her blankly. Nina seemed confused, and ashamed. 'I'm so sorry,' she said. 'I'll be all right in a moment. This place is your family's history, not mine. It's just that it brought it all back. His absence when we were happy, my mother and I, and then his presence. I'll just sit for a moment.'

'Of course.' They sat together in the sun. To their left stretched the double row of barbed-wire railings, not so high but bent inwards with china knobs through which electricity ran. A small wooden sign, hand-painted with a skull and crossbones, proclaimed HALT. A mockery, thought Fay, since so few had escaped and certainly not over the wires.

'Look,' said Fay. A small brown bird was perched on the sign, singing merrily. She had been aware of birdsong from their entrance, even spotted a butterfly resting lazily on the warm stones. Her voice was controlled. 'I wonder when these trees were planted.' The avenues of trees were orderly, like the whole camp. Prisoners were expected to leave their bunks tidy, a notice had informed them, even if they consisted only of a piece of sacking and contained two or sometimes four people.

'How different it is seeing the actual piles of glasses rather than photographs of them,' Fay continued. 'Did you notice the elegant ivory pair? And the lorgnettes? And the cheap ones made of wire? You can't help imagining the faces that wore them. Wondering what happened to them. Knowing what happened to them.'

'The faces are definitely the worst.' Nina stared at the bird still hopping and chirping. She seemed calmer now. In every block there were rows and rows of photographs, men, women, children, shaven-headed in striped prison dress, profile, front face, half-profile. Their eyes stared out with shocked disbelief. Some had survived only weeks, or even days.

'We are here to recognise their existence, I suppose.' Fay touched her breast where the cancer had been. It was tender. She withdrew her hand. 'Everybody has to die. But not like this.'

'I don't wish to hate anyone,' said Nina. A small stick, perhaps dropped by a bird, lay in the sandy grit near her hand. She picked it up and began to trace lines. Gradually the lines turned into a face.

'I'll carry on.' Fay stood up. Her duty was to see every horror, enter every brick-built torture chamber and record on her heart the dreadful histories that had been written inside. She had to keep moving. She realised she was tottering like an old woman.

Nina hardly noticed her going because the face had turned into the face of her father. She stared at it dazedly. Her father had lived in a place of death. What right had she to presume about hate? In no more than a few minutes she recognised the hatred she had stored up for him, and reached the understanding that made it possible for her to forgive him. Carefully, she leant forward and erased the face, smoothing the surface with her fingers. She sat for a few more minutes, head in hands.

Then she stood and went to find Fay. She felt more fitted now to be a comforter.

She took Fay's arm and they proceeded slowly, emerging from each block blank-faced and shaking, grateful for the sun that gave them back some strength. They saw the wall where men and women had been executed, the underground cells sometimes so small that prisoners could not stand, and the posts where prisoners had been hanged at roll call. They saw the crematorium, just outside the barbed wire, where prisoners were gassed and burned. The red-brick chimney and some of the ovens were still in good condition or perhaps had been restored. They saw where the first commandant of the camp had been hanged after the war and then they stopped again.

'Look.' Fay pointed. In one of the blocks, overlooking the wire, there were lace curtains at the window and flowers.

'Someone lives there? Who could bear to do that?'

Fay linked arms with Nina once more and they walked back to find their taxi. She reflected that this visit of theirs posed questions impossible to answer. 'Now we must go to Birkenau,' she said. 'That's where my grandmother was taken and where her relatives, my relatives, died. Her husband, her sister, her sister's husband, her son and others, I believe.'

They drove the few miles to Birkenau. Fay was struggling with dreadful thoughts. She was imagining her sons imprisoned, their bony nakedness invaded. There had been the photograph of a boy there who had looked very like Lex, a tragic attempt at defiance in his wide dark eyes. She leant her head against the taxi window. Her head and her whole body ached and yet felt pale and insubstantial at the same time. She wondered if the cancer in her breast so recently cut out would take the opportunity to spread throughout every cell. As a doctor, she had never accepted that cancer could be affected by psychological causes but, then, she had never imagined such an onslaught of horror. She was grateful as Nina put an arm around her. She leant on her shoulder. They leant on each other's shoulders.

Birkenau stretched over several hundred acres, its rows of wooden housing blocks widely spaced and set on brilliant green grass. Fay climbed slowly out of the taxi, followed by Nina. She stood for a few minutes, just looking. In the centre ran the railway line, entering through the much-filmed brick arch that rose to a tower, now open to visitors. Behind them, a coach drew up and a party of Polish schoolchildren poured out, their natural exuberance gradually turning into hushed whispers.

Fay turned away. 'I'm too weak,' she said. She got back into the taxi, helped by Nina.

For the journey back to Krakow, the road threading through pretty woods and pastureland, they did not speak. Nina was not sure if Fay had meant she was 'too weak' physically or psychologically. She herself had been extremely relieved to cut short their expedition. As they re-entered the city, winding past so many churches that she lost count, she found herself able to think quite clearly about her father. He had spent three years of his young manhood in a Japanese prisoner-of-war camp. He was there because he was a soldier, not because he was a Jew or a gypsy or a homosexual. His race or religion was unimportant and he was not part of a world-wide Holocaust. He was part of thousands not millions. Extermination was not the reason for the existence of his camp. There could be no comparisons with what had taken place in Auschwitz-Birkenau. Nevertheless, he had lived with brutality, torture and possible death. He had done things of which he was ashamed and had things done to him of which he had been equally ashamed. It had marked him and, by marking him, had marked her. The taxi stopped outside their hotel, just off the wide main square.

'Thank you for coming,' Fay said. Nina wondered if her face wore the same white strain of shock as Fay's.

'Yes.' Nina remembered another point of difference. Fay's grandmother had been the only one to survive from her family – apart from those like Fay's mother, already in America. She could not think about her father in the same breath as Fay's family. Such comparisons were disgusting, she decided. She noticed that she felt enormously hungry, as if her body were saying, Enough! You, at least, are alive.

They went into the hotel, Fay hurrying. 'I want to ring home,' she said, taking her key. 'Shall we meet in a couple of hours?'

Fay lay on her bed. She had ordered tea and a sandwich. Everything had been fine at home. Lex had been cast in a youth musical organised by the city. Jim had on loan a new computer programme in which you built an entire city. Ted had come home with a peanut-butter machine, which ground the nuts into paste that made terrific sandwiches.

Fay tried to remember how she had felt when Daniel had been killed, as if that might be the clue to reacting to Auschwitz. She had been mad with misery, anger, self-pity, she knew that, but nothing else was clear. Because of it, she had met Ted, and Ted and the boys had become her life. Was that the clue? Her grandmother had come over to America and made bread in their over-furnished apartment. How had she done that? Fay couldn't understand. Her mother had known about it but never spoken. She herself had known about it from an early age – flour catching a ray of sunlight and a sleeve falling back to reveal a row of blue-grey numbers. She had not wanted to know more and they, her grandmother and mother, had protected her. They had never mentioned Poland to her and certainly showed no wish to go back. So this was her burden, this going back, this remembering. Because she was strong enough. She would survive it. She was an American.

Fay closed her eyes but the long rows of faces, shorn heads, stricken eyes lined up to watch her. She sat up on the side of the bed and again felt her breast, the absent portion and scar. I will survive, she thought. I am an American. And then she thought of Daniel and even that didn't seem so certain.

1992

The mountain rose out of cloud so low and thick that only the shallowest slope was visible. Rain sluiced from the sky and ran down the various trails, tumbling looser stones and eventually joining two streams, cut deep into the rock and fringed by exuberant masses of brambles and fuchsia.

'We can't climb it in this weather,' said Leonardo, cheerfully, 'and even if we could, there'd be no view from the top.'

'We don't need a view to do the stations.' Connie's voice was mournful. Croagh Patrick had been a long drive from Lir. She stood by the statue of St Patrick and read from a placard.

' "First Station: Leacht Benain, the pilgrim walks seven times around the mount of stones saying seven Our Fathers, seven Hail Marys and one Creed. Second Station. The Summit. (a) The Pilgrim kneels and says seven Hail Marys and one Creed; (b) the Pilgrim prays near the chapel for the Pope's intentions; (c) the Pilgrim walks fifteen times around the chapel saying fifteen Our Fathers . . ." '

She stopped to watch Leonardo, who had walked away and was peering into a stream.

'It's an amazing colour!' he called. 'Brassy red, almost like blood.'

'And you call yourself Irish. Blood indeed. That water's coloured by the peat. Shall we try Knock, then, without the climb?'

Connie and Leonardo walked down the main street of Knock, past the souvenir shops tactfully called by saints' names. Connie wore a blue plastic cape with 'Knock' printed on the back. 'My aunt would have turned in her grave. Or would she?'

'Prosperity. That's all it is.' They looked up at the huge, ugly basilica built next to the original church where the appearances were remembered by a glass-worked chapel. Behind them a crowd gathered round the taps dispensing holy water. They were filling plastic bottles shaped like the Virgin bought for this purpose. A loudspeaker recited invocations to Mary – Mother of Mercy, Mother Inviolate, Queen of the Ocean, Star of the Sea, Virgin Immaculate . . .

'It doesn't put you off your priestly vocation, then?' Connie noted, with the shiver she never could repress, the large signs advertising confession.

Leonardo laughed. 'Mother, if this is the way some people like their religion, it's fine by me. The mass is the same everywhere. We'll go to that in a moment of two.'

'Let's get in the dry and have a drink first. I'm soaking wet and frozen.' So they did and when they came out, the clouds were streaked with blue and huge amounts of people, some in wheelchairs, some on sticks, of all nationalities and ages, were hurrying across the gleaming wet concrete towards the basilica.

'She would have been pleased, I think, Auntie Annie. Sister Oliver, I mean.' Warmed by the drink, Connie took Leonardo's arm. 'So much enthusiasm. So much faith. She died, you know, very soon after our visit here. She had an inoperable tumour. That's why she came back from missionary life in India and, presumably, why she came to Knock. I had the story from Eileen years later. I shall pray for her in the mass.'

'And I'll pray for you.' Leonardo smiled broadly as if he'd made a joke. Still arm in arm, they joined the queue entering the church.

Two weeks after her return from Auschwitz, Nina went into her studio and sat in her pink armchair. It was cool in the room, with the light turned green by the creepers covering the windows. For many years no one had been in there and dust and cobwebs covered the canvases propped against the wall. However, the large wooden easel had been cleaned and held a new canvas. After a while, Nina found a pad and began a letter to Connie.

My visit to Auschwitz has profoundly affected me. This is all the more surprising because we were there for such a short time. I went straight off, making no preparations, dragging along all the messy baggage of my life. I must say I'm amazed it has taken me so long to even begin to understand myself. I've only now thought clearly about my childhood when my mother and I tried to do everything the way my father would want, including, absurdly, the years he was far away from us, imprisoned in a jungle in Burma. Although of course we were happy then, my mother and I. After my father came back, I could never make myself important. He undermined everything. Well, you know all about my problems with painting. Then I married two men who were a lot too like my father to be healthy.

I expect you'll call it a kind of miracle but Auschwitz has made it possible for me to look at my beloved Rothkos again and still pick up my own brush. I've realised you don't have to be filled with hope all your life to bring hope to others.

I'd only dare write this to you, as my closest friend, because it seems blasphemous, to use your terminology, to respond in such a personal and selfish way to the horrific torture and murder of millions of innocents. On the other hand, I see no other way a human being can respond. Or, rather, this is the only way I can respond. I can't put anything right in the world, but I can do the thing I do best, paint. I imagine what Fay's grandmother must have seen in that nightmare place and it shapes my paintings. Sorry if I sound pretentious, but I'm determined to take myself seriously. It seems so clear now.

The day after I returned I wrote a letter of resignation to the board of Southern Painting. I hope it means I can still be a good wife to poor Gus. He's quite depressed now that he's retiring. I saw him nervously watching from behind a wall when I first unlocked my studio. It looks like Sleeping Beauty's palace with cobwebs everywhere. Wish me luck, dearest Connie. You have always been so much bolder than me.

Once more in her studio, Nina sat reading Connie's reply.

The great secret is not to pretend perfect happiness is ever within our grasp. The most cheerful people are also the most despairing, viz., St Francis. This is why I like Catholicism. It accepts human frailty, in fact it is just about founded on it. Vatican II took account of it and gradually changed the Church in Ireland from the one I grew up in to the one I know now. Recently I have been thinking about Kathleen very often and wondering whether she should know her real mother and her true relationship with Leo. The Catholic Church in Ireland goes wrong whenever it indulges in secrecy. I don't want to make the same mistake. At very least, I feel Merlin should know he is her father. Orlando only considers it from my point of view, fearing I will be upset, which is very sweet but not quite right. We will see. Incidentally, Fay cannot believe I have done nothing about it for so long.

I'm pleased you are painting again. I always had faith you would. Although, I have to admit, I never thought it would take such an age. Now you must sort out things with Gus. He's quite an ordinary fellow so you'll have to be leader. You can't go on denying your strong character. Holy Joseph (patron saint of families), forgive me, I sound like Fay. But you know much more about her now than I do. We always had a tricky friendship, although sometimes I have put my life in her hands. I don't think she'd ever do the same with me. If I'd gone to Auschwitz, I'd have wept over the shrine of Blessed Father Kolbe who gave his life so another prisoner should live. I expect that's why Fay didn't ask me.

How hard it is to appreciate murder and cruelty on the scale of the Holocaust. Even here, I might have lived content to let the troubles take their course without a thought from me if it had not been for Michael's involvement. And when one thinks of it, it was not Fay's Jewishness that made her want to confront the horror, it was the growing remembrance of her grandmother. When we saw most of her in the sixties, she never talked of such things and I'm sure she didn't think of them either. I was the one who alerted her to the evils of the Vietnam war and I don't believe she ever related it to what happened in the Second World War. Perhaps she did with Daniel, but if so, she never spoke of it.

Darling Nina, I mean to write about your painting and keep being diverted. You explain that you now understand that your principal reason for stopping painting was not directly due to Gus, or working at Southern Painting. You say it had lost any meaning for you some time earlier. You're not very clear but you seem to link this mostly to your father's influence but also to your passionate admiration for Rothko's work. Is this because you couldn't equal him or because, eventually, he committed suicide? I suppose if you make art a religion you're sure to hit problems like this. For sure, you can never expect your pictures to be useful. Or maybe you do? Then you write that Auschwitz unlocked all this. Suddenly you could paint again because, as far as I can understand it, such a scale of iniquity made ordinary good behaviour pointless and inclined you to reach for something outside it – in your case, painting. Is that what you feel? Put pen to paper, my darling.

Our household is filled with moral argument since Leo announced he wanted to become a priest. There is nothing more self-righteous than a male teenager stuck on religion. I find drink a great solace as usual and after a bottle of wine can survive Orlando and Leo's so-called civilised discussions with equanimity. I still see William when I'm in the North. He sends regards.

Goodbye my old friend. Remember you are more determined than Gus and do not answer my questions if they are crass.

Nina left the studio and crossed the garden. It was raining slightly, a cold drizzle. They'd already had supper and Gus was sitting by the fire, reading a newspaper, more asleep than awake. One slipper had fallen off but his feet were close enough to the fire not to feel the cold. Did she love him a little, a lot, not at all? Perhaps she even hated him. How important was he in her life? What did she expect of him? What did she owe him? These were all terrible questions to address, even if silently, to an off-duty, middle-aged man wearing one slipper.

'What are you reading?' she asked him, looking for clues.

Veronica, reading on the other side of the fire, looked up. Then, seeing the question was not for her, she put away her glasses, folded her paper and made for the door. 'Goodnight, my dears.'

When she had gone, Nina said, 'Did you hear me ask you what you were reading?' Maybe he was negligent, uncaring, insensitive. She tried to remember the accusations levelled at him in Connie's letter, before she realised that the only adjective Connie had used was 'ordinary'. They had been married for nearly fifteen years. Surely she should have worked out basic information about his character by now?

'Oh, did you?' He seemed unaware that he was on trial. 'Nothing worth mentioning.'

Now he got up, found his slipper, put away his glasses, folded his paper. He should have married my mother, thought Nina viciously, they have far more in common than we do. He won't tell me what he's reading because he knows I'll be bored by political gossip or sport.

'I'm going back to the studio,' she said abruptly.

Nina crossed the darkly dreary autumn garden and shivered more voluptuously than with cold as she entered her studio, which still smelt strongly of damp and disuse. It was ridiculous that she should feel it an act of rebellion to decide she felt like working at ten o'clock at night! She looked round the room, consciously avoiding, for just a little longer, the canvas that stood up so bravely on its easel. Her pink chair had sprung a leak, and trails of white flock, mixed with mouse droppings, led across the floor to a large hole in the wainscoting. So the studio had not been entirely uninhabited. Feeling cheered by identifying with the little creatures who had kept her place warm, Nina crouched down by the hole and stared into its black depths.

'Whatever are you doing?' Gus's voice was affectionately amused, which added to rather than detracted from Nina's anger. How dare he interrupt her in her private space? Hadn't she indicated as much when she told him she was abandoning Southern Painting for her own art? She was taking command of her life and if that made her sound like a strident feminist then he'd just have to get used to the idea.

'I'm painting.' She got up, irritatingly conscious that no woman of her size was seen to advantage crouched, bottom up. Yet why should she care about such things? What sex they had now was only habitual and a source of no more pleasure than stroking a cat. In fact, less. Sturdily she marched over to her canvas. Immediately her attention passed from him to the tentative shapes, indications of blocks and colours, that were all she'd managed so far.

'Why are you angry with me?' asked Gus. So he had noticed. She refused to turn round. How could she encapsulate the reason for her anger in a few civilised sentences? 'You can't blame me for the decisions you make about your life.'

'Yes, I can!' Nina found she had come in at top decibel. 'Don't you understand? I've hated you for years now! Loathed you! Not quite as much as myself certainly but going on that way. Why don't we just call it a day? Why don't we say we had a good time while it lasted?' Here Nina stopped, mouth agape. Her silence gave her a chance to see his face. She realised that what she most dreaded was that little-boy-lost look in his eyes, the one William had used to such effect. But, then, look how happily he had sorted himself out with Felicity!

'I don't recognise you.' Gus spoke quietly, but with some asperity. 'I won't ask you to calm down because I don't want you to. I want you to bellow it out. I want you to understand.' He rethought. 'Me too.' With that he sat down firmly on the exploding armchair.

'Don't sit down!' Nina hardly knew what she was doing. 'You'll squash my friends.'

Jumping up hurriedly, Gus surveyed with equal alarm the chair and his wife.

'The mice,' said Nina absently. 'That's who I was looking for. Oh, Gus.' As he moved away she now sank into the chair herself. 'How have we come to this?'

Gus stood with his back to her, staring apparently at the ectoplasmic painting. She had no idea what he was thinking. 'You mean you want me to go?' His voice was pleasant, as if such a thing could be said without weeping and gnashing of teeth.

'What do you mean, go?'

'I thought working for Southern Painting would help you. Why didn't you tell me?'

Surely, if he loved her, it should have been obvious? But then perhaps she had never let him see the real her because she wanted to keep her secret. Painting was a secret, obsessive occupation, not to be shared. Had she never allowed Gus closer than the rest of the world? Not even as close to her as Connie and Fay?

'You did stop washing.' He still spoke with his back turned, his tone

323

fair-minded, like the solicitor he had been. But she didn't want fair-mindedness. Being fair-minded had nearly ruined her life. She wanted to be extreme. That's the sort of person she really was. Extreme.

She began to yell again. 'Of course you made me secure and comfortable but it was the security of death, sterility! I might as well have swallowed a dose of depressants. I might as well have been locked up. You made me a prisoner. Yes! Yes! you should go. You took away fifteen years of my life. You're like a great mothball-smelling blanket smothering me. I can't exist with you near. I can't paint!' Now she was wailing like a child. But it wasn't quite true. She could paint. Even now with him in the room between her and the canvas, she had a longing to load her brush and stroke thick colour across those lines already laid. Inside she was exultant. Frankly, it hardly mattered whether he went or stayed.

Gus walked slowly to the door. She noticed that, despite her screams of hatred, she had not lost the habit of seeing him as a source of affection. She noted the baggy outline of his sweater round his slightly paunchy stomach, his shirt collar turned up a bit round his strong neck, his face with its regularity and rather noble brow increased by his baldness. She acknowledged that some part of her, at least, had not turned against him.

'But I have to be free!'

'Of course you do.' He paused, rubbing the door-knob with his hand. 'I feel free.'

'*You* do! I know you do.'

'You have to explain, Nina.' He came back to her and crouched down beside her. A patch at the knee of his corduroy trousers brushed her leg. She pulled back hurriedly.

'I can't. If you can't see that, then we should never have married.' She thought it odd that his supplicant position did not make him seem supplicant, rather calm and strong. 'You treat me like a child,' she added, although that was not quite right. 'You worry about me. Your worry wears me out.'

'But I love you.' For the first time his voice broke a little.

'You must love me without taking me over. I know what's best for me. I don't want to make love with you except when I feel like loving or fucking. Very often I don't want to talk to you. I'm a painter, not a wife. Not a mother, not a daughter.'

'And not a lover, you said.' Gus put a hand on her skirt and immediately she felt the breath of arousal. Was honesty such an aphrodisiac?

'There's nothing more I can say.' She let his hand lie there, almost interested that his fingers on her skin, even through her skirt, should have such an effect. She remembered the afternoon she had painted him in his shorts until he had become aroused. Their love-making then had led to such disaster: her pregnancy, her miscarriage, his anger, her guilt. Perhaps everything bad stemmed from that day.

'I should never have remarried,' she said. 'I'm sorry.' Their faces were close, both leaning forward.

'I will go away,' murmured Gus. 'But not for ever. I'll take Veronica for a cruise somewhere. Turkey. Greece. We'll leave you to paint in peace. When I come back we'll decide.'

'You've been remarkably fortunate,' the doctor told Fay.

'I'm a doctor, too, you know.'

He smiled. They were old friends. 'You're still fortunate. No sign of the cancer. A clean cut. No more radium therapy necessary. You're in the clear.'

Fay looked at the clean cut doctor in front of her – because he was clean-cut too. She had known him since medical school and a few years ago they used to run the opposite way round the park, wearing identical head-phones. Once they had made a plan to swap tapes but it never really worked out. He didn't feel like an appropriate confidant but Ted had had enough laid on him already. 'I don't feel I'm clear of it,' she said.

Adam, Dr Adam Windlass, looked surprised. 'The results are straightforward. Here, you can look for yourself.' He handed her papers, sheets of X-rays.

'Of course, I've looked.' She smiled tensely. 'Remember, that's my speciality. I can have them up on my office wall day and night if it suits me. I'm not talking about the tests, I'm talking about what I *feel*.'

Adam shifted his right hand on the desk in a way that suggested he wanted to look at his watch and would have done so, doubtless, if she had not been a friend and a fellow doctor. She knew perfectly well that feelings were not his province. Probably he would like to advise her to talk to her shrink. 'How can I help?' he asked eventually, disguising resignation under a kind, cheerful manner for which she was grateful.

'I just wonder if it's normal. After a successful cancer operation. Whether other patients feel as I do, as if you're being told a lie and you shouldn't let your guard down for a moment. I can't sleep.' She stopped abruptly. She would spare him her dreams, at least.

'You know, Fay, as well as I do, that everything is normal where

325

medicine is concerned. Yes, some patients worry. That's only natural.'
He talked a bit more reassurance and Fay listened, and after a while
allowed him to believe she was reassured. It wasn't fair on him, after all,
when she was only telling him the least important part of the truth.

Fay walked back to her office. It was autumn, normally her favourite
season, and she had bought herself a new cherry red jacket to celebrate
her recovery. The boys loved it, she knew, happily believing its cheerful
message. She hadn't told Adam about her visit to Auschwitz or, for that
matter, discussed it with her shrink. But then they were still working
through the death of her mother. When you're telling lies of such
serious omission to your shrink, you're in real trouble.

The same dream – nightmare – woke Fay almost every night, often at
exactly the same time, three twenty-eight. She was watching an
operation on a young boy, dark, very thin, about seven years old. His
face was slightly blurred but he seemed to resemble no one she had ever
known. The operation was being performed by a man, at least the
hands with the instruments, ungloved, were a man's. In the daytime
Fay could not bear to contemplate the horrors that were being
perpetrated on this defenceless boy who was alive and awake enough to
wriggle and jerk in reaction to his torturers. At night she was horribly
aware that she was witnessing Dr Mengele at work in Auschwitz but
that, at the same time, this was the kind of operation that she herself
had performed and the boy, although not recognisable, was yet like all
and none of the boys she knew or had known: Daniel, her own two
sons, the little golden boy who had died while she was operating on
him. Occasionally, there was a slight variance and the boy ended up
dancing at the end of a rope.

It was easy enough to analyse this dream. She could do it for herself
without the help of her shrink. It was about guilt. Guilt, a couple of
generations removed, about surviving Auschwitz, guilt about not
recognising this when her mother and grandmother had been alive.
Guilt that had never gone away, about the death of her little boy
patient, guilt that she had not managed to stop Daniel going to
Vietnam. Guilt that she had given birth to two sons, two more hostages
to fortune. In the day she recognised the simplicity of the message
delivered to her night after night. She knew perfectly well, without
asking Dr Adam Windlass, why she did not feel cured. She deserved the
cancer.

Her rational self disposed of all these arguments. Every one was
negative, purposeless and mostly without foundation. Her mother had
not wanted her to think about the tragic side of her Jewishness. She had

done her very best to save her patient, no one could have done better. Daniel had been twenty-seven, determined on his own life and determined to avoid any advice from her. Her sons had wonderful prospects, with doting parents, good health, enough money and sharp minds. Giving birth was a positive, creative act which – you could argue – a woman owed the universe.

But however much she rehearsed these arguments in the day, at night they dissolved into the same horrific scene, the same feeling of guilt and responsibility, of utter despair not just for herself but for the whole world and, in particular, her sons. Gradually, the sleepless hours – she lay still for fear of waking Ted – showed in her irritable behaviour and in her tense face. She knew that many of her friends suspected she was lying bravely about her cancer and that she had not recovered. It was possible Ted worried about this, even Lex and Jim.

Ted's life was changing even faster. At the age of forty-five he had found a passionate audience for his music. He had been taken up by the young. Last summer he had a concert in the Park which was written up in the *Times*; this autumn he had a date in Carnegie Hall. He said he had always written the same kind of music and fashion had caught up with him. This was not the moment to drag him down.

So Fay bought a brighter red lipstick and, going to the hairdresser, had the grey streaks, threatening to overwhelm the black, darkened several tones. She was back at work where, instead of making her hours shorter, she extended them. In her present state, the family were better without too much of her, she thought. Some mornings she looked in the mirror and saw a very old woman. Sometimes she saw her grandmother and those mornings she couldn't stop crying.

1993

The gallery was on East Second Street. Nina's paintings, still wrapped in brown paper, leant against the walls.

'Whatever happened to the Bowery bums?' asked Connie.

'I promise you, it's chic now. A place to see and be seen.' Fay ran her fingers down the whitewashed walls. 'They really try here. Look, perfect for hanging. Smooth. Not a bump.'

'Personally, I'd say it had the smoothness of a Westmeath field,' contributed Connie, 'but, then, I have a bit of a fondness for bumps and things that stick up in general.'

Nina waved a hand heavily stained with paint. 'Shut up, Connie. Honestly, Fay, you don't have to worry. I think it's amazing, considering my weird track record, that you've found a place that wants to exhibit me at all. In fact, I'd rather have this than the Tate.'

'God moves in mysterious ways!' Connie nodded sagely.

'I thought we'd decided this was a God-free trip.' Nina turned on her sharply.

'Thought you weren't as calm as you pretend.'

Fay looked at her two best friends and felt a hundred and five. How could they be so silly! Then, to her own amazement, she burst into tears. She sank down until she was crouching on the wooden floor. Nina and Connie stood back from her with horror. Fay never cried.

'It's nothing,' she sobbed, waving them away, unnecessarily since they still hadn't moved. 'I've let myself get run down. I'm working all hours. Worse than that, I absolutely hate my job. So much education stuffed inside my poor skull and all I want is to throw it all up and trail about after Ted like some silly musical groupie. I'm finished, absolutely washed up.'

'Wow!' Connie gasped, and came to sit beside her, wiped her eyes with a bit of Irish wool draped round her shoulders. 'You've missed your vocation. You could have been a weeping Madonna. There's one in Spain, although I guess she's black—'

'Connie!'

'Oh, don't stop her,' Fay told Nina. 'It was thinking how totally childish you two are that made me burst into tears. Sorry. What I mean is I've just got to the point when I can't go on—' Tears drowned whatever else she planned to say.

'Let's go somewhere else,' said Nina.

Holding Fay on either side, they walked her slowly to Washington Square where they found an empty bench heavily spattered with pigeon droppings. Knowing Fay's views on hygiene, Connie carefully draped it with her shawl. 'Now we'll just sit here,' she said. Nearby, two men played silent but bad-tempered chess. Further away two young women shouted at their children. On the adjoining bench an old woman, apparently wrapped in clingfilm, sat like a large food package. The sun, high and warm, cast variegated patterns through the wide greenish-yellow sycamore leaves. They sat quietly together until Fay began to recover.

'Thank you. I feel better now.' Fay stared at the mottled trunks of the trees and their long black shadows. She had told only a partial truth, simplifying her misery into what could be borne. Exhaustion, overwork, a weariness of spirit – just the normal signs of a mid-life crisis. But could she say more? She knew that the visit to Auschwitz had had a positive effect on Nina's life and, despite all the dreadful complexity of such an idea, she had accepted it and was glad for Nina.

The silence grew, the sun shifted a little so that the shade became deeper and the air cooler. One of the chess players pronounced an angry word in an unknown language. Nina took Fay's hand.

'I don't sleep,' murmured Fay. 'I haven't for ages.'

Connie flapped her hand at a beady-eyed pigeon. 'I would say that you have tried to save the world for long enough. Give it up, Fay, my darling, that's the advice from Mother Superior here. Go help Ted, listen to his music, watch your boys grow up. Be happy. If you want absolving from whatever devil rides you, then I'll send Leo along. He's very ecumenical.'

Fay thought that Connie couldn't help but interpret everything in absurdly religious terms and yet her words were oddly comforting. She held tight to Nina's hand. 'I knew I had to make things safe.'

'I know you haven't asked us,' Connie reverted to her more usual flamboyant tones, 'and I've already jumped in once, but I give it as my opinion that you have won the right to do exactly what you want with your life, and if that means you become a musical groupie, then let's sing Hallelujah!'

'I agree,' said Nina firmly.

Fay looked up at the trees, then down at her feet, so neatly shod, so very cramped and tired. Finally she laid an arm along the shoulders of Nina and Connie and leant back, eyes half closed. 'I guess there's all kinds of ways we can work our passage. I've done it one way long enough and now I'll try another.'

Nina sat on the aeroplane returning to England, looking at the clouds tinged with the remains of an abruptly curtailed sunset. We're going East, she thought, towards the rising sun, and she promised herself to be awake for it.

Connie, having experimented freely with the miniature bottles – 'Are these for dolls?' she'd enquired – was already curled up against Nina's shoulder. Her voice came from under Nina's chin. 'I am so glad you sorted out Gus. He was always a bit of a baby.'

'Oh, I love Gus.' Nina continued to stare at the last trails of ever-darkening crimson. 'I can't believe what a mess I nearly made of everything. You see, I hardly think about him any more. He's just there, like my mother's there. It suits him so much better too. I suppose,' she paused, as if struck by a new thought, 'I suppose the way I feel now is how a lot of men think about their wives. Just there. Just their wives. Nothing special. Anyway, it's an enormous relief. I can't think why it took me so long to work it out.'

Connie commented sleepily that it seemed to make quite a lot of sense for Nina, a grandmother moreover, although she couldn't imagine ever saying such a thing about Orlando. 'And now Fay's going to drop her career and cleave to Ted. Funny, really.'

Reluctantly, Nina had to admit that there was absolutely nothing left to see in the sky. Just a great black void. 'I guess we're the generation who know we're equal with men but find it hard work convincing our bones.'

That woke up Connie for a moment.

'Darling Nina! If that's your best attempt at gender studies, I think I'll tune out.' She closed her eyes firmly.

1996

Nina and Connie stood in the crowded foyer of Wigmore Hall.
'Everyone's so young,' commented Connie.

'I didn't know Ted was this famous,' said Nina.

'He should be famous by now if he's ever going to be. Allowing for eight years' age difference between him and Fay, he must be forty-eight.' Connie felt depressed.

'Where's Fay?'

'Holding his hand?'

'Could it really have come to that? I hope Gus and Orlando haven't sloped off.'

'They'll be here.' They looked through the doors to the cold frosty night from which people emerged bundled up and huffing energetically, to see Fay, neat in her buttoned-up coat, her hair now completely grey. Surely, thought Connie, disapprovingly, she believed in the bottle?

'Fay!' They rushed to meet her. 'Such a crowd!'

'*Quartet for the End of Time* is a real cult piece of music.'

'Is that what it's called?'

'Not Ted's. No. *The End of Time* is by Messiaen. Ted's comes first.'

'We haven't looked at the programme yet.'

'It's a modern evening. Atonality, post-modernism, polyrhythms, a touch of serialism.'

Connie made a face at Nina, which Fay intercepted. She laughed. 'I used to find it difficult too. Then I saw how the kids took it so easily and I let go of the anxiety.'

Connie recalled her own and Leonardo's adverse reaction to Lex and Jim on their visit to New York and rejoiced that they had changed into such intellectual super-brains.

'Ted's asked for a bit of concentration but the Messiaen's pure emotion,' added Fay.

Gus and Orlando came through the door just as Fay looked at her watch and asked to be forgiven for going on through, she liked to be in place and calm before it started. She and Ted, she told them, would not sit with them but up in the circle where he felt less pressure and could get an overview of how the concert was going. 'Sometimes I accuse Ted of making his work more complicated to prove he's not just a movie-music composer,' she said, before leaving, 'but he protests that's the manager in me talking.'

Fay had become Ted's manager. She had written to Nina, 'Since dedicating myself to Ted's career, I have never been happier. Each day I hear the music of the spheres . . .'

'Oh, God!' exclaimed Gus, who had been studying the programme. 'Any hope of a drink before we go in?'

'At least there's a cello.' Orlando smiled at Connie, who tapped his arm.

'Now, don't you go being inspired to pick up your bow. Do you know, he serenaded me on our first morning after? Although, truth to tell, it was after nothing.' Connie kissed his cheek. 'It must have been true love that I stayed with him.'

'That moment is sacred to me—'

'And there's no time for a drink,' interrupted Nina. 'We don't want to upset Fay.'

Fay watched the four of them come into the hall. Orlando and Gus were laughing, both men big, red-faced, reminding her slightly of overgrown schoolboys and very unlike her brilliant Ted. Connie and Nina were arm in arm, which gave her a twinge of jealousy. But she had chosen to be in the balcony, next to Ted, supportive in case he should need anything. They would have dinner together afterwards and she and Ted would spend a night at Lymhurst – all the time he could spare.

Fay stopped thinking about Connie and Nina and began to worry about Ted's composition. It was not first on the programme, Kurtag took that place, a witty, ebullient piece for piano and cello which she knew well. To be sandwiched between Kurtag and Messiaen was tough on Ted. It suggested a lack of confidence, perhaps, but to go first wouldn't have been good either and the piece was not long enough to fill the whole first half. Fay tried to relax, using breathing techniques learnt from one of Ted's singer friends.

'Hey, am I sitting next to a train?' Ted slipped in beside her. 'This isn't a première, you know. You don't have to be quite so nervous. At least, you do but for a different reason.'

Fay realised that her nerves were due to the presence of Connie and Nina – her friends. How ridiculous! They should give her confidence. 'What other reason?' she asked.

'The violinist's cut his finger. Bowing's OK. Plucking not so fine.'

'That's terrible.'

'He'll manage. But it will give you something specific to worry about. Did your friends come?'

Fay wondered at this description since he knew their names perfectly well. But the lights were beginning to dim and she felt that half-pleasurable, half-terrifying sense of anticipation that still reminded her of the seconds before an operation.

Nina listened to Kurtag with proper concentration and was pleased to discover she was enjoying it, although Gus expressed his relaxation by falling into a brief but comfortable sleep two or three times.

'You can't do that when it's Ted's piece,' Nina told him severely over the clapping.

'I've had a long day. Anyway, she'll never see me.'

'Don't you believe it. Fay's got very sharp eyes.' Nina turned round and looked upwards and immediately spotted Fay's bright silvery hair. They waved at each other.

'They won't see me when it's dark.'

'We're almost floodlit from the stage lights.' Connie smiled at Gus.

'I'm exhaustingly awake after all your haranguing,' complained Gus.

'It's called *After Life*,' Nina read from her programme.

'Better than *After-Birth*,' quipped Orlando.

At the same time Connie hissed, 'That proves he's a Christian.'

It was too late for Nina to point out the fallacy in this but it gave a context to her thinking as the music opened with a long solo from the cello. Despite its atonality, she could at once respond to its lyrical quality. Did Fay and Ted talk about his music? she wondered. Had the experience she had shared with Fay at Auschwitz, the confrontation of death in its most brutal form, been passed to Ted? She knew that the Messiaen quartet had been written from a prisoner-of-war camp in 1943. It seemed impossible that the juxtaposition of the two pieces was accidental. Over dinner, she would ask him. As the cello was joined by an oboe, used for a series of alarming shrieks, followed by a long silence until the piano took up some of the themes of the cello, Nina felt certain Fay's family history formed some part of what was being expressed. She reproved herself for looking for meaning in this crass way. How it annoyed her when people asked her to explain the meaning of one of her pictures! Even Gus had learnt to look without questioning. She never talked to him about her work: the most she would allow him were personal preferences. 'I like the dark one with the waves or possibly clouds . . .' Nina smiled to herself and was about to take Gus's hand when she saw he had dropped off to sleep again. Considering all four instruments were now playing in fervent disunion, the violin taking over the screaming at a higher pitch than the oboe, this was quite a feat. Nina gave him a sharp dig in the ribs. He jerked and turned to her apologetically. She took his hand anyway.

Connie was concentrating hard on hating the music. If she hated it enough, she would not be affected. Despite the occasional lyrical passage, usually taken by the cello, she felt the piece was filled with hatred, suffering and despair. Why was it necessary to write like this? she asked herself. The world had not become worse since the days of Bach and Beethoven. They knew how to turn anguish into art. If she'd such a gift, she wouldn't have wasted it. She considered all the years she'd worked to make Ireland a safer place – big ambition, infinitesimal success. If she had allowed herself such indulgent witness, she'd have achieved even less. Just last week she'd talked to a Catholic priest who went to comfort the relations of the dead or dying, even informed them sometimes. He did no weeping or wailing. He offered their tragedy up to God and tried to make the families put their suffering with Christ on the cross. I may be self-centred, thought Connie, but I know how to deal with pain.

Again, she reassured herself, the world is no worse than it ever was. But the sound continued to force itself on her attention, explosions, groans, chillingly beautiful strains of lament. This morning, in London, she had seen two youths whose legs had been smashed by a punishment squad of the Provos. Two weeks ago she had talked in the stables to a ten-year-old girl who'd lost her arm in a bomb. Not very long ago, Eileen had told her about a new recruit for the Sisterhood of Peace, a young Derry mother of four whose Protestant husband had been shot by the INLA. He'd been delivering bread to a Catholic – the woman's father. The Sisterhood of Peace had become a kind of refuge for women like this. It had no effect on the situation, admitted Connie sadly, to herself, so it might as well help in any way it could. The piano, cello and violin were playing now, a melancholy conjunction of notes. Tears formed in her eyes and rolled down her cheeks.

When the music finished Fay turned to Ted. She always wanted to thank him, but she knew he didn't like that. It was this piece, written three years ago, though never before performed outside America, that had finally convinced her to become his manager. She knew how much of her own anguish was in it.

Occasionally, she looked back with astonishment at the way they had come together – the doorman who had listened to her misery about Daniel. For years she had not realised that this extraordinary talent for listening and understanding was what made him such a good composer. He lived off sounds, which did not mean he was uncaring of the meaning. On the contrary, he interpreted meaning from sound then turned it back into sound again. That night when Daniel had died was expressed in this music, as well as Auschwitz, as well as other tunes she knew nothing about. She must not ask him.

'That was splendid!' Ted had not come to the bar in the interval so Gus congratulated Fay.

Connie had pre-ordered a bottle of champagne and was busy pouring it. 'Whatever happened to your face?' asked Nina.

'Tears,' said Connie, rubbing her face and gulping. 'Although I felt the conclusion was a little more tranquil.'

Fay felt an enormous surge of affection for Connie. 'It's very powerful.'

Nina took Fay to one side. 'I thought of our visit to Auschwitz. Can I say that to Ted?'

'You can say anything to Ted.' Fay began to love Nina too. 'As long as it's not stupid praise. Then he sort of disappears.'

Nina smiled. 'I'm afraid Gus specialises in stupid praise.'

Orlando kissed Connie's cheek. 'I don't deserve you. You feel things so deeply.'

'Is that an attack?' Connie swigged more energetically and Gus, overhearing, laughed.

Connie caught Orlando's look and took his arm. 'Let's go back and please supply me with a hankie in future.'

Fay felt very American at Gus's club. Because there were women present, they had to enter through a side door, and the dining room, although prettily decorated, appeared to be under ground.

'They serve the best club food in London,' said Gus.

Fay exchanged a glance with Ted. Did they look like people who cared about food?

'Were we a good audience?' asked Nina.

Fay tried not to be irritated. A little praise would go a long way, even if she'd hated the whole concert.

'The English are restrained but knowledgeable.' Ted smiled. 'At least, that's their reputation.'

'Listening to your piece, I felt unrestrained and unknowledgeable,' said Connie. Fay watched her complimenting Ted and felt unreasonably threatened to see it come from Connie. She leant so close and so sweetly, with that lovely Irish lilt, and still she wasn't ageing like ordinary women should. I wonder if I've always been jealous of Connie, thought Fay, the girl I never could be? Yet she's one of my closest friends, too. Strange.

'Ignorance is my most potent weapon,' said Connie. 'My education stopped at sixteen and before that I only learnt about the seven deadly vices.'

'Being English and middle class is far worse from the brain's point of view.'

'You should take Ted to see where Connie grew up,' Orlando told Fay, ignoring Nina. 'No running water, electricity, books, furniture, food, heating. It was like medieval England.' As Connie disclaimed some of this, Fay was reminded how Connie had always contrived to make herself the centre of attention.

Nina was determined to ask Ted her question. She chose a moment when Gus was busy with the waiter. 'Was *After Life* inspired in any way by Fay's visit to Auschwitz?'

Ted answered easily: 'Yes. More particularly, after Fay got involved with various survivors' organisations.'

'Not very involved,' interrupted Fay. 'I was just glad to meet a few people with experiences something like my own, who thought as I did.'

'We thought and read quite a bit,' said Ted. 'The kids were interested. Mostly in the lurid stuff. The films, too. *Schindler's List*. Painful stories.'

'I've ordered,' announced Gus. He faltered, realising his interruption.

'I hate choice,' muttered Connie.

'About unimportant things,' added Orlando.

'Food at this price is not unimportant,' Gus sat down after clapping Orlando on the shoulder.

'Dear Gus, I'm so rich that I should pay. All the Irish are rich now, whether they like it or not. We're nearly as rich and material as the Americans.'

'Thank you,' said Fay quietly.

'I consider you a European and Ted a citizen of the world.'

Connie laughed. 'How's Kevin?' she asked.

'He's had a hip operation,' said Fay. Fay and Connie began to talk about operations, Gus and Orlando continued their conversation about money until the first course arrived when they changed to food. Nina, pleased at communal peace, turned once more to Ted. 'What's your next commission?'

It had come from a Cologne businessman, Ted explained. His father had been killed in the war and he had commissioned Ted to write a commemorative piece for the sixty-year anniversary of the declaration of the Second World War.

'On the theme of reconciliation, I assume?' said Nina.

'Of course.'

'That's some challenge.'

'I'm not interested in anything less. What's the point when it's so hard even to write the merest jingle?'

Nina looked at her plate. Where did he get his confidence? Not from success. That had only come recently. She remembered when she had first met him, after Daniel's death. She and Connie had seen him simply as someone to make Fay less miserable. Even when his film music was being played everywhere, they had not taken him seriously.

'And you? You're painting, I assume?'

'Oh, yes,' Nina replied briefly, but she felt as if the question and answer had restored her to herself and spread a warm glow through her body.

Fay called across to her, 'Have you ever painted that old oak tree? The gigantic one we found in the wood.'

'Yew tree,' she corrected.

But her voice was lost in Gus's roar. 'I hope none of you are vegetarian?' A trolley bearing three huge juicy joints was wheeled up to their table.

1997

Connie felt like a tourist in London and suspected she was behaving like one too, paying extra attention to the kind of things most city-dwellers hardly notice: demonstrations, for example. She stopped to watch a small but lively group outside the gates of Downing Street. The scene was dominated by a white-bearded figure who held up one side of a huge banner with one hand and an antiquated megaphone with the other into which he bawled. 'The victory that stings can build you wings . . .' He seemed to be reciting a kind of poetry.

Coming closer, Connie recognised, with a thrill of shock and amazement, that it was revolting old Hubert. Still alive! When he had seemed so very old twenty-five years ago! He wasn't holding the banner straight enough for her to read more than three words. Guessing, she could make out 'Freedom' easily enough, but freedom for what, from what? Now she noticed that the banner, so inadequately held aloft, was slotted on two umbrellas, instead of the expected poles. The man at the other end had the unassuming physical presence of an intellectual, which was probably why he was so slack in his stretching duties, while Hubert, ninety if he was a day, was clearly more interested in lambasting the world with his terrible verse.

'What's it about?' Connie asked one of the demonstrators at her elbow, a woman rather smarter than the rest in a black suit with pearl drops in her ears.

The woman's face squared up to a serious issue. 'Censorship. Freedom to write.'

'But surely—' began Connie.

'Not here,' added the woman, 'in Myanmar. Burma to most of us. We're part of a world writers' organisation.'

Now a group of the demonstrators gathered beside a policeman who escorted them past the railings. Hubert was with them, his shambolic height and thick white beard giving him the air of a Russian sage or prophet.

'Who is that tall, bearded man?' Connie turned to the new person on her right, a bald, suited person who might have been a doctor.

'That's the Poet Laureate, Hubert Wyberley.'

With this information, the admiration in the man's voice, Connie walked away at once. She passed through Westminster Square without noticing the Abbey or the Houses of Parliament or Big Ben striking midday. She had clearly been in Ireland too long. Why had she not known Hubert had become famous? And why – she felt her heart beating, her face flushed – did it give her such a sense of exhilaration. She had no difficulty in thinking back to the time when they had, so disastrously, become lovers. Or, rather, he had seduced her, poor ignorant peasant that she had been, quite apart from his son's lover first. The images of their liaison had never left her: their first encounter in the hotel when he had publicly licked her salty arm and privately put his fingers up her knickers; his nightly appearance in the pub when he had used words to woo her and then their love-making, born out of self-hatred and despair (so she had decided), producing, after she became pregnant and had the abortion, more of the same mould. Self-hatred, despair and a rather puny attempt at self-harm. And now this sin-ridden instigator who should have gone down a fissure in the earth, screaming in agony, was the Poet Laureate and, odder still, was into good causes. It was enough to make you laugh. And, rather to her surprise, Connie found she *was* laughing, loudly enough for a passer-by to look at her oddly.

She strolled along the embankment of the Thames. This was a day to be recorded, not, as she had thought, an assignation with Nina at the Tate following a boring meeting. Perhaps this time she would *insist* on looking at the Rothkos. Nina always said she visited the room, with its vast red and black canvases, as a place to recharge.

It was Nina's religion, of course. Feeling in even better humour, Connie began to fly along like a child, only just resisting the impulse to widen her arms.

Carefully, Nina lowered her mother to the bench in front of the Rothkos. She hardly looked at them herself, unwilling even now to share her feelings, despite the long journey to bring her mother here. Instead, she became conscious of another painting – the shrunken old lady hunched between the great flowing canvases of red and black.

'It took me a very long time to come to terms with the fact he committed suicide,' she said.

'Oh, yes. I had forgotten.' Veronica stared at her, as if looking for clues. 'You wanted him to live for ever?'

'No, of course not.' Nina saw that her mother had warmed a little and was sitting straighter. 'But suicide. I know these paintings are dark. He painted them near the end of his life. But the others – the yellow, orange, scintillating—' She stopped, looked briefly at the walls and then back at her mother. 'You're not afraid of death, are you?'

'My death, you mean? I accept it.' Veronica's eyes were on the paintings. 'So must you. Now, shouldn't you find Connie?'

Nina went outside and stood on the great stone steps. Connie was always late but she liked standing here. The spring wind, buffeted off the Thames, crisped ripples on the water, shot clouds about the ugly buildings beyond the river, while Nina stood, hanging out her soul to air. Into my mouth, through my head and out through my eyeballs, she told herself, gulping slightly.

'What are you doing, darling Nina?'

Nina looked down and saw a slight figure, almost entirely covered in hand-knit shawls, layered over her like the petals of a flower. 'Connie! I was waiting for you.' They were close enough now to kiss, cheek to cheek. 'I've got my mother inside. In front of the Rothkos.'

'You've let her see the Rothkos? I hope she appreciates her good fortune!'

They began to walk back into the gallery through the high arched hall, passing slowly a pile of barbed wire and four dustbins stacked on top of each other.

'I used to be impressed that you've got a painting or two in here but when I see this lot, I'm not so sure.'

'You're returning to peasant conservatism, that's your trouble.' Nina held Connie's arm so she had to stop and pay attention. 'Actually, my mother's dying. Not just of age, I mean. She's got cancer. They won't even operate.'

Connie stopped to face her. 'So you're showing her the Rothkos.'

'Yes. I drove her up from Sussex this morning. I hope you don't mind her being included in our outing.'

Connie kissed Veronica warmly. They were about the same height,

Nina saw, since her mother had shrunk by several inches. 'Now, I want to see one of Nina's paintings,' said Veronica.

The painting was from Nina's apple-tree series. It was not hanging but they had been given special permission to go down into the basement and view it there. An attendant escorted them solicitously. 'This is where they keep the best pictures,' he said, winking.

Connie considered the canvas, which she had not seen for many years. It was split into two halves of colour, green on the top, the green of leaves, old lichen-encrusted branches, the green of the light through leaves, of apples not yet ripe, of yellow sun that had mixed in the blue sky; the bottom half was red, the red of a warm trunk, the red of earth, of shadow, the ripe apples that had fallen and mingled in the ground. None of this is explicitly there, she thought, none of it picked out for the viewers, but that is what I see, what I presume Nina wanted me to see. Or should I be thinking of the spirit and the earth? Or some other partnership or contradiction? Whatever it meant, she decided, it gave her a feeling of exhilaration.

'Thank you, darling,' said Veronica, turning to Nina. Whether thank you for bringing her to this spot, or some deeper acknowledgement of what Nina had given her, was unclear.

'Oh, Mummy.' Nina spoke absently, her mind, it seemed, still concentrated on the painting. She took her mother's hand, squeezed it tenderly.

Watching them, Connie wondered if it could have been like this if her mother had lived longer. Or if she had returned sooner. Too late for regrets. 'Now I'm going to tell you all my news,' she said to Veronica, 'before we all flee to the green hills.' What she meant was, before you die. She, Connie, was not afraid of death.

'My car never breaks down.' Nina looked at her mother with despair. They were on the M25. The blustery day had closed in, clouds massing darkly and about to bring rain.

'Try my mobile.' Veronica handed it over, a present from Helen on her eightieth birthday. There would be an hour's wait, she was told by the rescue service. Her mother sat patiently, hands in her lap.

Nina dialled Connie's mobile number.

'I've broken down.' Why was she so keen to share this news? It was most unlike her. Was it the new responsibility of managing her mother's illness and certain death?

'I've only just come out of the Tate. I'm standing on the steps, facing the river. I was thinking it's a very Irish sky.'

'It is here too. On the edge of the M25.' Nina thought of herself leaving the Rothkos to stand on the same steps. 'What else did you look at?'

'Not much. I met an old friend. He's with me now. He says it's not an Irish sky at all, it's a Poussin sky, which makes it French.'

'Anyone I know?' Nina thought how Connie, despite declaring that she lived a totally isolated life with Orlando, still seemed to move in a web of people. Perhaps it was her emotional intensity that drew others to her.

'It's Merlin. Dear Merlin.' Nina heard low laughter and a male voice.

'Merlin!' Nina tried to tone down her surprise. 'You mean Merlin de Witt? William's cousin?' A huge lorry passed, swallowing up, she trusted, any echo of what she was really thinking: Merlin, the father of your daughter.

'Yes, Merlin. Merlin to whom I behaved so badly.' It was obvious that Connie was talking for Merlin's benefit. 'He says he stopped hating me twenty years ago and, anyway, he has always had great regard for my work in Ireland. Although it's a mystery to me why he should know about it.' More background laughter. 'Do you know he was a knight all along, Sir Merlin Regis de Witt? I told him I'd be his Queen Guinevere. But he said I'd have to be his King Arthur because he's been a queen himself for the last fifteen years. Wasn't that a delightfully non PC declaration?'

Nina knew this conversation was too much for her, with her mother hunched in the car and the car itself rocked by the increasing load of traffic passing them continuously. She remembered that Connie demanded strength.

'The breakdown lorry's coming,' she lied.

'Merlin sends his love,' called Connie. 'Did you know his trust has bought two of your pictures?'

And that was true of Connie, too, thought Nina, as she put away the mobile, she brings good news.

'Merlin. Merlin. Merlin de Witt. Where are you taking me?'

'To Albany, of course.'

'The same flat?'

'Nobody gives up a flat like that.'

'Did you ever get married, Queen Merlin?'

'Once only. For three months, and we were apart for two of them. The best two.'

They were walking along the embankment. Connie in her petal

clothes, hanging from Merlin's stiff, tweed-clad arm. He wore, she noticed, a style of three-piece dressing, an almost Edwardian tailoring of narrow lines and high-waisted jacket, which reminded her of his youthful attempts at sixties' flamboyance. He was very nearly bald, with a few flickers of greying hair brushed up round his elegantly shaped dome. Perhaps he was more eighteenth century than Edwardian. 'And to think you gave me my break into journalism. You. Sir Merlin. Merlin Regis de Witt. In the swinging sixties. What a relief it must have been for you to escape from all that silliness!'

'You can probably give the credit to your fairy self.'

'I can?' Connie peered into his face.

'You may not remember but I followed you to New York.' As drops of rain began to spatter, he raised an arm to a passing taxi. Connie shivered a little. Did she really want their meeting extended? Could she bear it? Could she keep up this delightful light-hearted tone?

'As if I would forget your visit to New York. Did we not visit all the brightest spots in town? Those were the whirligig days before I washed myself clean in the waters of the Liffey.'

'Actually not,' said Merlin, beginning to laugh. 'We only met once because you were on your whirligig and had no time for a staid Englishman who made himself even more boring by being in love with you.'

'I only saw you once? What a misfortune! It's true I can't remember much about it but I drank like an Irishman in those days. My dearest Orlando liked to call me Princess Cirrhosis. He tried to convince me she was the heroine of a famous Victorian novel. Tell me, at this one meeting of ours, did I behave shamefully? Should I be asking for forgiveness?'

'Oh, yes. Because of your shocking treatment of me, your nice American friend said she would have nothing more to do with you.'

Connie withdrew her arm a little from his, although giving it a pat for reassurance. 'Do you keep champagne in Albany?'

They sat high up in the front of the breakdown lorry. Nina had stopped asking her mother whether she was all right. The lorry and its bulky driver would transport them and their crippled car to their front door. In this rain, with the wipers hardly keeping up with the sluicing water, that was the best she could arrange.

'Nearly there,' she said, as to a child. Her mother's eyes were shut but she gave no indication of being in pain, no uneasy movements, sighs or grimaces. Now she opened her eyes. 'Oh dear,' she said, with something between a frown and a smile.

A few minutes later they were in the driveway. With ridiculous pleasure, Nina glimpsed Gus in the vegetable plot, dressed in a shiny blue mackintosh belonging to her, and Jamie's childhood red bobble hat. He looked like an outsized and bedraggled garden gnome.

Merlin's room at Albany was even more grandly furnished than Connie remembered. French tables inlaid with marquetry, clasped in bronze, statuettes carved from the purest marble, clocks in which the sun and moon revolved slowly and a silvery bell chimed each quarter. Would all these beautiful and expensive objects fly apart at her story – if she were to summon up the boldness to tell it – as the discordant screech shatters glass?

'Champagne, Madam.' He brought glasses so delicate the bowls seemed to tremble on the stem.

We are old now. Well, he was certainly old, nearly seventy. Not as old as Hubert, who is a Methuselah among poets. She could not begin to imagine what was going on in the firmament when she should meet two such figures from her past on the very same day. 'Do you believe in the stars, Merlin dear?'

'I believe you are a star and always have been.' She watched his admiring eyes on her and thought that the news she just might tell him, although shocking and extraordinary, could also be glorious. But how to introduce it? Her heart fluttered and registered a sudden guilt that she was consulting none of those others concerned. Neither Kevin, Shirley, Kathleen herself, nor even darling Orlando, without whom she seldom made decisions these days or, to be more accurate, seldom played them out before informing him.

'Merlin, dear friend. You must often go to Washington. Those galleries.'

'And never without thinking of you.' He was the picture of old-world gallantry, seated like a peacock in a gilt and upholstered chair. A benign peacock, his ankles so elegant in thin silk socks. Only a few years ago she could dare despise him but now she felt indulgent.

'You are gorgeous, Merlin de Witt. Gorgeous. Tell me, did you ever think of passing your gorgeousness on?' Ah, now she had done it.

'A child, you mean? A *bambino* to lighten my old age? No. Certainly not. My Picasso etching is my son, my Lalique vase my daughter. I am far too selfish for anything more.'

343

'You know I have a son. A young man who treats me like royalty. Except that now he serves a higher good.'

Merlin stared into his golden bubbles. His voice had a bubble quality, thin and breakable. 'Just one child?'

'No.' Her heart seemed to have stopped with fright. She did not want to die on his sofa, she wanted to die in Orlando's arms or, if he happened to be unavailable, on the edge of the lake with the smell of wild sage all around her. 'Long ago I had a daughter. I'd like to say I was a young princess who let down her tresses to a handsome prince, but that wouldn't be true.'

'Is this a deep dark secret, beautiful Connie? I'm so glad you're still beautiful, incidentally. Because if it is secret, you may be certain I'll keep my mouth shut. I have to warn you I'm known in London as a wicked gossip – although that, in itself, is wicked gossip.'

'Of course, if you would rather I kept silent about these scenes from long ago?' They were dancing round each other, Connie apparently light-footed but also determined. 'She was adopted at birth. My daughter. She's a very good photographer. She plans to be a White House photographer.'

'The White House in Washington? Or the hotel of the same name off the Marylebone Rd?'

He could not suspect, Connie thought, and yet his evasion suggested some knowledge. 'I never saw the father afterwards. He never knew. I may say he was a most unlikely father, and I was so steeped in my own drama that I never even thought of him. Besides, he was in a rage because I didn't love him.'

'A rage?' repeated Merlin. Once again, the antics of Connie's heart threatened to end her life in Albany. She must say it out. She must put her hand on her heart, as if in some old-fashioned drama, and say it straight.

'You were her father, Merlin, my daughter Kathleen's father. You are her father, although she will never know or need you or want you. Oh, God! I'm sorry, Merlin, I didn't mean that rudely – she would absolutely appreciate you but you need do nothing. Indeed you should do nothing.' Inexplicably she found herself laughing. Terror. Excitement. Tension.

'Don't.' Merlin stood up. He came over to her and touched her shoulder. She stopped laughing immediately and only just managed to stop herself crying. 'Connie, look at me.'

'I can't! I can't. It's too much. I shouldn't have told you. Twenty-seven years ago.'

'Connie.' He paused. 'Can't you see me, feel my hand on your shoulder? I'm calm, Connie. You don't have to suffer on my account. I'm proud to have a daughter of yours. And such a daughter.'

'What do you mean? What do you mean, "And such a daughter"?' Connie felt her voice rising.

'Shall I sit beside you on the sofa?' He did. She saw he was what grown-ups are supposed to be, sensible, capable. How he had changed! 'About five years ago, I had lunch with William.'

'William as in Nina? My friend William.'

'My cousin William. Nina's ex-soldier, ex-husband.'

'I see him in Ireland. I stand in flowing rivers of water and try not to catch fish.' She heard herself talking wildly.

'He told me that you had had a mystery daughter and that, from something you had said, he believed she was mine. A year or two later, I was in Washington for a benefit and met your brother Kevin. He had his adopted daughter with him. Kathleen. She was at Georgetown University then. I guessed first – she looks so like you – and then I asked your brother's wife. I don't think she minded me knowing – she was even pleased in a way. But, of course, I told no one and never will. She was so lovely, Connie, so lovely. There you are. It's not so dreadful, is it?'

'No. No.' Connie stared. Was it possible there could be some lightening of this dark secret that she had carried so long? Orlando told her so but she had not dared believe him. 'She was no more mine than she was yours. At least, she was mine for about half an hour on the day of her birth when they laid her softness over my heart. But later it turned black and cruel. In the night I cried out to Nina but no one could help. I've only seen her once, at my mother's funeral. You've seen as much of her as I have.' She looked at Merlin, his wrinkled, puckish face, his clever kindliness. They would never have done well together. 'Do you have a partner? Do you have someone you love?'

'I did once. I have friends still. And, as I already told you, I have what you see around me.'

'Yes. Yes. So much art. She does not know anything, Kathleen. Our daughter.' Once more Connie found herself giggling hysterically. 'She believes my brother Kevin is her father, mother unknown. I've imagined so often . . .'

'But decided against it?'

'Yes. I deserve the sadness.'

Merlin smiled. 'That's far too Catholic for me. I promise I will never tell anyone.'

'At least we've talked. That makes me so happy.'

Merlin stood up. 'I'd like to give you something. A present for Kathleen's birth.' He walked slowly round the room, estimating the ornaments.

Connie extracted a handkerchief covered with green shamrocks and blew her nose several times. Then she found her bag, lipstick and powder. She crossed her legs and raised her beautiful face. 'What I'd really like is something to eat.'

Merlin, holding a tiny jade rabbit, stared at her. He saw she had recovered and glowed with vitality. 'I never keep much food around,' he began doubtfully.

Connie jumped up. 'It's too funny!' she cried. 'I bet it's still there. Don't look so bewildered, Merlin. I'm referring to the cake, the cake your mother wanted you to eat on your wedding day.'

Bewildered, he followed her into the kitchen where she pulled open cupboards energetically. 'There we are!' Triumphantly, she opened the tin and displayed the crumbled and largely mouldy remains of an iced fruit cake. Undeterred, Connie popped a chunk into her mouth. 'We're celebrating our daughter, Merlin dear.'

Carefully sliding the rabbit into his waistcoat pocket, Merlin came to join her.

The paintings were covered with a moth-eaten horse blanket. Veronica let drop her stick and pulled at a corner vigorously. 'I've been meaning to show you these for ages,' she said. 'Years and years. Not that they're anything special in terms of art.'

There were twenty or more unframed canvases, face to the wall, at the back of the old tack-room where Nina used to keep her pony's saddle and bridle and where Helen's two town-loved children now played let's-pretend-we've-got-a-pony.

'I never noticed them,' said Nina, turning the first one round.

'You weren't supposed to. They were painted by your father's mother.'

'I never knew she painted. When did she die?'

'About the time of my marriage. Your grandfather died much earlier. He never fully recovered after the Great War.'

'So much war,' murmured Nina. By now she had turned round a few of the paintings: pink, purple, green, mauve, crimson, scarlet, yellow, orange. 'Heavens, they're bright!'

Veronica looked at them doubtfully. 'Would you say they were impressionist?'

'More Fauve.' Nina pulled out some more. 'She certainly wasn't afraid of colour.'

'I believe she knew Vanessa Bell and that lot. They lived just a few miles away. But Daddy said she did her painting secretly. There were many more but he gave them away. Actually, now I come to think of it, he gave them to a forerunner of Southern Painting so they could re-use the canvas.'

'He certainly didn't think much of them!'

'No.' Veronica sat on an old stool and watched Nina as she carefully displayed each picture. The brilliance of the colours had at first made them seem more abstract than they actually were. Nina was beginning to recognise parts of the house and garden. There was the wall by the front lawn, a corner of the potting shed with a patch of vegetable garden, even the apple tree, *her* apple tree, smaller and less bent but still recognisable. The sight moved her in a way she couldn't understand. 'She's very bold for an amateur.'

'Oh, I think they travelled a lot,' said Veronica vaguely. She was beginning to have the grey, thin look that meant she needed to rest.

'I like them,' announced Nina, taking her mother's arm to walk back to the house.

'It's sad to think no one saw them till after her death.'

'Never too late. I'll hang some tomorrow.'

They walked very slowly, her mother leaning heavily on her arm. The garden glowed with yellow potentilla, scarlet rosehips, tall golden daisies, vine leaves tipping red at the edges, bunches of tiny grapes turning from green to purple, crimson roses, flowering for the third time, scarlet crab apples fallen in a circle on the grass, a few red apples below the big old apple tree. The shed changed from mauve to deep amber where rust had overtaken it, and the branches of the may tree shading it were decorated with tiny vermilion berries. 'I don't think she was exaggerating the colours,' she murmured.

Veronica misheard. 'I thought of showing you earlier, when you weren't painting but I didn't want to come between you and Gus.'

Nina looked at her mother. She wanted to say, 'So you put marriage above everything?' but it would have come out as a kind of accusation. Instead, she said, 'Yes. It was probably best I worked it all out for myself. You've done so much for me.'

'I like Gus. He does a very good cottage pie.' It was true. Gus had started to cook. 'Of course, I liked William too.'

Nina smiled. She was thinking about her grandmother's paintings. Without being sentimental, she thought they were rather good. They had achieved that trick of making her look at the world from their point of view. She wondered if knowing about this artistic grandmother when she had been struggling to turn herself from a soldier's wife into some kind of painter would have helped her. Perhaps, as she had said to her mother, she needed to fight her own battles.

'Well, maybe they'll give your Rothkos a run for their money.' They had reached the house and Veronica clutched the door-knob.

'Daddy behaved pretty badly.' Nina realised she had never said anything like this to her mother before.

'After the war, remember.'

After the war. Still special pleading. Nina remembered the morning when her mother had confided in her about her father's mistress. Lisa had then become her own cross. She looked at her mother's calm face and realised there was nothing to be said. She helped her into the house and up to her bedroom, where she lay down and shut her eyes.

Nina was bending over for a farewell kiss when she opened her eyes again: 'Perhaps Grandma Lettice's paintings will persuade you away from those very dark tones you're using, Nina. Life is not all black, you know.'

Nina smiled. Her present success was entirely based on the near blackness of her paintings. 'I'll think about it. I promise.' How she had loved colour in the past! But then it had let her down.

Nina went to her studio, passing through the rooms of the house slowly, touching objects, an oak table surface, a sagging armchair, brushing her hand across flower tops, rearranging the jugs on the mantelpiece, drawing a frayed curtain noisily because it was nearly dark now.

Gus was in London. She had hours to be alone. Choosing a small piece of card, she began to paint. Soon she had made a sketch, downcast blue that had entered the trees and leaked into shadows across the land. It was a worthy little illustration. Propping it up on the table where her tubes of colour lined up expectantly, she chose a new, much larger piece of board. Caressingly, she spread the surface with a warm gold, a soft brown. She paused, almost pleased. Above her head, a late butterfly dashed itself at the naked bulb of light. Such was its force – she stopped to stare and saw the orange stripe of a tortoiseshell – that

348

it caused the bulb to swing slightly, making shadows swell across the room.

Absorbed again, Nina painted over the warm earth, the golden autumn that would soon harden into winter. Nothing stays still, she thought, but equally, nothing is gone for ever. The shadows move constantly, the earth changes from brown to green to gold and back to brown again.

Movement had entered her picture: the shadows swept, like a pendulum, the trees from which they were suspended hung over them tenderly, and beneath it all the earth glowed. Nina put a hand to her head and then a hand to her heart. In both places her smeared fingers left an amber mark. She returned to her painting. In her concentration she did not notice when the butterfly stopped its battering and shut its wings, dropping loosely to the floor. The hours passed. The room was very quiet. Night came cool and misty, an owl whistled outside the window, its round eyes peering blindly into the brightness, before flying off out on dark patrol.

Nina's legs began to shake and her stomach, last fed on a sandwich at lunchtime, drew attention to itself with loud warbles. But her head was clear, and it was only when her arm, too, began to shake, and she could not make a smooth stroke on her picture, that she was forced to stop.

Abruptly, she collapsed on to the floor, beside the butterfly. Her head was filled with buzzings and whinings, a concerto of reproachful exhaustion. She lay with her eyes closed for a few minutes, allowing the noises to subside. She felt she had never been so happy.

'Nina. Nina.' Gus stood at the door, had been standing, perhaps, for a while. He came over to her quickly, helped her sit upright. He kissed her. 'You should come in to your mother.' He crouched down beside her. Nina looked at his face and saw that he had been crying. 'She looks so peaceful. Come with me now.'

1998

Connie only went into the town to buy some shoelaces, but once she'd found the main street she liked the lively look of it and decided to get something to eat – and drink, of course. It was a beautiful August morning and she needed to stretch her legs.

Over the years of running her holiday project for children from the North and South of Ireland, Connie often came to the North. It had become a kind of game to identify the difference between the South and the North. There were the more obvious points: the accent, the red post boxes instead of green, the constabulary instead of the Gardai, but there was something else, or so she thought, even with the Catholics. It was the same feeling she'd had when Leonardo had first talked of becoming a priest and she had tried to work out whether it was worth persuading him towards the Church of Ireland so he could marry and have children. He was, after all, their only child. But it was no good. She discovered that, however hard she tried, she could not make a Church of Ireland priest seem real, though he had the brains of Aquinas and the spirit of John the Baptist. Whereas a Catholic priest, disreputable, stupid or cruel, always seemed to be the real thing – that is, the representative of Christ on earth.

'I'm probably brainwashed,' she told Orlando, who did not deny it but commented that some might consider that a definition of faith. The argument had continued throughout the evening. Connie asserted that Orlando, as a late convert, could never understand the nature of true faith. Orlando suggested that her faith was all based on guilt for leaving her mother and her homeland (arguably the same thing). To which Connie replied, rather to his surprise, that he should have realised long ago that her faith arose out of contact with her Auntie Annie, who was probably a saint and martyr and had taken her to visit the shrine at Knock. Orlando insisted it was the first he had heard of this aunt, which put Connie into a sulk until later when they lay in each other's arms and she apologised for arguing with him when she was really arguing with herself.

The next morning, however, she had woken to find all her doubts resolved: Leonardo would become a priest, if that was what he continued to want, and she would be proud. It was in the blood.

Connie was thinking of Leonardo as she parked her car a short walk from the city centre. He was in Rome, at the English college. Before she left Lir he had e-mailed her a message: 'Just met Bishop O'Donald. He sent you love or the bishoply equivalent. He has a meeting in Dublin in the autumn and hopes to visit you for a night. He joked that, if he had been a marrying man, he'd have given Dad a run for his money.'

Connie smiled as she thought of all this. A bishop in love with you! Well, there was a thing to boast of – not that she had ever made the mistake of thinking priests outside ordinary human emotions. What if Leonardo fell in love? He had convinced her that he was strong enough to cope with such an eventuality. 'I shall just hand it over to the Lord,' he had explained, simply.

Heavens, I'm lucky, thought Connie, locking her car and walking into the bright sunshine. She had parked by a bus station. As she walked, she saw buses coming and going from the countryside. She read the names on their prows: Six Mile Cross, Duncannon, Angher – small villages bringing in mothers and children mostly, come for a pre-term shopping expedition.

The high street was modern with young, well-dressed men, women and children out shopping. It was a cheerful scene in contrast to the difficult meeting she'd just endured in a Belfast hall. She'd been trying to persuade a group of recalcitrant families that their children would benefit from a visit to the stables. Later she had met a Catholic priest who ran a similar organisation to hers, taking Protestant and Catholic children for shared foreign holidays. He was a cheerfully robust man but, at one point, he became sober. 'We all do this,' he said, 'we've been doing it for decades now, and we try not to notice the changed agenda.'

Connie knew what he meant. In the last few years, since Ireland had become so prosperous, it was not only the Unionists who wanted to keep the North attached to the United Kingdom. The majority of people living in the South, born a couple or more generations after the partition of Ireland, enjoying peace and an ever-rising standard of living, had no ambition to take on Northern Ireland with all its problems. Even the politicians only paid lip service to the great goal of a united Ireland. Everybody knew it – except, probably, the British.

The conversation with the priest had depressed Connie and was one of the reasons she decided to stop in the lively little town near the border. She wanted to remind herself of the goodness of people. Whatever the differences that she, being brainwashed by her upbring-ing, could neither define nor reject, she wanted to recognise them as her fellow countrymen. So she walked away from her car, a fifty-eight-year-old woman, who looked twenty years younger, into the main street.

Immediately, she saw someone she knew, a man who, as a boy, fifteen years ago, had come to the stables. He had kept in touch with her, recording his emergence from a violent family background into a university education, good job in business, married and two children. He was one of her success stories.

'Rory!' cried Connie with delight.

'Connie! What are you doing here?'

'I'm driving home.'

'Strange direction.'

'I'm running from an occasion of sin.' Connie laughed merrily. She had thought of visiting William but there was not much chance of sinning there. Really, she flattered herself.

They went looking for somewhere to eat. Rory had half an hour before a meeting about a site for a new factory. The sun was so hot and bright that when they went into the bar, dimly lit with red bulbs, it was like being in a cool, dark cavern.

Connie drank too much, as usual, ordering two large glasses of wine in the short time before Rory had to go.

'You shouldn't drink so much before you drive.'

'You sound like Orlando.' She laughed at him affectionately. 'I've been doing it all my life. I'll not meet many cars between here and Lir.'

'But plenty of police and soldiers.'

'Not so many these days, thank the Lord.' She waved at him jauntily. He went through the door and, doubling back past the window, he saw her once more, still smiling, tipping back the last of the wine.

If Connie had ever thought of her death, she had always assumed it would take place at Lir, in Orlando's arms. More recently, she added the expectation that Leonardo could give her the last rites. Occasionally forced herself to picture some disease taking hold from which her beauty would remain untouched, although she supposed she might have to suffer pain. She was not afraid of death.

'Hello, darling. You don't usually ring me on a Thursday.' Nina was proud of herself for noting this. Since Jamie had been posted to Northern Ireland, he was in regular contact: 'So that you don't worry about me,' he had explained, in his sensible officer's voice, which so reminded her of William (although Jamie was cleverer but less sensitive). In fact, she had hardly thought of being nervous before his calls, having no more interest or knowledge of the situation in Ireland than Connie forced on her. But this regular contact made her anxious. She had inherited from her mother the very old-fashioned view that the telephone is only for emergencies. More than that, ever since she had returned to painting full time, she had less and less interest or confidence in verbal communication. She avoided conversation as much as possible, seldom speaking at all between ten and four – her hours for painting. Jamie always insisted on speaking to her in person. For a period she entertained the idea that, unconsciously, he was getting his own back for the years when she had been less of a mother to him than Felicity – although that had been his choice.

'No. I know it's not my usual day. I'm afraid it's bad news.' His voice sounded more stiff than usual. 'Have you had the radio on or the television?'

'No.' Nina was surprised at the question. 'As you know, I detest both, and Gus has been outside all day pampering his tomatoes. He's growing them upside down in seaweed, which apparently is equivalent to serving champagne in a water-bed.' She looked out of the window and saw Gus picking runner beans for their supper.

'My battalion was first on the scene, which is why I can tell you in person.' Nina began to feel sick. Clearly, *he* was perfectly well, even if his voice had begun to sound a bit shaky. So what was the matter?

'Is Gus there?'

'Yes. I told you, he's with his vegetables.' Nina began to shout: 'Jamie, what is it? What's happened?'

'There was a huge bomb. Killed thirty or forty people. One of them ... Connie. She was killed instantly. I ...' He hesitated, as if remembering '... I was able to identify her. I have already spoken to Orlando, who's ringing Leo in Rome ...'

Nina had stopped listening. Images of Connie presented themselves in rapid succession: Connie thirty years ago in hospital, Connie in New York protesting against the Vietnam war, Connie at Lymhurst with Daniel at Christmas, Connie in Cork when she first met Orlando, Connie at her own wedding, at Helen's wedding, last year when she had left the Rothkos to talk to Merlin, just six months ago when she had come to her exhibition.

'Connie ...'

'No one's claimed it yet. But it looks like some republican splinter group. Not that it makes much difference. All those so-called paramilitaries on either side are murderers. Whoever planted it was probably hoping to upset the peace process ...'

'Peace ...' murmured Nina, and stopped listening again. It was impossible to believe Connie was dead. Yet she also found herself thinking that this was the way Connie would have had to die. She had lived her life so furiously, cramming in so much, so early. Yet when she could have led a peaceful life with Orlando, she had involved herself with the troubles.

'It wasn't – it wasn't aimed at her, was it?'

'Of course not. She's not so important. Orlando says she was driving back from Belfast. Perhaps she had been on her way to see Dad. There was no reason for her to be in the town at all. Just bad luck.'

'Bad luck.'

'I'm so very, very sorry. I'll telephone this evening.'

Nina made an effort. 'Thank you, darling. It was very thoughtful of you to ring.'

'It was chance I was in the area.'

'Lots of chance,' mouthed Nina, before putting down the telephone.

She gazed out at Gus, still picking beans – what would she do with so many, she wondered irrelevantly, before realising the entire conversation with Jamie had probably taken no more than a few moments. Connie had given her Gus, which, for many years, had seemed more like a disaster than a blessing. How ever would Orlando survive without Connie? How would she?

Nina walked out to the garden. It was August. The neatly shorn grass was pale. She preferred it longer and greener with daisies. But it was Gus's province, not hers. She remembered Connie's lawn, if it could be called that, a mass of flowers, not just daisies but blue periwinkles, buttercups, dandelions, clover, perhaps even shamrock.

Nina went to Gus and told him the news.

Nina rang Fay but Lex, very polite, informed her that both his parents were at the Tanglewood music festival where a piece of Ted's was being played. Nina knew she must not leave a message and put down the telephone. She felt she should do something else but she couldn't think what. She rang Helen, and when there was no answer there, she remembered they were having a family holiday in Cornwall. In her distraction, she couldn't find the telephone number.

Gus came to her and said she didn't have to do one thing and he would make supper. When she said she couldn't possibly eat, he said he would put her to bed and take a sandwich in front of the television. Nina thought that marriage can be such a consolation and then remembered what she had to do: ring Orlando.

She went hurriedly to ask Gus's advice and, even more hurriedly, he switched off the television. Nina realised he had been watching the news with a report on the bomb; she even thought she caught a flash of Connie's face but she might have imagined that. Gus explained (holding her hand tenderly) that Orlando would not be at Lir tonight. 'Then I will go to bed,' said Nina. She still hadn't cried.

Nina lay awake all night, making no attempt to sleep. Jamie had not rung back and she dreaded to imagine what horrors he had been involved in. After that first moment when he had given her the news and Connie had been so vividly before her, she had not been able to recapture her presence. It was as if even her memory had been blown away. Nina lay quite still in a kind of paralysis. Now and again, she found she had been holding her breath for several seconds and had to gasp.

It was raining in the morning and again she couldn't eat. Vaguely she remembered all the bustle of her mother's death, visiting the funeral parlour. For some reason the names of the coffins available sang like a dirge in her head: Chatsworth, Balmoral, Manor House. All so English.

At midday the telephone rang. It was Fay. She had seen the early-morning news in their hotel room. She would fly over. When was the funeral? Nina was amazed at her energy. 'Have you spoken to Kevin and Shirley?' she asked. She rehearsed the facts: the bomb had been totally unexpected. A peace agreement was supposed to be in force. There had been a warning but it had sent people towards the explosion. The majority had been women and children. The bomb had been placed by an organisation over which Sinn Fein had no control and for which, she pointed out to Nina, Connie's brother Michael had been suspected of hiding arms and explosives.

'I don't want to know of such things,' said Nina feebly.

'But what an irony,' continued Fay, inexorable, 'to be killed by your own brother. Although I admit he's probably been out of it for years now.'

'He lives with that drunken brother Joe on the family farm,' said Nina, wondering why they were talking like this when all she cared about was Connie.

'So, what about Shirley and Kevin?' asked Fay, returning to organisation mode.

'I haven't spoken to anyone, except Gus,' said Nina, helplessly. 'And I haven't spoken to him much.'

'Ted is going to offer a new composition for Connie's funeral,' said Fay, and she carried on talking. Perhaps, thought Nina, she can deal with this better than I can because she's fought off her own death. 'Shall I come to you before we go to Ireland?' Fay continued.

'I don't know. No. No.'

After Fay hung up, the telephone rang again immediately. It was Eileen. She started talking at once, making no introductory reference to Connie's death. 'Nina dear, you have to come to Lir at once. You and Gus. Orlando needs you. I'm very anxious about him, and Leo's having trouble getting a flight from Rome. We went up North to see poor Connie's body, or what remains of it, God rest her soul, and Orlando has been talking wildly ever since. He has not the consolation of the faith. He tells me he could never believe in heaven because his heaven was with Connie on earth and that he only pretended so he could please Connie. He says there's no point in him living on. I said he had Leo, but he said that Leo had God and didn't need him at all and started quoting the gospels at me. I'm afraid he'll do a damage to himself. He's out at the lake now and my Charlie trailing him a few yards behind. Oh, Nina, with all my work with the Sisterhood, I never knew what it felt like when it happens to your own.' Eileen began to sob, but through her tears repeated Orlando's need for Nina and Gus, Connie's closest friend and Orlando's old friend, too.

Nina agreed and went to Gus. Here was necessary action. But she thought that if Orlando asked her why he should go on living without Connie she would find no ready answer. She also thought that over all the years she had known Orlando, she had gained no clear picture of his character. She couldn't remember ever meeting him without Connie present, and Connie turned everyone else to shadow. The most complete picture she retained was at their first ever meeting in the seventies in Cork when he had been a laconic poet in thrall to his father. And then he had become in thrall to Connie.

Lir was unbearable. Nina saw at once why Orlando spent most of his time, day and night, at the lake. It was the only place where Connie had not impressed her personality. Gus must have noticed the same, for he suggested at once that they should have Orlando to stay after the funeral.

Trapped in her need to make pictures, Nina noticed the random arrangement of pots on the terrace, filled with mildly disparate plants, roses, grasses, herbs, orchids, palms, pansies. She noticed the colours in the living room, pale red, lime yellow, sage, a deep bluish purple she couldn't put a name to. In Connie's house, covers and curtains seemed to fade to order, a Chinese red striping to pink, a sky blue washing out to ice white. Above the mantelpiece hung the first of the series of paintings Nina had painted of Connie on her way to meet her mother after twenty or so years. The Sleeping Beauty. Looking at it now, Nina thought it excessively unlike Connie, who had boasted a positive aversion to sleep. Bracing herself, she set off to find Orlando at the lake.

He was standing on the lakeshore about half a mile from the stables. He waved her to him. His manner when she approached was not at all wild. She saw he had been looking across the glassy, still waters to the village on the far side, visible above the trees only by its church spire.

'You can tell me if Connie would have liked my plan,' he said, in a level voice. For the first time, Nina found she desperately wanted to cry but it was the one time she couldn't. She felt a pain all through her throat and head and heart.

'Bishop O'Donald and Leo will hold the requiem mass on the lawn inside a marquee,' continued Orlando simply. 'It's the only way to contain everybody who wants to come. Then her beautiful smashed body will be taken down to the shore and placed in a boat with just myself and Leo. No one else. We'll row ourselves across the lake to the church and there she'll be buried. We have a plot, you know. What do you think?'

'I think she would have been very pleased.' Unable to continue without tears, Nina walked away.

But Orlando followed. 'She told me about Leo's birth here. We both lay in the water. So ridiculous. It was winter too. Tell me, do you believe in life after death?'

'I don't know,' sobbed Nina, realising that her tears meant nothing to Orlando.

'Did Eileen tell you I'm considering drowning myself on the return journey when the boat is empty? I'll leave Leo at the church. My only difficulty is Connie. She became such a Catholic and Catholics believe suicide is a mortal sin. Just in case she is alive somewhere, I would hate to offend her. But, really, I can't see any point in going on without her. It's not as if I can set up something in her memory. She's done all that herself. Her Sisterhood, the stables. What do you think, Nina? You were very close to her.'

Nina thought, So he *has* asked me – albeit for Connie's opinion. They were ever nearer the edge of the water and while she tried to think of an answer, Nina noticed that some plants she could not identify were growing underwater, their flowers magnified and distorted. 'Connie would not have wanted her death to result in yours.' She spoke slowly, and before she had got out the words, she thought that they could easily be quite untrue. Connie might be eager for Orlando to prove that he could not live without her. 'Anyway, Gus and I want you to come and stay with us.'

'Thank you.' Orlando spoke gently, although she had no idea if he was convinced. 'If you don't mind, I think I'll have a swim.' At Nina's face, he almost produced a smile. 'No. No. Don't worry. I still have the funeral to come.'

Nina walked away as he began undressing. When she looked back he was far out in the middle of the lake. Nina couldn't help being reminded of his mad old father's favourite pastime. In the latter years, Nina remembered, Connie had sworn he carried pebbles in his trunks, which she had hoped were to sink himself to the bottom until she discovered he threw them at the swans. There were no swans this evening.

Fay had arrived in Nina's absence. She walked to meet Nina as she came up from the lake. They kissed quickly.

'You're freezing!' exclaimed Fay.

'It's all so dreadful. I feel so sorry for Orlando. I...' Unable to continue, Nina burst into tears.

She turned her back so that Fay could only see her heaving shoulders silhouetted against a background of dark laurel leaves. She thought that Nina had always liked to suffer privately. 'Here.' She opened her handbag and took out a clean tissue.

Nina turned round and took it. 'Trust you to have what's needed.' She blew her nose vigorously.

Fay knew she was thinking of that first visit to Lymhurst when Connie had led them in a dance by the ancient tree. 'We always were an odd trio.'

'I still can't believe it, actually. I suppose it's different for you, having been a doctor and everything. But it's true for me. I keep expecting to hear her voice making some stupid remark. It's the suddenness, I suppose.'

'Oh, yes,' said Fay sympathetically. But she thought that death had never seemed unexpected to her. On the contrary, she had lived in fear of it all her life. 'How was Orlando? Could you help at all?'

'No. No, I'm sure not. How could I?'

They started walking back to the house. 'I was so angry when she told me she'd slept with Daniel,' said Fay suddenly. She wondered what had put that into her head. Death, she supposed.

'What?' Nina sounded shocked.

'Didn't you know? That Christmas at Lymhurst. In the end, I was pleased about it.' And now they're both dead, Fay thought.

'But that must have been during her celibate period.'

'I guess that ended it.' They both smiled.

Fay could see the house now, the wide shaggy lawns, the terrace with its four stone urns overflowing with flowers and weeds. Something

358

nagged at her memory. 'There's something I've always meant to ask.' She turned to Nina, who stopped walking and looked at her with a strained expression. 'Oh, it's not so important. Do you remember when we first met at the hospital and there was a hopeless sort of garden?'

'Not very well. I looked at the clouds then.' Nina held up her finger.

'Yes. The point is, there was an urn on a terrace stuffed with sweet-peas and I used to imagine that one of you had put them in. I don't know why. I suppose I liked the idea. There were far too many and they were spilling all over everywhere.'

'Well, it wasn't me.'

Fay liked the seriousness of Nina's expression. 'In that case,' she said, 'I shall assume it was Connie.'

'If it was Connie,' said Nina, 'she'd have put in plenty of weeds too.'

'Pass. It's too long ago.'

They walked again, nearing the house in silence. As they reached the terrace, they could see figures silhouetted against a light inside the room. The tallest was Gus, standing awkwardly with his head bowed over the mantelpiece. Fay turned to give Nina a quick hug. 'Come on, darling. Let's help Eileen with supper.'

'Oh, Fay.' Again Nina burst into tears but this time she turned to Fay, and, although so much larger hung on to her as if she were a rock of strength.

Fay patted her shoulders. 'I feel kind of crazy myself. Travelling here I kept getting this weird image of myself pulling up beets from the garden and making soup for Orlando and Gus and anyone else who needed comforting. I had to remind myself that I had never been much of a Jewish mother and certainly couldn't cook borscht – even if Connie grew them in her garden, which by the look of it is wildly unlikely.'

Nina began to recover. She took another tissue from Fay and once more gave a manly blow to her nose. 'Right. In we go. From now on, I'll always look for you when I need to cry.'

'I had no idea Connie was so well known.' The morning before the funeral, Nina and Leonardo were watching the marquee going up on the lawn. It was warm but drizzling slightly, which neither of them noticed. As usual Fay was inside the house answering telephone calls, often from the press, but sometimes from Connie's old lovers. She said it was very distressing to hear grown men, sometimes old men, trying so hard not to cry. They were all planning to be at the funeral.

'It's lucky we opted for the bigger marquee.' Leonardo waved his hand at the slowly raising mass of canvas. 'My mother was much loved in Ireland.' Usually a controlled man, he suddenly burst out, 'I tell you honestly, I don't know how that Michael has the face to come round. I'll tell you, the biggest test of my faith yet is having to show him a bit of politeness.'

'I suppose priests are trained for that sort of thing.' Nina heard the ridiculous sound of her words. 'I'm sorry, Leo.' She laid her hand on his arm. This mourning son who was also a priest confused her. She realised that she had never quite believed in Connie's Catholicism. She had presented it with so much vilification and drama in her early life, but her conversion had been a much quieter affair.

They both turned to watch as various children from the stables arrived carrying bundles of flowers and what looked like whole shrubs dug out of the garden. A table was being set up to act as an altar and they began to pile the flowers at its base.

'Won't they die?'

Leonardo smiled. 'No one's claiming a miracle for her. They'll bring water in a minute.' He paused. 'And my father? How do you think he'll manage?'

Nina had been dreading this question. She had already confided her conversation with Orlando at the lakeside to Connie's mysterious Father O'Donald, now generally referred to as the Bishop. She had hoped he would talk to Orlando of the afterlife in a positive manner. But she was not very confident because he had commented sadly, 'Dying of a broken heart is no figure of speech.' To her objection that drowning at your own instigation was not the same as dying of a broken heart, he had only nodded and said that, after all, perhaps it was sometimes a figure of speech.

'We'll keep an eye on him,' she said to Leonardo. It sounded very feeble.

Fay sat with Nina, Gus, Eileen, Leonardo, Kevin and Shirley in the hall at Lir. It was the evening before the funeral, a splendid purplish evening with rooks and wood pigeons noisy outside. The Bishop had taken Orlando to see the preparations at the graveyard.

After a supper during which they had made valiant conversation, mostly about tomorrow's preparations, they had fallen exhaustedly silent.

Fay noticed that Leonardo seemed to be feeling under the sofa. He pulled out a book and looked at it anxiously. She recognised it at once, the 'no sex' book as Connie used to call it, with her zipper stomach on the front. Fay caught Nina looking in the same direction and both watched as Leonardo put it carefully back under the sofa.

Shirley stood up. She had become heavier and limped slightly from arthritis in the knee. 'I'm planning to make a pot of tea. Fay? Nina?' It was, quite clearly, a summons. Kevin began to talk to Eileen, questioning her, Fay overheard as she left the room, about Lir, the house, garden, land, the lakeside.

Untypically, Shirley didn't switch on a light in the large untidy kitchen. Evening blurred the outlines of the old-fashioned copper pots, the round of ladderback chairs, the window-sills decorated with fallen geranium petals.

'Please, let's sit at the table.' Shirley seemed both determined and very nervous. Fay and Nina sat obediently.

Fay said sympathetically, 'What is it, Shirley? Can we help?'

Shirley took a breath. 'If you don't mind, I'll just tell you it all at one go. Kevin asked me to talk to you. He gets too emotional. You see, we've told Kathleen that Connie was her birth mother. Before we left Washington. We think she had her suspicions and it was making her unhappy. Somehow the telling her has changed so much. We've just discovered today that Connie told Leo the truth some years ago on a train after a visit to us in Washington. So he's known for ages. Connie'd been upset by seeing Kathleen. Of course, Orlando has known more or less for ever. Kathleen decided not to come for the funeral but Kevin is definitely going to retire to Ireland so we're hoping to come to Lir. Kathleen thinks she could get backing to do a photographic project on the stables. Tara can come whenever she wants. They're both adults. Kevin can play golf, which is what he most enjoys. We've already spoken to Leo, who's very keen on the idea, and we plan to ask Orlando after the funeral.'

She stopped abruptly. Fay thought that all these new arrangements didn't disguise the most important information: a week after Connie's death, her daughter finally knew the truth. Fay saw that, like her, Nina was trying very hard not to cry.

'Don't leave it till too long after the funeral,' murmured Nina eventually. 'I mean, getting Kathleen over here.'

'It's a wonderful idea,' said Fay. She wanted to hear how Kathleen had taken the news. But Shirley stood up and began noisily filling the kettle at the sink. 'I'll tell you more later,' she said, over her shoulder. Fay realised she too was crying.

'I think it will make Orlando very happy to have Kathleen here,' said Nina.

'Is Kathleen all right about it?' asked Fay.

Again Shirley had her back to them as she heaved the heavy kettle on to the Aga. 'She's put a photograph of Connie by her bed.'

Fay thought sadly that it was a pity Connie never had the opportunity to acknowledge her daughter.

Nina looked up at the roof of the marquee. Some leaves had fallen from overhanging trees and lay in dark patterns on the canvas. They had nearly reached the end of the service. Soon Connie's coffin would be carried to the lake. Fay and she, sitting side by side, had whispered to each other information about the various mourners. Fay had recognised the infamous Hubert and they had both smiled sympathetically at Merlin, so effete, so elegant, so unlikely to be Connie's daughter's father. Hubert's son, the equally infamous Rick, was impossible to avoid since he had come with ministerial entourage plus bodyguard.

Fay and Nina giggled, despite their sadness, as they looked for the dreadful Trig but could see no one big or awful enough. 'He's probably a master of disguises by now,' whispered Nina. 'Did I ever tell you about Violetta Sugden pianoforte teacher?'

Again, Nina stared upwards and saw how some of the leaves were sliding a little and how, now and again, the shadow of a bird passed overhead.

Four of Eileen's sons were picking up the coffin. Led by the Bishop, Leonardo and Orlando, a procession started out from the marquee. Nina thought there'd be nearly enough mourners to stretch all the way from the garden to the lake. She walked between Fay and Gus not far behind the coffin. She turned to check Helen was all right and saw in passing Connie's dreadful brothers, Michael and Joe. There was no way she'd smile at them. She wasn't a priest.

A string quartet seated on the terrace was playing the piece Ted had composed especially, although he hadn't been able to come himself. Nina remembered how Connie had cried at the concert in Wigmore Hall.

'Connie would have loved all this, being the centre of attention,' she whispered to Fay. 'The music is beautiful,' she added, although, truthfully, she thought it far too difficult for the occasion. The bellowing of *For All the Saints* had been far more satisfactory.

As they neared the lake, the trampling feet filled the air with the scent of wild garlic and sage. Overhead a helicopter employed by a news service filmed the procession, but when they reached the lake it peeled away and everything became quiet. At the water's edge, the stables children, in untypically neat shirts with black armbands, formed the final guard.

The coffin was lifted into a small boat and Orlando and Leonardo got in and picked up the oars. They rowed slowly away.

'I've never seen the lake so still,' whispered Gus.

'It's in mourning,' Nina whispered back. She gripped Fay's hand.

Ten days after the funeral, Nina received a letter from Orlando. She took it to her studio and opened it with nervously shaking fingers.

My dearest Nina, I want to thank you for listening to me. You'll know when you listened and how I felt. Ridiculously, after our conversation, I found myself praying for help, for a miracle, I suppose, although I have to admit the Virgin's face looked deceptively like Connie's ... Well, you know the miracle. Just a little one called Kathleen but enough, I think, to keep me off the bottom of the lake. About Connie, I still can't bear to consider. The horror of what she might have seen and heard and felt was one of my tortures, even though everyone assured me her death would have been instantaneous. I wanted you to know one detail that has, in the end, given me some consolation. At the funeral, I was approached by a young man, called Rory, one of Connie's success stories from the stables. He was terribly moved, hardly able to contain his tears. I tried to avoid talking to him but he more or less dragged me into the laurel bushes. The laurel bushes that Connie hated, incidentally. She said they made her want to cry. He told me that he had been with her in a bar just before the bomb. He'd left her drinking white wine, very happy, he said. At first I was furious with him, although I managed to contain it. Furious that he had left her alone and not taken her off with him – he had gone to some meeting. Furiously jealous that he, not I, was the last person with her. But then I calmed down and questioned him more. She was sitting there, Nina, knocking back the white wine – he didn't actually say that in case it sounded

363

critical, but that's clearly what she was doing. We all know Connie and wine. She was on her way home to me after that sort of difficult meeting she believed was the point of being here on earth. I knew then she wouldn't have suffered a thing, a glass in her hand. Thank God I never tried to control her drinking! And thank God too (although I know it isn't the Catholic line) she didn't live on horribly maimed. Vanity was one of her strongest weaknesses, linked to lack of confidence and self-consciousness. And she was so beautiful . . . Enough. Enough. I will take up your offer to stay with you. But not quite yet. I must stay with Connie in Ireland. Her spirit is everywhere. My best love to you and Gus.

Six weeks after Connie's death, Nina received a second letter from Orlando. She noticed, as she opened the envelope, how like his writing was to Connie's large open hand. Happy couples were supposed to grow to look alike. Did it apply to handwriting too? She realised she was putting off reading the letter because she was afraid of what suffering it would disclose.

Among all the fall-out from Connie's death [wrote Orlando], one of the strangest is the emergence of her disappeared brother, Finbar. He read about her death in an Australian newspaper – he has lived there, it seems, for fifty years, going soon after the war. He has never married, or perhaps was married but now seems to be on his own. He wrote to Michael, or at least to the O'Malley farm address, and Michael answered. The upshot is that Michael accepted an invitation to visit – he who had never left Ireland in his life and barely left Mayo. He came to confide in me that he intends never to return. 'I shall die with my brother,' he growled, in his ugly, gritty voice, quite ignoring Joe who is still at Lir and certainly planning to die there. 'Kevin can take the farm,' he continued, 'and Connie's bastard can walk the fields like her whoring mother.' You can see, with such disgusting words in my head, how upset I became. I shouted. I never shout. Then I realised how terribly funny Connie would have thought it. Michael's self-banishment to some desert the other side of the world. Two tough old bachelors dreaming about Ireland and driving each other mad. So I stopped being enraged and saw how wonderful it was that Kathleen could go back to Connie's old home. She's an extraordinary girl. It seems too ridiculous to be true, but she and Eric – do you remember Eric who Kevin paid for to come from New York and run the stables? She and Eric have become fast friends. She's teaching him to swim; he must be the only American in the world who doesn't know how. He's teaching her to build a wall – not part of her previous education. Kevin and Shirley may now go to the O'Malley farm. There's a spectacular golf course nearby and regular flights from Knock and Shannon. Perhaps I can persuade them to take Joe too, although Connie's death has shocked him so deeply that whereas it would drive a normal man to drink, in his case it appears to have acted in reverse. I don't even bother locking up the whiskey any more.

Dear Nina, I hope you will not mind me writing now and again, instead of visiting. It helps me. Maybe I can persuade you and Gus to stay at Christmas. But I will not think of that now. I am glad that she had you and Fay for her friends . . .

2000

Fay felt self-conscious riding the hotel's elevator in her bathrobe. An observer might speculate she was back from an early-morning assignation, except that she was far too old. The elevator was filled with suits, four young men, one woman. She noted their newly showered hair, briefcases, name badges. They all seemed to be from the same company: all departed on the fifteenth floor, heading for conference rooms. She'd had that kind of expression on her face once, tense, engaged, keen to succeed.

The elevator made it to the fortieth floor and she stepped out, following arrows to the pool. Swing doors and she was on the top of a Toronto hotel heading for an early-morning swim. No one else had had the same idea. Just blue water, blue sky, bright sun and one middle-aged woman with grey hair and a partial mastectomy. Fay put her glasses in her pocket, slipped off her bathrobe and dived in.

She swam underwater with eyes open. Bubbles swept past her in cascades, then turned themselves into crystal flowers. She was glad Ted had gone off early to check out the concert hall, glad she was fit enough to swim backwards and forwards, glad to be alone.

Fay pulled herself out and walked round the edge of the pool. The parapet was too high to see more than sky and the tops of one or two even taller buildings. Then she spotted a telephone kiosk. 'Just so incongruous,' she said out loud, 'that I guess I have to use it.'

Nina was working on a patch of canvas that she'd already overpainted far too often when Gus called her. Picking up a palette knife she scraped clean the whole area. 'It's Fay. She wouldn't be put off.' He was apologetic.

'I figured it was your lunch-break.' Fay didn't sound as apologetic as she should.

'What's lunch?'

'Picture me. I'm standing in a telephone kiosk adjacent to a fortieth-floor pool.'

'Swimming?' Nina stopped being cross. She immediately thought of Connie. This was Connie's sort of scene, not Fay's.

'Just me, blue sky, water.' Certainly Fay sounded surprised at herself.

'No Ted?'

'Ted gets vertigo.' Fay paused. 'I began to think about Connie,' she said. 'Then I had a question. You, my oldest friend, seemed the right sort of person to answer it.'

'I'm waiting.' Nina accepted a glass of wine from Gus and with it more memories of Connie. She wondered how long it would go on, this feeling of a part missing from life.

'What's it all about?' Fay asked her.

'You don't expect me to answer that?' Nina laughed.

'First thought? That's all I want.'

'The meaning of life? Is that what you're talking about? Even you, Fay, can't expect me to sort that out. Really!'

'Oh, no? OK. No Wittgenstein, Jesus Christ, Gandhi, de Sade . . . Just you, me . . . old friends . . .' While Fay talked, Nina knew she did have some sort of answer. 'You think we're not old enough?' continued Fay. 'Not wise? Not read enough books? Not lived through enough?'

'I don't know.'

'Or you're not saying.' Fay laughed now.

'Don't be a bully. Just because you're standing on top of the world. Or, if you have got an answer, go ahead and tell me.'

'A kind of answer for me. It's to do with living. I thought I'd got it taped, being independent, becoming a doctor in a man's world, but after Daniel's death I began to understand I'd been running scared all my life. I guess you know about that. You came with me to Auschwitz.'

'Surely Lex and Jim are a good enough reason?' Nina sat down in the hallway. A sharp spring wind blew open the front door, which hadn't been properly latched, and gusted round her ankles. 'They must be reason enough for anything.'

'Did *your* children do it for you? Sure, I want them to be madly successful just like any other Jewish mother. Like my mother. But they have to die.'

'So, Ted? Does he do it for you?'

'His music. That's my best reason.'

'Music!' Nina heard her voice squeaking. Music as a reason for living? But that made them the same. How ridiculous! Art and music. When they had always seemed so different. Connie was the odd one out, then. Connie had believed in the spirit as defined by the Roman Catholic Church. But, then, Connie was an art form all on her own. Nina rethought. She and Fay were not the same. She made the art. Fay's husband made the music. 'I'll give you another reason,' she said.

Fay didn't seem to hear properly. 'Hey. Even my myopic eyes can see there's some kind of a gymnasium through a window here with a load of males pumping up their testosterone. Do they look foolish!'

'Friendship. I propose friendship.'

'What?'

'Friendship!' yelled Nina, but this time the word was blocked out even to herself by the front door slamming shut. 'Fay! Can you hear me?' There was no answer and she was about to put the phone down, thinking they had been cut off, when Fay's voice came clearly, if not very loud.

'Friendship. I heard you perfectly well the first time. I was just thinking about it. That's fine by me. Let's settle on friendship.'

'But what about Connie?' Nina was yelling again because Fay's voice had diminished to a whisper by the end of her sentence.

'Wasn't three decades enough for you?'

'No!' shouted Nina. 'I want years and years more. Your voice is fading out again.'

'I'm speaking softly,' whispered Fay, sounding cross. 'I think one of the testosterone males has spotted me out here and I'm feeling self-conscious.'

'Whatever for?'

'I'm not wearing a swimsuit.'

Nina began to laugh. The thought of precise, organised Fay caught with no clothes on was just so unlikely. 'Goodbye, my old friend.' But Fay had gone already.

Nina stood up. 'Gus! Fay's swimming nude in a public pool. Do you think the spirit of Connie can have entered her?'

The idea was so cheering that she didn't listen for an answer but went straight to her studio where she found her canvas had gained a mysterious radiance.